A Fall of Kings

ALEX CONNOR

First published in Great Britain in 2024 by Merisi Publishing. https://www.merisipublishing.com

Copyright © 2024 Alex Connor

The moral right of Alex Connor to be identified as the author of this work has been asserted in accordance with the Copyright, Designs and Patents Act, 1988.

A CIP catalogue record for this book is available from the British Library.

ISBN 978-1-7385363-7-5 (PB)

About The Author

ALEX CONNOR writes contemporary thrillers, always with a link to the art world. She has been published and translated in sixteen countries, had a world No 1 for CARAVAGGIO SAGA, and won the Rome Prize for Fiction. She is a working artist, historian, and FRSA. She lives in England.

A FALL OF KINGS is No 10 in her series of art thrillers.

Other Works By This Author

THE REMBRANDT SECRET
LEGACY OF BLOOD
THE MEMORY OF BONES
THE CARAVAGGIO CONSPIRACY
THE BOSCH DECEPTION
A WREATH OF SERPENTS
THE INCUBUS TAPES
A VINE UNDER GLASS
THE ISLE OF THE DEAD

Rich men look sad, and ruffians dance and leap
The one in fear to lose what they enjoy,
The other to enjoy by rage and war.
These signs forerun the death or fall of kings.

Shakespeare

'So I write these lines for you,
who have felt the death-wish too.
All the wires are cut, my friends,
live beyond the severed ends.'

(Louis MacNeice)

1

Prologue

Twenty years earlier

I remember. You might not, but I do.

I remember five men – princes then, not the kings you would become. You were celebrating an auction triumph. One of you had bought a replica of Rodin's 'Danaid'. I didn't know it then, but the sculpture depicts one of the Danaids of Greek mythology, who murdered their husbands on their wedding nights. Of course it was a nude - you were all collectors of the erotic and the strange - and I'd been hired to reproduce the pose. I didn't hesitate, not for a moment. I didn't suspect anything until it was too late.

It was a bitter November night. I'd been waiting for a second bus for a while, and decided to walk the last part of the way because I was afraid I'd be late. My shoes were sodden by the time I got to the house in Richmond, London rain coming in with me. I was nervous, in an unfamiliar city, with no family and scarce money. That was why I took the job. You understand? No, of course you don't. You thought I was just a model, posing for a group of wealthy men, who happened to be art collectors? You were the decent ones. Not me.

3

I'd never posed before. I was nineteen years old, naïve, and needed the money badly. For what, I'll explain later. I'd been working at an art school, had taken a cleaning job there, but my hours were reduced and I was soon struggling. I don't really know how the opportunity came about, only that my landlady, who had been very tolerant about my late rental payment, suggested it:

'It's at the house of Vincent Lund. He's a doctor and some kind of art collector. All you have to do is to pose like the sculpture one of his friends has just bought. Jesus, it's easy money, love. I'd do it. Fleece the bastards.'

When I arrived at the house, I was shown into a downstairs cloakroom and told to get undressed and put on a robe. It was some Oriental cover up with dragons on it. They had eyes like peeled lychees, tongues red and curling with smoke, or was it supposed to be water? I don't know. Maybe you do. Maybe the details have stuck in your mind. Maybe the robe was expensive, another auction triumph.

I was shaking, nauseous, my hands cold I couldn't feel anything and flinched when I brushed my own skin. There were – as I say – five of you. All talking, drinking, all well dressed in dinner jackets as though you were going to the theatre. I heard you all talking, mentioning how it was you, Vincent, who had set up this meeting of friends to celebrate your auction triumphs. I had the feeling it was something you did quite often. It was all your idea. And it was such a bad one.

Standing in the corner, I waited to be told what to do, as two servants – I suppose they were servants, God knows – turned the sculpture round so that it faced the group. Then they left, but not without one of them glancing over to me with an expression I couldn't read. And then it began. Someone gestured at the sculpture. It was of a young woman, lying down, curled up so that only her back was showing. I was told to copy the pose on the daybed, exactly as the woman was lying. A photographer had just arrived, preparing to take a shot for some glossy magazine. Apparently it was important and had to be right. You were all very proud.

I was relieved that only my back would be exposed and clambered onto the day bed, tripping awkwardly over the long oriental robe.

'Oh, for God's sake,' someone said, exasperated 'just take off the kimono.'

But I couldn't, and instead I sat down, facing them. Five pairs of eyes stared at me. Someone was smoking a cigarette, someone else put their head on one side, frowning, another man clicked his tongue with – what? Disgust? I didn't know. I was very young, naked under the thin robe, feeling exposed, vulnerable - and then they started to laugh. But I didn't leave. I didn't do anything when someone slipped off the gown and placed me like the woman in the sculpture.

My back was turned to them, I stared at the drawn curtains and a light went out inside me as my body was scrutinised. I didn't move, couldn't. No one touched me. Not then. You just looked, then one of you came so close I could feel your breath on the skin of my back and I knew I would never leave that house whole.

You remember now?

One of you was very drunk, the tall Dane, Vincent Lund, another dark skinned man with an American accent, was staring sadly like a wooden icon. I was counting inside my head like the ticking of an over wound clock. I stepped out of myself, stood back and

5

watched that little scrap of a girl, the white column of her body no longer her own, now the property of others.

It was later when the attack came. I wasn't prepared, and didn't react quickly enough. The hem of the gown was too long and I fell when I tried to get away. And behind me I could still hear laughter until one of the servants handed me my clothes and bundled me out of the back door. My shoes were still damp. I hadn't been inside long enough for them to dry off.

Oh, all you little Princes, later Kings, do you remember me now? It was November, 16th. For over twenty years I have watched you all. I never took the money you offered me. I don't suppose you noticed. The following day I left London.

But now I want my fee. Not in money, in something far more valuable. You ruled over me once, now I will rule over you and set in motion the fall of kings.

Book One

One

He would never marry again. Never. Irritated, Jimmy Nicholson tied his tie, looking at his reflection in the bathroom mirror as he murmured the words under his breath.

"*Never* fucking again."

He couldn't get the knot right and tugged at it, the silk creasing. It was tight around his neck, digging into his collar as he jerked it loose. His wife had bought him the tie two years earlier for his birthday. He hated fucking plain ties, he had told her that every year for the twenty five years they had been married, but she still bought them for him. Passive aggressive. So of course he had to retaliate, didn't he? She hated flowers, but every birthday he bought her roses.

They mean love, darling.

Roses aren't your usual flowers.

It's a symbol...

Oh yes, it was a symbol alright, a symbol of the fact he couldn't stand the sight of her. Inside all desire had curled like a dead leaf and all tenderness had left him. He was tied to a woman he no longer loved and

9

who no longer loved him – and the thought was a brake to his heart.

His career consoled him. As with many people who are lucky in their youth, Jimmy Nicholson had no suspicion that serendipity would one day desert him. His career was a cogent upward curve, his natural ability taken for granted. We inherit the genes we are given at birth and Jimmy Nicholson had a genius for sales. His gallery triumphed, his buys and auctions inspired by giddy skill. In his thirties he had made a name for himself by spotting a previously underrated English landscape painter, on a par with Turner, but with a tragically short – and undocumented - life.

Did this protégé exist? Who knew, who cared? Certainly not his clients who believed in Jimmy Nicholson's PR skill that had trumpeted an artist of limited ability into a sizzling talent. Talent that was then sold onto gullible and naïve buyers. After the elusive landscape painter, there were others, but not from England. Home grown talent could be investigated, better to throw his net further afield. If the rumours were true – and who was to say they weren't? – Jimmy Nicholson had created at least seven artists from the ether, giving the painterly ghosts names and backgrounds that were enticing, but never too extreme to invite suspicion.

Again Jimmy tugged at his tie, fighting despair. Not at the tie, but at the whole vacant hollow of his life; the sad contrast of the beauty in his career set against the dismal ugliness of his private life.

"We're seeing the Taylors tonight."

He turned: hadn't heard his wife enter and watched her lean against the bedroom door. "The Taylors?"

"You've forgotten, haven't you? You forget everything I tell you." Stella rebuked him, but her heart wasn't in it. "Just make sure you're home early, will you? We don't want to be late."

She turned. Left the room. He heard her footsteps walking away. Down the stairs. A pause at the bottom. Maybe a sigh, he couldn't be sure of that. Then silence. Jimmy turned back to his tie, finished the knot and moved into his bathroom, reaching inside the cabinet.

Late onset diabetes had hobbled him at forty five. He could have controlled it on tablets, but the lure of booze had proved too much for him and now he injected himself daily with insulin. Automatically efficient, Jimmy checked his blood sugar reading, prepared his insulin shot, pulled down his trousers and inserted the needle into his thigh. Then he depressed the plunger and waited as the insulin entered his body.

His heart reacted before the syringe was even emptied; blood fire coursing through his veins, his mouth opening without sound as he lurched forwards. Struggling to get a grip on the basin, he tried to cry out, but instead foam came from his lips, his torso in spasm. The pain and poison jerked him off his feet, his body breaking down whilst his mind continued to reason. But not for long and as his back arched, his bladder slackened, urine flushing down his legs as his hands lost their grip and he fell. Desperate, the dying man crawled on all fours to the door, but the spasms pulled him over onto his back, his hands clawing at his chest, the syringe still dangling from his bloodied thigh. It took Jimmy Nicholson exactly five minutes and seventeen seconds to die.

If he had lived he would have told people that his life had not flashed before his eyes; his existence had not been replayed to him. He would have said that the only image he saw was that of a pale white body on a cold night in London many, many years before.

When the Times published his obituary it spoke of an original and incisive mind, a loving husband and a respected colleague. It lied, as all the best obituaries do, enabling people to wipe their consciences clear and for unloving spouses to assume their grieving role. Yet the art world *did* mourn for the fall of one of its giants at the age of fifty seven. Those who had hated him felt unexpected sadness; those he had inspired expressed shock. But there was one question everyone asked – why was Jimmy Nicholson murdered?

No one realised then that his death was only the beginning.

Two

De Vries, Oakley & Wynam,
Lincoln's Inn,
London

Barend de Vries closed the private door of his chambers, his voice muted over the phone line. "Did you get one too?"

"A letter?"

"Yes, a letter! Don't bugger about, *did* you get one?" Barend snapped.

He could hear Tyland inhale; could imagine the thin, etiolated figure hunched over, the long fingers gripping the phone. Tyland Bray, art collector, suffering from Ehlers-Danlos syndrome, a condition which had resulted in severe early arthritis and numerous dislocated joints. A condition which, over the years, had made his normal life treacherous and painful.

"Yes, I got one. It was delivered yesterday by hand." Tyland answered, then asked. "Do you remember that night?"

Barend hesitated, shuffled through his mind's back catalogue and came up blank. "No…. It must be some kind of joke."

"Strange that you should forget, because I remember. We met up at Vincent's house. He'd just bought a reproduction of Rodin's *Danaid* at auction and was over the moon that *World Collectors* magazine were doing an article about it."

"I don't remember --"

"Your memory must be failing you, Barend, getting older does that." He responded acidly. "It was around the time Vincent bought a series of 18th Century anatomical drawings for his collection, long before it became what it is now. As for the Rodin, he said it fitted in because it was anatomically correct."

Barend replied, haltingly. "I remember something, but not much. We all used to drink heavily in those days –"

"And Vincent was very drunk that night. You *must* remember, Barend, think back. We were all there and Jimmy Nicholson arrived late. The same Jimmy Nicholson that's just been murdered --"

"*Murdered*!" Barend jumped in. "Not everyone thinks that. It could have been suicide."

"Jimmy would never have committed suicide. Inject himself with poison? Ridiculous."

"If I was married to his wife I'd have poisoned myself years ago."

"Stella didn't kill him either. His wife might have hated him, but she'd never murder her meal ticket. And you can drop the notion that Jimmy killed himself. He didn't." Tyland snapped. "His killer is the person who has been writing to all of us."

"You don't know that --"

"Hear me out, Barend! That's always been your trouble, you talk too much and don't listen enough. Typical of a bloody barrister." Tyland paused, rubbing the knuckles of his swollen left hand. "The writer has spelt it out - '*Now I want my fee. My recompense for that night. Not in money, in something far more valuable.*'"

Barend shook his head dismissively, clutching the phone, his podgy hand shaking a little. "It's a threat, no more. Women don't kill."

"What about Arlene Wuornos? She murdered seven men." Tyland retorted. "Are you *sure* you don't remember much about what happened that night?"

"I was drunk --"

"You weren't that drunk. You were sober enough to talk to the journalist and pose for a magazine photograph. Always been a snob, haven't you, Barend?" He pulled the letter towards him and stared at it. "She said it happened at Vincent's house over twenty years ago. How can anyone remember that far back?"

"Maybe she's trying to blackmail us?"

"For what? I thought you didn't remember anything."

"I don't!" Barend retorted, unnerved. "I don't know what the fuss is all about. It was about some sculpture –"

"The *'Danaid'*, Rodin's sculpture based on the tale in the Metamorphoses of Hypermetria, eldest of the Danaïdes. They were daughters of Danaos, made to fill up a bottomless barrel with water in punishment for killing their husbands on their wedding night – another damn fool Greek myth." Tyland could not resist brandishing his knowledge. "I remember the piece well. Camille Claudel had talent and became an important sculptor in her own right, even if she was a woman. Indeed, there is still some argument as to whether the original was actually by her and not Rodin. Nonsense, of course, and I stand by my opinion."

"Yes, you always do."

"It was a difficult pose to reproduce," Tyland continued, ignoring Barend's remark. "I remember saying that we should have hired a professional model."

A memory was slowly shifting into place, the diminutive Dutchman frowning. "It's coming back to me now…but what's it got to do the letters?"

"The writer was the girl that posed as the *Danaid*. For God's Sake, Barend, put two and two together! Vincent won the auction for the Rodin and I was going to display it at my gallery, but there had been a water leak just before the Private View, so Vincent held it at his place. After all, he had enough room."

"So it was Vincent who hired the model?"

Tyland became thoughtful. "Actually, I think I did."

"*You?*"

"Yes, I seem to recall we couldn't get a professional model at short notice and someone was talking about a girl working in one of the art schools, who needed money." Tyland rubbed his shoulder, grimacing in pain. "Perhaps my secretary recommended her –"

"Ask her."

"It's over twenty years ago! I don't even know where she is now."

"So you think it's the girl writing the letters?"

"Who else?

"But if she'd had a problem, why didn't she mention at the time?" Barend replied. "Did you… do anything?"

An Artic blast came back. *"Did I what?"*

"She's suggesting something… she says she was attacked…"

"And you think it was me?" Tyland replied, his voice intimidating. "Maybe it was you."

"No! I didn't do anything –"

"Apart from drinking too much and having a convenient lapse in memory." Tyland countered. "Of course, it could have been Leo or Vincent –"

"Leo's gay."

"The woman says she was attacked, doesn't specify if it was sexual. You're the one putting that spin on it."

"I'm not putting a spin on anything!" Barend protested. "Mind you, we were a lot younger then. Not as powerful as we are now. She probably thinks she can come back and try to rip us off --"

"If she wanted money she would have asked for it. She wants something else, revenge."

"I say it's bullshit, a practical joke --"

"Jimmy Nicholson is dead. How funny is that?"

Rattled, Barned began to panic. "We should go to the police. The woman's obviously insane."

"Now you *are* joking," Tyland replied, "You really want the police involved? You want them to go back to that night, picking over our lives for twenty years? Our backgrounds? Our families? We're public figures, none of us would welcome that. And there's another thing you should consider - our collections. Not everyone would understand. To the police they might be obscene. You have that Courbet --"

"It's a masterpiece! Jesus, this is 2024, people are open minded. They don't give a fuck about sex. Mind you" Barend paused, his tone becoming furtive "you'd be in trouble, wouldn't you? People are never open minded about *crime*. I suppose it wouldn't do your career any good, you hoping to be the next Minis-

17

ter of the Arts, if it came out that you'd once smuggled artefacts out of the Far East --"

"Or that a soon-to-be King's Counsel was once an impoverished Dutch kid running around Harlingen with his arse hanging out of his trousers." Tyland replied, giving time for the insult to hit home.

"*You bastard!* I told you that in confidence."

"And I've never repeated it--"

"But obviously never forgotten it!" Barend snapped, Tyland interrupting him before he could continue.

"We all have a lot to hide, and we can tear each other apart, or join forces. You're a barrister, you know how the law works. How the truth is scuffed up, however deep it's buried. We must keep quiet about these letters. You hear me?" He paused. "Have you spoken to Vincent?"

"Yes, he got one this morning."

"Hand delivered?"

Barend sighed. "Yes, like the rest of them."

"So how has this person never seen? Vincent's house has got security cameras everywhere, Jimmy Nicholson's place had numerous lights around it, and we all have alarm systems."

Tyland stared ahead into the narrow chamber with its arched ceiling, one of only two private residences in London that sported such cathedral-like architecture. A ceiling that Tyland had restored painstakingly over the decades, a bevy of specialists employed to meet his fastidious and, at times, neurotic standards. It was to be his legacy, he declared, and who left a legacy vulnerable, open to destruction?

"As for Leo," Tyland continued "he travels all the time, but his apartment is never empty. He has staff, the place is never deserted."

"When I rang Leo I was told he was in London, but that he'd gone out for the evening. I left a message for him to call me back." Barend paused, wary. "Has he had a letter?"

"I don't know. I haven't spoken to him yet."

In unison they thought of the fifth member of the group, Leo Parks, African-American publisher of an interior design magazine. Philanthropist, charity event organiser, owner of one of the largest collections of homosexual art in Europe. Dividing his time equally between New York and London, Leo Parks had raised over $5,000,000 for charitable causes. *That* Leo Parks.

"Ring me when you've spoken to him, will you?" Tyland said, concluding the call. "And make it clear to him that there must be no involving the police. I'll talk to Vincent later and tell him the same."

Barend was beginning to bluster. "There is another way to look at this. If Jimmy Nicholson did something… if… well, *if* he did, he's dead now."

"Meaning, that he was guilty?"

"The evidence points to that."

"You're not in court now, Barend." Tyland replied. "He wasn't named in the letters."

"But if it *was* Jimmy, then the woman's got her revenge. It's over."

"Really? So why did she write to *all* of us? She could have killed Jimmy Nicholson and that would have been that. But she didn't, she made a point of accusing everyone."

Barend's hand gripped the phone, his palm sweating. "You think she's *really* coming after us?" He forced an unconvincing laugh. "You think we wouldn't be able to outsmart a woman? One woman pitted against five men?"

"*Four*," Tyland replied. "Remember, she's already killed one of us."

Three

New York

Leo Parks clapped his hands together, then spread them, palms showing. Silence fell over his audience, the packed room of illumini waiting for the auction lot. Leo had learned the value of suspense. As a younger man he had failed to make his mark as an actor, but had taken from his failure kernels of value. He might not play Broadway or appear in London's West End, but he could command attention and hold it like a bull dog with a chop. His broad face, with its oblique eyes, Moorish nose and cropped hair hijacked attention.

"Ladies and gentlemen, this is the last lot of the evening, and we have something I know all of you" he paused, smiled, "will bid for. And bid well," Laughter, nods of approval. He is so remarkable, who can resist Leo? What a showman, and it's in such a good cause. He knows what they think, plays them. They know he is a philanthropic salesman, and they play him. All will feel morally sated by the exchange. "This is extraordinary. So exquisitely beautiful, Bulgari..." and on he went, conjuring interest in an emerald necklace that he knew could transform into sack of money for his cause. Which was? An irrigation system in Niger.

Leo Parks had a quixotic relationship with failure. He didn't fear it, or resent it. He shifted through every failure panning for insight, shaking off the lumpen dirt to uncover the speckles of gold. There was always something priceless in the detritus, he realised, the trick was finding it. Whilst other men hid, or were shamed by their failures, Leo Parks revelled in his; each a medal of honour, proof of character.

On the dais he was assisted by a striking young woman, pointing out any bids he might have missed. To another other man she would have been a distraction, but Leo had no sexual feeling for women. He could admire their beauty, but their bodies did not have the enticement of a man's. His homosexuality was not hidden, nor flaunted. People suspected, but no one pried, because he was a good man, a humanitarian, altruistic to his African American bones.

The Bulgari exceeded its estimate, members of the audience clamouring to outbid each other, to prove their wealth under the cover of charity. Finally Leo closed the auction to applause, slipping out of the hotel and into the back alley where he lit a cigarette. Steam rose from a drain nearby, kitchen noises background accompaniment to the traffic as Leo remembered the letter he had been left for him. Taking it out of his pocket he read it, looking for a date, then a signature. There were neither. His great brow furrowed, he stared ahead down the alleyway and thought back.

Barend de Vries might have forgotten, Tyland Bray might affect a detached logic, but Leo felt only a snap of shame. It was easy for him to remember the night twenty years earlier. He had been newly initiated into the London group, impressed by the glamorous Dr Vincent Lund and by Tyland Bray's reputation, already firmly established in the art world. The dealer's illness was not apparent then. He was just starting to develop symptoms, the dislocated shoulder that required surgery, the heavy softness of skin around his elongated neck. When Ehlers-Danlos syndrome was diagnosed Leo reminded Tyland that Paganini had suffered from the same condition, even bought him a print of the virtuoso violinist. He sought to flatter him; as though he had picked his illness to share with another great man.

Leo's memory shifted back to the letter, to the girl who had been their model that night. He had been surprised that Vincent had not chosen a painting, but settled on a sculpture instead, Rodin's *Danaid*. The pose was beautiful but difficult to hold, the model naked, only her back exposed, her head turned to one side. An exquisite position. And, Leo had thought, one that would be exquisitely uncomfortable.

Her expression as she had been shown into the library was unreadable, her gaze moving to the life size reproduction of the Rodin and then back to the assembled men. She had been a touching figure, poignant, slight in the overbearing room, where successful men in dinner jackets lounged in leather chairs and talked amongst themselves, greeting her politely but without warmth. She was to be their model for the night, their disappointment hidden, but obvious to her.

And her discomfort had touched Leo, trying to catch her eye to smile reassuringly... Unnerved, his thoughts boomeranged back from the past into the present. *He had done nothing.* He had committed no abuse, no violence. There had been no reason to object. And besides, he had been careful not to offend, afraid to be ostracised by his new allies, aware that his perch on the exclusive ledge was narrow and precipitous....

Vincent had been drunk. Not boisterous, but drowsy, and only half present; Barend laughing, Tyland berating the girl. And Jimmy Nicholson, stout, unappealing Jimmy Nicholson, bumptious and angry that the girl offered no response to his flattery.

The other models had been professionals, quick to replicate the image that had been chosen for the evening in order to celebrate a new auction purchase. Usually in Tyland Bray's gallery, where he would invite his most influential collectors to attend this exclusive Private View. Sometimes it had been Manet, or Titian, even Velasquez, the poses in the paintings made flesh by models usually employed for professional artists or in Academy schools. They were beautiful and eager to work for a good fee. Content to stand or lie and daydream, never touched, merely admired.

The whole idea had stemmed from the Renaissance, Vincent the originator, explaining how collectors had held such displays to see how the original painting had been conceived. That was how it had begun. Naturally it had appealed to Vincent's medical curiosity to know how a pose had been arranged, and held. He would diagnose the original painting or sculpture and tell his guests that the pose showed signs of some unusual curvature of the spine. It was slight, he would say, but when the model became older it would bother her. Beauty more in the bones than in the body.

As for Tyland Bray, he had no interest in flesh or anatomy, only culture. A woman might stand before him and he would see only how well she imitated the pose of an early Degas. His ill temper, caused by frequent pain, had dried up his sexuality and beauty did not stimulate him personally, only his wallet.

Leo then thought of Barend de Vries. He had always arrived late, harassed, chuntering about his cases and clients, gradually soothed by cognac and finally becoming calm. Perhaps because his wife was supremely beautiful, Barend had developed an appreciation for pulchritude, along with an impressive collection of erotica. Yet no woman, however stunning, could have tempted him away from his partner. He would consider the model's appeal and then leave the house later knowing that he had married a greater beauty.

As for Jimmy Nicholson, what of him? ... Leo closed his eyes against the memory, but remembered all the details. Indeed, had never forgotten them. Despite all the generous irrigation systems in Niger and food drops in war zones: despite all the charity balls and auction feeding frenzies. Despite all his multifarious, bloated raising of money, the girl had remained eternally present, hovering over him like a premature memorial.

And now she was back. Just as Leo had known she would be, one day. He had tried to forget, but could not. He had hoped she was relegated to the past, but knew she was timeless, of yesterday, today and tomorrow, and he had been right. Exhausted, emptied of his earlier auction triumph, he held the letter in his hands and saw – only inches down his own lifeline – his fate awaiting him.

Four

Vincent Lund read the letter twice, finally laying it beside Jimmy Nicholson's obituary notice. *What happened?* He said to the dead man's photograph. *It was so long ago, no one meant to hurt anyone. But apparently we did. I did.* **You** *did…* His memory was already waiting for him; a fish at the top of the water, looking to be fed. Their exclusive club had seemed arcane and unconventional, five young, wealthy men discussing art and their private collections. At once liberal and elitist. But although the lure of erotica was appealing, Vincent's attention had soon concentrated on medical artefacts, antique surgical instruments and Victorian wax anatomical figures used to train students in anatomy. Dummy figures of the faux dead, their torsos opened to reveal internal organs, or the moulded workings of a wax womb.

He was a doctor, after all. Initially his interest had been piqued by the Hunterian Museum, a collection of medical oddities and physical deformities which resided in the belly of Lincoln's Inn. As a barrister with chambers nearby, Barend de Vries had first drawn his attention to it, Vincent captivated by the plethora of the weird and touched by the poignancy of deformity. It had not been to Barend's taste – Barend drawn to tame Victorian erotica and the likes of J W Waterhouse – but Vincent had been mesmerised by the quirks of humanity and the inner workings, the blood and bone under the soft skin.

"Vincent?"

He flinched, slid the letter under the newspaper and smiled as his nephew walked in. Milas Hansen, the son of his estranged sister who had died in a car accident alongside her husband. Vincent had not heard about their deaths until Milas had sought him out, arriving at the hospital one humid July morning.

'I'm your nephew.'

Vincent had paused, in scrubs, surgical mask dangling by his chin. Hurried, not expecting a child, now grown, to emerge in a hospital corridor.

'Milas?...'.

Well, what could he say? He just used his nephew's name, clasped his hands, tried to express some regret that should have come years earlier. But never had.

'Milas, sorry,' he stammered.... But how do you say that when the word has lost meaning? Too past its usefulness; too small for comfort...

They went to the hospital canteen, drank some coffee that needed more milk, fiddled with sugar wrappers, both embarrassed and amazed by the finding of each other. Vincent, with no son, a daughter instead, now looking at a young man in his thirties who would be a son. Perhaps. Maybe. Was he hoping for too

28

much? Was he rushing? Would Milas stay or was he just passing through?

Stay, please stay....

Milas was fair haired, like him, slender, wearing glasses that slid down his nose because his skin was damp in the heat. And Vincent tried to explain the bitter estrangement, make amends, wanting to incorporate this elegant fledging into his stagnant nest.

He loved his daughter, Charlotte, but she was unlike him, and he had no ally.

Until that morning when Milas came to him.

"Are you alright?"

Vincent nodded. "Just a bit tired." His gaze moved back to the hidden letter and then returned to his nephew. "What was all the noise about?"

"Charlotte's laptop broke down. You know how she gets. So upset about everything."

Vincent's daughter had suffered from asthma since the age of six; barking, gasping episodes tamed by inhalers. The illness had left her frail, remote from other children, her childhood affection concentrated on her mother. The same mother that had left. And then what else could Charlotte do but switch sides? Cling to her father, a little too much, a little too desperately. But Vincent had welcomed it and saw Charlotte's affection as revenge for his wife's leaving.

For a while Nancy had chopped up her affection into portions, doling it out fairly to her husband, daughter, and Milas. Perhaps another woman would have resented the inclusion of her husband's nephew, Nancy did not. It had no bearing on her life. On those endless shifting travels of her career. What was another person in a house with so many rooms? And besides, Milas asked nothing of her. When she left Vincent, citing *'irreconcilable differences'* – even though they both knew it was down to her adultery – the house seemed unchanged without her.

She kept in touch because of their shared daughter, but the spaces between contact elongated, a swimmer always heading further away from shore. Vincent never mentioned her affair; that shabby instance of betrayal. Occasionally he had entertained the idea that he would match her treachery, but fell back to his work instead, to the soft comfort of success.

"Get someone in to fix the laptop for her, will you? I don't want Charlotte upset."

Milas nodded. "Someone's coming this afternoon." He was wearing a green t shirt and jeans, narrow leather band around his neck. "I wanted to talk to you. It's important."

"What is it?"

"It's… probably ridiculous." Milas paused, drew in a breath, puffed out his chest like a pigeon in a city square. "Do you think I could..."

"Could *what?*"

"Nah, forget it, it was a stupid idea."

Vincent wasn't going to let it pass. "Don't do that! We can talk about anything, you and I. Come on, what is it?" He leaned forwards, gesturing for Milas to sit down, but he moved to the window instead, looking out. His back was tense, his shoulder blades interrupting the line of his t shirt, his hands picking at the window blind.

"Can I help you with your research? Not the writing obviously, I couldn't do that, but I could find out facts for you. Help you out with the donkey work." He was tugging at the blind, mortally embarrassed. "I've drifted all my life, I'm too old to be a waster. A man in his thirties should be settled, have a proper career –"

"I'd welcome help," Vincent said, surprised. "if you're sure that's what you want."

"I *do*, but…" he seemed embarrassed. "It's a stupid idea. Everyone knows I'm Vincent Lund's nephew it would just be seen as nepotism. As if you haven't given me enough already."

"You don't owe me anything," Vincent replied, "Your coming to live here is one of the best things that's ever happened to me. I regretted the fight with your mother for years, I should have tried harder to reconcile."

"She found it hard to forgive."

The ache of old wounds. "Did she ever talk about me?"

Milas shook his head. "No. I used to asked her about you, but she never explained why you two fell out. But I guessed it was because she was jealous, angry that you'd left Denmark."

Vincent thought back to the clammy estrangement which had separated his family from that of his sister. Years of no communication, of distance, only solved by the death of a woman he had almost forgotten. Adela had been a part of his upbringing and life in Denmark; but the closeness they had had as children dissolved when he left for London to train at St Thomas's Hospital. She had remained in Denmark, marrying Noah when she was twenty two. A while later Adela wrote to her brother and told him about the birth of Milas, his nephew, and they exchanged photographs, Vincent sending images of his daughter. Their connection did not gel and they began to make excuses; Vincent was coming to Copenhagen, they could meet up.

Adela was coming to London, they could re-connect. But the siblings were too dissimilar to breach their differences and then came the summer when Vincent finally visited.

It was hotter than he remembered, air clear, sun high, waiting to do damage.

She poured him a drink and sat beside him in a garden which needed attention, behind the house Adela had inherited from their parents.

Why not? Vincent was rich, successful, established in London, his munificence was automatic.

She threw the line at him: 'You know you broke their heart?'

Sun overhead, knifing him through the skull and the blond hair.

'What?'.... Vincent turning, spilling the drink she had given him, seeing the cat look in her eyes, the expression of old hatred.

'Our parents, you killed them with your indifference...'

She was a martyr in a deckchair, rounding the corner to middle age, spite marinated in the long years.

'I'll never forgive you.'

His financial support, his achievements, the pride he had supposed they felt in his success turned to crematorium ashes, urns of dead parents and the dry barking of guilt.

'They never forgave you and neither will I.'

"I didn't know your mother wanted to leave Denmark."

"You were supposed to guess." Milas replied. "My mother expected everyone to understand her. I never

32

did." He turned, held Vincent's gaze. "It's hard living up to you. I know I can't, that's not what I expect. But I want to make you proud of me."

"Why didn't you stay in touch after your parents died?" Vincent asked. "I tried to contact you, but you never replied to my calls or messages. And then you left Denmark. I did try to find you, but realised that you didn't want me to --"

"It wasn't that." Milas interrupted. "I just felt that you wouldn't want to know me."

"But you're family and I'm proud of you," Vincent insisted, "and I'll help you with anything you want to do. If you want to do research for me, I'd be more than happy. As I say, you're family, Milas, you belong here. Always remember that."

He wanted so much to pry, to know more about his nephew, but he was fearful of creating another rift, terrified of losing someone he had grown to love. Afraid that Adela had shared her bitterness and resentment, how dangerous would it be for him to wriggle amongst the silt of old hatred?

Vincent glanced at the letter hidden under the newspaper, his throat nerve-dry. What would Milas think of him if he read it? If he knew what had happened twenty years ago? He was a winner to his nephew. To the son he had never had. To the young man who had returned. Milas saw him as Vincent *wished* to be seen. Not as a failed husband, an uncertain man afraid of exposure, but as a hero.

He would do anything to preserve that.

Five

Rubbing his forehead with the tips of his dry fingers, Tyland Bray stared at the photograph in the auction house catalogue. *La Mujer Barbuda*, aka 'The Bearded Woman,' the original painted by Ribera in 1631. It was coming up for sale listed as either an unknown version by the artist, or a copy by a follower, possibly a student. Tyland scrutinised the image, making a mental note to visit the auction house and see the painting before the sale took place, having had a lifelong admiration for *La Mujer Barbuda*.

The subject of the painting had been a woman called Magdalena Valentina, born in Abruzzi, who had given birth to three sons before suddenly developing a full beard at the age of thirty seven. When Ribera painted her in Naples she was fifty two years old, and had become famous, her image known throughout Europe. She had fascinated and repelled people in equal measure, her dignity and defiance inspiring Ribera to paint her the portrait.

The portrait Tyland wanted. Just as he knew the other members of his coterie would want it too. Vincent would see it as an oddity, a hormonal irregularity which was an obvious addition to his medical collection. Barend would see it as some bizarre female failing from grace, a shift in sexual key. As for Leo, a woman turning into a man would intrigue him. Was *La Mujer Barbuda* still female, or had she undergone some emotional metamorphosis along with her switch of gender? He could imagine the American's fascination, his compassionate curiosity.

Oh yes, Tyland thought, they would all want it. For different reasons, but they would all want it and bid for it, pushing up the price... He winced, rubbing his shoulder and taking a couple of pain killers. His doctor assured him that his condition was being managed 'robustly' and that the disease 'was not progressing quickly'. It felt quick to Tyland. Despite what the medic said, pain didn't have a speed; it was just pain. His attention moved back to the painting. Perhaps his colleagues were pre-occupied, too anxious about the death of Jimmy Nicholson to care about the Ribera. But Tyland knew better. Collectors all had a dark taint of obsession and the whiff of *La Mujer Barbuda* would concentrate their minds nicely.

Having decided he would view the painting at the auction house, Tyland was just about to leave his gallery when a short, podgy man with thinning sandy hair blocked his way.

"Mr Bray?"

Tyland had the advantage of height, and used it. "Yes. And you are?"

"Detective Sox."

"As in 'shoes and socks'?"

"No, as in S-O-X."

Tyland stood back to let him enter, then guided him towards his office and shut the door behind him. "Unusual name, Sox."

"It has an unusual history. No one's very sure where it originated, possibly England," he explained. "It's mentioned in the 1852 census, although it was known in the USA before then. In fact, my grandfather was an American."

"Oh, I am sorry." Tyland replied, his face impassive.

He had been expecting a visit from the police for the last few days. After all, Jimmy Nicholson had been a friend of his, but he was surprised by the smiley little man now seated opposite him.

"So, what can I do for you, detective?"

"Mr James Nicholson was murdered, as you know."

"A tragedy. He was a very gifted man."

"You knew him well, I believe."

"You have reason to believe that?"

Sox nodded. "That's what I was told by Mrs Nicholson. You were friends and colleagues. Mr Nicholson dealt in…" Sox flipped open his notebook and ran a stumpy finger down the page, then paused. "... Italian paintings." He snapped the book shut. "I've often wondered what the difference is between Italian and Spanish painting."

"A few hundred miles." Tyland replied dryly.

"Depending on how you travel. Or how the crow flies. You ever wonder where that expression comes from? I do." Sox replied, laughing wheezily, then getting serious again. "Always been fascinated by entomology."

"Bugs?"

"Pardon?"

"Entomology is the study of insects. I think you mean *etymology*. That's term for the origin of words and expressions."

Sox laughed. "You mean I've been using the wrong word all these years? Oh dear, I must have looked like an idiot...."

Tyland said nothing.

"... People thinking I studied bugs. Life really is laughable at times, isn't it?"

"Not if you're Jimmy Nicholson."

Sox sobered up. "No, Mr Bray, not if you're Mr Nicholson. Which brings me to the point nicely. Did Mr Nicholson have any enemies?"

"Not that I know of."

"But people could have been jealous of his success?"

"Maybe, he had a fine brain, he was very learned in his field. But you don't murder a man to steal his brain, do you?"

"Well, it's not a motive I've ever heard of." Sox agreed, moving on. "Now, what about these *private* pictures."

"I don't understand."

"Mrs Nicholson said her husband collected art, paintings and sculpture, nudes in particular...."

Bloody fool woman, Tyland thought, Stella Nicholson should have kept quiet about the collection. If she hadn't wanted it, she could just have sold it on and made a huge profit. There were several William Ettys he would have bought from her. In fact, ever since he had heard of Jimmy's death he had been thinking of approaching Stella – in due course – with an offer for the collection. Before Vincent or Leo did.

"... Mrs Nicholson said the paintings are very erotic."

"They're nudes, not kittens in a basket."

"I think" Sox went on, leaning forward, one elbow on the edge of the desk "that she doesn't care for them."

"She *hates* her husband's collection. But I don't think she killed him because of his taste in art."

"Oh, Mrs Nicholson has never been a suspect." Sox replied, leaning back. "She was talking to their housekeeper when her husband died, and she had been at her hairdressers before that. Besides, she never handled Mr Nicholson's insulin vials or his syringes. He wouldn't let her, and she was afraid of needles."

"Stella doesn't like anything to do with illness. When Jimmy was first diagnosed with diabetes she said it was all in his mind and refused to discuss it ever again. Strange woman, very cool indeed."

"Did Mr Nicholson have a mistress?"

Tyland raised his eyebrows and tipped his head to one side. "Now *why* would you ask me that?"

"Did he?"

"How would I know?"

"You were his friend."

"But not his confidante."

Sox nodded, then glanced at the open catalogue on Tyland's desk. "You're a very respected art dealer, even more so that Mr Nicholson. Were you rivals?"

"No, we collected art from different schools and times."

"But you both have *private* collections."

Bloody Stella Nicholson, Tyland thought, the woman had been indiscreet. The questioning was getting a little too intrusive, a little too close to the marshy past. Tyland didn't want Sox to know about his collection, but then again better to throw him one bone rather than deny him and have him dig up all the others.

39

"I do collect eroticism and have done for decades. Unlike Joe Public, I see nudes as artistic and seldom obscene. We seem to have a fear of sexuality than has never left us, even in the twenty first century."

"Gender bending."

"What?"

Sox pointed to the open catalogue.

"Sex and gender, all that stuff. Seems people can't seem to get enough of it at present, all the woke beliefs becoming common currency. But human nature is basically the same as it ever was. It's not surprising how many murders are prompted by sex. Same sex, opposite sex, trans sex, deviant sex." He paused, his expression regretful. "It's like we opened the flood-gates when we became so liberal."

"You want homosexuality to be illegal again?"

"Oh no, you misunderstand me! I'm just a copper. I clear up the mess of peoples' sex lives, I don't tell them what they can – or can't – do." He looked back at the catalogue. "Funnily enough, I know that paint-ing. You see my wife teaches art, not at your level of knowledge, of course, but to secondary school pupils." He tapped the photograph with his podgy index finger. "It's called *'The Bearded Lady'*."

Tyland was trying to gauge the little man, won-dering if his guileless manner was just that, or a benign ruse to make people let down their guard. Neither his collection, Vincent's, Leo's, or Barend's were obscene or illegal, but they would inspire curiosity if they became public. Important men in important positions were scrutinised; which was exactly why they had always striven to keep their collections private. But now here was this funny little policeman asking ques-tions, digging away like a cross-bred terrier, ratting out their secrets. And whilst he did was he wondering just how connected those secrets were to the murder of Jimmy Nicholson?

Tyland decided to tackle the notion head on. "Do you have any idea who killed Jimmy?"

"Not yet. We don't know the motive either. He wasn't worried about anything, was he?"

"Not that he mentioned."

"Nothing suspicious had happened to him lately? No threats? No phone calls from numbers he didn't recognise? No arguments? Disagreements with clients? No money worries?"

"He was a rich man."

"What about his past?"

Tyland was beginning to sweat. "Jimmy and I knew each other, as did our wives, we socialised, sometimes we did business, but he wasn't an intimate friend."

"Even though you had known each other for over twenty years?" Sox continued. "Mrs Nicholson said you met up frequently --"

"To talk business."

"What kind of business?"

"Art business."

"Not about your collections?"

"Sometimes," Tyland paused, took in a slow breath.

He thought of Stella Nicholson with her dogmatic refusal to acknowledge the arts, in direct contrast to Jimmy's innate culture. He had often wondered why they had married, why a sexual man had chosen a woman with such a vicious undertow of self-righteousness. Perhaps they had stayed together for the sake of their son? But if so, the sacrifice had been pointless because the Nicholson's only child had moved to France years before, married, had a family of his own, and never contacted his parents. Tyland even wondered if he would return to London for his father's funeral. Would the estrangement still persist when there was a will and a fortune at stake?

"You have to realise that the art world is very small, very insular." He explained patiently, his thoughts returning to the policeman. "Every one knows each other, but that doesn't mean we're like a family."

Sox smiled, then glanced back to the open catalogue. "Are you going to buy the painting, Mr Bray?"

"That depends. It's not the original Ribera, of course, but there is a slim chance that it might be by the master. Sometimes a painter will many several versions of a picture. Or it could be an excellent copy, done by one of his pupils, but a copy none the less."

"I suppose others will want it, it being so rare? I mean, the subject matter makes it desirable – for certain collectors." Sox went on. "Poor Mr Nicholson would probably have wanted to add it to his stockpile."

"Strange word."

"Strange painting," Sox responded. He was unnerving Tyland, shifting around the edges of the frozen lake, avoiding the thin centre ice, dancing his little gnome jig. "I suppose there are others who would want it too?"

"Maybe."

"Perhaps other collectors you know personally?" Tyland stayed silent as Sox glanced at his notepad again, although Tyland was certain he didn't need to check his facts. "Mrs Nicholson said that her husband was friendly with Mr Barend de Vries, a barrister. Do you know him?"

"Yes."

"Is he a collector too?"

"Yes."

"As serious a collector as Mr Nicholson?"

"Depends on what you call serious."

"Is his collection valuable?"

"Yes, but not as valuable as Jimmy Nicholson's."

"Which is now about to move on."

Tyland could feel the shift in atmosphere, the sensation that he was on the edge of a nasty fall. "What d'you mean by that?"

Sox flipped his notepad closed. "Oh, I see you haven't heard."

"Heard what?"

"It's not common gossip yet, so perhaps we should keep it to ourselves for the present.... Mr Nicholson left his collection to an ex-lover. I think you know her, she's married to another friend of yours. Or so I'm told – Alicia de Vries."

Six

London

It was past four when Leo arrived and made his way to Vincent's consulting rooms. Patiently he waited in reception, glancing at a year old copy of Country Life and pretending to read. Occasionally his attention wandered, his head going back, glancing at the ceiling. It was typical for Wimpole Street, stuccoed Adam style, an opulent ceiling rose surrounded by a cornice of egg and dart moulding, an over varnished landscape sulking over the fireplace.

His flight had been easy, or was that simply because flying was commonplace for him?

> *Boarding pass, sir, thank you, turn left. Another blanket?*
> *Of course. Shall I turn on the light over your head so you can see your papers more clearly?*

And yet suddenly all the journeys he had done so willingly had begun to melt into one great sink hole, a yawning chasm soaking up stills of photo shoots, material swatches, extravagant trimmings and the dim seduction of ambient lighting. *Leo Parks has an eye, you see. He knows about interior design. Knows a hat stand from a handsaw….*

Smiling, Vincent walked into the waiting room as his last patient left, showing Leo into his consulting room and closing the door behind them.

"It's good to see you."

Leo didn't reply, the words bolting from his lips: "What are we going to do about her?" There was no need for Vincent to ask who he was talking about. "Perhaps the letter was just a threat?"

"You believe that?"

"No." Leo paused, glancing around nervously, "what *are* we doing to do? I mean, what do we know about her? Who was she?"

"The professional model was ill that night, the girl came in her place."

"Who sent her?"

"I don't remember, Leo. Calm down, we have to think this through without panicking." Vincent replied. "When did you get your letter?"

"The day before yesterday. It was delivered to the hotel where I was holding an auction. When I asked at Reception, they couldn't remember who handed it in. It was just left anonymously." He paused, sat down, Vincent taking the seat behind his desk. On the mantelpiece an Edwardian clock ticked sonorously, someone whistling on the street outside as Leo spoke again. "Have you talked to the others?"

Vincent nodded. "Barend is panicking. He claims he can't remember anything."

"But he wasn't that drunk! You were, Vincent, and you were pre-occupied. You'd been arguing with your ex-wife." His tone was sympathetic. "You have some excuse."

"I have no excuse. It happened in my house."

"If anything really happened."

"You doubt her? She talked about *'an attack'* in the letter --"

"She could be lying." Leo's shoulders tensed. "She could. People do, all the time. But *if* it happened... *if...* it would have been Jimmy who assaulted her."

"And Jimmy Nicholson is dead." Vincent said solemnly. "Murdered."

Leo's head snapped up. "Has that been confirmed?"

"He didn't commit suicide, you and I both know he wasn't the type. There was nothing in Jimmy's life that would have pushed him to kill himself. Nothing out of the ordinary had happened – apart from a threatening letter reminding him of a night more than twenty years earlier. Jimmy's conscience didn't kill him, *she* did."

"No," Leo said, his voice unsteady. "She was only a girl –"

"She's an adult now," Vincent retorted. "Over twenty years have passed, people change. We're not what we were, and neither will she be."

"But she can't have killed Jimmy!"

"He was *poisoned.* Murdered after he received that letter... Come on, face facts." Vincent took a long drink of the whisky. "She killed him."

"Then he *must* have been guilty."

"So if he *was* guilty, he deserved it?" Vincent countered. "What now, Leo? You think that's the end of it? She got her revenge on Jimmy Nicholson, it's over. Think for a minute, if that is the truth then why did she send the letter to *all of us?"*

"God…" Leo slumped back in the chair, the handsome face puffy from a lack of sleep. "Perhaps we were all complicit. If something *did* happen, Vincent, we should have known! The girl was nervous, I could see that, and then she ran off so suddenly."

Vincent reached into his lower desk drawer and brought out a bottle of whisky, then filled two glasses and pushed one over to Leo.

"Drink that –"

"It was bitterly cold that night, and raining," Leo continued, his voice muted. "I thought I should have run after her, checked she was alright, but I didn't…I *should* have gone after her." His eyes fixed on Vincent. "What do you remember?"

"About that night?"

"About her."

Pale, tall, thin. Long hair that was loose around her shoulders, just like the Rodin girl in the Danaide sculpture.
She wasn't crying. No, not crying…
She had an accent, not foreign, maybe Northern.
Fine white hands picking at the dragons on the Oriental gown…

"Did she say anything?"

"Not that I remember."

"She still had her shoes on, and they were wet." Leo said dully. "It was raining that night."

Yes, the rain… she had said the buses were running late.

'Hurry, run for it, they'll be waiting'... *Wild*
white moon under a yawn of trees outside the
window of a great white house owned by a
handsome Dane.
'Fleece the bastards'.

"One of us should have seen her home afterwards." Leo looked away, ashamed. "She just left so
quickly. Did anyone see her again?"

"No." Vincent shook his head. "Well, I didn't,
you'd have to ask the others. But I don't think anyone
saw or heard from her. Until now."

"No name?"

"No," Vincent said, emptying his glass. "I never
knew her name. It's a long time ago."

"And how would we recognise her after so long?
Maybe she's isn't poor now, maybe she's powerful.
She could walk up to us, pass us in the street, she could
be a patient of yours, a client of mine – and we'd never
know." Leo felt a chill run through him. "Maybe Barend has interrogated her in court? Or defended her?
Maybe she was a witness, or maybe she went to Tyl-
and's gallery and admired his paintings." He was trying to steady his nerves, but it wasn't working. "We're
presuming she's just materialised out of the past, but
what if she's been moving amongst us all these years
and we never knew it?" His voice rose. "She could
be stalking us. She could know *everything* about our
homes, our lives --"

"You have to stay calm."

"We have to tell the police what's happening!"
Leo interrupted him. "I know Tyland and Barend don't
want that, but it's the right thing to do. It's what we
have to do."

Vincent turned away, thinking. He could imagine the fall out, the resurrection of past lives, secrets, that cold November night exposed. One night that could topple decades of success, the good drowned in the sludge of one error. His daughter would know, his nephew, *his heir,* would know, both releasing that what they had admired was fake. And as the police keep digging, what other dry bones would come back and shake their buried fingers?

He would do anything to prevent it. *Anything.*

"We'll be ruined if we tell the police about the letters. If we do, it will open up a can of worms," Vincent said, warningly. "It would bring us all down. Tyland will never be Minister of Arts, Barend will never make KC. Your business will suffer --"

"*I don't care!* I should have done something at the time."

"Like what? We didn't *know* Jimmy had done anything until she contacted us." Vincent paused, reading the letter again. "There's something strange about it. She doesn't go into detail. Doesn't describe what happened, just says that she was '*attacked.*'" Vincent hesitated. "Maybe it wasn't written by the woman herself, maybe it was written by someone she'd confided in. Someone who didn't know the whole story. Someone who elaborated on what happened --"

"*We don't know what happened!*"

"We can guess!" Vincent retorted. "It's not spelt out, but Jimmy is dead, murdered. That seems pretty conclusive, doesn't it? And as much as we might have forgotten about that night, she hasn't." He refilled his glass, his hand shaking. "Did you ever discuss it with Jimmy?"

"No, no one ever mentioned it."

"No one said anything?"

"No! You were drunk, arguing with Nancy – you were out of it - and the rest of us just pushed it to the back of our minds and went on with our lives." Leo hung his head. "Charity…"

"What?"

"I've spent all these years raising money for charity, pretending to be the good guy. What a fucking hypocrite I am. I didn't show any charity that night."

"I don't remember –"

"Stop fucking saying that!" Leo snapped, uncharacteristically sharp. "Just because you have the Get Out of Jail free card –"

"No one's going to jail," Vincent said coldly. "No one's panicking either. You're innocent –"

"No, I'm not! I didn't go to the girl's defence. I was a coward, I didn't want to lose face in front of our little club." He was talking too quickly, spittle forming at the side of his mouth. "I didn't want to be exiled --"

"*Exiled?*" Vincent ed, incredulous.

"It's nothing to you, is it? You're not a gay black man and American to boot." He smiled ruefully. "It's not such a big deal now, but twenty years ago it was. I was *proud* to be part of your exclusive little English 'gang'." His voice wavered on the edge of bitterness. "You welcomed me, Jimmy and Barend thought of me like a kid brother, and you – even though we were around the same age – who couldn't be impressed by the wunderkind of the medical world?" Leo paused, clasping and unclasping his hands, an old mannerism he slipped into when he was nervous. "I was a little in love with you."

Vincent paused, then nodded. "I know."

"*You knew?*"

"Come on, Leo, you're not the only person that can be impressed." He replied honestly. "You impressed *me*. I genuinely liked you, liked your style, your artistic flair. I collect art, but I can't create it --"

"Making curtains and covering sofas isn't art."

"Don't start with the self-pity, that's not your style," Vincent replied. "What happened that night *cannot* come out. Do you hear me, Leo? It can't. And that's not just because of how much it could damage our careers."

"And you don't want it to come out about our collections?"

"No, I don't." Vincent nodded. " People wouldn't understand."

"You're safe. You collect medical specimens, I'm the one that collects gay erotica."

"That's hardly unusual, is it?" Vincent replied, raising his eyebrows, then staring intently at Leo. "Is there anything else you should tell me?"

"I don't know what happened that night –"

"About what you collect." Vincent interrupted him. "Tell me everything, Leo, I have to know. I *need* to know, otherwise I can't help you. I need the truth. The whole truth."

"You think I'm some freak? A *paedophile?*"

"I didn't say that!"

"You didn't have to!" Leo replied. "You thought it –"

"I didn't think it! I just wanted to know about your collection."

"What if I said – 'Yes, I'm the worst of the worst. I'm filth, if they look at what I collect I'll be thrown in jail and buggered by every man in there'." Leo's eyes filled. "No, I'm not what you think! I am **not** what you think –"

Reaching out his hand Vincent touched Leo's shoulder, then pulled him into a hug. "I didn't think it. I *didn't*, believe me, I wasn't suspecting anything to do with children. I know you couldn't do that, Leo, I was just trying to find out how hardcore the pornography was. If there was anything –"

"Nothing that you couldn't see in liberal art galleries." Leo replied, stepping back and wiping his eyes with the back of his hands. "But I still wouldn't want some of the photographs made public. They were – *are* – friends. Lovers."

Vincent nodded. "Ok. But some people are still homophobic, don't kid yourself, Leo. Your business would suffer. It could ruin you." Vincent paused, unwilling to ask the next question. "Is there *anything* in your personal life that would be damning?"

"No!" He said emphatically, turning the inquisition onto Vincent. "What about you? People will ask questions about your life too, your collection. Your patients will wonder, maybe stop trusting you as a surgeon --"

"You still think this is just about my work?" Vincent retorted. "This is more than my career. My nephew lives with me and I'm finally making up for what happened between me and my sister. Adela turned him against me - but now she's dead, and Milas has come to me. I'm the only family he has. He's like a son, the boy I never had." Vincent paused, taking in a breath. "He admires me, Leo. I *can't* let him find out the kind of man I really am."

"You did nothing wrong –"

"The sin of omission. The sin of pleading ignorance. Jesus, Leo, it happened at my house, I should have known." His voice faltered. "And if all this came out, what about the effect it would have on Charlotte? She couldn't take the gossip, the back stabbing --"

"Maybe if we spoke to the police in confidence?"

"And say *what*? That Jimmy Nicholson was killed by a woman he raped?"

"Jesus..." Leo said dully. "are you sure he raped her?"

"I don't know. I didn't see it. But if rape *was* the motive for Jimmy's murder we have to stop it coming out."

"To protect ourselves?"

"To protect us, and all the others it would affected. What about Stella, Jimmy's wife? And their son? What about Barend and his wife, and their daughter? What about you?" Vincent shook his head. "Think about the damage that would follow if the truth came out. If Jimmy raped that girl, he's paid for it. She's had her revenge. Barend didn't rape her, Tyland didn't, you didn't and neither did I. Why destroy so many lives for the actions of one man?"

Leo was listening, but not convinced. "If she'd only written to Jimmy I might agree with you – but like you said, she wrote to all of us. So she must blame all of us."

"All the more reason to hide it."

Leo hesitated, his hands clasping and unclasping. "I can vouch for you, Vincent, tell them you were drunk at the time, arguing with Nancy, that you didn't know what was going on --"

"You think anyone would believe that? It would look like I'm trying to avoid responsibility. Jimmy Nicholson is dead and people would say that we made him the scapegoat because he couldn't defend himself."

"You didn't assault her."

"Neither did you."

"But we both failed her! I keep thinking that if it had been my daughter what how would I judge the men that didn't help her? I'd want to punish them, I'd want to kill the likes of Jimmy Nicholson –"

Vincent put up his hands to stop him, changing tack. "Why's she come forwards now, after so long?"

"Maybe she's seen how well we've all done. Maybe she's had to struggle, and she wants to punish us. Maybe she feels she *has* to do it."

"*Has to kill*?" Vincent asked incredulously. "Murder as justice? Why didn't she just expose what happened at the time?"

"I don't know! But it was Jimmy that attacked her. Perhaps she's just trying to scare the rest of us. There's nothing to say she intends to go any further." Leo paused, his hands going through his hair. "It's a week since Jimmy was murdered, maybe she won't kill again."

"You think one murder was enough?" Vincent stared at his old friend. "No, she's kept her nerve for over twenty years, she's not going to back off now."

They both fell silent, the clock ticking behind them, the street outside the window quiet. In the distance a car horn sounded, and across the road someone turned on a light in a penthouse flat. It shone through the glass dome of the roof, a great cold eye begging for mercy from the darkness above.

Seven

Marina Bray had spent her life in blinkers. They had kept her focused and cut out any peripheral vision. Which included the past. Long before the notion of 'mindfulness' Marina had perfected the attention span of a flea. It had protected her from the grief of being childless and married to Tyland Bray.

She found that life could be pleasant if you were willing to perform your own frontal lobotomy. A certain sweetness was possible, even pleasure, if it was not held up against memory or expectation. But the sight of the glamorous Alicia de Vries walking up the front steps of her house unnerved Marina so much that she ducked out of sight behind the porch door.

"Don't be bloody silly, Marina, I saw you!" Alicia said, calling through the letter box. "Let me in. We need to talk."

Smiling wanly, Marina opened the door. "I was just --"

"Hiding."

She flushed, then showed her unwelcome guest into the morning room. It was drowsy, with yellow walls and a bowl of pink peonies which clashed with the curtains.

"You'll never guess who was at my house this morning, sneaking around with my husband." Alicia walked through the archway into the kitchen and over to a coffee machine. "Can I?"

"Oh, yes, yes," Marina replied, hurrying behind her. "Do you want a biscuit?"

"You think I could get into these jeans if I ate biscuits?" Alicia replied, looking pointedly at Marina's wide hips. "I know a great nutritionist if you want their number, and a good trainer."

Marina flushed and changed the subject. "You said you had a visitor."

"Your husband."

"Tyland?"

"That's who you're married to, isn't it?" Alicia replied, moving over to the window and kneeling on the cushioned window seat. Her hair was piled up on her head, her dark roots just beginning to show at the base of her neck. "I like your house, always have. You would let me know if you were thinking of moving?" Her tone was sly. "Or if you were getting a divorce?"

"A divorce!" Marina repeated, watching Alicia laugh.

"I was just teasing you! Honestly, you're so easy to bait." She sighed, sitting down and crossing her legs, the mug of coffee in her right hand. "What did your husband want to see Barend about?"

Marina stared at her, her voice soft. "How would I know?"

"You're his wife."

"You're Barend's wife, why don't *you* know what's going on?" Marina replied, uncharacteristically sharp. "I mean, you usually know everything that's going on."

"Not this time." Alicia replied. "Anything unusual happened lately?"

Marina sat down, her skirt covering her knees. At twenty she had been bosomy, full lipped and drowsily sensual, but her fifty year old breasts were now disguised under loose clothes, her lips asexual, thin with disuse. Somewhere, her flamboyance had slipped to timidity. She couldn't have said the precise moment when the shift began, only that she felt like someone who had asked for directions and been given the wrong route.

"Well," Alicia repeated, *"has* anything unusual happened?"

"Such as?"

"Anything unusual! Jesus, Marina, it's not hard, you're not giving evidence in court."

"Who said anything about court! Am I in trouble? Is Tyland?" Marina pulled down the cuffs of her sleeves, her hands shaking. "Why did you come here, talking about divorce and court?"

Alicia stared at her, baffled. "Calm down!"

"I *was* calm, before you came. You've confused me," Marina got to her feet, glancing at the clock. "You'll have to leave. I can't deal with this… Tyland will deal with it."

"With *what?* That's what I'm trying to find out. *What's going on?*"

"Tyland needs me to be calm. He needs his home to be calm. He's not a well man," Marina turned to Alicia. "It's very wrong of you to upset him."

"Are you off your fucking head? I'm talking to you, not your husband. I haven't said a word to him."

Flustered, Marina's voice became plaintive. "You're always trying to make trouble, everyone knows that. You can't stop interfering in people's lives."

"Since when?"

"There's been gossip," Marina said, flushing. "You and other women's husbands. You and Jimmy Nicholson. And, of course, Vincent Lund."

Alicia shook her head, trying to appear nonchalant, but Marina knew the dart had scored.

"That was a long time ago. Besides, Vincent's divorced –"

"He wasn't then."

"The marriage was over long before our affair, Marina. And anyway, his wife cheated on him and I was separated from Barend then."

Marina wasn't about to lose the point. "But it wasn't just Vincent Lund, was it?" She said, her voice wavering. "Tyland said that Jimmy Nicholson was crazy about you. People talk, you know. They have done ever since you married Barend."

"Of course people talk! I didn't fit it, did I? I still don't. You and your little clique of good wives."

"You didn't try to fit in."

"I didn't *want* to."

"Tyland said --"

"Jesus, Marina, have you never had a thought in your head that was your own? Or does Tyland think for you?"

"You've nearly broken up two marriages --"

"Only two? I must be slipping," Alicia replied coldly, "Look, I know you don't like me. You never have, but we should join forces and work together."

"Doing what?"

"To try and find out what's going on."

Marina glanced down. "You should be at home, looking after your family, not coming here throwing around accusations."

"Your jealousy's showing." Alicia replied, adding. "What wouldn't you give to *have* a family?

"I wouldn't want a daughter like yours!"

Her eyes widening, Alicia leaned back in her seat, swinging her left leg. Her painted toenails caught the morning light, deep pink, almost the colour of the bowl of peonies. Marina could feel the swim of dislike emanate from her and regretted her words. Alicia de Vries wasn't a person to insult.

"We shouldn't argue."

"Who's arguing?" Alicia asked, watching Marina over the rim of her mug as she sipped her coffee.

"Tyland is not a well man."

"Marina, I didn't come here to upset you, or your handsome husband. I just wondered what was going on."

Her words had been picked with care, the threat obvious.

… handsome husband… I could take your wretched, sickly, gangly husband and make him crawl on all fours to me. If I wanted to. If you gave me reason to…

"I don't know anything" Marina blustered, but her voice had a whine to it. "Honestly, I don't know why Tyland would be at your house talking to Barend."

"Pity." Alicia put down her mug and stood up. "Well, I've got to get to the gym. I'm late as it is."

"I'm sorry…" Marina's voice had lost its power. "… if I was rude."

"You called me an interfering troublemaker, an adulteress, and you insulted my daughter - why would I think you were being rude? Don't worry, Marina,

I've never been one to hold a grudge." She moved to the door and paused. "But do think about hiring a trainer, darling. I'm sure you'd feel much better if you did something about the way you looked. And I'm sure Tyland would appreciate it."

Eight

As soon as Leo left his consulting rooms Vincent made his way over to St Thomas's Hospital. Working there as a reconstructive surgeon, he had the advantage of being on the spot and immediately sought out the pathologist who had undertaken Jimmy Nicholson's post mortem.

"This must be very difficult for you, but there's no easy way to say this. Your friend was poisoned."

Vincent nodded. "I won't ask if you're sure."

"I'm sure and I'm sorry." Dr Andrews said, passing him the medical file. "It's all in there."

"What was the poison?"

"Belladonna –"

"Belladonna?"

Andrews smiled grimly. "I know, one of the old favourites, but lethal. Comes from deadly nightshade, taken from the berries. People are using it as a recreational drug now. Ridiculous, causes far too many overdoses."

"How does it work?"

"Belladonna contains tropane alkaloids. Some block the neurotransmitters in the central and peripheral nervous system." He looked at Vincent, then paused. "You want to know more?"

"I'm a doctor, go on."

"It disrupts heart rate, breathing, causes intense sweating and involuntary spasms in the muscles of the gastrointestinal tract. You get poisoned with belladonna and you lose your balance, can't stand the light, vomit, suffer hallucinations and die."

Vincent's mouth was sandbag dry. "So Jimmy would have suffered?"

"I'm afraid he would. Poison's a nasty way to go. It's a nasty way to kill someone too. Usually it's a woman's choice. That's been my experience anyway." Vincent didn't react, the pathologist continuing. "Most of the famous poisoners of the past have been female. Belladonna was supposedly used by Lucrezia Borgia."

'A *woman's* murder weapon.' Yes, it was, Vincent thought. He was right there. "I've been trying to work out how the killer managed it."

The pathologist frowned. "Huh?"

"Think about it. Someone would have had to take the insulin vial, drain the dose, then refill the vial with belladonna." Vincent explained. "Someone who had access to Jimmy's bathroom."

Andrews nodded. "It wouldn't be that difficult to do. A bit fiddly, that's all."

"But the killer had to get access. A stranger couldn't get into the house."

"Maybe it wasn't a stranger? Your friend was a rich man, the family must have had staff. Maybe it was one of them?" Andrews offered, putting some surgical instruments into the steriliser and turning it on. The machine made a slow wheezing sound. "I can't tell you who did it, I wish I could. I just examine the bodies and leave the rest to the police." Curious, he glanced at Vincent. "There's been a lot of publicity about the case, hasn't there? I mean, Mr Nicholson wasn't famous, but it's caught the attention of the press. That's unusual."

"Poison is unusual too."

The pathologist nodded. "You know, sometimes I wonder why it's not used more. I mean, poison's efficient and silent. Not like shooting someone, is it? Or stabbing them? That would be noisy, bloody. They might run away, cry out for help."

"Maybe Jimmy cried out for help?"

"He wouldn't have had time. The pain would have buckled him. You can't call out when you're lungs are exploding and your mouth is full of blood and foam. He had no chance to save himself."

Vincent took a moment to reply. "Would the person who killed him know that?"

"If they did their research and had chosen the method deliberately." Andrews paused. "Nasty way to die. Takes long enough for you to know what's happening - but not long enough to get help."

Shocked into silence, Vincent was thinking that if the woman got to Jimmy Nicholson so easily, how easily could she get to him? It was true that he was always surrounded by people, but in a hospital full of patients, medical staff, drugs, surgical instruments. A place where people were endlessly moving. A place where surgical masks covered faces and disguised identities. And then Vincent realised that could be standing next to the woman in the operating theatre and wouldn't know until it was too late.

"Have you got any idea as to why someone would kill your friend?"

Jolted out of his reverie, Vincent shook his head. "No."

"There's no DNA evidence?"

"Nothing. Well, what little there was didn't belong to anyone on police records."

"What about a motive?"

Vincent didn't look at the pathologist, didn't dare to. "The police have no theory about a motive." He lied. Didn't felt proud of it, but lied anyway. "God knows why anyone would want to kill Jimmy Nicholson."

"Well, they did. And they have. They planned it meticulously, and carried it out with skill." Andrews turned up the thermostat on the steriliser unit. "It will come out eventually. I always comes out in the end."

"What will?"

"Who did it," Andrews said simply, "and why."

Nine

Richmond

Tilly de Vries was hanging round the end of the road where Vincent and his family lived. It was only a hundred yards away from her home, near enough for it to seem perfectly understandable that she would walk her dog there. But that wasn't the reason she was hesitating, the little spaniel tugging at its lead, eager to be gone.

"Wait!" She told the dog, "just a bit longer. He'll be out in a minute."

Tilly was right, only seconds later the slim figure of Milas Lansen turned the corner, bumping directly into her.

"Oh, sorry! *Tilly?*"

She smiled, as though surprised to see him. "I was just walking the dog, she was whining and I had to take her out." Her long hair fell across her face as she petted the animal, then straightened up again. "What are you up to?"

"I was just going to get the paper." He replied, Tilly falling into step with him. "Vincent's pretty shaken up about Jimmy Nicholson's death and wanted to see if there was anything new reported."

"It would have been on the internet first."

"I know, but he sent me anyway and to be honest I'm glad to get out of the house." Milas continued. "I don't think he can believe it happened. They'd been friends for a long time. It's tough, sad."

"Yes, I suppose…."

"You suppose?"

"I didn't like Jimmy Nicholson," Tilly said flatly. "I always thought he was creepy. You know the type. Always staring, eyeing you up. A bit too smooth. I mean, he wasn't handsome, but women really liked him, and he liked them. Enough to feel miffed if someone rejected him."

Milas absorbed the information, looking at her. "Did *you* reject him?"

"*God no!* Jimmy was friendly with my father, he'd never have dared to try it on with me. That would have been too much like shitting on his own door step. He wasn't stupid. Over-sexed, but not stupid."

She twisted the dog lead around her wrist, taking a sideways glance at Milas and remembering the first time she had seen him at Vincent's house. It had been seven years ago, the newcomer welcomed at a special dinner party. The whole de Vries family had been invited over for dinner, along with the Brays and the Nicholsons, Stella Nicholson watching behind her glasses, the Sphinx of Richmond. And as usual, Jimmy Nicholson had been banging on about a painting…

'You should see it, Vincent, I mean, hell fire, this is a great piece. Lord Leighton…' He had paused, let the boast mingle amongst the roast lamb and buttered asparagus.

Milas had been quiet, newly arrived to live with the Lunds, hair the colour of a Pietmontese calf, glasses with dark rims... Take them off, Tilly had thought, I want to see your eyes....
Fine hands, narrow palms, open necked shirt with a crease in the left collar. About thirty, thirty two.
Oh, Mr Lund you have such a hand-some nephew.

Milas hadn't paid her much attention, but that was alright, he was a newcomer and besides, Jimmy Nicholson had taken over the conversation, boring everyone about his bloody picture. But when they left later Tilly – aged twenty four – kept thinking about Milas Nicholson. Aged around thirty two. And wondering about him.

But although they lived nearby Tilly had had no real opportunity to get to know Milas, no reason to seek him out. Until now. Now was the ideal opportunity. The death of Jimmy Nicholson had got everyone talking and mixing in a way that only a murder draws people together.

"It makes you think though, doesn't it? Jimmy's house is not that far away from here." She glanced over to Milas again. "No one seems to know why he was killed –"

"Are you frightened?"

Her expression was scornful. "Frightened! Why would I be?"

"I just asked –"

"It was a fucking stupid question! Jimmy Nicholson was probably killed by some jealous husband. They say he was poisoned. Hell of a way to go." She looked at him, surprised. "That was odd - asking if I was scared. I mean, why? Do I look like the nervous type?"

"It was a stupid thing to say." Milas replied quickly. "It's just that – like you said - Jimmy Nicholson lives near to you."

"And near to you! Look, this is London. I imagine if you lived anywhere someone would have been murdered nearby." She tugged at the dog's lead, encouraging it to keep walking with them. "You must think we're all very strange in England."

"No." he smiled, relaxing "why would I?"

"Well, you come from Denmark."

"I haven't lived there for ten years! I've been in London for a while now."

"We don't see much of you," she wheedled. "I mean, living close by we should be friends. And I should know more about a friend. Didn't Vincent say you were a librarian?"

"Yeah," he smiled again. "But I've done a lot different things. I worked in a café in Paris, and in London I was working in a bookshop. I liked that, but I have... I think it's called a 'lack of ambition.' It never worried me until I came to live with Vincent. Now I see him and how successful he is and it's made me think I should do something with my life."

He was easy to talk to. Open.

"You've no family then?"

"Only Vincent, and Charlotte. Are you two friends?"

"Who?"

"You and Charlotte. You must be about the same age."

Tilly gave a wry smile. "No, your cousin's the quiet type! I think I'd be a bit too colourful for her -

although Vincent's always trying to encourage us to be friends. Charlotte and I are completely different. Anyway she's always busy with her translation work. A real book worm… I don't read much. People should stop writing books, it's old fashioned, no one reads anymore."

They paused at the kerb then they crossed over, heading for the newsagent.

"What about you, Tilly? D'you have a job?"

"I'm the idle offspring of the rich. My stepfather made me take a degree in Art history, but God knows what I'm going to do with it. I've worked in one gallery, but I didn't like it much. Still, I suppose I'll end up in another one gallery somewhere, smiling at the clients. I think – when I was much younger – that Barend had hopes that I'd going into law," she laughed loudly, "but that was never going to happen. I'm not clever, you see."

"You seem smart to me."

Was that a compliment, Tilly wondered? She changed the subject, eager to know more. "Don't you have a family of your own?"

"Never been married."

"Relationships?"

"Yeah, I've have relationships!" He admitted. "But nothing permanent and no kids. Not met the right woman, I suppose. To be honest, I'm more concerned about getting a career going now. Enough dithering about, playing at it. I want to work more with Vincent, help him. Full time, I mean, not part time like I've been doing. He needs a dedicated researcher for the book he's writing." Arriving at the newsagent, Milas glanced down at the dog. "She doesn't look like she's enjoying the walk much."

"Oh, she loves walking!" Tilly lied. "I walk her every day."

"In that case, no doubt we'll bump into each other again," Milas replied, smiling and walking into the shop.

And that was it, Tilly left standing outside with the distinct impression that she had been politely, but firmly, dismissed.

Ten

"So when exactly when were you going to tell me?"

"I've only just found out myself!" Alicia snapped, Barend pink faced, burning with anger as she turned on him. "How did I know Jimmy Nicholson was going to leave me his collection? I didn't care about his bloody collection. Never even saw it!"

"I find that hard to believe!"

"Well, it's true." Alicia replied, watching her husband throw his legal papers onto the sofa, his voice raw.

"Were you still fucking him?"

"No! That was over three years ago, you know that –"

"I don't know anything anymore," he replied and slumped onto the sofa, limp with anger.

His wife – his bloody cheating wife – was going to inherit Jimmy Nicholson's collection! The thought raged inside him, firstly, because it implied that their affair had been ongoing, and secondly, because it would mean gossip. Unavoidable gossip, which would lead to surmise, questions about the *nature* of Jimmy Nicholson's collection, and those of the other friends. Secrets would start to bleed out: secrets about private collections and old sins.

Stella Nicholson would have plenty to say about her husband's will. Her dislike of Alicia was well known, but had it had been curtailed by English manners and contempt. But the loss of a large chunk of her husband's fortune was another matter.

"I thought you loved me. I thought we'd get over this."

"We did. We *have*." Alicia said, sitting beside her husband.

Immediately he stood up and walked away from her, pouring himself a drink. He wondered if – somewhere in the universe – there were couples who could confide and trust each other. If – somewhere in that same universe – a man could confess a secret and expect forgiveness. Recriminations, certainly, but then pardon, spousal clemency. Perhaps he could have told another woman – another wife – about the letter. About that night twenty years earlier.

> *'We were wrong... but no one thought it mattered. And she said nothing. Not then...*
> *Wet shoes, I remember her shoes being wet. They left prints on Vincent's carpet, but Vincent was drunk and wouldn't have noticed.'*
> *'Were you drunk?'* ....
> *(Would he lie to this woman?*
> *This other wife? Risk honesty and banishment?)*
> *'Tipsy, not drunk. But it was Jimmy that did it... it was Jimmy. Only Jimmy...'*
> *(And this other woman, this other wife, would look at him, and she would ask – would have to ask:)*
> *'If that's true, why is she coming after all five of you?'*

Barend stared into his drink, loneliness a yawn in his gut as Alicia walked over and sat next to him. He didn't move this time, didn't walk away… Her affair with Jimmy Nicholson had been brief, her interest soon waning. But the pepper mill of gossip had ensured that their fling had been ground up and sprinkled far and wide, a nasty burn searing into their marriage. Barend had accepted his wife's reassurance that she loved him, not Jimmy Nicholson. And he had believed her; just as he had believed her two years later when she said she didn't love Vincent Lund. He had believed her in his mind, but his heart had sniffed out the lie.

A dazzling intellect inspired envy, but a man's sexual currency was his looks. Barend knew he might have a beautiful wife, but he also knew he was outranked, that she could, at any time, leave him. The thought made him alternately bitter and desperate.

"I didn't know he'd left me his collection, Barend."

"When did you last seen Jimmy?"

"A month ago. You remember, we went to dinner at his house. Stella made that awful casserole."

He turned to her, caught hold of her hair and pulled her towards him. His mouth was only inches from hers.

"Why are you such a whore?" She didn't try to escape, instead she leant into him, Barend resting his head against her shoulder. "Why are you such a bloody whore?" he repeated.

"I love you."

"Why do you do it?"

"They don't mean anything," Alicia consoled him, her voice low. "Nothing. It's just sex, nothing else."

"They're my friends."

"Jimmy was no one's friend." Alicia said quietly. "As for Vincent, we'd split up when I went to him. You can't blame me, Barend, you'd walked out –"

"I wanted to shock you! I wanted you to know how much it hurt to be rejected. I wanted you to beg me to come back. But you didn't. What *did* you do? You slept with Vincent Lund instead --"

"We weren't together! You'd left me, Barend. I didn't know if you were going to come back."

"I should have *stayed* away! I should have divorced you. Cut you off without a penny. Taught you a bloody lesson you'd never forget… You're a fucking whore." His voice fell, muffled against her shoulder. "I hate you, you bitch. I hate you, you fucking, whoring bitch."

He was crying, sobbing, his teeth sinking into her shoulder through her blouse.

And then she knew she had him.

Eleven

The last person Alicia expected to see when she visited Jimmy Nicholson's collection was his wife. In fact she had been there for nearly a minute before a dark shape emerged from behind a carved screen, Jimmy's widow wrapped up a padded winter coat, her hands in leather gloves.

"Come to look at your spoils, have you?"

Alicia stared into the dim light. Four thirty on a winter afternoon, twilight come early. "I can't see you, where's the light switch?"

Stella ignored her, just kept talking. "Jimmy really was a stupid man, wasn't he? Ruled by his prick, as ever." Her accent was upper class English. "He was besotted by you. I knew that, of course. Everyone did. But it didn't matter, you were a tart and he was an old letch. You were made for each other, and as long as you didn't threaten my life in any way I let him get on with it. Saved my having to endure his grunting and humping." She was standing by the screen, imperious. "But I never expected him to give you anything, apart from a good screw."

"Where's the bloody light switch?" Alicia repeated, looking round. "This is ridiculous, talking in the dark."

"But that's where you do your best work, in the dark." Stella replied. "In the ten days since my husband was killed I've been thinking and wondering *why*? Why would Jimmy leave you his collection. Of course I had no interest in it, vulgar paintings, all his sordid little fantasies hung up for him to come and visit and *enjoy*. I didn't want them, I'd have been ashamed to have them in the house. They were Jimmy's dirty little secret and as long as they *remained* a secret, I was happy. But now the police are digging around, and the press will follow, his sexual proclivities soon to be exposed --"

She coughed suddenly.

"You've got a cold."

"Sorry to disappoint you, Alicia, but I don't intend to die from it."

"Oh come on, Stella, I didn't know Jimmy had left me his bloody collection."

"Apparently he changed his will four years ago – when you two were an 'item'. I get everything, the house, the cars, the money, but you get the paintings. Some of which are valuable. And that rather annoys me, Alicia." Her tone was steely. "But I can't do anything about it. Jimmy was in his right mind when he made the will - so I suppose I have to live with it. Just seems so odd. You see, my late husband was a mean bastard. Apparently up North they have an expression *'short arms and low pockets'*. That was Jimmy all over. He dealt in fortunes at the gallery, never missed a trick at auction, but he counted every penny at home. You think my dinners were nondescript? They were, but he didn't give me much housekeeping and no money for caterers. You think I really liked the 'shabby chic' look? I didn't, it covered up his meanness. Jimmy could never get over the fact that I found him repulsive and his miserliness was a way of punishing me. He wanted the classy wife, but he never understood that any woman with breeding would find him a pig..."

Alicia was still looking for the light switch as Stella continued.

"... I even started to wonder if the motive for my husband's murder was staring me in the face. Perhaps he was killed for his collection?"

"I didn't kill him!" Alicia retorted. "Like I said, I didn't know he had left me anything until the other day."

"He said nothing? No hints? No murmurings on the pillow? No promises between the sheets?"

"It wasn't like that --"

"What *was* it like, Alicia?" She asked, her tone vengeful. "You weren't the first, just one of many women he fooled around with. Poor Jimmy, with the sex drive of a spotty teenager, forever groping and pawing females. But you – *you* – were the only one who ever got anything out of the old goat."

"If he was that bad, why didn't you leave him?"

"And walk away from a fortune? I'd earned it, I intended to keep it. A divorce would have been costly – for him, and for me. And public. Mean and unfaithful Jimmy might have been, but he was a powerful man. Important. Respected in his field. Which is why.... " she flicked on the light switch "... I don't want people to know about *this.*"

Blinking in the sudden bright light, Alicia took a moment to adjust, then drew in a breath. It was a gallery, but not like the gallery Jimmy Nicholson had run on Cork Street. These walls were hung - no, crammed – with pictures and etchings, nudes cheek by jowl with each other, grand oil paintings suspended from metal chains, in carved gilt frames. It was obvious that he had been collecting for many years, an Egon Schiele nude – genitalia in full view – hanging beside a Courbet painting of sleeping lesbians. Stunned, Alicia looked around, Stella watching her, then pointing upwards.

Above their heads was a painted ceiling of a Bacchanalian orgy, homosexual poses and overtly graphic depictions of oral and anal sex. In silence, Alicia walked down the gallery. Between the images on the walls towered two cabinets, in which plaster moulds of vulva and penises were carefully dated and labelled.

"Jesus," Alicia started to laugh. "he *was* dedicated! Some of this stuff is porn --"

"I wouldn't know, pornography isn't something with which I'm familiar." Stella walked over, tapping the glass of one of the cabinets. "Boys and their toys. What can you do?" She flipped a velvet cloth over the glass to cover the exhibits. "Personally I don't find it funny."

"Jimmy collected *all* this?"

"Over many years. He and the others."

Alicia's eyebrows rose. *"Others?"*

"You didn't know about their collections?" Stella asked, her turn to be amused, "but you had a fling with Vincent Lund, surely you knew?"

"Knew *what?"*

"Vincent, Tyland Bray, Leo Parks, Jimmy and your husband are all collectors of erotica."

"Well, I know Barend has some paintings, and Vincent collects surgical instruments and prints, but I didn't know it was serious."

"It started a long time ago, when I'd been married to Jimmy for only a few years. The five of them became friends and after a while they banded together to share an interest in art. Erotic art - and they amassed a fortune." She folded her arms, angular face, widow's eyes. "After all, both Tyland and Jimmy were art dealers, they knew what was coming up for sale and some pieces they bought privately. They went to auctions worldwide, and collected, and *kept* collecting. They were in the business, perfectly placed to tip off Vincent, Leo and Barend."

"So what? That's not illegal."

"No, it's not. I'm sure it was merely titillating for young men, but young men become middle aged men, and tastes become jaded. The thrill soon becomes commonplace, the libido not so easily satisfied. So they started to collect more *unusual* pieces. Not purely sexual paintings." She glanced around her, sighing. "In time, it became more varied. Vincent's taste for eroticism waned and he began to collect medical instruments and anatomical figures. Life size wax replicas of dissected patients, very popular in the Victorian era, I believe. Apparently they were used for training purposes, quite understandable for a doctor."

"Vincent?"

"Have I shocked you, my dear?" Stella replied, cold to the bone. "Jimmy bought an iron penis shaft in the Ukraine. As for Tyland Bray – that pinnacle of propriety – he has a stash of condoms dating back to Hogarth."

"Unused, I hope," Alicia replied smartly. "So, what d'you want, Stella? This stuff isn't to my taste, but I could make money and sell it on. It would be a nice nest egg for me. It's not that long ago I was a single mother, struggling to raise Tilly on my own. Life's unpredictable, if anything happened to Barend

I wouldn't want to find myself back in my old life. I've fought too hard to get out, I intend to *stay* out."

Stella's crystal sharp vowels remained intact. "But why should anything happen to your husband?"

"Why did anything happen to yours?" Alicia countered.

There was a shift in the atmosphere, a sudden malice. Stella's grey eyes were unreadable behind glasses, her arms folded, head tilted back. She had a memsaab's stance, an arrogance that comes from old money and good breeding. Alicia could feel the dislike emanate from her, her height imposing, her contempt palpable. Stella Nicholson might have privately despised her husband, but she was determined to protect his public persona.

"Why do *you* think Jimmy was killed?"

"I don't know." Alicia admitted. "I'm sorry though --"

"Oh, spare me! I don't need the fake grief." Stella snapped. "I have a son, did you know that?"

"Barend said you'd lost touch."

"Sad, isn't it? Dominic was a good child." Stella continued. "But Jimmy resented him, even insisted he was a thief and drove him away. *'...You have to write some things off in life. People and situations that don't serve you. They have to be sacrificed to keep order...'.* It was fine for him, but too big a sacrifice for me." She was surprised she had shown weakness and rallied. "My husband was a success. He died a success, and he will *remain* a success - unless his reputation is sullied."

"By some pins ups and an iron dick?"

"Christ, you *are* stupid, aren't you!" Stella replied, waving her hand around the gallery "I wouldn't have bothered to talk to you except for the fact that we have this *connection* now. Your husband is set to become a

KC, unless something spoils his chances. My husband will remain prominent and respected, unless something spoils his legacy. You see where I'm going with this?"

Alicia nodded. "You want me to keep shtum about my little windfall?"

"Exactly. If you keep quiet, you can keep the collection. Say one word about it, try to sell any of the pieces publicly, and I'll make it known that your husband has his *own* collection. As you say, my dear, it's not illegal, but it's certainly not an advantage for a barrister hoping to become a King's Counsel." She put out her hand. "So, do we have a deal?"

Twelve

Four anxious men met up the following evening at Vincent's house, one by one ushered into the study where a fire burned in an oversized grate. Morose, Leo stared into the flames and remembered another night when there had been a fire burning in the same grate, a night that had ended abruptly when an irate Jimmy Nicholson left.

Rubbing his aching shoulder, Tyland stood by the mantelpiece, his expression sour as Leo entered and sat down.

"So when are you going back to New York?"

Leo sighed. "Not New York, Los Angeles, later this week."

"I hate travelling by plane, never enough leg room," Tyland grumbled, his gaze moving to the door as Vincent walked in. "Where's Barend?"

"On his way." Vincent replied, "You seem irritable."

"I'm in pain."

"Sorry about that."

Tyland brushed the words aside. "Have you talked to the police, in particular a little runty man called Sox? Short, bow legs, looks like a badly painted gnome."

"He's coming to see me tomorrow, at the hospital."

Leo looked up from his seat on the sofa. "The police haven't approached me yet."

"They will, they're talking to all of Jimmy's friends and colleagues." Tyland explained. "Fishing around. I was asked if I knew if Jimmy had any enemies, or if I could think of any reason why someone would kill him."

"What did you say?"

"That I didn't know of any people who had a problem with Jimmy."

"That was a lie."

"Really? Perhaps you would have confessed, Leo? Told the police what happened and the letter we all got. .... *Yes, officer, I can think about a motive. Twenty years ago....*"

"Ok, Ok, I get it." The American slumped back in his seat, Vincent hearing the front doorbell ring and returning a few moments later with the portly Barend in tow. "We're all here now."

"Oh, goodie," Tyland replied meanly, wincing as he rubbed his shoulder.

Barend was immediately on the defensive: "I know what you're all going to say, and no, I didn't know anything about Jimmy leaving his collection to my wife."

"I don't suppose she'd consider an offer?"

They all looked at Tyland.

"*What?*" He asked, bemused. "Business is business. With all due respect, Barend, your wife is not a collector. I wouldn't cheat her, I'd give her a fair price. And anyway, what would she want with Jimmy's hoard?" He paused, sarcastic. "Or maybe she's a secret connoisseur. Maybe *she* killed Jimmy for his paintings?"

"Piss off." Barend replied, taking the whisky Vincent offered him and sitting down opposite Leo. "She didn't know anything about the will until today when the solicitor told her."

"What about Stella Nicholson? Did she know?"

"She's not said anything --"

"She wouldn't," Tyland replied, "but I bet she'll contest the will."

"I doubt it, Stella always hated Jimmy's collection."

"She hated your wife more."

"You're a spiteful bastard, Tyland."

"He's in pain."

Barend looked at Leo and shrugged. "He should be."

"This is getting us nowhere," Vincent interrupted. "There are more important things to discuss."

"Like our collections?" Tyland replied. "The detective knows about them. Well, he knows about Jimmy's, I think he was just feeling his way to find out about the others. The trouble is that Jimmy leaving his collection to Alicia will mean gossip – and that means that the police will start poking around."

"The collections aren't illegal --" Leo said, plaintively, Vincent interrupting him.

"We all know that, but we also know how it will *look* if it comes out." He turned to Barend. "What does Alicia want to do with her legacy?"

He shrugged, round shouldered, round cheeks reddening. "She's going to view it tomorrow."

"She hasn't seen it before?"

"No." He looked from one man to the other. "I expect all of you will be after Jimmy's stuff, but you can't hound Alicia. You go through me."

"It's her legacy." Tyland was still massaging his injured shoulder. His narrow bony face grim. "I'll make a fair offer for the whole lot –"

Exasperated, Leo shouted. *"What the fuck are you talking about! Are you off your minds? Jimmy's been murdered,* all of us have been threatened. We're covering everything up - hiding the motive and lying to the police – and you jerks want to talk about *pictures*?"

"Oh, drop the fake outrage," Tyland sneered "you'd love to get your hands on some of the loot to sell on to your little clients --"

"Shut up!" Leo's voice drowned him out. **"For God's Sake, shut up!"**

They all fell silent. Leo Parks was leaning forwards, his elbows on his knees, his eyes sharp as fish hooks. *"Who is the woman coming after us?* Isn't that what we should be talking about?"

Calm, Vincent took over. "Leo and I have been trying to remember anything about the girl. A name, a voice, any detail…" he paused, Tyland was staring at him, Barend blank faced. "Think back. There must be something. We have to work this out, we can't just leave it and let her come for us." He could see their reluctance; a refusal to accept what was happening. "She got to Jimmy. She broke into his house and killed him. She used deadly nightshade. The choice of poison wasn't accidental. Belladonna means 'beautiful lady.'"

"I feel like I'm listening to *Gardener's Question Time*."

Vincent turned on Tyland. "Make a joke of it, if you want, but you – *we* - should all think about what she did. It took Jimmy a while to die. He suffered. He didn't have time to get help, didn't even make it out of the bathroom." He paused, looking at each of them in turn. "You want to die like that?"

"Oh, fuck." Barend moaned.

"We have to stop thinking of her as the harmless girl we met that night. That was over twenty years ago, she's an adult, a woman approaching middle age now. She'll have changed – and we have *nothing* to go on unless we can remember something. Unless we can find her and stop her before she stops us."

The four men fell silent, Vincent leaving the room as Tyland glanced over to Barend.

"You talked to her."

"I don't remember anything. Just some girl standing next to that Rodin statue that Tyland bought –"

"The statue!" Leo interrupted them. "Who has it now?"

"I sold it –"

"You sold it, Tyland? Why?" Leo asked. "Why would you do that?"

"I never intended to keep it, it was a replica, not a Rodin, not even by Camille Claudel."

"You spoke to her too." Leo said, his tone condemning. "You told her she wasn't posing right."

"What?"

"The pose," Leo repeated "you got angry with the girl, and she moved and tripped up –"

"You remember a lot more than you're letting on," Tyland said wryly. "I don't remember anything like that."

A long silence fell over the group of men, all of them intent on their own thoughts, Barend at the window, Tyland wincing in pain as he tried to get comfortable on a sofa by the fireplace. And Leo, mute as a ghost, staring into the flames. The house grew silent around them, the curtains muffling the sound of falling rain, the fire crackling, a faint echo of footsteps sounding overhead.

After a while Vincent re-entered the room and laid a large print down on the coffee table in front of Leo. Signalling for the others to come over, he then pointed to the photograph of Rodin's statue.

"This was the *Danaid*, the pose we hired her to copy."

"She was too thin," Tyland said sharply. "Far too thin. You could see her ribs."

"And she was shaking with nerves," Leo stared at the painting. "She wasn't smiling, she wasn't relaxed, she was cold, her skin was covered in goose bumps."

"I don't remember any of this," Barend said, shrugging. "Seriously, I can't remember anything."

"She was wearing a Chinese gown," Tyland added. He had stopped rubbing his shoulder, his long back bent over the coffee table to look more closely at the photograph. "It had dragons on it... Have you still got it, Vincent?"

He shook his head. "No. It disappeared a long time ago."

"Maybe she took it... How much did you pay her?"

"I don't recall."

"I'm not surprised, you were pretty drunk that night," Leo said, turning to the others. "Remember? He'd been newly promoted at the hospital and had been celebrating. Nancy had come back from a business trip to Hong Kong and then they'd had a fight. We could hear raised voices coming from the kitchen."

He looked back to Vincent. "She stormed out and after that you kept drinking."

> *'Come on, have a drink with me, I'm celebrating, Come on, Nancy, for Christ's Sake, you're my wife, be happy for me'...*
> *'You don't need me to be happy for you, you're happy enough without my help.'*
> *Angry, wearing a black jacket, long auburn hair, gold hooped earrings.*
> *And he had poured himself another drink....*
> *Charlotte, their daughter, came down to see what the arguing was all about.*
> *'Daddy'... Short of breath, wheezing, Nancy getting her inhaler.*
> *Him bending over their child...*
> *'You're so good at being the doctor, Vincent'...*
> *She was gone in the morning on the first flight.*
> *Left the hooped earrings in the bathroom and Never came back for them....*

"There must be more we can remember. We have to keep trying --" Vincent insisted, Barend cutting him off.

"*What's the bloody point!* We don't know who we're looking for. She knows us, we don't know her. She has the upper hand." He got to his feet, angry, losing control. "I've had enough of this bullshit! All of it. If the bitch wants to come after me, she can. I hope she tries something. It's ridiculous, some crazy tart who can't let the past go." He looked round at the shocked men. "**For fuck's sake!** What did we do that was so bad? Women get worked up over nothing. She was hired for a job, she was well paid. It's in the past, it

91

should stay there! It was all Jimmy's fault anyway. *He was the one who went after her, he was the one who landed us in this mess. I told him to leave her alone, I warned him, but he wouldn't listen…..*"

Barend trailed off, realising he had said too much, Leo staring at him, incredulous. "You *warned* Jimmy? *What* did you warn him about?"

He ignored the question and hurried to the door, Vincent following and grabbing hold of his arm.

"I thought you didn't remember anything--"

"I don't!"

"You're lying."

Barend's expression was brutal. "And you're not?"

Thirteen

De Vries, Oakely & Wynam
Lincoln's Inn
London

Barend was going to return home, but changed his mind. Home was Alicia. Home was questions. Home was nothing any longer. So instead he headed for his Chambers, knowing everyone would have left for the evening. Taking short cuts Barend hurried along through the sudden seven o'clock mist, passing under the lamplights and crossing the square. A few homeless men shuffled after him, asking for change, Barend moving past, then doubling back and emptying his pockets, piling money into upturned palms. He hoped such an action might buy him some Karma, some moral protection, but felt only a sense of encroaching despair.

The letter tormented him. He had an astute brain, was used to looking at evidence, adept at meticulous shuffling through a maze of claims and counter claims. In court, if a witness lied to him he chipped away at the falsehood until it was exposed. He prided himself on his lack of judicial emotion, an incisive examination of facts, an avoidance of confusion.

Precision had served him; his career had progressed until his reward hovered before him - King's Counsel. Not bad for a poor boy from Holland.

'Hadn't Rembrandt been a miller's son? So why should I be ashamed of being the offspring of a baker?'
But his father had been more; a wretched, drunk from Harlingen...
Barend had worked his way up, little, round lad, looking innocuous. Lucky that...people didn't fear him, dismissed his Happy Camper persona, Barend's brain catching them unawares, propelling him to the upper reaches of London's legal hierarchy.
'King's Counsel - take that, you bastards. And I married a beauty. A slut, but a beauty'...

His hand shaking, Barend unlocked the door of his office and walked in. Somewhere in one of the back rooms he could hear the whir of a computer, someone working late. Some young barrister putting in the hours, trying to make an impression.

It won't matter in the end. You'll get olderand impotent and walk past the brass plaque without even seeing your name on it. Because somewhere, sometime, you fucked up badly, and it'll come back on you....
King's Counsel...I am an honoured, round, little man with a round little medal coming. Round like a clock face, like a stalker moon....

94

Barend moved into his office and slumped into the easy chair by the window, looking out onto the square below and remembering how the squatters used to congregate in tight clumps under the lamplight. Then tents were erected when the light failed, cropping up like mushrooms in amongst the grand legal terraces and the varnished front doors. But no more, the tents and the homeless had been moved on to some other bedding-down along Park Lane.

He could *feel* his future slide away. His marriage, his career, all exposed for what it was – trompe l'oeil – a trick of the eye, a forgery of the life he had led. He was a legal man; knew the police, the system. Knew that his past would come out. His unstable marriage. His art collection. A little weakness of his which – in prosperous times - would be seen as a naughty eccentricity, but, when weighed against a sexual assault, an authentication of guilt.

And then there was the letter; evidence of his complicity. He might have torn it up, but that didn't matter, the words could be written again.

Barend leaned forward and breathed on the window pane, then inscribed his name in the vapour. The streetlamp outside haloed it, but a moment later it was gone. He sighed. Perhaps the woman had sent a copy of her letter to the newspapers? Or the police? Perhaps it was now about to blaze up on the internet? He wanted – no, he didn't – he *thought* he wanted the police to be involved, but knew that wouldn't save him.

Then he thought of the Ribera painting coming up for auction. The marvellous copy of *The Bearded Woman*. Only a week before Barend would have longed to own it; would have competed with Vincent at the auction. Because the doctor would want it so badly. Unlike his own collection, Vincent's was kept at his home, in what used to be a guest house but which had been turned into a private museum. And there, in amongst the exhibits of anatomy, the depictions of bone malformations and skin conditions, was the antique poison cabinet Vincent prized, along with some of the earliest English medical bags. But those exhibits paled against the full and palpable glory of the skulls. Arranged on four shelves, craniums of differing sizes, male, female, children, some ancient, some relatively modern. Cleaned and ordered: choir stalls of the dead.

Not unusual - for a doctor who specialised in maxillofacial surgery. Merely a reference tool. But amongst the practicality there were paintings too. Depictions of barbarism, Goya's nihilism and *The Gros Clinic*, demonstrating the fallibility of humanity. Vincent's taste for eroticism was limited and tinged with remorse; aftermaths of seduction, women changed by men's deceit and the loss of innocence. Which was why Barend knew Vincent would want the painting of *The Bearded Woman*, not merely because it represented a medical condition, but because she was courageous, poignant, and he would admire that.

Still staring out of the window, Barend thought of his wife. Would she sell Jimmy Nicholson's collection? Or use it as leverage to effect a reconciliation with Vincent? Because she wanted him. In fact, she *longed* for him and had taken his rejection hard. No man rejected Alicia. She might not have confided in him, but Barend knew the blow to her pride would have gone deep. Perhaps she had truly hoped for a future with Vincent Lund, the failure of her marriage lessened by her moving on to another lover. And it was only after much pleading that she had finally returned to Barend.

But despite Vincent's rebuff, she had never *stopped* wanting him... Barend understood why. Of all of them Vincent was the most admirable. Celebrated for his surgical skills, respected by his colleagues and patients. No round little man challenging the big boys, he was a strapping Dane, blond, ambitious, cuckolded, but hopeful – always hopeful – to achieve a heroism of sorts. He had seen it in Vincent's eyes, the doleful hope that his nephew presented, an opportunity for redemption. Something in which Barend had long ceased to believe.

He paused, the noises from the room beyond had stopped, the computer silenced. Maybe the young pretender had left for the night. Maybe he was happy thinking that he had been noticed by one of the partners. ...*Mr de Vries saw me working late*... he would think to himself, hoping Barend would pass his virtue on.

Then there was another noise, footsteps moving around, Barend irritated because he wanted to be solitary. Sighing, he rose to his feet and moved out into the passageway.

"Hello?"

Silence.

"Hello?"

The noises had stopped, the light down the corridor turned off. He walked to the bottom of the stairs, looked up, and caught the shadow of someone moving on the landing overhead. Then the figure paused, silent, its dark outline thrown on the wall above his head. Unmoving, waiting.

And he knew, before he saw her, before he had chance to escape, that she had come for him.

Book Two

This is my second letter to you all.

*I know you will have wondered why I didn't go into detail about that night twenty years ago. I wasn't that I didn't remember every detail, I just wanted **you** to remember – all of you. I wanted my omission to act as your reminder.*

Jimmy Nicholson wouldn't have remembered much. The event would have been unimportant to him. I had always known that, but wondered if the rest of you might start to face up to what you did and take responsibility. No? Not yet. Maybe you will now.

It's very easy to move around when no one sees you. I know I have the advantage, I can watch you and yet none of you would know me if we shared a taxi or queued at an airport Departure Gate. I've changed a lot, you see. But then all of you have changed too. Poor Tyland Bray, your disease is making you irritable, out of temper. I imagine you shout at your wife, which you shouldn't, Marina isn't the type to retaliate. Or is she? I mean, what do we really know about anyone? When she rubs your shoulders or straps up the ankle you turned so painfully last month does she feel pity? Or resentment? Maybe she longs for that family you never gave her. Those children you withheld.

And Leo Parks, what about you? Charity fund raiser, globe trotter, humanitarian – why no partner? No lover that stays. I know you've had your share of lily white boys, but who sits with you when you plan the next cover of your magazine? Who shares the monthly midnight deadlines? Who cares about the Biedermeier sofas and the Aubusson tapestries? Who waits for your key in the lock or leaves notes hidden in your luggage?

You're such a lonely man, Mr Parks, lonely in so many ways.

You didn't protect me, but I know you wanted to. I could read that in your eyes, but you lacked the courage. No courage to intervene, no courage to love. Poor wanderer. I know one thing for sure – you would have remembered the Oriental gown I wore that night. It would have appealed to you, concentrated your mind with its beauty when everything else was so sordid… You use charity and beauty as carapaces, but neither are reliable: charity is resented and beauty rots in time.

*As for you, Vincent Lund, still using the excuse of drunkenness? How drunk **were** you that night? Did your wife leave you because of your drinking or your ambition? Or that hazy middle ground you inhabit, the place where you hope to impress your nephew. You're not hero material, don't you know that? Don't you know Milas will find you out?*

I blame you the most. You gathered those men together. It was your idea to start the collections and you encouraged them. It was at your house, under your roof, that my life changed. It was wrong of you, Vincent Lund, you should have been more careful in choosing your friends.

The clock is ticking, gentlemen. In London, New York, Copenhagen, in every room you sit and down every road you walk. It's ticking…

Fourteen

Detective Sox was waiting for Vincent outside his consulting room, the shoulders of his coat wet with a London downpour. As Vincent showed him in, he took the coat off, hanging it over the back of his chair, water dripping onto the wooden floor.

"Thank you for seeing me, Dr Lund," he said, glancing towards the window. "It's a grim day. In more ways than one. I'm sorry about your friend, Mr de Vries, his death must have been a terrible shock."

Vincent nodded, not trusting his voice. The murder of Jimmy Nicholson had been traumatic, but the death of Barend, coming so quickly afterwards, had rocked him to his core. A darkness was falling, the shadow lengthening and threatening to engulf them all as Vincent ran his tongue over his dry lips. In his pocket was the letter he had received that morning, posted through his letter box at home, the writing ominously familiar.

Sox was still talking: "I have to ask you some questions, I'm afraid. It's always difficult, but we have to get to the bottom of this. Two deaths of two important men, two friends of yours, make me anxious for your safety..."

Vincent remained mute.

"…Apart from your being friends I need to know if there is any other connection you have to each other."

"No."

"No threats?

"No."

"Nothing unusual?"

Vincent cut him off. "How did Barend die?"

"He was stabbed. In his chambers at Lincoln's Inn." Sox said evenly. "His body is being examined now by the pathologist. The press haven't got hold of the news, not yet anyway." There was a moment's pause, but if the detective expected Vincent to talk, he was disappointed and continued. "Sometimes there are things people keep secret. They have their reasons, but where murder is concerned no secret is worth dying for."

"Barend didn't confide in me."

"He was a friend –"

"Not an intimate friend."

"My mistake, I thought you were close." Sox wrote something in his notepad and then continued. "So you don't know if he was worried about anything?"

"No, I don't." Vincent replied, his tone robotic. "He wasn't an intimate friend."

Sox nodded. "Yes, you said. But perhaps he had mentioned some personal difficulties? Health? Work? Financial problems? Martial difficulties?"

"No, nothing."

Sox wasn't convinced, Vincent Lund had the look of someone struggling to function.

"I don't believe you, doctor." He was almost apologetic. "You see, I've spoken to Mrs de Vries and she says that you and her husband met up last night --"

"Barend wasn't worried about anything."

" – and your housekeeper, Mrs Brooks, told me that Mr Bray and Mr Leo Parks were also at your house. All four of you met up last night."

"We're friends."

"Close friends?" Sox queried.

"Long time friends."

"Isn't that the same?"

"I don't think so," Vincent replied, "I'm still in touch with people I went to school with, but I wouldn't call them intimates."

Sox nodded and smiled, as though relieved to have the point clarified. "But am I right in believing that you were *all* friends of Mr Nicholson?"

Vincent paused before answering. "We mixed in the same circles."

"And now both Mr Nicholson and Mr de Vries have been murdered." The detective stared at his notebook, podgy hands wet from the rain making damp patches on the imitation leather. "How long have you and Mr de Vries known each other?"

"For many years."

"Twenty? Thirty?"

"About twenty five years."

"Long time."

"Yes."

"So how did you all meet?"

"I met Tyland Bray through Jimmy Nicholson. We have – we *had* - similar interests…" Vincent trailed off. "There's no crime in that surely?"

"In being friends?" Sox asked, smiling wryly. "No, no crime in that, or we'd all be arrested. I have friends who like the same things as I do, same hobbies. I love golf, but I can't play well. I don't have the height for it. It's attractive in a women, what do they call it? *Pocket Venus*, yes, that's it. But in a man, being short is not good. Especially if you want to play golf." He shifted gear. "Tell me, what kinds of interests *did* you share?"

Vincent faltered, shuffling in his seat. "Theatre, books –"

"Art?"

"Yes, don't most people have an interest in art?"

"Not me, I don't like galleries, they always seem depressing places." He leaned towards Vincent. "As for dealers, if you don't mind me saying this, I find them a pompous lot. Mr Bray, for instance. I know he's a very learned man, but not very friendly. I told my wife that I'd met him and she was impressed, being an art teacher herself. Wanted to know what he said about the painting coming up for sale," he looked at his notes, "*Magdalena Ventura, The Bearded Woman,* by Ribera. Very odd picture, don't you think?"

"Beautiful in its own way."

"And what way would that be, Dr Lund? As a curiosity? I suppose it would appeal to a medical man. But not to most people." There was a long pause, Vincent glancing away as Sox spoke again. "You haven't asked me about your friend's death."

"You told me he was stabbed."

"Twelve times, with a long knife. Like a bread knife, which made me think – how likely was it for someone to be walking around with a bread knife in their pocket? A flick knife, a Stanley knife, yes, I could see that. But a bread knife, that's unusual." His coat was still dripping water onto the floor, both of them could hear it. "You know the Chambers where Mr de Vries worked?"

"I've been there many times."

"They have a kitchen?"

Vincent nodded. "On the ground floor at the back of the building, yes."

"So the murderer could have got a knife from the kitchen?"

"I don't know, maybe."

"Maybe they'd been hiding there, waiting for Mr de Vries to come in, then attacked him." Sox paused, shaking his head. "Did he often work late?"

"Sometimes."

"But not regularly?"

"I don't know Barend's timetable, why don't you ask his assistant or his secretary?"

"Would they know?"

"They should."

"But when he left your house last night Mr de Vries didn't say he was going to his Chambers?"

"No."

"Did he say he was going home?"

"He just left."

"But with his wife and he having had an argument I suppose it was a good guess that he wouldn't want to go home straight away."

Surprised, Vincent stared at him. "I didn't know they'd argued."

"Oh yes, Mrs de Vries said they'd had words. Apparently her husband wasn't too pleased that Mr Nicholson had left her his painting collection." Sox drummed his puddy fingers on his notepad. "I'm going to see it later. Have a look at what all the fuss is about." Vincent could feel the ground becoming unsteady underfoot and was relieved he was sitting down. "Where were you last night, doctor?"

"Here, as you know. As my housekeeper told you –"

"But Mrs Brooks left at nine. What about *after* that?"

"I was with Mr Bray and Mr Parks."

"And when did they leave?"

"Late, very late." Vincent replied mechanically.

"And you were with them all the time?"

"Yes, but I went to the hospital after they left."

"At night?"

"One of my patients needed to be seen."

"So you have witnesses?"

"Witnesses?" Vincent's voice was curt. "Do I *need* witnesses?"

"Do you have any?"

"I went into the clinic, visited a private room, checked my patient's notes and medication, and left. I doubt anyone saw me."

"No nurse on duty?"

"There was a nurse on duty, but she was attending to another patient."

"Well, at least *your* patient can vouch for you."

Vincent hesitated. "He was asleep. Still recovering from his anaesthetic."

"He was asleep…" Sox tapped his front teeth with his pen. "And then you came home?"

"I wrote up my report in my consulting room and then came home."

"And when you were in your consulting room did anyone see you?"

"No."

"And how long were you in your room, Dr Lund?"

The water had stopped dripping off the detective's coat.

"About an hour."

"It must have been a long report."

"Difficult case… Why are you asking me all these questions, detective?"

Sox sighed. "It was something Mrs de Vries said."

"What did she say?"

"That you had been a close friend of her husband. And that you had once been her lover" Sox replied without emotion "which sounds very much like a motive to me."

Fifteen

Charlotte Lund was just walking up the drive towards her house when someone stopped her. Someone she didn't know, a man with a whippet face who had followed her through the gates.

"Miss Lund?"

She turned, pale in the cold. "Yes?"

"Can I ask you some questions?"

Nervous, she hesitated. "What?"

"You father was a good friend of Barend de Vries, wasn't he?"

Caught off guard, Charlotte was uncertain of how to reply, but noted the past tense and felt uneasy. She had known Barend most of her life; never really liked him, thought him clever but comical, a little tubby, verbose man. As for his wife, Alicia was too awesomely glamorous to be comfortable around. Charlotte had heard the rumours about her father and Alicia, but had never referred to them. Vincent loved her, she knew that, but they weren't confidantes. Milas might share her father's secrets, but not her.

And after her mother remarried she asked Charlotte to visit her in Marseilles. But they had both known it wasn't going to happen. Charlotte was a nervous traveller and unwilling to regain a closeness which might be curtailed again. In the years since her mother had left, family life had become stable - but the murder of Jimmy Nicholson changed everything. The atmosphere at home had shifted, her father remote, spending more time at the hospital to avoid conversations with her or Milas.

Nervous, she stared at the man who had accosted her. "Who are you?"

"I work for *The Evening Standard*--"

She didn't even let him finish his sentence. Instead she ran away, making for the front steps that led into the safety of the house.

-o0o-

From an upstairs window Milas has seen the exchange and pushed away the notes he had been working on, walking downstairs to the study. Vincent was sitting still, head down, silent. Only an hour earlier Milas had watched Sox leaving, the sandy haired detective pulling on his coat against another threatened rain storm, hurrying towards his car and making some notes before driving off.

"What is it?"

Vincent looked up. "Oh, Milas, hello...I didn't hear you come in."

"What's the matter?" He could see his uncle struggle to gather his composure. "That was the police, wasn't it?"

"Yes."

"Any news about Mr Nicholson's murder?"

He could see the stagger of a hesitation, Vincent glancing away. "No, nothing."

"No news at all?"

"Not about Jimmy, no."

He sat down opposite his uncle. "So what else has happened?"

"Barend de Vries has been murdered."

Milas took a moment to reply. "But he was here last night."

"Yes... he was killed at his Chambers, after he left here."

"So what did the police want to know?"

"Where I was last night."

"They can't believe that you were involved?"

"Detective Sox seems to think I might be." Vincent replied uncertainly, glancing over to Milas. "I wasn't."

"Of course you weren't!"

"I didn't have anything to do with it."

"I know that!" Milas replied "what's going on?"

What's going on? Vincent wondered. What do I tell you? How much do I tell you? I can't tell you anything really, can I? Not the truth, certainly not that. I don't want to see that look in your eyes, the same look my sister had. That judgement, that negation of my life, my success. I don't want to fall from your grace because where would I fall to? If you knew me – really knew me – I would never stop falling. I'm fifty five, too old to be called to account by a ghost.

"Jimmy Nicholson and now Barend... *why* were they killed?" Milas asked, leaning towards his uncle.

"I don't know."

"Are you in danger? I mean, they were friends of yours," Milas continued, "is someone going to come after you?"

"It's co-incidence, Milas, nothing more."

"Bullshit! Why don't you tell me what's going on?"

"There's nothing going on."

"Do you need protection?"

Only from myself, only from the past.

"Talk to me!" Milas said, his voice rising. "Two of your friends have been murdered. Why? Why were they killed?"

Sunlight came in through the study window, then backed away as the rain started again. It began drumming on the glass, at an angle, making water slides.

"Come on, tell me." Milas pushed his uncle. "Why *were* Jimmy Nicholson and Barend de Vries killed?"

"I don't know!" Vincent snapped. "I don't know and you can ask me the same question over and over again and I'll say the same thing – *I don't know."*

"Has it anything to do with your private collections?"

Vincent flinched. *"What?* They're a hobby. Other men play golf."

"Other men don't have two of their friends murdered." Milas countered. "You all collect valuable stuff. I don't mean just the erotic pieces, but all of it. There's a lot of money tied up. God know how much *you've* spent at auctions over the years, and Jimmy Nicholson always bragged about his erotic paintings. It's a miracle none of you have been robbed before –"

"Jimmy and Barend weren't robbed. They were killed."

"Yeah, I know… I just thought…" Milas shook his head. "I'm not criticising how you live. You help enough people and you've work hard for a long time to earn the money, it's up to you how you spend it." Milas picked up with catalogue on Vincent's desk, open at the painting of Magdalena Ventura. "I know this painting, *La Mujer Barbuda.*"

Vincent's eyebrows rose. "You speak Spanish?"

"A little, I lived in Spain for a while years ago. I saw the original in the Hospital de Tavera, the museum in Toledo –"

"You've never seemed to have much interest in art."

"I don't really, but the painting was fascinating. It made an impression on me when I saw it."

"What were you doing in Toledo?"

"Working for a bookseller there. I was studying restoration, the conservation of old manuscripts." Milas paused, shrugging. "I didn't stick at it, just stayed in Spain for a while, and moved on. That's been the pattern of my life. I get can't settled anywhere for long."

"I want you to settle here." Vincent replied, "You're part of the family now."

"Oh, I don't intend leaving London. I've found my home here." There was a genuine warmth between them, Milas pausing for a moment before returning to the previous topic. *"Are* the murders connected to the collections?"

Without showing his irritation, Vincent answered. "No, why would they be?"

"What did Barend de Fries collect?"

"Barend liked the female form, Victorian painters mostly. Nothing obscene, if that's what you're asking."

"I wasn't," Milas replied, looking back to the Ribera painting. "So he would have wanted this painting?"

"Yes, he would."

"And Jimmy Nicholson?"

"Yes."

"What about Tyland Bray and Leo Parks?"

"It's a unique painting, so yes, they'd be interested." Sighing, Vincent shook his head. "Why all the questions?"

"Oh, come on!" Milas replied, "don't treat me like a child. Perhaps this painting has something to do with what's going on. I mean, doesn't it seem odd that it's coming up for auction and the murders have begun? It's like someone knew the five of you would want it for your collections."

The thought had never occurred to Vincent. "It can't be related. The painting's may not even be a version painted by Ribera –"

"Maybe it's not the painting, but the subject?" Milas suggested. "Maybe it's because of some connection to Spain? Or the painter himself?"

Vincent thought of what he knew. *La Mujer Barbuda* had been commissioned by the Duke of Alcala in 1631, the Duke being the Viceroy of Naples and Ribera's patron. According to legend, the Duke's picture collection had been decadent, many paintings depicting figures engaged in grotesque behaviour, including a portrait of an individual who 'ate everything placed in front of him'. As for Ribera, his fascination with the bizarre was well documented; *The Clubfooted Boy* and drawings of sexually ambiguous figures with grotesque warts and the ears of a faun. Years earlier Vincent had bought a reproduction of Ribera's black chalk drawing of a man suffering from a form of neurofibromatosis, 'Von Recklinghausen's disease', one of the painter's sketches of *Five Grotesque Heads*. A series of particular interest to a doctor who specialised in maxillofacial surgery.

But a connection with the murders? No. Vincent thought. No, that was something else entirely. Something Milas could never know.

"How was Barend de Vries killed?"

Vincent flinched, his thoughts coming back to the present. "He was stabbed."

"Are you sure you're not in danger?" Milas asked, anxious. "Shouldn't you have some kind of police protection?"

"Not if the police think I'm the killer."

"For God's Sake! Why would you murder two of your closest friends!" Milas retorted heatedly. "It doesn't make sense, you'd have no reason to kill them. The police are fools. They're looking at the wrong person."

Yes, Vincent thought, they are.

Sixteen

"Will we lose the house?"

"Tilly!" Alicia snapped, staring at her daughter. Well, with her maternal attitude what could she expect other than a materialistic child? But her daughter's cold heartedness still came as a shock, Tilly sitting on the sofa looking at her i phone, unperturbed.

"I don't know why you're angry with me, you didn't love Barend." Tilly replied, "You were always talking about leaving him."

"People say all kinds of things when they argue. You'll know that when you get married."

"I'm not getting married," Tilly replied, "It doesn't work. You taught me that, running off and having affairs with Vincent Lund and Jimmy Nicholson –"

"You don't have any right to judge me! I've made mistakes, I know that, but you don't have the right to sit there and criticise me. I made sure you had a cushy life, Tilly, you owe me some gratitude for that at least."

She fell silent, sullen, still looking at her i phone. "Well… *will* we lose the house?"

"No!" Alicia shouted, "the house is mine."

"You've got Jimmy Nicholson's collection too --"

"How the hell d'you know about that?"

"Oh, God, Mother, *everyone's* talking about it." Her expression was smug. "I suppose you could sell it to Vincent Lund and get back in his good books – now you're a widow."

Alicia grabbed her daughter's arm and hauled her to her feet.

"Watch your mouth! You're twenty two years old, when I was your age I was a single mother earning a wage to keep us both going, not lounging about doing sod all with my life."

"Meaning what?" Tilly countered. "That I should be grateful for being the daughter of the neighbourhood whore?"

Without pausing to think, Alicia slapped her. Hard. Tilly running out, her feet pounding up the stairs as she made for her room. Breathing hard, Alicia slumped onto the sofa, trying to calm herself. Her soft little nest in the world was suddenly jagged, open to the elements. *Barend was dead.* Murdered. *Her husband was dead....* To her surprise she felt real sorrow. It was true that she had never loved Barend with any deep passion, but he had loved her and provided her with a lifestyle she had relished. His devotion had been a nuisance at times, but also a security, a knowledge that she was not alone in the world, that she had a man who would excuse her, forgive her, and always return to her.

She would never have admitted it to Barend, but she had been proud of his accomplishments and could understand Stella Nicholson's defence of her husband's legacy. Jesus, why did anyone want to kill you, Barend? What did you do? Alicia thought blindly. People didn't die in their fifties. They weren't supposed to die at that age. They certainly weren't supposed to be murdered. Barend hadn't deserved that. Not to be carved up, not in his Chambers, left for dead in amongst the trappings of power. Barend de Vries, prominent barrister, soon to be King's Counsel, but stopped in his tracks.

The detective had been the same one who had talked to her after Jimmy Nicholson's death, the same one who had discussed her inheriting Jimmy's collection. A funny little man, offering his handkerchief, patting her shoulder, talking in a low voice which was meant to be soothing. But all along his eyes had been alert. Others might be fooled by him, but Alicia knew men; knew that unattractive men developed other talents, like brain power. Sox looked benign, but she was wary of him.

Surprised by a sudden threat of tears, Alicia glanced across the room, unconscionably touched by the sight of Barend's scarf on a side table. Silk, of course. 'Taking Silk' the award of King's Counsel, the reward he had waited for and earned. But now he was in the morgue, bled out. The little round Dutchman falling like Humpty Dumpty, never to be put back together again.

And question was *why?* Why had Barend de Vries been murdered. Why had Jimmy Nicholson? They were friends, but other than that what else did they have in common? Their collections? Their interest in art? Alicia put her head back against the sofa cushion. Above her head she could hear Tilly running a bath, then rock music began, then silence, as though even Tilly realised that was callous.

What else did they have in common? Alicia asked herself again, struggling to think clearly. Tears she had never thought she would shed had dried her out. She knew she would find others, that there were always tears waiting, cold salty little demons that a person tore from themselves. Late night tears; afternoon tears; tears that came unbidden, unstoppable, from a grief that had never been suspected.

Alicia closed her eyes, pressed her emotions into submission, turned back to her previous thoughts. What was the shared motive for killing two successful men? Absent-mindedly, she toyed with the fringe on one of the cushions, thinking back. What did she know about Barend's past? Everything over the last ten years, but before that? Before they had married? Very little. Had he done something that had finally caught up with him? She opened her eyes and stared ahead, the moulded ceiling reflected in the mirror over the fireplace. Had Barend done something illegal early in his career? Or had he prosecuted a criminal who had held a grudge and come back to level the score? She knew Barend had defended several murderers - but he had got them off, so what argument could they have had with him?

Then she remembered something else and stopped twirling the fringe. Hadn't Barend once mentioned a case, long before they married, where he had prosecuted a killer who had murdered their employer? She struggled to remember the details. The woman had been young and had cut her female employer's throat, claiming insanity, which Barend had challenged. As a result, the insanity plea had been dropped, and the woman had been sentenced to life.

But life wasn't life, was it? It was a *part* of life. A *bit* of life. A *portion.* You served jailed life then you left prison and you got on with serving free life. Had someone been released? Someone who had harboured revenge for years? Someone who had hated Barend de Vries enough to stick a knife into him repeatedly until the blade broke against his spine?

Alicia got to her feet, rummaged in her bag for Detective Sox's card and then tapped out his number.

Seventeen

Bray Art Gallery
Central London

The rain had given way to sleet, freezing sleet coming hard against the windows in W1, the streets emptied of people on a six o'clock Friday. In the summer Central London clamoured with tourists, office works, shoppers and art dealers; the pubs overfilling, the surplus drinkers sitting outside at the worn trestle tables, under a blowsy overhang of baskets trailing their plumage of geranium and ivy.

But not in January. In winter the streets were quiet.

Tyland Bray wouldn't have noticed before. Usually early winter evenings meant the examining of new stock or the planning of a forthcoming exhibition to keep his attention distracted, but this silence was different. He even regretted having let all the staff go home early, the accountant incubating a heavy cold and the porters bemoaning a Tube strike. Their company was usually unwelcome, but this Friday was different, *this* Friday Jimmy Nicholson and Barend de Vries were dead. One in the ground, already buried in Richmond, one in a Chapel of Rest.

Reluctant, Tyland had visited his old friend, standing outside the ante room as the undertaker showed him in. The coffin was been closer to the door than Tyland had expected, shuffling past it before he turned. And then a ghastly fear welled up in him. Barend's eyes were closed, but Tyland had the feeling that at any moment they might open, Barend der Vries rising up from the moire silk lined casket to challenge him.

'Look, soon this will be you.'

And as Tyland stared, mesmerised, he felt the first shock of real fear.

There were no visible marks on the barrister's body, no wounds to his face. The damage lay under the Armani suit and the Garrick Club tie. Tyland remembering the first time they had met, Barend five feet six, rounded as a snowman.

> *'I hear you're a barrister, up for Silk.'*
> *Barend had nodded, black eyebrows raised.*
> *'I hear you're an art dealer.'*
> *Scintillating conversation, Tyland had thought snidely.*
> *But Barend had a wicked streak, gesturing to his wife as though to say, 'Don't dismiss me, look at what I married.'*
> *And by contrast Marina had been there, dithering around with a sherry, midcalf length dress and a bad haircut - hardly a work of art in anyone's eyes. Least of all her husband's.*

"You were a bloody liar."

In the corridor outside, the undertaker heard him, coming to the door. "Sorry, sir? Do you need anything?"

"No, nothing." Tyland replied hurriedly, embarrassed to be found talking out loud. "Everything's perfectly fine, thank you."

When the man left, Tyland looked back into the coffin. Their exclusive little coterie had never talked about death. None of them. Perhaps supposing - being such wealthy and important men - they would be spared, or given a longer lease than most. Or maybe his friends *had* thought about their demise, Tyland mused, although he never had. Despite his psychical ailments he hadn't been troubled by the notion of dying. Until now, studying Barend de Vries and thinking of the murdered Jimmy Nicholson.

And then that inescapable watchman suddenly became real to him. Death - silent and patient - standing close by.

It *couldn't* be just about the girl, Tyland thought incredulously. It couldn't be. It was too long ago, who held a grudge for decades? In the cold anteroom his shoulder ached, his disease all the more noticeable in the morbid space, his gaunt form aching like a rotting tree.

You were a bloody liar, Barend, he repeated silently, *you lied, you lied. You know it, and I know it.*

Tyland's confusion persisted. It had all happened too fast! Two murders within ten days. It was too fast. Panic came unexpectedly, his previous arrogance mocking him:

"A woman, pushing forty? You think we wouldn't be able to outsmart her? Honestly, you can't believe she'd really have a chance. One woman pitted against five men?"

And then he had remembered Barend's reply.

"Not five, four now. Remember, she's already killed one of us."

But he *still* hadn't taken it seriously. Instead Tyland had consoled himself – it was Jimmy's fault. He had been the worst offender, it was down to him – and had stupidly hoped that with Jimmy Nicholson's death it might be over. Arrogance had always been his Achilles heel. It was someone else's fault. It was only a woman. What woman killed?

She did....

For another ten minutes Tyland stared into Barend's death face, trying to read animation into the locked features. He even wondered about the old wives' tale, that the retinas of the eyes held the last image the victim saw. In a moment's insanity he almost reached out, tempted to lift the closed lids and read what was written there, but instead Tyland Bray reeled back and hurried out of the Chapel of Rest.

Eighteen

New York

When he turned off his mobile Leo's hands were shaking. All the strength left his legs and he almost stumbled, clutching the back of his chair and lowering himself into the bed. *I am an old man, he thought, I am suddenly, irredeemably, old. Emptied of life, because life is seeping out of me.* Had he just heard correctly? Barend de Vries had been murdered. Barend, Barend, after Jimmy now Barend. He knew that he had to accept the news, but couldn't. Tried to postpone understanding, to grip those last few moments before reality. But instead the news had sounded like an early Matins bell wrenching him out of sleep.

His first coherent thought was to run, and he stumbled around his bedroom, tossing clothes into a suitcase along with his passport. Yes, he would run, would run from this woman, this killer. But where could he run to? Back to London? Was she there, did she only kill on her own territory? He had returned to New York, so maybe he was safer staying there. She didn't have money, she couldn't afford to make the trip.

What was he thinking? What did he know about her? Wasn't that the whole reason they had gathered

127

together, to try and prise some recall out of their collective memory? Who knew what this woman was now. Over twenty years had passed since that night, in twenty years where had she been, what had she done?

Her image had never left him. If he had had the skill he would have drawn her, the long white column of her body, thin, too thin, her ribcage showing, her breasts small, only temporarily glimpsed when the Oriental gown fell away. Her hair had been very long, thick, dark auburn around the spectacular face. Oh yes, she had been spectacular, much more beautiful than the girl in the Rodin sculpture, the one she had been hired to mimic. As a gay man, her sexuality had not moved him, but her beauty had been riveting, her eyes fiercely dark against the white skin. Had she spoken? No, not at first, instead she had looked at him, seen into him, and pleaded silently.

And he hadn't responded, because she wasn't important and Leo had made new friends that he wanted to keep. Friends who were influential, who knew about art and culture, men who didn't reject him for his homosexuality or his colour. He had found a home at Vincent Lund's and he didn't want to be exiled because of a girl he hadn't known and would never see again.

But he *would* see her again.

And, if he was honest, Leo had always known that. He could light candles in St Patrick's in New York or in the Vatican in Rome, but the little flames stayed earthbound with his prayers. He could plead with God, say:

'I was poor too, I suffered too. I've changed, I've helped many people often. Isn't it enough?'

But he knew the answer and jumped when his mobile rang.

"Hello?"

"It's me, Ruby. You sound weird," her voice was strong, but crazed like an old painting. Ruby Schulman, charity fund raiser, millionaire widow, fearless. "What's going on?"

"Barend de Vries was killed." Leo heard the croak in his voice and repeated the name. "Barend de Vries."

"Who?"

"He was an old friend of mine, a London barrister. I told you about him, he was set to become a KC."

"Yeah, yeah," Ruby said, taken aback. "Did you just say he was *killed?"*

"Murdered."

"Shit," she replied simply. "Didn't another friend of yours get murdered too?"

"Yes, Jimmy Nicholson."

"You should keep better company," she replied, thoughts running on. "Hang on a minute, I recognise that name. Nicholson's an art dealer –"

"He *was* an art dealer." Leo corrected her. "He isn't anything now, but dead. Two of my closest friends are dead."

"I'm coming over to the UK. I'll stay at the Holland Place flat."

"I'm Ok –"

"Shut the hell up, I'm coming! If everyone around you is getting killed you need company." She paused. "Leo?"

"Yes?"

"Don't fret. You're not alone."

And with that, she hung up.

-o0o-

Impassive, Stella Nicholson started to empty her husband's wardrobe, folding the suits neatly and packing them into large boxes along with his shirts and shoes. Never a sentimental woman, she didn't linger over his pyjamas or his dressing gown and only paused when she spotted her late husband's glasses on his desk. Strange, Stella thought, he should have been buried wearing his glasses as he always wore them. But she had never seen a corpse in glasses at all the open casket viewings she had attended. Jewellery, yes, but glasses, no.

Moving steadily, Stella entered the landing. The obituaries had all been gracious and impressive, Jimmy's nasty little habits mercifully undisclosed. She *had* been anxious after the will: it had been unpleasant to learn that the trollop Alicia de Vries had inherited Jimmy's collection. There had been local gossip, but the press hadn't mentioned it – although now she wondered *when* the coverage would start, because now Barend de Vries had been murdered.

Stella paused, her late husband's washbag in her hands. Alicia wouldn't jeopardise her legacy by talking, or by selling any of the collection and thereby exposing it to the market. But the press would be bound to start making connections between the two murders. Two friends killed within ten days – no one would believe that was a co-incidence.

Stella certainly didn't. Deep in thought, she moved on to Jimmy's bathroom, noting with distaste that the carpet had not been properly cleaned. She wanted to feel pity as she looked at the place where her husband had died, at the patch of soiled carpet where he had squirmed and fought to breathe, but Stella had long since lost all love for her husband and her heart remained closed.

Jimmy would never have understood why she disliked him so much. If he had thought about it, which she doubted, he would have put it down to his affairs, his overheated sex drive, but he would have been wrong. Stella's loathing had first taken root when Jimmy rejected their son, Dominic. It was true that he hadn't been academic, impressively stupid at school, but he had had a sweetness of nature which Stella had treasured. Her parents had been British upper class cold, her friends superficial, but when her son was born she had found contentment.

He was engaging, charming, amusing, loved by everyone – except his father. Jimmy saw in Dominic a rival; someone who would compete for Stella's attention. They hadn't been married long with their son arrived. Had it been later – when the martial decay had begun – it wouldn't have had the same effect. But in those early wedded years Stella and Jimmy had had some semblance of closeness and his jealousy roared into life. His son became his scapegoat, the reason for his affairs. Even the beginning of his private collection dated from the time of Dominic's birth. Jimmy had found that motherhood made his wife asexual, her breasts no longer solely his property, her affection hijacked by an infant he resented.

And so Dominic grew up, but he remained unscholarly and immune to the appeal of his father's art business. He didn't have an instinct for culture, found the gallery tedious, his interests leaning towards computer games, computer graphics and AI. For a father who relished the Old Masters a son admiring *Dragons and Dungeons* was intolerable. Dominic soon started to drift away, finding a girlfriend who shared his interests and then, one early autumn, he visited home and told Jimmy that he was married and about to become a father.

Stella never knew what was said; she had only her husband's version and doubted its veracity. Apparently they had argued and Dominic had taken money from his father's wallet and left. The only address Stella had for her son was no longer valid, the mobile phone disconnected. When she pressed Jimmy for an explanation he told her that their son was a thief and that he never wanted to see him again. He lied, high spots of colour on his cheeks, and said he was glad Dominic had gone and that their marriage would be better without him.

She hated him from that moment, and she kept hating him. And when – years later - Dominic made contact she hated her husband even more. Jimmy had lied, forcing and encouraging the estrangement between mother and son. He had told Dominic that his mother was ashamed of him and his wife, and that she didn't want anything to do with her grandchild... Coolly revengeful, Stella had tried to repair the damage, but the trust between mother and son had gone and Dominic slipped away. And this time, he stayed away.

Angered by the memory, Stella moved into her husband's bedroom and snatched up his dressing gown. She folded it, then paused, feeling something and reaching into the pocket.

And there she found it.

The first letter Jimmy Nicholson had received.

From the woman who had killed him.

Nineteen

Detective Sox scratched his thin ginger hair and thought about what Alicia de Vries had just said. It was a theory certainly, but was she trying to trick him? Or genuinely trying to find her husband's killer? He liked Alicia de Vries. Not just because she was beautiful, but because she was a chancer, an opportunist, one of those women who walked a spiral through life. No straight lines for Alicia de Vries.

Naturally he had looked into her background and found nothing he hadn't expected. A pretty woman using her looks to get a rich husband. So far, so predictable, and her later affairs were just as foreseeable; married for a while, bored, testing that her appeal was still there. But her choice of lovers *had* interested Sox. Jimmy Nicholson not so much, he was a player, but Vincent Lund? That *was* a surprise… Sox scratched his head again then scratched irritably at his ear. It was the shampoo. He had told his wife that anti dandruff shampoo made his skin itch, but she had still bought it, two for the price of one. Of course it was on offer, he'd said, rubbish was always cheap.

*'What d'you prefer?' She'd replied. 'To be itchy
or covered in dandruff? It doesn't look good for
a detective to go around with dandruff on his
collar...'*
Sox had stared at her balefully:
*'It's not good to see him scratching like a mon-
key either...'.*

He would wash his hair again when he got home,
but in the meantime Sox's thoughts turned back to
Alicia. It was lazy having affairs with your husband's
friends. Lazy and brutal, because Barend would have
been sure to find out eventually. Or maybe that was
why she kept her sins close, so that her husband *would*
find out. Maybe it titillated him. Sox had heard about
such things before. Or maybe not. Maybe it would
make him want to kill the other man. But that didn't
make sense either, because now Barend de Vries was
dead and if he had been after Alicia's lovers Vincent
Lund would be the one in the coffin, not him. Which
brought Sox back to Alicia's suggestion that it might
have been some criminal Barend had prosecuted, or
failed to acquit. Some crook with a grudge.

It was feasible. If you discounted the death of
Jimmy Nicholson. He had been a gallery owner and,
despite Sox's digging, had no criminal associations.
Rivals and competitors, yes, but nothing illegal. The
two murdered men had been friends, had shared the
same woman, but they had nothing else in common –
except for their collections.

Sox scratched his ear again, his nails raking the
skin. How many times did he have to tell his wife
about the shampoo? It was the same with bacon. He
hated bacon, he had loathed bacon all their married

life, but she still made it – every Sunday breakfast. That was marriage, he decided, petty torments and little niggles. Which was fine unless they covered something fundamentally wrong. Which brought him back to Barend de Vries.

So what had the barrister *really* thought when he found out that his wife had inherited Jimmy Nicholson's erotic art? Had he been disgusted or enraged? No, that didn't make sense, Sox thought, it didn't tie the men together with a joint motive. Try again. So was it something to do with their own collections? Or maybe he should check out what the lovely Alicia had suggested? That somewhere along the line there *had* been someone familiar to both Jimmy Nicholson and Barend de Vries, some vengeful criminal. Possibly some case in which both men had been involved.

But the collections kept popping back into Sox's head. Those treasured possessions the five men had relished for over twenty years. Art was money, art was competition. Great wealth – the kind that meant men could indulge their tastes without restriction – inspired envy.

Theft.

Possibly even murder.

Twenty

With the letter tucked deep in her pocket Stella arrived at the Bray house. She had to hand it to Tyland he had made a substantial fortune, profits he had flipped back into brick and mortar, the house regal and overstuffed with weighty pieces of furniture garnered over a hundred auction sales. As she was shown into the drawing room a massive chinoiserie cabinet faced her, large enough to hide a body, an armchair the size of a sedan hogging the fireplace. By contrast the sofa facing it was a delicate, carved French antique, its overstuffed cushions teetering on fine gilt legs. Blue and white Chinese pottery urns – round bellied, depicting scenes of long dead warriors – stood to attention on either side of the bay window, whilst a piano, lid up, bared its yellowing teeth.

The aggressive opulence offended Stella, and as she looked round she heard the door open and Marina walk in. She entered nervously, as though *she* was the visitor and Stella the house owner, her hair limp from a hurried shampoo, her feet shuffling in new shoes that were too tight for her.

"It's good to see you, Stella." She said uncertainly, "I'm so sorry about Jimmy, are you getting over the shock?"

"No," she replied crisply, "but you don't have to make any fuss on my account. Isn't Alicia here yet?"

"I'm… I'm expecting her any minute. Would you like to sit down?"

Stella took the armchair, making a note of Marina's pained expression. Of course, Stella had guessed that it was Tyland's chair, it had to be. That was why she had picked it, staking her claim to being the master of ceremonies.

"Everything's very difficult at the moment," Marina continued timidly, "Your poor husband… and now Barend being killed … I don't what to think. Tyland said --"

She stopped talking as Alicia entered. Although fully made up and apparently composed, her eyes were puffy from crying. Nodding to both women the newcomer sat down, her gaze falling on a tea tray already set out. "What's this? Alice in Wonderland?"

"I thought tea --"

"We need to talk, all three of us," Stella cut Marina off in mid-sentence, her autocratic gaze raking over Alicia's casual outfit. "The police don't seem to have any idea what's going on, so I wanted to ask if either of you did."

"Did *what?*"

"Have any idea why our husbands were killed?"

Alicia stared at Stella suspiciously. The two women disliked each other, but were drawn together by a mutual bond and forced to communicate.

"I don't know anything." Alicia replied, toughing it out. "Have you got any ideas?

Oh, Stella had plenty of ideas, but she wasn't about to confide. She wanted the other women to tell her what *they* knew. Her only intention was to make sure that the truth implied in the letter didn't come out. Jimmy might have been an indifferent husband, but she wasn't about to let his grubby actions ruined her life. Or the new life she had planned.

Ever since his death Stella had found herself plotting. She wanted her son back, wanted a family around her as she grew old: a grandson in whose life she could be included. Her late husband had shattered the family, but Jimmy was dead and now she had a chance – if she was clever – to get that family back. Stony faced, Stella thought of the letter and its damning contents. There was a woman out there who was determined to get revenge. She could understand that. But not a subtle, slow burning revenge: this woman wanted to kill - and she had already proved she was serious.

It had worried Stella that she might expose the men publicly and ruin them that way, but after a lot of thought she had realised that wasn't the plan. The murderess wasn't interested in ruining lives, she was interested in taking them. And although the only person mentioned by name in the letter had been Vincent Lund, Stella guessed the identities of the other four men. Two of whom were already dead. And, if the woman carried out her threat, Tyland Bray, Vincent Lund and Leo Parks would follow.

Her first instinct was not to save them, but to save herself and her future. Any loyalty she felt to Jimmy was to his legacy, not to him as a person. The story of that night twenty years earlier could not be allowed to become public, the motive *had* to remain secret. Which meant that another motive had to be found, something which would convince the police and turn scandal away from her door.

The only problem was the other women. Did they know about the letter? The real motive for the murders?

"So," Stella repeated. "*Do* you know why they were killed?"

"Perhaps when Tyland gets home we could ask him --"

"*Tyland has nothing to do with this!*" Stella snapped imperiously. "I want to find out if either of *you* have any idea what's going on."

"I suppose there has to be a link between them." Alicia offered, lighting a cigarette. Marina looked about to protest, then slumped back in her seat. "And they only had one thing in common – their bloody collections."

"Which is hardly a reason to kill them. Even an art critic wouldn't go that far," Stella sneered. "There must be something else, something more serious."

"Like what? Ok, so Jimmy and Tyland are art dealers, but Vincent's a doctor and Barend was in the law." Her voice cracked on her husband's name. "Maybe it's someone with a grudge against high ranking professionals."

Stella's tone was cold. "You hardly seem to be grieving, my dear."

"I don't see a tear on your cheek either." Alicia retorted. "Jimmy always fooled around, Stella, you know that. He could have pissed off a dozen people. Maybe it was a jealous husband who killed him. Or some criminal with a grudge against Barend."

So Alicia *didn't* know the truth, Stella thought, satisfied. Alicia had no idea what had happened, or that the killer was a woman. And obviously neither Alicia or Marina knew anything about the letter. The thought was comforting.

"If it was a jealous husband," Stella suggested. "perhaps Barend killed Jimmy? I mean, you two had an affair."

"And then what? Barend committed suicide by stabbing himself to death bread knife?"

Marina let out a moan. "I don't see that this has to do with me or Tyland...."

"They were all friends --"

"That's not enough of a reason!" Marina replied, stricken, her hands clasping together. "Tyland is a good man, he's done nothing wrong. And he's sick --"

"Terminal, if he's not careful." Alicia replied dryly.

"How could you!" Marina said, her face flushed. "How could you be so cruel? You never cared for your husband, but I love mine. We're happy, and he's worked so hard to get where he is. Tyland will be Minister of the Arts, everyone knows that..." she trailed off, looking from one woman to the other. "Why would anyone want to hurt him?"

For a fleeting instant Stella was almost sorry for what she was about to do.

Twenty One

New York

After buzzing to be let in, Ruby Schulman pushed open the door to the lobby and made her way to the lifts. At nearly five foot ten inches in height (age having robbed her of her six foot status) she still walked with a long looping stride and waited impatiently for the elevator. In the reflection of the steel doors she turned her head from right to left, admiring the ageing Nefertiti features and the aureole of white hair.

Leo was waiting for her on the 10th floor, kissing her on the cheek in greeting.

"You look incredible."

"You look fucking terrible." Ruby replied, following Leo to his apartment. He closed the door behind them, sliding the lock and the chain bolt. As he did so, Ruby sat down, ensuring that her best profile was on view. "I want to know everything."

"They were killed in London --"

"You said murdered."

He nodded. "Yeah, murdered."

"Why?"

"If I knew that I wouldn't be so worried," Leo replied, glancing away. "It's unbelievable. Two of us dead —"

"Two of us?" Ruby repeated. "Two of *who*?"

"There's five of us. You know about this, Ruby....." He paused, shrugged. "We became friends because we're all collectors."

She nodded, thinking about Leo's private collection, the one people knew about, but hardly anyone had seen. Apart from her, of course, because they had been friends for over fifteen years; Ruby widowed, loving gossip and spending money, Leo overjoyed to have someone with whom he could plan his charity balls and society auctions. Aside from her New York brownstone, Ruby had a flat in Holland Park, and a spacious studio apartment which she sometimes rented out. But never when she was over in London for the summer, never then. Because that time she dedicated to Leo and his magazine. Gleeful, she would willingly spend half a day tracking down a specific lamp for a magazine photo shoot, working her way around Park Avenue with her long giraffe gait, firing instructions and demands. Spending so much money, she was indulged, Leo's aesthetic style working its magic. Catnip to a panther. Ruby Schulman hadn't helped Leo with one cover of his magazine, but dozens. And over the years she had become that most elusive of all creatures: a stand-in mother with impeachable style.

"What's collecting got to do with your friends being murdered?"

"I don't know."

"You're a terrible fucking liar, darling!" She reproached him. "Spit it out?"

"There's nothing *to* tell, Ruby. I don't know why it's happening."

The lie caught her off guard. Leo – of all people – was deceiving her. Wary, she changed tack: "Isn't Vincent Lund part of this circle of chums?..."

Leo nodded.

"... I haven't seen him for years. He used to be my doctor when I lived in London."

"I know, you told me. He always sends his best wishes."

"Frigging best wishes, my arse!" She laughed loudly, "I was a pain in the neck. Poor Vincent, so patient with my maladies."

"You don't have any maladies."

"That's why he was so patient, darling!" She nudged Leo sitting next to her on the sofa. "You're missing one."

"What?"

"The fifth member of your coterie." She counted them off on one manicured hand. "There's you, Vincent, poor Messrs Barend and ...... what was the other one's name?"

"Jimmy. Jimmy Nicholson."

"Oh yes, I bought some Courbet drawings off him a while back. Never liked him. Fucking letch." She returned to her previous thought. "You nearly left out the gangly Mr Bray, that creaking scarecrow of a man."

"You seem to remember him well enough."

"Because he's a brilliant dealer! That man never misses --"

"And he's tipped to become Minister of Arts."

"With that dull wife of his?"

"You're cruel, Ruby."

"But honest, Leo." She teased him, her tone becoming serious again. "So out of five friends of yours, two of you have been murdered." Her expression hardened. "This isn't funny. What do the police say about it? Have they got any suspects?"

"No, I don't think so."

"Clues? Evidence? There must be evidence."

"Not that I know of."

"How did they die?"

Leo swallowed. "One was poisoned… the other was knifed."

"Dear God," she took in a breath. "So there *must* be evidence, DNA."

"None the police have found. There's nothing, no clues, nothing…." He bowed his head, remembering his conversation with Detective Sox over the phone.

'Yes, we were friends. I've known Barend and Jimmy for twenty years, but I didn't see them often.'

(I am talking too quickly? I can't tell, there are pauses in our conversation over the long distance line. Does it make me sound shifty? Stay calm. Don't tell the police that once - in Vincent's great drawing Room - we hired a girl to recreate the marble replica of a Rodin sculpture. We were just emulating the patrons in Renaissance times. It was creative, inspirational, something we did for magazine shoots and photographs. It was all perfectly harmless.)

Sox hadn't told him anything about evidence, just denied that there was any. And Leo had nervously asked about the knife. Had it been left in Chambers or taken away after she –

(No, don't say she! I'm not supposed to know the gender of the killer)

– after they murdered Barend.

'Did they bring the knife with them, and take it away again?" Leo had asked tentatively. "A bread knife? That would mean blood, a lot of blood."

Sox had paused on the line: not asking further questions, just answering Leo's in a manner that warned him to be careful and talk slowly. Like someone with nothing to hide.

"No fingerprints in Barend's Chambers?.... I see. What about Jimmy? No fingerprints there – even though the killer" *(not **she**, Leo warned himself, I shouldn't know that)* "had to go through the house to get to the bathroom?"

"What about you, Mr Parks," Sox had interrupted "do you know Mr Nicholson's house well?"

Leo had taken his time to answer; thinking about the detective, wondering if he could sense every lie slithering out of his mouth like snakes from a sand pit.

"Leo!" Ruby said sharply, breaking into his thoughts. "What the hell's the matter with you?"

He looked at her helplessly as she took hold of his hand. "Talk to me, Leo, we can fix this. Whatever it is, we can fix it. You need money? You need help? Tell me, darling, tell me what you need and you've got it."

"It's not something money can fix."

"Then it must be bad," she joked, her voice sympathetic. "Is it some young guy? Someone blackmailing you, Leo?"

"No, nothing like that."

"Is someone trying to steal your business? Take over the magazine?" She tilted her head to one side. "Come on, Leo, tell me! Are you gambling? In debt?"

"No."

"Are you ill?" She asked, suddenly anxious, then correcting herself. "No, it can't be something that concerns just you if two of your friends are dead. So it's something that involves *all of you*. Was it a crooked business deal?"

"It's nothing to do with my career!"

"D'you need some advice?" She pressed him. "A good lawyer?"

"I don't want a lawyer!"

"Just tell me, I'll stand by you." Her voice rose. "I'm not going to let anyone hurt you, Leo. They'd have to kill me first."

He glanced down, fighting emotion. "Ruby, if anything *did* happen to me --"

"I won't allow it!"

"Hear me out. Please, listen. I've seen a lawyer and made a will. I've left you my collection."

"Darling, I'm not gay," she teased him "it would be lost on me."

"So sell it, do what you like with it. The rest of my stuff I'm leaving to charity."

"I'm not discussing this anymore!" Ruby increased the grip on his hand, scrutinising his face. "Don't talk about dying. You're too young to talk about dying --"

"Jimmy is dead and now Barend is dead! I *have* to talk about dying because someone wants to kill me." Leo looked at her, his tone steady. "Don't you understand? Someone is after **all of us**."

"So tell me why!"

"I can't."

"How can I help you unless I know the facts?" She snapped, unnerved. "How can the police help you unless they know?"

"They don't. And they won't."

"Be reasonable, Leo! If someone's aiming to kill five men they need to be stopped."

"They won't stop until it's over –"

"Until the five of you are dead!" She shouted, "So that's it, is it? You're just going to sit around and wait to be killed? Fuck you, Leo, where's your fight? I don't care what you say, whatever's going on we can stop it."

"No, we can't. Not this."

"Not *what?* Tell me what it is and I'll tell *you* if we can't fix it. I can't do anything until I know what we're up against. I've lived too long and done too much to be shocked. You can't have done anything that bad, you're not the type. You're no fucking gangster." But she was spooked and leant towards him. "I don't believe you'd do anything unforgivable. I don't believe Vincent Lund would either. Neither of you are wicked."

"Not wicked, weak."

"Weakness isn't a criminal offence!" Ruby snorted. "And whatever it is won't change how I feel about you. Anything you say to me is between us – and *stays* between us. I won't judge you." She lifted his chin and looked into his eyes. "I'll ask you one last time, Leo, *what have you done?"*

"I damned myself.... And worse, I thought I could get away with it."

Twenty Two

It was past nine in the evening when Vincent decided he was not going home and instead would stay the hospital. So he called Milas, had a brief chat with Charlotte, then rang off, labouring under the strain of sounding normal. Detective Sox, with his irritating probing, had unnerved Vincent and he knew that the perky detective would have investigated his past, the previous hospitals where had had worked, and his old colleagues.

He could probe as much as he liked, Sox would find nothing. Vincent Lund's career was exemplary. His research papers were excellent too, his expertise in the field of maxillofacial surgery acknowledged in UK and USA. A few years earlier Vincent had been offered a consultant post at a hospital in New York, but had resisted, unwilling to leave St Thomas's and uproot his family.

Ambitious, yes, he was always ambitious, but not to the detriment of his daughter. Charlotte had been unsettled by her parents' divorce and had struggled with her feelings of rejection, her mother leaving her behind in an emotional baggage drop. And so Vincent had no desire to unsettle Charlotte again, relieved that

Milas had entered their family and been assimilated so easily.

Milas… Vincent reached into his bottom desk drawer and poured himself a whisky. He wasn't on call, there would be no emergencies that night. Not with his patients anyway. Sipping the drink, he scooted his chair over to the window and looked down three stories onto the hospital courtyard below as a gaggle of nurses passed under the awning and made for the side entrance. Bugger bloody Sox, he thought bitterly, you can dig all your like, but you won't find any misconduct in my career. No inappropriate affairs with patients, no medical mistakes, no legal cases brought against me. Dig all you like, my career's pristine.

> *But then you'll dig into the **collection,***
> *won't you?*
> *'The Bearded Woman,' yes, I want it, yes, I do.*
> *Should it matter, when I could be dead any*
> *day now?*
> *A painting, fifty paintings, medical cabinets,*
> *skulls, all the pickings of auctions and curios –*
> *to what end?*
> *And what of my daughter if I'm killed?*
> *Pale eyelashes on a paler cheek, asthmatic,*
> *finding breath difficult at times….*
> *What will I leave behind me?*
> *To my daughter, I leave worry.*
> *To Milas, I leave disgrace.*

"Bugger you," Vincent said out loud, thinking of Sox again. Thinking that in the detective's beady brain he might be cunning enough to work it all out. But not if the three of them stayed quiet. If they stayed silent, mute, dumb, they could get though it… Vincent watched as an ambulance pulled into the car park, a drunk fighting with a male nurse as they got out. He was almost envious: drink made you reckless, but then he had been drunk *that* night… Vincent took another sip of his whisky and felt the warmth comfort his gut… He shouldn't worry, Tyland Bray wasn't going to expose them, neither was Leo. Both men had too much to lose. Tyland professionally, Leo morally.

Then Vincent thought of the Rodin sculpture and the girl they had hired that fateful evening. Where had the *Danaid* gone? He couldn't remember, but supposed Tyland had sold it on. It had been a replica, after all, an exquisite replica certainly, but Tyland was never interested in copies, however extraordinary. So if it wasn't in his collection, who owned it now? He thought back. Jimmy Nicholson had initially wanted it, but after that night he had suddenly changed his mind and Leo had also lost interest.

If Tyland Bray had sold it, where was it now? Twenty years on, would he remember who the buyer was? It could be important. Perhaps -Vincent felt a sudden hope - perhaps there was a clue there. Some opening which would lead to the killer. He wasn't going to give in, be cowed, backed into his own death, even if the others might begin to flounder. When he had spoken to Leo the previous evening the American had been weary, resigned to his fate. But Vincent wasn't ready to die. And he knew Tyland Bray wasn't going to go gentle into any good night… Vincent kept staring down into the hospital courtyard as the ambulances came and went. Leo needed support, the weakest link of the trio. Perhaps, under too much pressure, he might go to the police. He had always been religious, would he seek redemption in the face of judgement? Would his conscience compel him to confess? If he went to a priest they would be safe, his confession sacrosanct, but if Leo confessed to the police they were finished.

Vincent's heart rate speeded up. He had to get Leo back to London where he could watch over him; he was too far away in New York, hiding. No more travelling for Leo Parks. Since the murders had taken place his life had been curtailed, sucked dry between the four walls of his apartment. He had told Vincent that he prayed, sent out for his food to be delivered, and – most tellingly – had handed over running of his magazine to his editor in chief, claiming ill health, grief over the deaths of two close friends.

Perhaps it *would* be better to get Leo back to London... Vincent's gaze moved over the car park, lost in thought. Then a loud noise startled him and he looked down to see a couple of nurses laughing. The sound had been a car backfiring, that was all, he told himself. The nurses were laughing, it was nothing to worry about. Relax... Suddenly the hospital clock chimed ten, Vincent surprised to realise how long he had been sitting there, his attention caught by a bright light.

It was a piercing beam of light, like an ultra-strong torch, shining round the courtyard then up the walls of the Cardiac Unit opposite, moving erratically like a quick white insect. Curious, Vincent watched. It darted about, shone on windows and on the roofs of the ambulances and then, unexpectedly, it swung round, the full impact of the light catching him sitting at the window.

An instant later the light went out. But it had been long enough for Vincent to realise what it meant; he

154

was being watched. Spooked, but angry, he ran down the four flights of stairs to the EXIT doors, slamming them back as he hurried out into the courtyard. The nurses had gone, there were only two ambulance drivers chatting beside the entrance to the A & E.

"Did you see that?"

One of the ambulance drivers looked over to him. "*What?*"

"A light, a very bright torch light. It was being shone round, it came from down here. Someone was shining a light from this yard." Vincent paused, looking from one man to the other. "You can't have missed it! It was bright, *piercing*."

"There's a full moon --"

"The light was being moved around! Someone was swinging it round and it came from down here." Vincent persisted. "You *must* have seen it!"

"When was this?"

"Just now."

"Well, there's only been me and Gary out here for the last five minutes. There's been no one fooling around with a torch."

His companion joined in. "Are you sure it came from down here?"

Vincent was losing his patience. "*You can't have missed it!*"

The two men exchanged a glance.

"We didn't see anything, doctor. Nothing. No one's been here. With - or without - a torch."

Twenty Three

Bray Gallery
London

"You must have records."

Irritable, in pain, Tyland gestured for Vincent to follow him, then closed his office door behind them. "It's past ten at night, what are you doing here?"

"I want to know if you have records that go back twenty years."

"Jazz or classical?"

Vincent smiled wryly. "Records of your customers."

"People who buy art aren't customers, they are *collectors* –"

"Have you got records?"

"Why d'you want to know? This isn't about Leo, is it?"

He reacted to the name. *"What* about Leo?"

"I spoke to him earlier, he was in a bad way." Wincing, Tyland gripped his shoulder.

"Is the pain worse? D'you want me to have a look at it?"

"No, I don't like doctors."

"You're in a nasty mood, even for you." Vincent replied, "what did you mean about Leo?"

"I'm worried about him," Tyland's long fingers dug onto his shoulder, pummelling the flesh to get some relief. "He's weak. We'll have to watch him, he's won't hold out if he's pressurised."

Vincent had been thinking the same. "Did you get the second letter today?"

A moment's pause.

"Yes… and obviously you did too."

"That's why I want to see your records, Tyland. Can you look up who brought the Rodin?"

"The one we –"

"Yes, *that* one."

Tyland sighed, "It might take me a while, I can't remember off hand who bought it. Jimmy was keen, then he went off the idea. I always wondered about that." He paused, stared at Vincent. "You want me to look it up *now?"*

"Yes, now. If we find out who bought it, it might tell us something."

Groaning, Tyland moved to the door. "I'll have to go upstairs and dig through the old files. I can't promise anything, but I should have a record."

"Tyland?" He turned, Vincent's voice sombre. "Are you scared?"

He *was* scared, but he wasn't going to admit it. "Don't be absurd, I've never been scared of a woman in my life."

"But she's not an ordinary woman."

Tyland was disdainful. "You think she's some all-powerful Nemesis? For Christ Sake, she's human –"

"She got to Jimmy and to Barend."

"But she won't get to *me*. And if you keep your wits about you, Vincent, she won't get to you either."

Tyland was gone for a while, Vincent waiting in his office and hearing the dealer moving around upstairs. There were sounds of filing cabinets drawers being opened, then slammed shut, followed by the noise of a door creaking open. Then silence. Finally, half an hour later, Tyland re-emerged with an old sales slip, the cuffs of his white shirt dirtied.

"How you any idea how grimy it is up there?" he said, his tone irritated. "I hope Marina can get the marks out of my shirt –"

"Did you find anything?"

"I did." Tyland said, nodding. "Mrs Ruby Schulman, of New York City."

"You're joking."

"No, why the name mean something to you?" Tyland said, thinking back. "I remember her well when she was living in London. She complained about the frame, said there was a break in the moulding and insisted it happened in transit. Threatened to sue me. The Americans are like that, childish. Is the old bag still alive?"

"I don't know, but I think so. She's a good friend of Leo's."

"Really?" Tyland smiled dryly. "You don't think *she*'s our murderer, do you? Or perhaps she has an illegitimate daughter that's coming after us?"

"None of this is funny."

"Am I laughing?" Tyland replied, rubbing his shoulder and reading the invoice slip. "The painting was shipped to New York soon after Ruby Schulman bought it. I imagine she still has it, but you'd have to ask her. Probably a dead end."

"It's all we've got to go on."

"Slim Pickings."

"So what do you suggest?" Vincent retorted. "That we sit here like three ducks on a wall waiting to be picked off?" He thought of what had just happened. "Someone's watching me. Someone was at the hospital earlier, they wanted me to *know* that they were watching me."

"Then you must be next."

"You're a callous bastard," Vincent replied, "don't you care about anything but yourself?"

"I've worked and waited for decades to be made Minister for the Arts. Barend might never have made KC, but no bloody woman's going to destroy my career. I've had a new alarm system installed here and at home --"

"What about Marina? Does she know anything?"

"*Nothing!* She'd panic, you know what's she like."

"Have you confided in anyone?"

"No."

"Then I suggest we keep doing what we're doing and *keep* quiet."

"I agree, besides, the police have nothing to go on --"

"That's what worries me." Vincent interrupted. "There's no obvious motive so they're going to keep digging until they find one. That detective Sox is wily, not the type to lose interest, he won't give up…. Has he seen your collection?"

Tyland nodded. "Earlier today. He didn't say what he thought of it and I didn't ask for his opinion. What about yours?"

"Not yet, but he'll be round. He keeps harping on about *The Bearded Woman* painting coming up for auction tomorrow."

Tyland's eyes flickered. "I'd almost forgotten about that."

"You're a liar. Are you bidding for it?"

"Are you?"

"It interests me." Vincent replied cautiously. "It's a medical condition, it would go well in my collection."

"It's a fine painting, it would go well in mine."

"But it's only a *copy,* Tyland. You're never usually interested in copies."

"It might be a copy, or it might be another version by Ribera. It's not a fake knocked up in some garage in Ealing."

"What a snob you are."

"Guilty as charged" Tyland nodded. "So what do we do about Leo? Get him over to London where we can keep an eye on him?"

"I'll call him tonight, he can stay with me at the house."

"Two sitting ducks under one roof. You realise you might be making it easy for the killer?"

"Or there could be safety in numbers," Vincent replied, getting to his feet. "I'm sending Charlotte to stay with her mother, I was wondering if Milas could use your flat upstairs for a while, until all this is over?"

"It's been empty for a long time and it's full of books, but if you want him there, he can use it." Tyland replied, his tone momentarily faltering. "You think our families are in danger?"

"No," Vincent replied quickly, too quickly "but if something happened I don't want Charlotte or Milas witnessing it. I don't want them finding my body. I certainly don't want my daughter having the cope with anything like that... What about your wife, are you going to send Marina to stay with her parents?"

"I need her at home," the dealer replied, affronted. "I'm not well, I need my wife to take care of me. Marina is the only person who can manage my illness, she wouldn't want to leave me. She takes her duties as a wife very seriously."

"You could have your condition managed in hospital --"

Tyland's eyebrows rose. "Hide out in the London Clinic? Don't be absurd."

"You'd be safe there."

"Really? You're working at St Thomas's everyday - I'll wait and see how you get on there before I make my decision."

Twenty Four

St Thomas's Hospital
London

The previous night Vincent had dreamt of the hospital courtyard, filled with torch lights. Beams which shone up and down the walls, and tracked him as he tried to escape. The courtyard had closed in, walls stretching fifty feet on either side of him, a ceiling over his head, lights shining down on him from above. And he panicked, ran around like a tortured rat looking for an escape route, some darkness to hide in, or a break in the wall. And then the lights became flames and the heat and the fire tore into him as he spun, endlessly screaming himself awake.

Exhausted by the nightmare, Vincent later arrived at the hospital to find that one of his patients had haemorrhaged, and was prepped for surgery. He scrubbed up, avoiding his own reflection in the mirror, and nodded curtly to his colleagues. The images of his dream kept coming back, but he suppressed them and moved into the operating theatre where the sedated patient was lying on the table. An unresponsive, silent body... Without warning, Vincent thought of Barend, then wondered how his own body would look in death.

Five of his colleagues – his surgical team - were waiting for him, five faces turned to him, five pairs of eyes watching. And Vincent wanted to ask them to remove their surgical masks. So he could just see – for an instant – that they were who he thought they were.

Of course he didn't and unsteady walked over to the operating table. The haemorrhage was due to a ruptured blood vessel. Meticulously Vincent clamped and repaired it, then put out his hand for the surgical needle he would use to suture the wound. The nurse stared at him. Eyes above a mask.

"I need to suture the wound."

"Dr Lund?"

He didn't know her. No, he didn't know her. She was a stranger, he didn't know those eyes… His hands shaking, Vincent repeated what he had just said.

"I need to suture the wound."

"But—"

"Just do as I say!" He snapped, his hands sweating in the surgical gloves, his body oozing sweat from every pore.

Who was this woman standing in the middle of his operating theatre, Vincent thought, fighting panic. Who was it hiding behind a white mask, defying him? He tried to compose himself. She could do nothing, not here, not amongst his surgical team. If she rushed at him, stabbed him, she couldn't get away. They would catch her.

She can do nothing here, Vincent assured himself. Not here, not here…. Unless she doesn't care, unless she doesn't care if they catch her.

"Nurse!" He snapped. "Why don't you listen to me!"

"I *am* listening --"

As Vincent gripped the side of the table, his surgical team watched him, the nurse – the woman he didn't know – confronting him.

"I'm sorry, I don't understand, Dr Lund, what do you want?"

"I want to suture the patient's wound."

Whose voice was that? His? No, not his. He was talking like another man. A wavering, frightened man, his voice losing its footing. Vincent could feel the sweat trickle down his spine, his head overheated under the surgical cap. And all the time the nurse was looking at him, her eyes steady.

"Dr Lund, are you alright?"

'You see, Milas, it's a vocation, being a doctor. It's all I ever wanted...'
He is looking at me with admiration, hero worship.
I never worshipped a god, had no reason, no belief, I found God in the body, in the divine engineering of blood and bone.

Vincent slumped against the operating table, his voice far away, in some other country, some other space of mind.

"I need to suture the wound." He repeated dully.

"Dr Lund, please."

"I need to suture --"

"You've already done it!"

In hazy slow motion Vincent looked down, saw the neat stitching around the patient's jaw, then saw, in his hand, the used surgical needle which fell - almost without making a sound - onto the theatre floor.

Twenty Five

Polishing her glasses, Stella Nicholson looked at the papers on the table in front of her. It was surprising how perfectly it all fitted together, better than she could have hoped. In the hallway outside she could hear the cleaner moving around. It was good to have domestic help: something Jimmy's parsimony would have prevented if he had still be alive. But now Stella could indulge herself and had hired a daily and a gardener. She had also bought some exceptionally extravagant food, filling the freezer and dumping the packets of cheap pasta in the bin outside.

Times were changing, she thought, then glanced at the photograph of her late husband, the silver frame throwing a reflection on the polished mahogany sideboard, and thought of the letter. A letter Stella had read many times, filling in the blanks with her imagination and knowledge of her over-sexed husband.

Dominic would have been around seven at the time that the events in the letter had taken place; still that plump, dim child Stella had adored. She wondered if he was still plump, or if having a family had sheared off the fat and left him lean with worry. She also wondered if the private detective she had hired would find him. Or at least an address or phone number by which she could contact her son.

Jimmy would have been enraged to think that his money was being spent in such a way. A private investigator looking for the son he had so skilfully banished... Stella's gaze rested on the photograph.

*'He's my son too, how could you drive
him away?*
'He's a thief, a liar --'
*'The only liar is you, Jimmy!' And then the
banging of the door and the car leaving. Off to
his cronies or his gallery. Mucky little man with
his mucky little ways....*
*Years go on. Yes, they go on, and now they sleep
in separate bedrooms and she reads all night
whilst he whispers to his whores on the phone
downstairs.*
Mucky little man...

"But we'll keep your secret, hey, Jimmy?" She said quietly, still looking at his photograph. "I'm saving your skin, well, actually I'm saving my own. No one will find out, and you want to know why? Because you won't drag me down with you. I won't let your actions give my son another reason to stay away."

Fifteen minutes later Stella said goodbye to the cleaner and locked the front door behind her, then moved into the breakfast room and dialled a number.

"Hello?"

"Is that Detective Sox?"

"Speaking. Who's this?"

"Stella Nicholson," her crystal sharp tone was imperious. "I think I might know the motive for the deaths of my husband and Mr de Vries. Could you call round? Shall we say three this afternoon?"

-o0o-

The Lund house

"No, I'm not leaving here!" Milas snapped. "Not when you're in trouble --"

"Who said I was in trouble?"

"For God's Sake, Vincent, don't treat me like a bloody child!" Milas retorted. "Look at the state you're in."

"I'm just not sleeping --"

"I'm not surprised. If you're worried, send Charlotte away, that's a good idea, but I'm not going anywhere."

"I don't want to have to worry about you."

"Why would you worry about me? I wasn't a friend of Barend de Vries or James Nicholson --"

"No, but you're my nephew."

"And I'm in my bloody thirties! Don't you think I might be useful to have around?"

Vincent sighed, shaking his head. He had hoped that Milas would agree to moving into Tyland Bray's gallery flat, but he wasn't having it. "Just leave until the problem is over --"

"*'Problem!'* Two murders are what you call a fucking problem?" Milas raged. "Perhaps if you confide in me all this would make more sense!"

"I don't know what's going on or I'd tell you," Vincent replied, regretting the lie as he said it. "I'm inviting Leo Parks to stay here and it would be easier for me if you weren't around."

"The house is plenty big enough for three men --"

"It's not a question of space!"

"What *is* it a question of?"

"There's an auction coming up, Milas. The painting we were talking about, *The Bearded Woman,* Leo wants to bid for it."

"And he has to stay *here* to do it?"

"He has business in London and wants to stay here. Why not? He's an old friend. And I think he's got some personal problems too."

"He isn't the only one, is he?"

Vincent flinched. "What's *that* supposed to mean?"

"You can keep your secrets, if that's what you want. If you don't trust me --"

"Milas, it's not a matter of trust."

"Of course it's a matter of fucking trust! If you trusted me, you'd confide and let me help you. But you don't trust me, you think I'm like my mother, your sister. You didn't trust her and you don't trust me --"

"This has nothing to do with Adela!"

"It has everything to do with her *and* the past. You think I haven't guessed?"

The words went through Vincent like an electric shock. *"Guessed what?"*

"That you're in danger," Milas replied, "Is Leo Parks in danger too? Is that why you're inviting him here? You think you'll be safer if you club together?"

"You don't know what you're talking about!"

"Obviously not. Apparently you've no idea why your friends were killed, or what the motive is." His tone was pure sarcasm. "Ok, stick to your story, Vincent! Pretend, lie to me. Protect me, protect Charlotte, keep up the charade that you 'have no idea what's going on.' *But I don't believe you.* I think you know *exactly* what's going on, you just won't admit it. Even to me."

Enraged, Milas then snatched up his jacket and walked out of the house.

-o0o-

Seeing Milas across the road, Tilly hurried towards him, calling his name. But when he didn't turn, she quickened her steps, tapping his arm as he rounded the corner.

He jumped, startled. "Oh, Tilly, hello."

She was crushed by his ill-disguised irritation. "Yeah, well, I'm pleased to see you too."

"Sorry, I'm just not in the mood to talk."

She tipped her head over to one side. "Is there a problem?"

He was too angry to be discreet. "All this going on – your stepfather murdered, Jimmy Nicholson killed, and Vincent trying to send me and Charlotte away to 'protect' us – without telling us what he's protecting us from." He paused, looking away from her, then looking back. "I'm sorry, you've got your own problems…. How's your mother coping?"

"Like the trooper she is," Tilly responded sourly, seeing Milas vulnerable and making a move. "Look, you want to have a coffee? We could commiserate together."

This time Milas didn't rebuff her and instead they walked to a nearby café and moved to a table at the back. Outside the temperature was dropping, brushing zero, but inside the café was hot, swollen with people, the steam from the coffee machines creating vapour on the windows. Taking off his jacket Milas ordered two coffees, Tilly pulling off her woollen hat and shaking

171

her hair loose. She knew it was her best features, thick, long and ash coloured, but Milas hadn't noticed and was staring morosely into his coffee instead.

"*Are* you going away?"

He looked up, stirring his coffee. "What?"

"You said Vincent wanted you to move out of the house – are you going to?"

"No. If my uncle's in danger, I want to be here. I'm not afraid."

"I am," Tilly confessed. "I mean, I wasn't when it was just Jimmy Nicholson, but now Barend's been murdered. It's scary… I keep wondering what's going on, but no one's got any idea about why it's happening. The police don't know anything and neither does my mother." she shuddered. "I was reading about in online, they had *photographs* of the crime scene. Fucking photographs! I know those Chambers, my mother used to take me there when I was younger, I knew the room where Barend was killed…."

"That must be hard."

"Yeah… he was Ok. Barend. I mean. He could be a shit, but he was Ok most of the time… I just don't know why someone would kill him like that… My mother thinks it's some criminal he prosecuted in the past who's come back to get even."

"Could be," Milas said, realising that she was upset. No longer trying to brazen it out under the hard-nosed exterior. "D'you want something to eat?"

She shook her head. "No, I want to talk, because I can't talk to my mother. She's hyper, all over the place. One minute she's fine, the next shouting. I hear her crying at night, but in the daytime she pretends that nothing's happened. I think she really loved him… but she won't talk about it."

"She trying to protect you."

"From *what?* No one's coming after me. This has nothing to do with me. Although…." She leaned over the table towards him, her voice low. "I've been thinking about it. My mother had a fling with Jimmy Nicholson – that's why he left her his paintings – and she also had an affair with your uncle." She stopped short, staring at him. *"Don't say you didn't know?"*

"I didn't actually."

"Oh, sorry."

Milas shrugged. "It's Ok, go on."

"Well, my point is this – is she the one thing they all have in common? My mother was married to Barend, had been involved with Jimmy Nicholson and Vincent – perhaps she'd had an affair with the other two?"

"Tyland Bray?" It was the first time Tilly had seen Milas laugh. "He's not the type, he's not fit enough for a start. And Leo Parks is gay."

"He could be bi?"

"He could, but no, I don't think that's the motive. And you're being a bit hard on your mother, aren't you?"

Feeling chastised, Tilly looked away. "The Nicholson's house isn't far away from ours, what if the killer lives nearby?"

"Your stepfather was killed in his Chambers. That's a long way from Richmond."

"But the Brays live three roads away from us. Your uncle's house is five minutes away. That's a bit of a coincidence, isn't it?"

"Leo Parks lives in New York."

"But he comes over to London every month… maybe it's something to do with Leo Parks? Maybe he's done something criminal? Maybe we're all suffering for something *he* did?" She was surly, folding her arms as she looked at Milas's impassive face. "Ok, so what d'you think the motive is?"

"I don't know."

"What about the collections? The five of them were always talking about their stupid paintings, or that medical freak show of your uncle's. Barend loved going to auctions too, he relied on Tyland Bray and Jimmy Nicholson to advise him. He loved the nudes." She warmed to her theme. "Barend never thought I'd seen them. But I did."

"His collection?"

She nodded. Finally she had stimulated Milas's interest. "I stole his key once and went to look. He never knew... Barend had a flat in Barnes. Apparently he used to rent it out, but then he began his 'collection' – this is years ago - and kept it all there." She had Milas's full attention and ran with it. "Nudes mostly, a few Egon Schiele drawings. Some of them pretty explicit. And some big oil paintings.... Honestly, why bother?"

"How d'you mean?"

"Why bother collecting porn when you can go online and get it for free? You don't even have to pay for most of it." She paused, Milas was staring at her with a cold look on his face. *"What?"*

"I don't think your stepfather wanted porn, I think he wanted art. I think he wanted to be moved by something that was erotic and beautiful too. I think he knew the difference between sex and sensuality."

She shrugged. "Same thing."

"No, it's not. And if you don't know that by now, you should."

Annoyed, Tilly got up. "Fuck you, Milas." She said simply and walked out.

Twenty Six

At precisely three o'clock Detective Sox pressed the front door bell of the Nicholson house, Stella letting him in. As ever, he was surprised by her height as he followed her down the shady hallway, passed the vacant breakfast room and into the drawing room beyond. The atmosphere was solemn, like a Methodist church, the table by the window clear, apart from a small stack of papers.

"Please, take a seat," she said, pointing to one of the dining chairs and watching as the detective sat down. "This is not a pleasant business."

"I'm very sorry for your loss."

"I'm not talking about Jimmy's death. Not directly anyway. I called you here to give you information, detective..."

Sox had the impression that he was not being told something, but taught.

".... Something which has troubled my conscience for days. But I have to do the right thing. I'm sure you understand that." She didn't give him time to agree before continuing. "You know Mr Tyland Bray?"

"Yes, the art dealer."

"You know he was a friend of my husband's?"

"Yes."

"And I imagine you know that there were five men who were all close friends?"

"Who met to talk about art and discuss their collections. Yes, I know."

Stella could see the crack in the ice and nudged him away from it.

"This has nothing to do with collections." She tapped the table with her index finger as she passed, making a dull thudding sound. "I'm finding this very difficult. I know Marina Bray well and we've been friends for a long time. The art world is a very closed shop, people involved in the business know each other and know what's going on, but people outside are barred. It loves to keep its secrets."

"You have a secret to tell me?"

Her expression betrayed nothing. "Tyland knew my husband very well, they did business now and again." She paused, turned to the window, her glasses catching the light and obscuring her eyes. "Many years ago Tyland was involved with some unsavoury people."

"Unsavoury?"

"Crooks."

Sox raised his sparse eyebrows. "Really?"

"Tyland was already successful in the art world, but when he was younger he allowed himself to get drawn into a deal which turned out to be illegal. Fakes. The forgeries were being sold in London, New York and Paris and Tyland was ..."

Sox leaned forward in his seat. *"Yes?"*

"... selling them as originals."

Yes, he was taking the bait...

She could see it slide like a bug down his throat.

Be good, little man. Swallow, swallow.

"A man called Clive Shawcross was arrested. He had accomplices, but he wouldn't divulge who they were. He would only say that he had dealt with dealers in London. Shawcross was brought to trial and defended by the senior barrister in Barend de Vries's Chambers --"

"Mr Barend de Vries?"

"Yes," Stella continued. "Apparently Tyland had confided in Barend and he had organised Shawcross's defence, pro bono, in return for Shawcross denying that Tyland Bray had any involvement with the fakes."

"You said you believed you had uncovered a motive for the murders, so where did your husband come into this?"

"Jimmy was caught out in the fake dealings. He didn't know he was doing anything illegal, but Tyland had used him. Apparently Shawcross was putting pressure on Tyland and he needed outlets for the fakes and…"

"And he used his friends?"

She nodded, turning away from the window, her eyes visible again.

"Yes, Tyland used Jimmy, Barend, Leo Parks and Vincent Lund as buyers for his fakes. Oh, he wasn't that much of a villain. They might have protested at first, but they knew they were forgeries and agreed to help him. Of course they all swore to keep it a secret. Apparently Tyland needed to sell the forgeries on quickly to pay off Shawcross and his associates. He was afraid of passing them through dealers who might spot them as fakes."

"But your husband was a dealer, a respected one."

"Indeed he was. But Jimmy only found out that he'd been used when it too late. He'd been on a busi-

ness trip and when he returned to London Tyland confessed, but by that time Jimmy's partner at the gallery
had sold on the fakes and Jimmy could only get two of
the three back. The third painting disappeared."

*Are you following this, little man? Are you
taking it all in? Show me some reaction. No?
You're more clever than I took you for.
Come on, get on the hook…*

"So all four men," Sox said, head tilted to one
side, "your husband, Barend de Vries, Leo Parks and
Vincent Lund were conned by Tyland Bray?"

"It wasn't as ruthless as it sounds. Tyland was desperate. He was sure he could raise money elsewhere,
pay off Shawcross, and get the fakes back and no one
would be any the wiser. It was meant to be a temporary
solution."

"So how did Shawcross get caught?"

"He was careless, went to a dealer who spotted
the fakes straight away. As I said, through Barend -
who needed to protect himself - a prominent barrister was hired to defend Shawcross and get him off. In
return for Shawcross taking all the blame."

"Was Shawcross acquitted?"

"No. The defence should have won, but…" Stella
paused. "… Shawcross was given a four year sentence."

"Did he serve his time?"

"Yes, he did. And he kept his word, never
exposed Tyland, but when Shawcross left prison he
disappeared."

Sox leaned back on the dining chair, it creaked,
Stella hiding a grimace as she watched him. He thought
back to the suggestion Alicia de Vries had fed him sev-

eral days earlier and wondered if the two women had been talking, either comparing what they knew, or working out a plan together. Several moments passed before the detective spoke again, taking out his notepad and sitting, poised awkwardly, with his pen over the paper.

"Shawcross, you say?"

"Clive Shawcross."

"I'll check it out." He wrote the name slowly, in block capitals. "Did Shawcross know that Tyland Bray had involved his friends?"

"I imagine so."

Sox's sparse ginger eyebrows rose. "This Shawcross seems a very noble man for a criminal. What did he get out of keeping quiet?"

"I told you, he was hoping to be acquitted."

His pen still poised over the notepad, Sox let out a sigh. "Now, Mrs Nicholson, you're playing with me, aren't you?"

She stared at him, glasses high on the bony nose. "I don't understand what you mean, detective."

"You're missing lots of little bits and pieces out of this pretty pattern. Like the motive you promised me."

"The motive is obvious --"

"Not to me."

"Only because I haven't finished telling you what happened, detective. Although he was bitter, Shawcross *was* prepared to serve his time. I imagine – you must be thinking this too – that he had money or some fakes put away for when he got out of jail. And so he was content to wait. He probably planned to blackmail Tyland Bray and his friends when he was released, threaten to expose them and ruin their careers if they didn't give him money. God knows, he must have had

179

plenty of schemes planned. He had four years to think it out, after all."

"Then what happened?"

Stella paused, shook her head. "As I said, Shaw-cross was content to wait - but his wife wasn't. The day after Clive Shawcross was jailed, Jenny Shaw-cross hanged herself."

The detective's eyebrows rose higher. "And you think he's coming back to get his revenge? Murdering the men who used him? But why now? Why not sixteen years ago?"

She shrugged. The movement was hardly discernible.

"I don't know the answer to that. Perhaps he's ill or dying. Perhaps it's not Clive Shawcross, after all. Perhaps he's dead and it's one of his children –"

"He had children?"

"So I believe. Two sons," she paused, "maybe they're taking revenge for the misfortunes of their parents. The eldest would be in his thirties now."

Good girl, Stella, use the pronoun 'his'. Don't slip up now.
The little detective is thinking, wondering. But he can look it all up and check. It's the truth.
My version anyway....
Tyland Bray brought to book after so long would be justice.
No chance of becoming Minster of the Arts now.
Sorry, Marina, it's your turn to lose....

Sox paused, studying Stella Nicholson. She didn't flinch or look away. "*Now* do you see the motive, detective? *Now* do you see it?"

Twenty Seven

Back in his car, Sox considered what he had been told, scratching his head absent mindedly. Was Stella Nicholson telling him the truth? Or after Alicia de Vries's suggestion for a motive, was it just another ploy to whet his appetite? Alicia's tale of the woman who had cut her female employer's throat, Sox had already investigated. It was true, Barend de Vries *had* prosecuted the woman, but she had died of a heart attack in jail long before her sentence was finished. No avenging Nemesis there.

His mind turned back to what Stella Nicholson had just told him. Her motive theory was more subtle than Alicia's. If the five men *had* been involved, two couldn't deny it and the three left alive would hardly admit it. Sox was intrigued. The story seemed plausible and it would be a strong motive, but how could he prove it? If Clive Shawcross had refused to expose Tyland Bray and the others at his trail, where was the evidence? There was nothing on record. To all intents and purposes Shawcross had been working alone, or with his own, unnamed, cohorts.

But if it *was* true, Tyland Bray must have been a very worried man, constantly wondering if the truth would come out and knock him off his arrogant pedestal. He – along with his four friends – would have lived with the threat of *if*, or *when*, Shawcross would expose them. Tyland Bray's chance of becoming Minster of the Arts would be obliterated if he was exposed; as for the others, their exalted positions and status would be toppled.

If it was true.

Sox looked at the name he had written down – *Clive Shawcross*. He could investigate the claim, see if there *had* been a forgery trial, but after that Mr Shawcross seemed to have disappeared. Which was more than a little convenient. Of course Shawcross might well have changed his name and moved abroad after he was released. Or, as Stella Nicholson suggested, he might be dead. The tragedy of his wife's suicide would certainly have been a motive - along with his having to serve a jail sentence he had been assured he would avoid. But why had he waited for so long to get revenge?

Sox flipped his notepad closed and stared out of his car window into the street. An expensive neighbourhood, off limits to most, the houses set well back from the road, drives barred with iron gates, the entrances protected with alarm systems. Impregnable – but not quite. Someone had broken through to get to Jimmy Nicholson and kill him. Someone had murdered Barend de Vries in his Chambers, and Sox knew that all the alarm systems in the universe couldn't stop someone determined on revenge.

If he was still alive, Shawcross would be in his late fifties. But, as Stella Nicholson said, his sons would be in their twenties and thirties. Had one of them taken up the role of avenger? Certainly no one would know them, or see them coming. They might have recognised Shawcross and remembered him, but any child of his would be a stranger. Easy to discount. Who could pick Shawcross's offspring out if they visited Tyland Bray's gallery? Or St Thomas's hospital where Vincent Lund worked? Who would realise they were a danger if they ambled into Leo Parks's publishing office in London? Or New York?

The detective's thoughts turned back to Barend de Vries. He could easily find out who had defended Shawcross, but it was another matter to prove if Barend had been involved in the forgery scam. And it would be difficult to prove if Jimmy Nicholson had been involved. Two dead men, keeping a secret and a scandal to the grave. But he *could* ask Vincent Lund and Leo Parks.

A tap on the car window made Sox jump, Vincent looking down at him. "I thought it was your car, detective. Aren't you parked too far away from my house? Or didn't you want me to see you coming?"

Sox smiled. "I am heading your way, doctor, but I just had a meeting with Mrs Nicholson." He gestured to the passenger seat. "Can I give you a lift?"

"I've got my own car, thanks. Is there some news?"

"Should there be?"

"You said you'd been talking to Stella Nicholson, so I wondered if there was any news about Jimmy's murder." Vincent paused. "Is there?"

"Shall we talk at your house?" the detective asked, starting up his car and then following Vincent's Mercedes.

At the entrance to his drive Vincent buzzed open the automatic gates, then drove up the front door and waited for Sox. The temperature was still dropping, past zero as the light fell, vapour coming from the detective's mouth as he parked his car and then stood, looking at the house. On the second floor lights were turned on, the curtains drawn downstairs, a massive Georgian lamp turned on over the front entrance.

But instead of entering the house, Sox walked around it, Vincent watching him from the front steps, his hands in his pockets, a biting wind blowing his hair across his forehead.

"Are you looking for anything in particular?"

The detective smiled, turning back to Vincent. "Is your house alarmed?"

"Yes. The garages too."

"And you need a remote control to open the gates?"

Vincent nodded. "I thought I was a suspect, but now it seems you're worried about my safety."

The little detective ignored the remark. "You have a lot of trees around the house. Bad for the foundations, you know. My wife nags me about an ash tree we have, too close to the back wall, she tells me, it'll cause damage. It's just a matter of time."

Vincent's face was unreadable. "Shall we go inside?"

"The trees are bad for another reason," Sox continued. "They'd be a good hiding place, you know. Anyone could secret themselves there --"

"They'd have to get through the electric gates first."

"Or climb over the wall."

"It's fifteen feet high."

"Ever heard of ladders?" Sox replied, smiling. "Although I take your point, doctor, someone would be bound to notice a person with a ladder climbing over your wall. Or would they? You'd be surprised what people *don't* notice. They see someone with a ladder, but if he's dressed in workman's clothes and he looks like he might be cleaning windows or fixing telephone wires, who'd stop him?"

"I doubt anyone in this neighbourhood *would* stop him, but they'd certainly call the police." Needled, Vincent opened the front door, Sox finally following him inside. Overhead they could hear footsteps coming from the bedrooms and at the back of the house someone was moving around in the kitchen as Vincent showed the detective into the drawing room.

"So what did Stella Nicholson tell you that made you think I wasn't a suspect now?"

"Sorry?"

Vincent tried to sound nonchalant. "You don't seem to think I'm a person of interest anymore, and you've been talking to Stella Nicholson... I just put two and two together."

"Really?" Sox replied, blowing his nose, then tucking the handkerchief back in his pocket. "Don't you find the cold weather always makes your nose run?"

"What did Stella tell you?"

Unfazed, Sox answered. "It was very interesting, all about Tyland Bray." He glanced around him. "Can I see your collection now?"

Realising that he wasn't going to say more, Vincent nodded, leading the detective through a side door and across the garden towards a low outbuilding abutting the garages.

"Ah, now I understand why you have the garages on the alarm system, doctor."

Unlocking the door, Vincent walked in and turned on the light, Sox following. Then Vincent took out another key and opened the interior door, pushing it back so that the detective could enter. Before them was a screen which block their view, Vincent ushering Sox to the left and then into the gallery beyond. He paused, enjoying the detective's amazement. Sox didn't say anything, but his breathing quickened as he moved along, then turned to the row of glassed cabinets, finally pausing in front of the wall of skulls.

"Amazing, truly amazing... How long did it take you to collect all these?"

"Not that long really. When people know what you're looking for they alert you to auctions or sales. Dealers offer you things, not so much the skulls, but the anatomical models." Vincent pointed to a wax body lying horizontal in a glassed walnut cabinet with its stomach eviscerated.

Sox studied it for a long moment. "What's this?"

"They were teaching tools for the hospitals, to show medical students the workings of the body. Of course, we don't need them now, we have computer imaging, but I find them fascinating. Even if they are redundant now."

"No shortage of cadavers to practice on?"

Vincent's expression was professional, detached. "People often donate their bodies, and besides, as I say, we use computer graphics to make three D images at lectures."

"But your speciality is the face, isn't it?"

"Face, jaw." Vincent agreed. "I do a lot of recon-structive work on car accident victims or deformities."

His attention taken elsewhere, Sox walked over to the far wall, staring intently at portions of faces and jaws – human – suspended in formalin. They were all meticulously labelled on a series of shelf, beginning at eye level. But not eye level for a short detective, Cox rising onto his toes to see more clearly. He found them macabre, gruesome, grotesque, of obvious interest to a surgeon, but disturbing none the less. His attention was then caught by a series of sketches of the sexual organs, male circumcision, and female genital surgery and mutilation. Finally he moved along to the last wall, pausing by a mahogany vitrine and staring at an object on the second shelf.

"Is this what I think it is, doctor?"

"I don't know, detective, what d'you think it is?"

"A poison cabinet."

"Yes, it is." Vincent nodded, folding his arms. "It's over three hundred years old, Italian –"

"They were great poisoners."

"They are famous poisoners," Vincent corrected him, "the great poisoners are the ones that are never caught."

Genuinely amused, Sox nodded. "Good point, good point." He leaned forwards, studying the vials. "But the bottles are empty; none of the original poisons survived."

"None."

"Not even a trace of Belladonna?"

"No, detective, no Belladonna. Not even a trace." Vincent replied, "I know what you're thinking, but I didn't poison Jimmy Nicholson --"

"So you wouldn't mind if I had them tested?"

"Actually I *would* mind. I've co-operated with you all the way, even though you've intimated that I'm involved in these murders. Then tonight you've had a volte face, and now you seem concerned for my safety." Vincent said coldly. "Don't insult me, detective, if there had been any Belladonna in the cabinet I'd have disposed of it long ago if I'd been Jimmy's killer. But if you really want to have the bottles tested, you'll have to get a warrant first."

Sox blew his nose again, sniffing loudly. "I seem to have annoyed you."

"I don't like mind games. I don't like mixed messages, hints, innuendoes. If you've something to say, say it. Jimmy and Barend were friends of mine, this situation is not funny to me."

"Especially as you might be in danger." Sox said quietly. "But you have to understand where I'm coming from, Dr Lund. I don't like confusion either, but detective work is all confusion which, if we're lucky, we make clear in the end. At the moment I have a riddle – five friends, two of them dead, brutally murdered. They had little in common, aside from an interest in art. They didn't follow the same professions."

"I don't see your point."

"Don't you?" Sox said, his tone regretful. "They didn't have anything in common apart from their collections, and the fact that Barend de Vries and James Nicholson were either married to, or having an affair with, Alicia de Vries. But I don't have anything that connects all *five* of you. Apart from your collections –"

"We collect different things."

"But it's all art, even medical art," Sox replied, waving his arm around the room in a half circle.

"I don't understand your point, detective, many people collect art."

"Many rich people do, and all five of you are – or were – rich. But you're right, doctor, a liking for paintings isn't a crime, not enough to cause the murder of two men. So the motive has to be something else. Something big enough to incite butchery." He chose the word with care and saw a flicker in Vincent's eyes. "What I don't have and what I most need is a motive..." Vincent was silent, waiting for him to continue. ".... Which Stella Nicholson might well have provided me with."

'Watch her, watch out for Stella Nicholson, she's
poison....Listen to me for once, Vincent, I'm
your wife and I can sense things about women.
Stella Nicholson is a dangerous bitch'....
They were at a party at the Nicholson house,
Hot August, night lights in the trees, Stella, tall,
with her bony nose and glasses, watching Jim-
my resting his hand against Alicia's thigh.
Long hot night, fireworks streaking across the
swallowing Richmond sky.....
'Women like her wait, wait for years, decades,
for the right moment to strike - then they go for
the kill'....

Vincent kept his arms folded because his hands had started to sweat. There was a slow buzzing in his ears, a sense of foreboding.

"What did Stella say to you?"

"It was about Tyland Bray, about how, over twenty years ago, he was involved in fakes –"

"Bull shit! Tyland's reputation is impeachable."

Buzzing in his ears and a sense of being
plunged underwater...Little detective looking
down on him from dry land.

"Apparently Mr Bray was under a great deal of pressure," Sox continued "out of his depth, you might say - and in order to get out of trouble he needed to raise money fast. So he sold some fakes as originals."

"This is absurd!"

I am drowning in my head... breathing underwater... My lungs are full of stones and feathered weeds.

"Mrs Nicholson was emphatic and gave me details. Apparently Mr Tyland Bray then sold the forgeries to his friends. One of which was **you.**"

Vincent's face was impassive. "Nonsense."

"Now you see, that's my problem. I can find out about Shawcross - the man that Tyland Bray was involved with when they were dealing in the fakes. His crime, his trial, his prison sentence - I can prove that part of the story, it would be on record – the Shawcross portion, that is – but how can I prove the rest? That five of you were involved in an illegal forgery scam?"

"**We weren't!**" Vincent snapped, regaining his nerve when he realised that Sox wasn't onto the truth, but onto another track altogether. The relief only lasted for an instant. The detective was heading somewhere; he wasn't just ambling along and Vincent's initial relief quickly shifted to unease. What was he leading to? And why was Stella suddenly in charge? He knew only too well that she would protect her dead husband's legacy, but at what cost. Would she really try to ruin four men to serve her purpose. Or was the story an ingenious smoke screen to hide the real motive. And if it was – how much did the redoubtable Stella Nicholson really know?

"You look worried, doctor."

Vincent ignored the comment. "I wasn't involved in any scam, and neither, to my knowledge, were my friends, Besides, how would Stella Nicholson know all about this?"

"Perhaps her husband told her?"

"Jimmy's dead, so he can't confirm or deny the story."

"But *you* can."

"Well, then let me be clear, *I deny it.*" Vincent said firmly. "As for this Shawcross man, if the story was true why didn't he expose us?"

The detective smiled, tapping the side of his nose. "I've told you enough for now, doctor, you must allow me a little secret of my own." He moved to the door, then turned. "I'll send someone to pick up the poison cabinet tomorrow. Around twelve be alright for you?"

Twenty Eight

Several days passed without news, or any visit from the unnerving detective Sox. Four o'clock had punched in cold and because of the rain the light had faded early as Vincent stood at the double doors of the conservatory. Around him ferns stretched out their filigree limbs, palms trees stabbing upwards into the dying light. His calm had deserted him; he was a child again, afraid of the dark, afraid of what he couldn't see.

For two weeks Vincent had survived by ignoring his fear, but now it had pushed aside his self-control and beggared his logic. The incident at the hospital had told him what he already knew – he was out of control, unfit for service. Every time he closed his eyes he saw Jimmy Nicholson fighting for his life, crawling on a bathroom carpet, unable to cry out for help. And now Barend, round, clever, barrister, brain-sharp and cunning, had been gutted like a landed carp.

What had he felt as the knife went in? Pain, shock? What moments left of his life had been terrifying, that little portion of time when he moved from sentient being to corpse? Vincent felt his stomach lurch and sat down, his head in his hands. The room was suddenly alien to him, the sounds of the housekeeper moving around deafening. Mrs Brooks was making food. She was making food.

Was she the woman? Was she now putting something toxic into his evening meal? Maybe under the crisp skin of lamb there was a bitter poison he wouldn't taste until it was too late. Perhaps she would wait outside the door, listening for him to fall, to retch, to attempt to spew up the venom. Then there would be silence, him left staring upwards into the moulded ceiling. She, dormouse quiet, counting him out as the third death, the third felled.

No, it *wasn't* her, Vincent told himself, it wasn't Ellen Brooks. He knew her, she had worked for his family for decades, he knew her and her husband, Arthur. The man who looked after the garden, tended the conservatory, waved to him when he looked out from the window. They were known to him, trusted by him.

But what if it was them? Someone trusted had gained access to Jimmy Nicholson's house and his medication. Someone trusted had managed to get into Barend's Chambers. A stranger – in both instances – would have been challenged.

Vincent thought back to what Sox had said.

'You'd be surprised what people don't notice. They see someone with a ladder, but if he's dressed in workman's clothes and he looks like he's might be cleaning windows or fixing telephone wires, who'd stop him?'

Sox didn't know that it was a woman coming after them. He was still searching for a man. Vincent paused, thinking of the women he knew. Or *did* he know them? Who was Alicia de Vries really? And what of Stella Nicholson? Or even the timid Marina Bray? A memory came back to him suddenly, about

Marina having a sister. Where was she? Were any of them connected to that girl from so long ago?

We stop seeing people after a while, Vincent realised. *We stop seeing the familiar...* He then thought of the hospital; how he walked around St Thomas's without taking notice of people he *expected* to see. The mind didn't register them. He was used to his patients needing him, to their dependency – but what if there had been one amongst them who had fooled him?

No, not a patient! He told himself. They couldn't falsify their illness. So maybe it was a relative? Someone who accompanied a patient. Visited a patient, came onto his wards, perhaps spoke to him. The caring mother, wife, sister, some woman smiling, shaking his hand with the same hand that had poisoned Jimmy Nicholson and driven a knife into Barend's gut.

'*Thank you, doctor, for what you've done.*'

His mind faltered. How many women had entered his consulting rooms, studying him whilst he attended their relatives?... Vincent dug his fingers into his scalp, pressing into the flesh. Or maybe it *was* one of his medical team, face was obscured by a surgical mask. Or a ward nurse. He passed them every day, going to and from theatre, but he didn't know who they were. Nurses who nodded greetings, voices, but no faces. And they changed regularly, different shifts, some sourced from outside agencies, drafted in to support the surgical teams. A nurse would know how to deal with poisons, how to tamper with a syringe. A nurse would know where to stab a man fatally.

No, Vincent reassured himself, Barend's death had been bloody, his wounds numerous, not precise. Vincent had seen the photographs, Barend had been slaughtered, his skin ripped, multiple defensive wounds on his hands. Or maybe that had been the point, to *make* him suffer, jabbing a knife into him repeatedly, letting him bleed out, until she delivered the coup de grace.

Vincent thought of Barend's rooms in Chambers; the leather back volumes of legal books in their serried rows, the Edwardian desk, the window looking out over the square. All bloodied now, every surface spotted with red dots, like SOLD tickets at an auction… Vincent's thoughts shifted. *Auction,* what about the auctions? Jesus, was it someone who worked at an auction house? Or a gallery he frequented? There were always assistants, porters, receptionists in such places, people who fitted in. People who excited no interest *because they belonged there.*

His hands dug into his scalp, his head bowed. He couldn't go to the hospital, he couldn't risk leaving the house. He couldn't risk operating. He would hide instead. She wasn't going to get to him, not if he locked himself away.

> *'Have you ever thought about dying?'*
> *He had laughed, because they were newly married.*
> *'What kind of a question is that, Nancy? I'm not going to die, I'm going to be immortal and live with you forever…'*
> *She left. Love passed away.*
> *Nothing was immortal.*

Vincent swallowed dryly. No, he couldn't hide, he had responsibilities. He had a family. If he panicked what would happen to them? Worse, if he panicked, he might reveal himself – and the motive for the murders. He couldn't let the truth come out. He couldn't endure the shame he would bring on Charlotte, or the disappointment Milas would feel at seeing the fall of his hero.

It took several minutes for Vincent to compose himself, but finally he sat up and smoothed his hair. The fear which had threatened to buckle him was losing its grip; fading as a plan began to form. He was going to *find* her. He was going to find the red haired girl. Vincent didn't know how he was going to do it, but the decision gave him strength.

Arthur and Ellen Brooks were drinking tea as he walked into the kitchen, Ellen getting to her feet. "Did you want something, Dr Lund?"

"No…" his voice cracked. He tried again. "No. I just wanted a word with Arthur." The gardener was sitting in socks, his muddied wellingtons by the door. A contented man, drinking tea in a warm kitchen next to his wife. "I want you get the trees cut down around the house."

Arthur blew out his cheeks. "All of them?"

"As many as you can. I know some will be protected by Bylaws, but I'll get Milas to check that out for you. In the meantime, cut back the bushes, especially those around the house and the outbuildings."

"It'll take me a while."

"Hire some help!" Vincent snapped, then apologised. "I'm sorry, Arthur. Get all the help you need. Just do it."

Twenty Nine

"Deny it all you like, but I know you were keen on Milas," Alicia said, watching her daughter. "What happened?"

"He talks like an old man."

"What did he say?"

Tilly shrugged. "I was telling him about Barend's collection and he went off on some 'holier than thou' rant."

Alicia glanced away. She was smarting from Vincent's lack of response to her messages. He was courteous, offered his condolences for Barend's death, but had drawn back from any intimacy. She had thought, wrongly, that her situation might incite some interest from him; had even mentioned Jimmy's collection in the hope that he would want to talk to her about it. But apparently he didn't. Perhaps he thought her behaviour was inappropriate for a new widow. Or perhaps he didn't care for her anymore. Which hurt, because she cared for him.

The previous day the three remaining friends had attended Barend's funeral, Leo Parks on a brief visit from Los Angeles, Tyland Bray and Vincent talking solemnly outside the church before the service.

Dressed in stately black, the first widow, Stella Nicholson, had remained aloof, Marina holding a handkerchief to her face. Was she crying? Alicia had wondered. Surely *she* should be the one crying, it had been her husband. Tyland Nicholson was still alive. Barend wasn't. He had told her years earlier that he wanted to be cremated.

'Don't spend a bloody fortune on a wooden box with flash handles. Don't bury me. Burn me.
I want to go up in smoke...'

"I don't know what Marina's got to cry about," Stella had said, moving over to Alicia.

"She's worried. If anything happened to Tyland she wouldn't be able to cope on her own."

"He'd leave her plenty of money."

Alicia had sighed, her gaze fixed on Vincent. "Money isn't a bedpan on a cold night."

"No, but money can buy an expensive electric blanket."

"You've got a hard heart, Stella."

"Says the woman who slept with my husband. *Do* stop staring at Vincent," she had continued "he's not looked in your direction once. Perhaps you were more appealing when you were married, my dear. Now you're a widow he seems to be distancing himself."

The barb hit home and Alicia had changed tack. "I had a word with that detective, the little ginger one --"

"Really? What were you talking to him about?"

"The motive," Alicia had then outlined what she had said, an elastic moment stretching out before Stella spoke again.

200

"You think that the killer might be one of Bar-end's old criminal cases? How interesting. But a woman? Hardly."

"Why not a woman?" Alicia had persisted. "I've known some real bitches in my time."

If Stella had caught the inference, she hadn't shown it.

Alicia's attention was jerked back to the present when her mobile rang. It was Tilly, her daughter still smouldering over their argument, and announcing that she would be staying overnight at a friend's house. Relieved, Alicia poured herself a drink and replayed what Stella had said earlier, scrutinising it word for word - especially the explosive motive she had put forward. She had seemed to hesitate before confiding, Alicia stunned to hear about Barend being involved in the forgery scandal. Of course, it had happened long before they had married, but Barend had never said anything about a scam, a deal which had involved all five men. Then again, Alicia thought, why would he? The men were long-time friends, they had closed ranks to protect each other. Everyone had secrets, things they wished to hide. There were too many egos and fortunes at stake to risk exposure.

It should have seemed like the perfect motive, but where Stella Nicholson had intellect, Alicia had instinct. And her instinct was humming like a wasp trapped in a hot car. She was angry too. Enraged that Stella could endanger the reputations of all the men and throw Vincent onto the pyre like an Indian widow committing sati. She wanted to know the truth and there was only one way to get it. Talk to the three men still alive.

And she would start with Vincent.

Thirty

Charlotte had never been talkative; her instinct was to listen, consider, ponder. At school she had been considered slow, but that was mainly because she had missed a lot of teaching because of her illness, the asthma which had hindered her since she was six years old. It still hampered her adult life, but it hadn't prevented her going to University and getting a degree in Modern Languages.

Vincent had not been proud, he had been ecstatic, and always supportive, had greeted her mediocre grades with delight. His own remarkable achievements were never allowed to overshadow his daughter's modest triumph. Although she had had some ambition to teach, Vincent had gently steered her away from the notion, knowing it would be too strenuous for her, instead encouraging Charlotte to work as a translator. Perhaps she had *wanted* to be guided away from teaching, certainly she took to her new career with enthusiasm.

She had just been translating some German poetry for a publisher in Munich when she heard the front door slam shut and walked downstairs to find Milas making a sandwich in the kitchen.

"D'you want one?"

Charlotte shook her head. "No, thanks, and you should eat more, you're too thin." She paused before continuing. "Are you angry about something?"

"What?"

"You don't usually slam doors."

"I had a run in with Vincent." He admitted, biting into the sandwich as he sat down at the table.

"Is it to do with the research for his book?"

"No, that's going well. He likes my work."

"So it's about the murders." Charlotte said, taking the seat next to him. "You don't have to worry, I can talk about it. I won't fall apart or panic. I'm not a baby."

"That's funny, because I used the exact same words to Vincent earlier when he wanted to send us away."

"What d'you mean, *send us away?*"

"Because of the murders. He's worried, and he wants us to be safe."

"Are we in danger?|"

Milas shook his head. "No, I don't think so… of course not"

She looked unconvinced. "You don't know and neither do I. And I imagine my father and the police have no idea either. So what would be the point of leaving here?"

"It would put you out of harm's way."

"Where is Harm's Way? It sounds like a gloomy place, Harm's Way. Not at all a place where anyone would feel at home."

He was amused and smiled. "I still think you should do what your father wants. Go and stay with your mother for a while, until all this blows over."

"I don't want to leave here!"

"It would stop Vincent worrying about you."

"If you're not going, then I'm not."

He sighed and put down his sandwich. "It wouldn't be for long."

"How d'you know that?" She countered. "How does anybody know anything about what's going on? Dad won't talk to me, just tells me not to worry. Only two of his friends are dead. They didn't die like many middle aged men, from diabetes or heart attacks, they were murdered. Poisoned, carved up... So tell me, Milas, how can I *not* worry?" She toyed with her hair, twisting her fringe absent mindedly. "My father should have protection, What are the police doing?"

"They're working on it."

"Giving advice about cutting down trees!" She said, her tone mocking, "You think trees will stop anyone who is determined?"

Milas noticed the agitation and tried to contain it. "Vincent won't be alone, I'm staying here with him. I'm not going anywhere --"

"But what if something happened to *both* of you?" Charlotte asked, stricken. "What consolation is that? I don't understand any of it. It's all over the internet and the papers. Every time I go out someone stops me and asks questions. Some journalist was here earlier --"

"A journalist? What did you say?"

"I didn't say anything, how could I? He probably knows more than I do." She paused, traced her finger along a crack in the surface of the wooden table. "My father's never done anything bad. He's a doctor, he looks after people, he cares about people –"

"I know."

" -- you think that it's some patient who's got a grudge? I mean, you read about it all the time. Someone thinks they weren't treated right. Law suits about negligence."

"Has Vincent ever told you that he's had trouble with a patient?"

She shook her head, relieved to have someone to confide in. "No, he's not talking about his patients. Hardly ever does. But I know they've always been devoted him. I resented it, until now."

"Why's it different now?"

"Because now I understand. If your father's a doctor, you can only ever expect half of him. If that. When I was little, I thought he was away so much because he didn't care for me, or my mother, but it was just his work." She sighed, looking down. "Maybe it was in his past?"

"What d'you mean?"

"Maybe it was something that happened *before* my father came to England?" She glanced at Milas, her pale grey eyes steady. "Was there any trouble when he was in Denmark? I don't want to dig up old wounds – I know Dad fell out with my aunt – but I just wondered if he'd had any trouble in his *career*. You know, at the hospital, or with his patients. You'd know about that, if anything had happened."

"I never heard anything. Nothing was said at home."

"But *would* you have heard, wouldn't you?" She changed the subject. "Dad really regrets what happened, you know. He used to talk about it a lot. That's why he was so glad you came to live with us. He thinks it goes someway to make up for the past and besides, he's very fond of you…. Why did they fall out?"

Milas hesitated before replying. "It was an argument between my mother and my uncle. I don't know all the details, only that my mother felt aggrieved that she was left to care for their parents. She thought Vincent got off lightly, coming to London and making a success of his life. She was jealous of him."

"Was she a doctor?"

He laughed. "God, no! She couldn't put a plaster on straight. She was a housewife, had a lot of friends, very sociable. She was the sporty type, she liked tennis and swimming."

Charlotte nodded. "Were you lonely when you were growing up? I mean, I'm an only child too, I get lonely. Were you?"

"Sometimes."

"So why didn't you marry? Have children?" She stopped, flushing, the fine skin on her forehead revealing a vein at the temple. "I'm asking too many questions, aren't I? I shouldn't, it's a bad habit. People think I'm shy, and I am, but I'm still interested, still curious about people. Especially my only cousin."

"In answer to your question, no," Milas replied. "I never married or had children."

"Yet."

"Yet." He nodded. "Maybe I will, one day. But some people aren't the marrying kind. And besides, I wouldn't make a good father."

"You don't know that --"

He stood up, Charlotte immediately apologetic. "I'm sorry, did I say something wrong?"

"No, you didn't say anything wrong." She thought he was going to say something else, but the moment passed. "I just have to get on with my work, Vincent wants some papers finished by tonight." He moved to the door and turned. "But think about going to stay with your mother for a little while, Charlotte. It might be a good idea and it would take pressure off your father."

She watched him go, her gaze falling on the half-eaten sandwich. She had irritated him without meaning to, talking about the past was obviously unwelcome. But there was something else which niggled at Charlotte, something Milas had said about his mother.

... she liked tennis and swimming...

It had made an impression because she remembered what her father had told her many years before, when she was learning how to swim.

"Don't be like my sister, she never learnt" he had said. *"Adela was afraid of water."*

Charlotte shrugged off the thought. She had been mistaken or had misheard. Or perhaps Adela had got over her anxiety and ended up becoming a keen swimmer. After all, people changed and Milas knew his mother better than she ever would.

Thirty One

New York

"Are you sure you want to go back to London? I thought you were just going for the funeral. Do you need to go back again?" Ruby asked, her voice concerned. "Honestly, Leo, is that wise?"

He had wondered the same thing, but realised he couldn't spend the rest of his life locked behind his apartment doors. Another week had passed and although he followed the reporting of the murders on the internet, there were no new developments. His mood alternated between hope and despair; perhaps the woman had come to her senses, stopped the killings. Perhaps she had been killed herself, or perhaps she was now making her way over the Atlantic to come for him.

So after another bad night, it seemed sensible for him to return to London and stay with Vincent. Perhaps he *would* be safer in England, certainly he wouldn't be alone.

"It's a stupid fucking idea!"

"I'm going, Ruby." Leo said firmly. "There's a painting coming up for auction that I want to bid for."

"Oh well, that makes perfect sense! What sane man wouldn't risk his life for a lousy painting?"

"Hey, be fair, I have a business to run --"

"Something you conveniently forgot until now. Why the sudden change of heart? And why are you going to be staying with Vincent Lund? Why don't you stay at my apartment in Holland Park?"

Leo was dodging her questions like bullets. "Vincent's a friend, you know that."

"Friend, or ally?" Ruby asked, perceptively. "I don't worry, Leo, I'm not going to pry, you'll confide in me eventually."

"Vincent's going to be ringing you."

"Really?" She countered. "I haven't spoken to him in years. What does he want?"

"I don't know, he just said that he needed to talk to you."

There was a pause before Ruby spoke again. "Ring me when you get to London, will you? Let me know you're safe."

"You know I will."

"You better, Leo, you better."

Resigned, he finished packing then went to his desk. Finding the second letter he read it again, the words burning into him; a hot iron on his skin.

> *You're such a lonely man, Mr Parks, lonely in*
> *so many ways.*
> *You didn't protect me. I know you wanted to;*
> *I could read that in your eyes, but you didn't*
> *have the courage. No courage to intervene, no*
> *courage to love. Poor wanderer...*

The clock is ticking, gentlemen. In London, New York, Copenhagen, in every room you sit and every road you walk down. It's ticking...

And then he realised that she would never stop and that he wasn't going to escape. She had set her revenge in motion and would see it to the end.

Two men down, three to go.

-o0o-

London

Detective Sox had washed his hair three times, but there was still some residual itching, some irritable niggle at the crown of his head. Blasted shampoo, he thought, rearranging his thinning hair over his bald spot. His gaze moved over to his computer as an e mail came in, the name CLIVE SHAWCROSS catching his eye.

He read it with care, taking in the details, which correlated perfectly with what Stella Nicholson had told him. Yes, twenty six years earlier a man called Clive Shawcross had been found guilty of trading in fakes and jailed for four years in Wormwood Scrubs... Sox scrolled down the report... Shawcross had been defended by Oakley Benedict, senior partner in the Chambers of *Oakley & Wynam,* Lincoln's Inn... So De Vries hadn't been a partner then; still working his way up. Many years to go before King's Counsel beckoned. Sox read on, going over the court transcripts. Shawcross had said he worked alone and had refused to name any of his cohorts, let alone the five prominent men who had supposedly been inveigled into his scheme by Tyland Bray.

There was *one* direct reference to Tyland Bray. He had been called to give evidence about the London art market. Already a prominent dealer, his opinion respected... Sox leaned back in his chair, scratching his head with a pencil. Bray had had some nerve giving evidence. He must have wondered about the man sitting in the dock across the court. Wondering, as he pontificated, if Shawcross would suddenly expose him. Public disgrace had been shimmering only feet away, his whole life and status reliant on a thief keeping his word.

And how likely was that? Very likely, Sox concluded, if there had been a sufficient incentive. A huge pay off, a few forged paintings stashed away for when Shawcross left prison, that would be enough to pay for his secrecy. But *that* wasn't the motive Stella Nicholson had put forward... Sox continued to read. Then scanned Shawcross's medical report whilst he was imprisoned. And there it was. Shawcross had been hospitalised, heavily sedated and kept under suicide watch for 48 hours after he had been told of the death of his wife.

Looking through the glass door which lead out into the squad room, Sox beckoned for a junior officer to come to him.

"Yes, sir?"

"I need information on a Mrs Jenny Shawcross. I've just forwarded the report on her husband's case, so check your e mails. I want to know *exactly* how she died, when she died, and what happened to her children. Two sons, I believe, find out for me." Sox paused. "And whilst you're at it, do a search on Tyland Bray too."

"I've already done one on him, sir."

"Yes, I know that, constable." Sox said patiently. "We've checked the backgrounds of Messrs Bray,

Parks and Lund, but just check out the *Bray Gallery,* will you? See who owned it before Tyland Bray bought it, or inherited it. And, most importantly, find whatever you can on the wives."

"Wives?"

"Yes, lad, wives. You might have one of your own one day. Just don't let her buy the shampoo." Sox said drily, then checked his notes. "Forget Alicia de Vries, I've done that one myself, but I want you to find everything and anything on Marina Bray and Stella Nicholson. As for Mr Leo Parks, he's not got a wife, but he might have a partner somewhere. Check that too." He looked at the officer then waved his podgy hand to gesture he should leave. "Well, go on, move it!"

-o0o-

Bray House

Marina put down the phone, her hand shaking. Panic was doing its little jig in her chest as she moved into the bathroom and took another pill. Anti-anxiety, or was it anti-depressant? One of those, something that was supposed to smooth out her nerves like a well made bed. Only it didn't, *they* didn't, and changing the prescription or the drug hadn't made any difference. She was still jangling like a tin chime.

Tyland wouldn't tell her what was going on and she had not dared to press him and risk his temper. So the previous night she had waited until she had been massaging his back – and he had finally relaxed – to broach the subject again.

In response he had reared up, clutching his dressing gown, one bony hand gripping her arm. "Stop panicking and asking questions about these bloody murders!"

He had snapped. "You have to calm down, Marina, the stress is bad for you, you know how hysterical you get. Leave it all to me. It's nothing I can't handle."

She had nodded, too terrified to speak.

But she hadn't believed a word he said.

His bullying, his gas lighting, his manipulation, had all had an effect over the last fifteen years and the woman she had been was now cordoned off to the past. Marina knew she had mislaid her glamour: she didn't know where, or she would have reclaimed it like lost baggage. Because Tyland *had* loved her sensuality when they met. Loved that lush soft yield of flesh which had always welcomed him.

Maybe it was his illness that had scuppered their marriage. Maybe the pain and the discomfort Tyland suffered daily had been the problem. Pain was a mistress no woman could defeat. A real living woman was something tangible, someone you could confront. Pain was a spectral whore. Dark, all-devouring, obsessive. Fifteen years earlier Marina had been a wife; but over the last decade she had been demoted to her husband's part time nurse. And full time whipping boy.

> *'It would be different if we had children...'*
> *He had set his face against it from the start;*
> *'You're not strong enough, your nerves wouldn't*
> *be up to raising a family...'*
> *But I didn't have 'nerves' then, Tyland.*
> *I still hoped and thought miracles happened.*
> *Such a long time ago, when I was myself and*
> *believed all the empty bedrooms would be*
> *filled....*

*In the end they were filled with shadows,
every drawer and cupboard stuffed with spent
promises.
And I grew old before it was time.*

Marina heard the front door close and tidied her
hair, standing beside the dining table like a waiter in
her own home. When she noticed the knife was crooked at Tyland's place setting she corrected it just as he
walked in.

"Hello, my dear."

He pecked her on the cheek, wincing at the same
time. "My shoulder isn't getting any better. I could
hardly sleep last night, you must have heard me walking around."

*Separate rooms, I didn't know that would happen when I married you. Cold sheets, closed
doors, a wedding ring loose through weight
loss... Or was it nerves?...*

"I'll massage your shoulder for you later, if
you like."

He spun round. "What d'you mean – *if I like?* Of
course I don't like! I'm in pain, Marina, don't you realise what I'm going through? Of course not, you don't
understand what it's like, you've always been in good
health. People in good health are always callous."

"I didn't mean to upset you, dear."

Angered, he sat down at the dining table, rubbing his forehead. "I work all day running the gallery,
tending to collectors and exhibitions, is it too much to
expect to be able to relax when I come home? Not to
be verbally attacked as I enter the door?"

I should have left him whilst I was still strong
Found someone else. Left him before he became
the full blown tyrant. He's shouting, his lips
moving.
I'm not listening. But he's worried, I can see it.
I can see how he broods about the murders....
I could reach out, to hold him, offer comfort,
grip his hands only inches from mine.
But he's too far away.
Inches are continents between enemies.

Without saying a word, Marina went to the kitchen and returned with two plates, laying one in front of her husband. If he noticed her hands shaking, Tyland didn't mention it. Instead he ate his meal in silence, Marina sitting at the table beside him toying with her meal and staring blankly at the window reflection of a woman she no longer recognised.

Thirty Two

Clive Shawcross's file arrived on Sox's desk later that day. A bulky file, with its extended history of fraud and theft. Apparently Shawcross had begun his career in the North of England as a thief, then, via Strangeways and several short prison sentences, had changed his location to London. His instinct for thieving had not changed; but his tastes had become more expensive. The art market – with its under belly of crooks - had been a perfect home for an opportunist like Shawcross and he had soon found his forte as a runner.

A runner, Sox thought, so Shawcross had been hired by private individuals or dealers to *find* the works of art they desired. Stealing to order. But how would a novice like Shawcross know about art? Perhaps a runner didn't need to know the aesthetics, just know what they were expected to steal… Sox read on, jolted by the mention of Tyland Bray. Apparently, many years earlier, Shawcross had been accused of stealing a drawing from the Bray gallery – charges which were later dropped.

Ah, Sox thought, there it was! The connection he had been looking for. The entrée to the art world for Mr Shawcross. Perhaps Stella Nicholson's story was true, certainly it was beginning to look more likely. If Bray *had* dropped the charges against Shawcross he might well have used it as leverage against the Northerner later. Perhaps Bray wasn't so much a participant in the forgery, but had *initiated* it.

Sox read on. Shawcross's wife had come from the North too, Jenny Shawcross giving birth to two sons. When she committed suicide the day after her husband was imprisoned she had been seven months pregnant. The baby had died with her.

Hanging was a hard way to go, Sox thought, looking at a newspaper cutting which had been included in the file.

> *Mrs Jennifer Shawcross, aged 32, was found hanged at the family home on 45, Holland Street, Rochdale. Her husband, Clive Shawcross, is presently serving a four year jail sentence in Wormwood Scrubs. Two sons - Freddie, 11 and Gary, 4 - have been placed in care.*

Sox considered the Shawcross boys. Freddie would now be in his early thirties. Tragically Gary had been killed in a motor bike accident, as for Freddie, there were no records of him. Puzzled, Sox called his assistant over.

"This is it?"

"All there was on the Shawcross family." The constable replied, "I dug around, but that was all I could find. And after Clive Shawcross came out of jail, he disappeared."

"People don't disappear."

"He did."

Sox raised his sandy eyebrows. "Have you checked the death records?"

"No record of him being dead. But if Shawcross died abroad, we couldn't find that out." The officer hesitated. "As for the wives --"

"Ah, the wives," Sox said, leaning back in his chair. "What of the lovely ladies?"

With a triumphant smile, the young officer pushed another set of notes across the desk. "Lots to see there, sir."

"Well, before I get to those, did you check up on the Bray Gallery?"

"I did. There's a bit of information about Mr Bray in those notes," he pointed to the file, "as for the gallery – he inherited it from his late father. Who'd inherited it from *his* father. Family business really."

"Thanks," Sox said, glancing back to the notes. "I'll call you when I've finished."

There was enough to keep Sox occupied for the next half an hour. He started with Stella Nicholson; the cold martinet who had been born into an Army background and raised in the nest of the Home Counties. An only child, she had been Head Girl at school - naturally, Sox thought, she was perfect head girl material – and had trained as an accountant. Again, to be expected, Stella Nicholson weighed up everything in terms of profit and loss.

She had met Jimmy Nicholson and married him soon after, giving birth to their only child, Dominic, three years later. Her parents were still alive, living in South Africa, although her husband's parents had been dead for some years. An active member of the Rotary Club, Sox groaned, she was also a Justice of the Peace and a keen golfer. A busy, sociable woman, left well provided for after the death of her husband.

A proud woman, very aware of her status. *So* aware that she was quite prepared to ruin Tyland Bray, Vincent Lund and Leo Parks to maintain it. Of course, the men would deny that they had been involved in any criminal activity, but she must have realised the police would investigate them and check them out. Just as she would know that Tyland Bray's chances of becoming Minister of the Arts would be destroyed by even a hint of a forgery scandal… Oh dear, Sox thought, Stella Nicholson was not a woman to have as an enemy.

Marina Bray was another matter entirely. Sox hadn't spoken to her in any depth and their only conversation had been stilted. He glanced at the photographs of Marina Bray, taken thirty years apart. When young, a rather luscious girl; when middle aged, drawn, colourless, mousy. Her background was the biggest surprise. Marina's father had been an artist, her mother a potter, so her early life had been surrounded by creativity – natural then that she would circulate in art world circles. Natural she would meet the dealers and fall in love with one. But *Tyland Bray?*

They seemed an odd match and after her marriage Marina had become withdrawn. The gregarious girl turned into an introverted woman. The artistic talent she had once enjoyed had seemed to dry up too. Sox could imagine how that could happen married to Tyland Bray, the art world's top dog. He could picture Bray's dismissive attitude to his wife's work when he dealt with the Old Masters. As his reputation soared, so hers remained earthbound. Obviously in the Bray household there was only room for one ego.

Flicking over the pages, Sox found some older notes and a medical report from a clinic in Yorkshire – where Marina's family had originated from. He had expected as much. The clinic was for psychiatric patients, no doubt it had been somewhere Marina found solace for her anxiety. But what Sox *didn't* expect was to find that the person admitted for treatment was called *Rachel*. Not Marina at all. But her sister, Rachel.

Sox peered at the notes. Although Rachel would now be thirty seven, at the time of her admission she had been eighteen years old, her condition labelled as manic depression.

"Bi-polar." Sox said out loud, "now there's a turn up."

He continued to read. Rachel had been admitted several times, the last entry – five years earlier - declaring that she was well controlled by her medicine and had been summarily discharged. The only other information about Rachel was that she was unmarried, and had had no children.

Sox drained his mug, then grunted, picking some tea leaves off his tongue. He hated loose tea, always ended up with a mouthful of slurry.

"Hey!" he shouted, the young officer hurrying back into his office. "Chase up the lab reports on Vincent Lund's medicine cabinet, will you?"

"Will do, sir."

"And get some bloody teabags while you're about it."

Thirty Three

It was a freezing morning, frost on the grass and rooftops, the gravel ice-coated as Alicia made her way up the Vincent Lund's front door. Whatever he had to say he could say it to her face, no more ignoring her. She was tired from another night's wrecked sleep, exhausted by anxiety, by the questioning looks from her neighbours and the journalists who left messages on her answer phone.

> *Why don't you want to talk about your husband's murder?...*
> *Do you think it was something to do with one of his cases?....*
> *Is it true that Jimmy Nicholson left you his art collection?*

Questions, questions, questions – all without answers. And she had had enough. Better to know the worse, to face reality, than to spend another day wondering. Alicia rang the bell then walked past the housekeeper as the door opened.

"Tell Dr Lund I'm here will you, and don't tell me he's left for the hospital already."

She moved into the drawing room, hugging her coat around her, facing a cheerless unlit fire as the sound of rain hit the conservatory roof.

A moment later Vincent entered. "I can't talk now --"

"*Really?* Well, you're going to have to, Vincent. Did you know that Stella Nicholson's gone to the police and exposed Tyland Bray in some old forgery scam?"

He closed the door and motioned for her to sit down, playing for time. "What are you talking about?"

"And it's not just Tyland, she's hung you all out to dry. If the press get to hear about it you're all finished." She paused. "Is it true that Tyland involved you in a scandal years ago?"

"It's rubbish --"

"**Wrong answer!**" She snapped. "My husband's dead and so is Jimmy Nicholson and from what his bloody wife's being saying so are the rest of you if this comes out." Her tone softened. "I don't want anything to happen to you. Vincent."

"Alicia –"

"Oh, don't panic, I'm not trying to start our relationship off again, I'm just trying to find out who killed Barend. You think I didn't care for him - you're right, but only up to a point. Truth is, I did care, just not *enough*. I cheated on him" she stared at Vincent "*we* cheated on him, but Barend and I were separated at the time. And I did it because I cared for you and because I was lonely." She sat down, still huddled in her coat. "You look knackered. Are you Ok?"

"I've been better."

She nodded, then shivered. "Can't you feel it?"

"Feel what?"

"The atmosphere. Like something else is going to happen." She narrowed her eyes, studying his face. "What's going on?"

"I don't know what you mean."

"*Bullshit!* There have been two murders. Both friends of yours. Same killer, of course it is. So who's doing it, Vincent? Who wants to kill you?"

"*Kill me?*"

"Oh, so you're *not* under threat?" Her expression was combative. "You're immune, are you? What about Leo and Tyland? Are they going to be spared too? I mean, when the police investigate what that bitch Stella told them --"

"Surely you don't believe what she said?"

"I'm not sure, she'd say anything that would serve her best. She'd sacrifice anything or anyone." Alicia paused, her voice rising. "Don't you get it? I'm scared. My husband's been murdered, Vincent! He was cut up, and I want to know if my daughter's safe. *I have to protect her!*"

"Tilly will be alright –"

"**How do you know that?**" Alicia snapped. "What aren't you telling me? You *have* to tell me what this is all about, I need to protect my daughter - and myself!"

"Why would anyone come after Tilly or you?"

"Why would they come after Jimmy or Barend? Or you?" She countered. "Because you think they are coming for you, don't you? You looked petrified, Vincent, so you must believe you're in the firing line."

He stood up, moved to the window, looking out. "You're jumping to conclusions –"

"Has this got to do with your bloody collections? I've guessed that much." She interrupted, moving over to him. "All five of you were friends, but not that close. Your only real link is art, your collections."

"You don't know what you're talking about –"

"Was Stella Nicholson right? Are you dealing in forgeries again? Are you collecting and dealing in fakes?" She asked, incredulous. "Is that what it's all about –"

"This has nothing to do with fakes!"

"Then what the fuck *does* it have to do with?" Alicia shouted, grabbing his arm and pulling him round to face her. "Why is someone after you?"

"I don't know." He said simply, moving away, Alicia watching him as he slumped into a chair.

"'You don't know'? ... So what are you going to do? Wait for the police to find the killer?"

"It's their job."

"And you're going to wait for them to do it, hey?" She sneered. "What if someone's out there now, watching you? They could come from anywhere and be anyone. Barend wasn't expecting it, even after Jimmy was killed." She paused, her tone suspicious. "Or was he? Perhaps all five of you are expecting it... What have you done, Vincent? What did *all* five of you do?"

She could see him hesitate, taking a moment to answer.

"I don't know who, or why, someone is coming after us," he said finally "but I'm sending Charlotte away from here, to be on the safe side. I wanted Milas to go too, but he won't leave."

"Should I send my daughter away?"

"She's safe."

"How do you know that?"

"They are after us! There are after five *men* --"

"And only *three* are left." Alicia countered. "Jimmy and Barend are dead. What about the others?"

Vincent hesitated before speaking again. "Leo Parks is coming to stay here, with me. I'm expecting him tonight." He glanced at her. "And in answer to your question, the one you haven't asked, but want to. Yes, I'm afraid."

Her hand reached out, laid on top of his. "Can I do anything to help?"

"No."

"You won't trust me?"

"I can't."

"You *can't?*" She withdrew her hand. "Or *won't?*"

"I won't. It wouldn't be fair on you."

A moment fluttered between them, Alicia sighing bitterly. "So you *really* have no idea who's doing is?"

"No."

She knew he was lying and left.

-o0o-

Bray Gallery
   Grafton Street, WI
Tyland Bray was just opening the front entrance doors when there was a tap on his shoulder. Startled, he jumped and turned to see his assistant hovering.

   "Stop creeping up on me!"

"Sorry, I was just --"

"Creeping about," Tyland snarled, letting them both inside.

The gallery was unwelcoming and cold, the radiators banging as the boiler shifted into gear. Around the walls were paintings in crates or bundled in shrouds of bubble wrap, a large Epstein bust glowering from an iron plinth. The pleasure Tyland would usually have felt was dimmed, his ideas for the new exhibition unforthcoming. For years he had preceded over prestigious shows and Private Views, entertained royalty and film stars, given advice to Russian oligarchs and their spoiled wives, but he felt no pleasure in his standing any longer. He was vacant inside, drained by pain and fear, waiting for the next person, the next phone call, the next shadow to move in his direction and attack.

He had never experienced terror before. But now the length of the nights seem to have had trebled. Over-medicating himself on pain relief, he dreamed of dark corridors which narrowed whilst he walked down them, of doors which opened onto brick walls, of windows where people stood and watched him. And in amongst the faces, always in amongst the faces, was the blank visage of a woman.

She was there every night and when Tyland woke sweating, clammy in cold sheets, she was standing beside his bed, or waiting in the hallway as he stumbled to the bathroom. His terror made her into a ghost; something real, but unreal, and when he moved back to bed he would lie with his eyes open waiting to feel someone, or something, climb in beside him.

"It's about the Ribera painting --

"What!" Tyland snapped, turning to his assistant.

"The picture coming up for auction this morning, sir, *The Bearded Woman*. You wanted to bid for it, you told me to remind you."

Tyland nodded. "Yes, of course, of course."

Without his usual enthusiasm, an hour later he left for the auction. His legs weren't functioning properly. They felt numb, but grossly heavy at the same time, his steps down Bond Street laboured. An old man stumbling ahead over a pavement that seemed to be melting underfoot. Fighting to control himself outside the auction house, Tyland paused, then straightened up and entered. Nodding to several dealers he knew, he sat down, pretending to read the catalogue and then glancing towards the raised dias. The painting was erected on an easel, perfectly illuminated, *The Bearded Woman* image intimidating. To his surprise, he was momentarily taken aback; had not expected the image to be so skilful, nor so large, dwarfing the auctioneer on his plinth beside it.

"Bidding, hey?"

"What?" Tyland glanced at the dealer who had sat down next to him. "I am bidding, yes, but I doubt it's a version by Ribera. It's a fine copy," he continued "an important one."

"You don't usually go for copies, Tyland."

"The subject matter interests me," he replied, but his mind was playing games, his usual eloquence escaping him. "It's… good."

Oh Christ, he thought, control yourself.

"I'm sorry about Jimmy Nicholson," the dealer continued "he was a good friend of yours, wasn't he? Being poisoned like that, in your own house too. Police got anything to go on?..."

Tyland couldn't find an answer.

"… and you were friendly with Barend de Vries too. I remember you bringing him to a sale last year. God, it's bloody terrible what's happening in this city. Murder. Two prominent men, respectable men, men we both knew. It's a lot worse for you, of course --"

Tyland flinched. "Why?"

"They were friends of yours. And I can see how shocked you are," the dealer continued, misunderstanding Tyland's distress. "You never know what's coming in life, do you?"

The bang of a gavel brought everyone's attention to the opening of the auction, a capacious video screen allowing the people at the back of hall to see the lots clearly. To Tyland's relief, the auctioneer was preparing to start the sale with *The Bearded Lady*. All he had to do was to bid for it, secure the sale, and then he could leave, get back to his gallery. And there calm down. But to Tyland's irritation, he wasn't the only person interested in the painting. There were a few other dealers after it, Tyland guessing that Vincent would be bidding online and suspecting that Leo might be doing the same. Piqued, his competitiveness shuffled into gear, the bids rising, Tyland's eyes fixed on the painting. But instead of seeing its beauty, he felt unexpectedly afraid, alarmed by the macabre image of the woman, the oil paint appearing to swim under the overhead lights, his mind wandering.

She was very thin, very thin, too thin....
'Hurry up, just pose there, that's all you have to do, girl, just copy the Rodin pose.'
Jimmy Nicholson, red around the jowls, sweating as he came back into the room.....
'It was all your fault. You did it. You did it...'
Oriental gown wrapped around the thin white pillar of her body... and Vincent, already drunk, getting more wine from the cellar.
'It was all your fault, Jimmy... all this is your fault.'

Rigid in his seat, Tyland stared ahead. And there she was, on the dais, her face superimposed over the face of *The Bearded Woman*. White as a lily, still, dark eyes challenging him. And then Tyland felt the room swirl like a vortex around him and swallow him whole.

Thirty Four

Her voice lowered, Charlotte turned to Milas for support. "I don't want to go to my mother's! Can't you talk to him? He listens to you. This is my *home*."

"And no one's trying to push you out, it's just that…" Milas stopped talking, watching as Charlotte pointed out of the window. "Oh look, that weird little man is back again. Is Dad in his study?"

"He was earlier, but I don't know where he is now."

"Maybe we should lie, tell the Detective Sox that he's out." She whispered. "I don't like him."

She moved to the door, immediately stepping back as Sox was shown in. "Good morning, Miss Lund."

Charlotte said nothing in reply, Milas looking at her in surprise as he addressed the detective. "Morning, what can I do for you?"

"That's a wonderful old expression '*what can I do for you?*' You know, a long time ago – long before people said – 'have a nice day' – people in shops would always say it. *What can I do for you*? I always thought it was polite, welcoming, but not overdone." Still silent, Charlotte watched him as Sox continued. "I've come to have a word with the good doctor. Is he in?"

She was about to say no, when Milas intervened. "I'll find him for you, if you wait in the sitting room."

Surprised, Charlotte ran after him and tackled him in the hall. "Why did you say that? Why didn't you say Dad had already left?"

"Because it's lying, that's why. And his car's still in the drive." Milas replied. "And if Vincent suddenly walked into the room it would look suspicious. You worry too much. Sox is probably here about something and nothing."

"I don't like that detective."

"Yeah, I got that much."

"He says too much and too little at the same time."

Despite several other bidders vying for the painting at auction, Vincent had managed to buy *The Bearded Woman* over the phone and was looking round his gallery for the ideal place to hang it. For the first time in days his attention was not on the murders or the woman, so when he heard the outer door open he turned, irritated at being disturbed.

Especially when he saw who it was.

"Morning, Dr Lund," Sox said, ambling towards him, Vincent glancing at the antique medicine box in his hands. "How are you today?"

"About to go out –"

"Well, I'm glad I caught you. Your nephew was looking for you, but I guessed you might be here. Took a chance, and got lucky."

"Have you any news?"

"Oh, yes, I've got some news," the detective replied.

"And you've brought my exhibit back. Thank you. I said you would find nothing." Vincent put out his hands, but Sox hesitated. "What is it now?"

"Belladonna. Deadly nightshade, death cherries, the devil's berries. The Roman used to poison the tips of their arrows with it, and women used it to enlarge their pupils and make their eyes more alluring. That's how it got its name, *Beautiful Lady*." Sox paused, laid down the box on a glassed cabinet. "You said there was no Belladonna in any of the bottles."

"There wasn't. There never has been."

"We found some."

Vincent stared at the detective, uncertain he had heard correctly. *"What?"*

"One of the glass bottles had held Belladonna recently --"

"That's not true!"

"I have the toxicology report to prove it." Sox replied, handing Vincent a printed piece of paper. "Read it for yourself."

He took the report, scanned it, and shook his head. "I don't understand, there's been a mistake. There were no poisons in that box. All the bottles were empty when I bought it. And the list of what had previously been in the cabinet did *not* include Belladonna."

Sox regarded him thoughtfully. "Mr Nicholson was poisoned with Belladonna."

"Oh come, on!" Vincent replied scornfully. "Are you accusing me of something?"

"Should I be?"

"When I bought that medicine cabinet there were no poisons in it, no belladonna, nothing. If you found belladonna that means that someone put it there."

"You?"

"Would I be that stupid, detective? If I'd poisoned someone would I really leave the evidence for you to find?" Vincent was agitated, his voice rising. "Have you checked it for fingerprints?"

"There were none. Wiped clean, which is odd in itself."

"Well, that proves it wasn't me, doesn't it?" Vincent countered. "I've handled that bag many times, taken the bottles out to clean them –"

"Why?"

"Why what?"

"If there was nothing in them, why clean them?"

"If the cabinet was displayed open, which sometimes it is, then dust would have got on the bottles. And I would clean them."

"Inside and out?"

"I wouldn't need to clean them inside, there was never anything in them."

"Apart from the belladonna –"

"*Which was never there!*" Vincent replied sharply.

"The laboratory found some –"

"How much?"

Sox glanced at his notes. "A trace."

"How much of a trace? And how long had it been there?" Vincent asked. "If it was a minute trace it could have been there since I bought the cabinet. It could have been there all the time and I wouldn't have known about it –"

"Unless you washed the bottle inside."

Vincent's patience was exhausted. "*I never washed inside the bottle!* If I had, there would have been no belladonna."

"Ah, I see," Sox replied, "no more belladonna, because you would have washed it away?"

Vincent frowned, confused. "No, that's not what I mean! Look, I didn't know about any belladonna –"

"So someone else put the belladonna in the bottle?"

"It wasn't me –"

He was interrupted immediately. "Apart from you, who else has a key to this gallery?"

"There's only one key. Mine."

"And it's locked all the time?"

Vincent nodded. "I lock it at night, when I'm at the hospital, or when I'm travelling. I don't lock it when I'm at home because I sometimes spend time in here. Or take delivery of a new piece. It would be insane to lock it every few minutes when I'm coming in and out."

"So others could do the same?" Sox said, smiling. "Come in and out, I mean."

"You mean a stranger?"

Sox raised his ginger eyebrows: "You think it's a member of your family?"

"Of course not!"

"What about your housekeeper, your gardener?"

"Why would they want to come in here? They'd have no reason." Vincent was struggling. "And anyway, I'd *see* them. The gallery's only yards away across the drive!"

"*Would* you see them? It's winter, it gets dark early. Say you been in here in the evening and then popped back to the house for something. Someone could have taken their chance then. You say you'd have seen them, doctor, why are you so sure about that? Do you have outside lighting?"

Vincent hesitated. "We usually do, but the system failed a week ago. Someone's coming to fix it today."

"So whilst the lights were broken, and it was dark, a person *could* have slipped into this gallery unnoticed?" Sox paused, clicking his tongue. "I did say before that your house is surrounded by trees and bushes, perfect coverage for someone sneaking about."

"The gardener's on to it. We're having them cut back tomorrow –"

"You see, they could have been hidden, watching, waiting for you to go back to the house, and then take their chance to plant evidence in here and leave." He stared at Vincent, widening his eyes. "Then how would you know they'd even been in here? You weren't likely to check on the medicine box, or the bottles, would you? I mean, you'd have no reason to. Would you?"

"So you believe that I didn't have anything to do with Jimmy's death?"

"I believe," Sox replied, "that you are an educated, intelligent man, who – if he *had* chosen to murder a close friend – would not have planted evidence on his own premises to incriminate himself. I also believe that the person who did this knew full well that we wouldn't really suspect you."

Vincent was floundering. "I don't understand."

"It's too clumsy, too contrived." Sox said, his voice amused. "This wasn't meant to fool the police, this was meant to throw a scare into *you*. Just to show you how easy it is to gain access. It was meant to point out how vulnerable you are." He looked round the gallery, then turned back to Vincent. "How did the auction go?"

"What?"

"The auction? Did you get the painting you wanted?"

"Yes," Vincent nodded, gesturing to the picture covered by a dustsheet. "Yes, actually I did."

"Odd picture, not one I'd want in my house, but there you go." Sox tipped his head to one side, like a curious bird. "Why did she have a beard? The woman in the painting, I mean. She was married, she had three sons - then she developed a beard. It made me think, I can tell you. I said to my wife that if *she* suddenly grew a beard I'd be worried."

Vincent smiled stiffly. "It's a condition called hirsutism. Women who have unusually high levels of androgens in their blood can develop a heavy growth of facial hair. Sometimes it's an abnormality in the ovaries, adrenal or pituitary glands, or polycystic ovarian syndrome." To his surprise, Sox was listening avidly. "It's not that common, but there are some rare tumours that affect the androgen hormones."

"What d'you think the woman had in the painting?"

"Magdalena Ventura? Who knows for sure, but the beard developed after her sons were born so it's a pretty good guess that it was a change in hormone levels."

"A woman with a beard...strange."

"She was considered a freak in her time," Vincent replied, "These days she'd have be able to get treatment."

"But still," Sox continued, "it would be odd to wake up to a wife that looked like a man. Funny thing about gender, isn't it? I've often wondered what it would be like to be a woman. They think so differently, don't they? They're kinder, as a rule. Although a violent woman is worse than any man...."

Vincent's antennae was alerted. Was Sox implying something? Or was it just a chance remark?

"...in my experience women don't murder that often. It's not in their nature. It's *against* their nature, and that's probably why it is all the worse if they do

237

kill. Poison, that's often their weapon of choice." Sox leaned on the display cabinet and pushed the medicine box towards Vincent, smiling as he did so. "Well, I'll be off now. When I've got any news I'll be in touch."

"Detective?"

"Yes?"

Vincent had opened the lid of the box and was looking inside. "One of the bottles is missing."

"Yes, the one that had the belladonna in it. We've kept it for evidence."

"But that makes the exhibit incomplete." Vincent said, irritated. "It's not valuable incomplete."

"Dr Lund, with due respect, that's the least of your worries."

Thirty Five

Carefully positioning the angle of her head, Tilly took a selfie, checking the image afterwards and then repeating it five times until she was satisfied. Her unexpected notoriety had been a surprise; her status as stepdaughter of a murder victim singling her out among her friends. Tilly liked that. She had inherited Alicia's good looks, but without the blatant sexual allure, the added appeal which made men stare and woman despair.

Competitiveness had always marred their relationship, Tilly developing young and throwing a dent into her mother's confidence. Their bond – always erratic – worsened when Tilly ran away from home, forcing Alicia to temporarily relegate Barend to second place in her affections. But not for long, Tilly soon looking elsewhere for attention. She was an adept flirt, but – like her mother – took rejection badly. So when Alicia returned home and Tilly prised out a recall of her conversation with Vincent, she was overjoyed at her mother being rejected.

"He doesn't want to know?"

"You don't have to sound so bloody pleased about it!" Alicia replied, "it's not like you're having a roaring success with Milas."

The words hit home, Tilly smarting. "I don't even like him."

"The hell you don't!"

"I think he's gay."

"Oh, for God's sake, Tilly, of course he isn't!"

"How d'you know?"

"Because I do," Alicia replied, her thoughts moving on quickly. "I don't trust Stella Nicholson --"

Tilly ignored the comment. "How d'you know Milas *isn't* gay?"   "I just know." Alicia replied shortly. "He's too old for you anyway."

It was the impetus Tilly needed. If her mother had failed with Vincent she wasn't going to fail with Milas. Supposedly dismissing the idea, she made them both some tea, passing the mug across the kitchen table to her mother.

"Everyone's talking about what happened to Barend. All my friends are asking me about it." She began, but when Alicia didn't reply, continued. "There are lots of rumours."

"Like what?"

"You know, *why* he was killed."

"Listen, Tilly" she reached out for her daughter's hand. "I don't want to you fret, or be afraid. Don't worry about any of this, nothing's going to happen to us."

"Oh, I'm not worried about that!" Tilly retorted. "Should I be?"

"No. We're fine. The police will find out who killed Barend."

"Do you miss him?"

"Yes." Alicia nodded. "Yes, I do, but not as much as I should…. What about you?"

"I suppose so."

"He was always good to you. Good to *us*." Alicia went on, her voice becoming gentle. "I know he could be difficult at times, but Barend was a generous man. What happened to him wasn't fair."

Tilly had already slipped back to her original train of thought. "People are saying that it was probably a robbery that went wrong."

"You shouldn't be talking about it --"

"Do *you* think it was a robbery? I mean, why would someone have killed him in his Chambers? There's no money there, is there?"

"Maybe they thought there was." Alicia shook her head, felt the fall of her hair against her shoulders. Barend had loved her hair, admired it, often in public. Women hated her for that; for that open devotion he had expressed.

"Or maybe it's something to do with what you were saying the other day." Tilly continued. "Maybe it's someone Barend prosecuted in the past. Someone who wants revenge."

"I don't want you talking about that to anyone!" Alicia said sharply. "Don't gossip, Tilly –"

"I'm not gossiping! But I can't say nothing, can I? Not when people keep asking me about my step-father's murder. Not when I get stopped by journalists every time I leave the house." She folded her arms across her chest, petulant. "*'Don't gossip!'* You've got to be joking, I can't *avoid* the subject."

Alicia took in a breath. "I mean, don't talk to journalists. I don't say anything to them, because they twist your words, dig around in your life, *our* life. Just ignore them. Don't say anything."

"I don't."

"People lie, especially the media. You could be misquoted, Tilly, so keep quiet. We both have to be discreet."

"But I've got friends, I can't just shut them out."

"Say you don't know what it's all about."

"Well, I *don't* bloody know, do I?" She countered. "Milas doesn't know anything either."

Alicia flinched. "*You've talked to him about it?*"

"We bumped into each other when I was walking the dog. And we had a coffee. He's worried about Vincent. His uncle said he wanted him to live somewhere else until it was over."

Alicia's interest ignited. Moments earlier she had been against her daughter having any involvement with Milas but now a plan was forming. If she couldn't get to Vincent directly perhaps she could get access via Tilly?

"So Milas confides in you?"

Her daughter felt a quick thrill of power. "Yeah. We talk."

"Does he have any theories about the murders?"

"He's not saying much." Tilly had the upper hand and liked it. "Not much at all. But he's determined to stay at the house, he doesn't want to leave Vincent if he's in danger."

"How noble," Alicia said dryly. "Are you planning to meet up with Milas again?"

"Maybe."

"Don't be sly, Tilly, not with me." She leaned across the kitchen table. "And don't repeat what I'm about to tell you to anyone. D'you hear me? I care about Vincent Lund --"

"Everyone knows that."

" – stop throwing the past in my face! Your step-father and I were separated when I had the affair with Vincent. And afterwards I went back to Barend."

"Only because Vincent didn't want you to stay."

"You can be such a bitch!"

"I had a good teacher," Tilly replied, smiling to defuse the insult. "I understand what you're saying. Vincent Lund is glamorous and good looking –"

"It's not just that. I really cared – *care* – about him. You can laugh all you want, Tilly. I'm sure it seems pathetic to you, but even if he doesn't care about me anymore, I still want to help him, if I can."

It was true, up to a point. It was also true that Alicia wanted Vincent back and was prepared to do anything to restart their relationship. Even if that meant pushing her daughter into Milas's arms. And confidence.

"I need your help."

The words had exactly the effect Alicia had hoped, Tilly smugly magnanimous. "Ok, what kind of help?"

"If Milas tells you anything about what's going on, tell me, will you? Whatever he says, however unimportant it seems, tell me." She stroked her daughter's hair. "You're really finding out about life now, darling, and there's one lesson you *really* have to learn - family always sticks together."

-o0o-

"All the trees?" Ellen Brooks said aghast, looking at her husband. *"All the trees?"*

He shrugged. "That's what Dr Lund said and that's what I'm going to do. I've got some more men to help me tomorrow. The biggest trees need chain saws to fell them and a bloody great truck to take them away – even if we chop some of them up. It's a hell of a job. What d'you think brought it on?"

"The murders, what else?" Ellen replied, "He's scared, you can see that. I mean, who wouldn't be? Two close friends killed, that's got to have you worried."

She put some sliced carrots on to boil and checked on a stew simmering in the oven. Her considerable weight made her slow, but it didn't affect her cooking, the aroma leaking from the kitchen and snaking round the ground floor of the house. After moving from the North of England to London, the couple had been employed by the Lunds for eighteen years, living in a flat nearby and coming to work every day, apart from Sunday. Over the years Ellen had cooked for numerous dinner parties and events – with and without hired catering staff - her husband occupied with the garden and the growing collection of conservatory plants.

They had watched Charlotte grow up and witnessed the acrimonious divorce of her parents, had enjoyed Vincent's prominent success, and accepted the arrival of Milas. The house was spacious, what was one more person? And besides, Milas was the surrogate son Vincent Lund had always wanted. The couple were discreet, but missed nothing. The Brooks might talk to each other about events in the Lund household, but never gossiped to outsiders. The latest happenings however were different. The murders had affected their employer, his usual urbanity replaced by uncharacteristic nervousness. And the press had annoyed Ellen for the last two weeks with their intrusive questioning. When she arrived in the early mornings she found them idling against the electric gates, trying to get through as she entered. They had never managed it; Ellen weighed thirteen stone and had sharp elbows.

As the days passed, she had grown anxious about Charlotte. Afraid for her father, the girl had suffered frequent asthma attacks, luckily finding an ally in Milas. A confidante, something she had missed since her mother left. Which always brought Ellen's thoughts back to the same question - why hadn't Vincent Lund married again? A wealthy professional man should have his pick of women; a wealthy, attractive professional man should never have been alone.

"You think the doctor is really worried?"

Ellen glanced over her shoulder towards her husband. *"What?"*

"That someone might be after him? I mean they killed two of his friends. There must be some connection."

"It's not for us to think, let the police do the thinking."

"Maybe…. What about that detective?"

"The ginger dwarf?"

"Oh, Ellen, that's harsh."

"He's got red hair and he's short." She poured some boiling water over the carrots and turned up the gas under the pan. "Oh come on, we've been saying it ever since Mr Nicholson was killed – these murders have to be connected. The victims were all friends." She dropped her voice. "What if it's something to do with their collections? I mean, the doctor's got some pretty weird objects. I won't go in there. Refuse to clean the place. I went once and couldn't stomach those skulls and wax figures watching me."

Arthur laughed. "He's not a Satanist!"

"How do we know?" She countered. "How do we know *what* it's all about?"

"It's art."

"Art to them and smut to us." Ellen replied. "And what does Leo Park collect, hey? Not *Country Life* and that's a fact. I don't see the point of hoarding. There are always paintings and objects coming here for the doctor, for what reason? Just to collect things? That can't be all there is to it –"

"He enjoys it. He has the money to indulge himself –"

"I might have believed it before, but after two of his friends have been killed, I'm not so sure." She shook her head. "Those things Dr Lund collects, they're bloody odd. Wax bodies with their insides hanging out."

"'Anatomical dummies'."

"I know what they are! I'm just saying, doctor or not, they're strange things to have around. And God knows what his friends collected. Jimmy Nicholson was --"

"You shouldn't speak ill of the dead."

" -- I'm talking to *you*, Arthur, no one else. And I'm not going to speak ill of the dead, I'm speaking the truth, Nicholson was an old letch. I hated him." She folded her burly arms. "He was exactly the kind of man a woman wouldn't want to get stuck in a lift with."

"Maybe you're right, but don't go saying that to the police." Arthur warned her, pulling off his socks and putting on the slippers that had been warming beside the boiler. "Keep your mouth shut, Ellen."

"I'll remind you to do the same. And don't mention Mrs de Vries coming over here either." She glanced towards the kitchen door and kept her voice low. "I mean, they had a thing going on, didn't they? The doctor and her. Who's to say *that* didn't cause a problem."

"You think Dr Lund stabbed Barend de Vries to death?"

"*I don't mean that!*"

"Well, what *do* you mean?"

"What if it's all to do with *her?* Alicia de Vries is trouble. You know as well as I do she had an affair with Jimmy Nicholson too. And when he died she inherited his collection – I wonder how that made her husband feel? I'm only saying it to you, but maybe *she* killed him?"

"Killed her husband? Don't be stupid!"

"Why's it stupid?" Ellen retorted, leaning on the back of a kitchen chair. "If she'd her sights set on Dr Lund and her husband was in the way –"

"And I suppose she killed Jimmy Nicholson too?"

"She could have done! Maybe Nicholson wanted her back and she didn't want him anymore. Maybe he took it badly, threatened her with some kind of exposure. People make tapes all the time, it's always in the papers. If he had something embarrassing on her, she could have killed him to keep him quiet."

"You should stop watching Netflix documentaries –"

"You can mock all you like! But you don't know women. Men *never* understand women. A man's brain can only think of one thing at a time. A woman's brain can juggle, manoeuvre, plot --"

"Your stew's burning."

Sighing, Ellen heaved herself over to the oven and took out the casserole. Lifting the lid, she sniffed and nodded. "It's good."

"Of course it's good," Arthur said, "everything you make is good."

She ignored the remark, intent on her previous thought. "Jimmy Nicholson was poisoned. Now that's a woman's weapon. It's calm, cruel. But stabbing? Now that's another matter. For a woman to stab a man – especially her husband – she'd have to *really* hate him." Ellen raised her eyebrows. "How much would *you* have to hate someone to look them in the face and drive a knife into them repeatedly?"

"God Almighty, Ellen, give it a rest!"

"I'm just saying --"

"Yes, and 'just saying' can get us into trouble. Keep your theories to yourself, and don't say anything to the police." He paused, thinking for a moment. "If it does have anything to do with Mrs de Vries, the killings should stop now. I don't suppose she had an affair with Tyland Bray - and Leo Parks doesn't go for women."

"Who's to say it's sex related? People kill for a lot of reasons. Sometimes trivial things they've brooded on for years." Ellen shrugged. "But I'll say this – innocent or guilty, Dr Lund should steer clear of Alicia de Vries."

Thirty Six

There was a fall of leaves about her head, a shuffle of dry twigs, a sky melting into the deep pit of loss, disappointment, despair. Stella Nicholson stared at the papers she had been given minutes before. The leaves kept falling; she could hear the sound of her brain tear. The private detective she had hired had found her son. Found an address, a phone number. He had found Dominic. But no longer softly gentle, reaching out, now hands closed, arms folded.

'I'm sorry, he said he didn't want to see you.'
He was my baby, my only child. Smelling of
soap, sweet skinned. You made my heart open.
A safe unlocked and a bird flew out,
Making for high ground....
*He **must** want to see me.*
'No, Mrs Nicholson, he said no.'
He said no.
Like his father. Like Jimmy always said no.
Father and son. Always no.

The leaves were falling heavily now, shifting about, shuffling around her ears, her blood pumping, the vein in her neck filling, swelling.

> *What did I do?...*
> *I thought it would bring you home,*
> *I did it for you. For you, for the yielding skin*
> *the out reaching arms. For you...*

The twigs are heavier now: they hurt as they fall, as they strike against her head, her forehead, the mounds of her cheeks, her eyes closing against the hurtling, injuring leaves that have no place here.

> *You were supposed to come home.*
> *And you said no...*
> *Another door closes, only old age*
> *And the silence of musty rooms.*
> *Old age coming like a stalker down lonely*
> *streets*
> *And empty gardens where once flowers grew...*
> *I did it for you.*

Book Three

Tell me, are you ready now?

I've been ready for years, many years, changing, waiting until the time was perfectly poised, like a dancer. I was a dancer once. You don't know that, but I was. I danced in bars and clubs for men that you would see as less than yourselves, but they weren't. They were you, all of you, just cheaper suits and shoddy jobs, no Kings, no Princes, just men.

While I read about you in the newspapers and later online, whilst you were feted and admired, I made a little life amongst the streets that you would never had gone down, with wives who would have been shamed to be seen there. I saw doctors. Yes, Vincent, doctors. Some you know, some you don't, talking and trying to make myself whole. And I remembered, as you do, if you'll just let yourselves.

Too hard for you? Of course, I understand, what's that quote? 'Human kind cannot bear very much reality' it's true, but my kind have only reality, that's what we face whilst your kind talk of becoming King's Counsel, Minister of Arts and having a wing of a hospital named after you. You're a healer, Vincent, aren't you? That's what heroes do, they heal.

No one even remembers that I had been hurt.

You can blame Jimmy Nicholson, but you were all to blame. He was the worst, but all of you knew what his intention was. You had a Christmas tree in your house, Vincent, with parcels under it, for friends, family, colleagues, I suppose. Mr Parks, you saw him take me in the other room, and you, Mr Bray, with your fading wife and Vincent, with a glass in your hand, full, always full. Do you still drink? Do you still pretend you can't remember?

*That Rodin sculpture, the Danaid, that I was hired to copy. Such a wonderful pose, but Rodin was a genius, wasn't he? I didn't know that then. I was ignorant then, but I have learned. Just as I've learned that the sculpture might not have been created by Rodin, after all. Oh, I know it was a replica that night, I'm talking about the **original.** Now they think it might have been sculpted by the poor wretch, Camille Claudel. Such a brilliant and beautiful woman. Rodin loved her, and then he broke that china doll face, and her porcelain heart. Another of the art world's victims.*

And lately I've been watching you all wanting to buy that painting Magdalena Ventura, 'The Bearded Woman', that pitiful freak. But then again, we are all freaks to you, aren't we? I certainly was. Poor and pitiful. Jimmy Nicholson found that out and couldn't forgive me, or himself.

I wondered if he told you. Did he? I suspect he must have done. Perhaps he laughed with you, Vincent. Or perhaps his masculine pride prevented his ever mentioning it. He was ashamed. No more than I was, as I stumbled out of that house, past that florid Christmas tree, into the chilling night with the Oriental robe stuffed in to my bag.

*I've returned it now. With interest. And I'm wondering, Vincent, how you will react. You see, I blame **you** the most. Jimmy Nicholson was what he seemed, crude, animal, amoral, but you, you were the better man and yet you let it happen in your house. Under your roof, drinking yourself forgetful, strutting your peacock ways.*

And now you're wondering, aren't you? Wondering who's next. Tyland Bray? Leo Parks? Or you, Vincent?... Leo is coming apart like a dying bird, all falling feathers. Bray is using his bully boy tactics, but the nights are long for him and all his new alarms can't keep his ending away. As for you, your nephew still admires you, worships the clever idol you present, but the plinth is rocking under your feet and the fall is coming.

Remember this - we are all freaks, Vincent.

But some are more obvious than others.

Thirty Seven

"Oh, my God, is she alright?"

"Of course she's not alright! She's had a stroke." Alicia said, taking the tea Marina had handed her. "Stella Nicholson, of all people."

"Is she going to… going to die?"

"Don't whimper, Marina! No, she not going to die. She should be out of hospital in a few days, they're just keeping her in for a while to check her out. It wasn't a serious stroke. Well, I suppose all strokes are serious." She sipped her tea and grimaced. "Bloody hell! You make terrible tea, it's so flaming weak."

Marina's eyes filled.

"Oh, I didn't mean it, sorry. Everyone's jumpy…" Alicia murmured, "It doesn't matter, don't cry, I didn't want tea anyway –"

"It's not the tea."

Alicia leaned towards her. "Speak up, Marina, I can't hear you if you whisper."

"I said it's not the tea! *It's Tyland*. He fainted at the auction. He said it was because he'd taken too many painkillers. That's what made him dizzy… And he said the room was hot… Very hot. That's what made him pass out."

"Well, I wouldn't worry," Alicia said half-heartedly "if that's what he said."

"But Stella's had a stroke --"

"It's not catching," Alicia replied, putting her arm around her. She was surprised how thin Marina was under all the layers of clothes. "What did his doctor say?"

"That it was because he was over working," She looked at Alicia imploringly. "But it's not that, is it? It's worry, too much worry, about everything that's going on. The murders... You know, Jimmy Nicholson and your husband..." She flushed, mortified. "I'm sorry, I should be supporting you, not the other way around."

"It's Ok. I know you're worried about Tyland."

"He's not well, you know. He isn't well at all."

"But he's tough, he isn't a pushover."

"I don't know how strong he is now. He walks about at night. For hours sometimes. And then he goes to sleep and I hear him cry out. He brushes it off, says he was just dreaming, but it's frightening and I can't help him." She wiped away tears that threatened to overflow, her fingertips wet. "It's my nerves, you see. I'm no good to anyone. No help at all. Tyland always says that - '*it's your nerves, you should be pleased I can look after you.*' And he's right. I keep wondering what I would do if anything happened to him." She tugged at the hem of her skirt, distracted. "I never thought something like this would happen. Even though he's not well, I still didn't think it would happen. Not to Tyland."

"He's just tired."

She shook her head. "No."

"Marina, listen to me. He's under stress and not sleeping, you said it yourself. He'll be fine if he gets some rest."

"No, you're wrong," she said, her tone panicked. "He's not tired, he's waiting." She stared at Alicia, her voice lost. "He's just *waiting.*"

"For what?"

"For the end." Marina said, her expression anguished. "He knows it, and I know it. It's going to happen, and we can't stop it. Neither can that policeman, no one can stop it. Because no one knows who it is, where it's coming from, or why. No one expected it, Alicia, did they?"

"No," she agreed dully, "no one."

"They're just working out the order."

"*What?*"

"The order of the deaths." Marina answered, her expression frantic. "If it's random, who'll be in first, second and third place? But if it's alphabetical and they're going on Christian names, it will be Leo first, Tyland second, and Vincent third." She paused, stricken. "But if they're going on surnames, who'll be first then? *Tyland*, that's who'll be first! Tyland **BRAY**!"

Thirty Eight

New York

Seated at the dinner table with her guests, Ruby was listening for the phone to ring. When it did, when she knew Leo had arrived safely in London and was at Vincent's house, only then would she relax. Until then she was suspended, between a vacuous lawyer on one side and a loquacious actress on the other. It was a woman Ruby had always liked before, but tonight their conversation was strained, Ruby's concentration erratic, as giddy as a kite.

Taking a mouthful of food, Ruby chewed thoroughly, turning it round and round like sand in a cement mixer, tasting nothing. The verre verte on the walls around the table reflected the guests, the candlelight giving a bilious feel – she had never noticed that before - silver and gold lights darting like mosquitoes. For the first time Ruby felt the rigidity of her chair seat. Wondered if, somehow, the stuffing had gone and only the bare wood remained.

She shook off the notion. It was just her discomfort that was turning everything into a petty torture. When Leo rang she would be alright, the world would be whole again. A recognised place... The sound of sirens outside reminded her that the city was still moving, just as the clock was, just as the plane was. Moving towards London. With Leo on board.

Without anyone noticing, she stole a glance at the clock. Old, Gustavian, reliable and stolid as a farmer, striking on the hour... Leo was late. Yes, he was late now. Allowing for the plane to have been delayed, allowing for his going through Customs, allowing for a slow journey to Vincent's house he was late... The actress next to her was talking about Broadway, gibbering about the honour of appearing on such a blah, blah, blah... Ruby watched the woman's lips move, trying not to think about the worst that could happen: a life without Leo, without the person who meant the most to her.

Then the phone rang in the hall outside. The landline that Leo teased her about, mocking her for not getting a mobile. At once, Ruby excused herself and hurried out, her maid passing the phone towards her as she snatched it up:

"You're late!"

"For what?"

A crunch of disappointment.

"Who is this?"

"Vincent, Vincent Lund."

"Vincent? Put Leo on the phone."

"He's not here."

She dropped her voice, leaned against the wall, tried to sound normal. "He should have arrived at your house by now. I've been waiting for his call."

"His plane was delayed. Leo phoned me to say he'll be along later."

Were her eyes filling? Ruby wondered. Was that relief? Or old age? "Shit, Vincent! You could have said that first instead of leaving me hanging out to dry."

"You didn't give me chance to speak."

He was weary with worry, the last letter delivered only hours before. The writer – that anonymous, vindictive female - was provoking him. The thought tormented and shamed him at the same time. Why shouldn't she torment him? Perhaps he deserved it.

"Vincent, are you still there?"

"Yes, I'm here… how are you, Ruby?"

"Old, over made up, with bad knees. How the hell are you?"

"I wanted to have a talk with you. Is now a good time?"

"No, not at all, but I'm glad of the excuse to escape." She gestured for the maid to take the phone, then walked into the study, closed the door behind her and picked up the extension. After waiting for the click on the line that told her they could not be overheard, she turned her attention back to Vincent. "Leo won't tell me what's going on with these murders and I suppose I'd be wasting my breath to ask you?"

"Yes, you would."

"Fuck you, Vincent," she said simply. "Just look after my boy, will you? And yourself. So, if you don't want to confide, what *do* you want to talk about?"

"You bought a sculpture from Tyland Bray twenty odd years ago, it was a Rodin nude. Some said it was by Camille Claudel, his pupil. You remember it?"

"I'm not senile, darling, of course I do. I've spent half the night looking at it. It's in the dining room here –"

"It's in New York?"

263

"Yes, and it's odd that you should ask me about it because I had it in storage for years and only had it brought back to the house last week."

Vincent was relieved and didn't know why. "So you didn't sell it on? Thank God... Does it have a label on it?"

"*A label?* It's a work of art, not a hand of bananas."

"It should have a brass plaque on it."

"Oh, yes, there's one of those. It's grimy, needs a clean, but I like it dusky, adds to the atmosphere. I was told that you had to be very careful with the attribution on a plaque, she said you had to be sure it was correct. I think it's because no one knows for certain if it was Rodin or Camille Claudel."

"*She.*" Vincent said, alert. "You said *she*. Who's she?"

"She was Rodin's lover and pupil –"

"Not Camille Claudel! I meant the specialist. Who was she?"

"Oh, some sort of art consultant --"

"From where?"

"London, of course. She was sent to me by Tyland Bray, recommended by him."

"What did she look like?"

"*What did she look like?*" Ruby echoed, mystified. "Like an ordinary woman –"

"Was she tall?"

"Do you have to be tall to be an art consultant?"

"This is no joke, Ruby, tell me what she was like."

"Average height, dark hair around thirty."

Relax, Vincent told himself, she was too young. Thirty was too young. And she was average height, dark haired. It wasn't her. It was just some specialist recommended by Tyland, and had nothing to do with

the woman who was coming after them. Calm down…
Another thought followed on. Had Leo seen the sculpture in Ruby's house? No, she had just told him that she had kept it in storage until the previous week.

"Could you look at the plaque for me?"

Ruby laughed down the line. "What the hell for!"

"I don't know, but I might be something or nothing."

"I haven't spoken to you for years, Vincent, and you ring me out of the blue with some fool request. If you think I'm going rush off to do your bidding --"

"Whenever you can."

She sighed extravagantly. "Is it important?"

"It might be. But then again, it might mean nothing."

"That's exactly the way to get my attention, isn't it?" She glanced towards the closed dining room door. "As soon as they've left I'll have a look. Then I'll call you back."

Her guests stayed on. As people always do when you wish them gone. They chatted at the table, in the drawing room, and then at the door before leaving. An endless confetti of trivia. Finally, around midnight, Ruby said her last goodbyes and moved into the dining room and over to the sculpture in the alcove. Having waited for nearly two hours Ruby's curiosity was at fever pitch as she put on her reading glasses and bent down to look at the brass plaque. It was barely readable, Ruby rubbing her finger over the writing and making a note to have it cleaned it in the morning.

She had no idea what she had been looking for, but felt vaguely disappointed with what she had found. "Reporting in," she said, ringing Vincent later.

"You timed that well, Leo's just arrived. He's exhausted, but he's fine."

She smiled down the phone line. "Give him my love and tell him to call me tomorrow."

"I will. Did you --"

"Yes, I looked. But I can't read it, it's too dirty. I'll clean it tomorrow, see if it's readable then."

"What about a date?"

"Oh, I'm spoken for, darling."

He laughed. First time in two weeks. "On the sculpture, Ruby."

"No, can't make out the date either. I'll have another look when it's clean." She slipped off her shoes, and sat down in a dining chair, toying with a discarded bread roll. "What did you expect to find?"

"I don't know. I was just hoping there was a clue there."

"To what?"

"To a mystery."

She laughed, throaty, amused. "You and Leo are both fucking mysteries."

"Has Leo seen that sculpture?"

She thought for a moment. "Not here, no. Now I think about it, Leo's never seen it because I loaned it out to a gallery in Switzerland for years, then to a place in France that was doing a show about Camille Claudel –"

"And Leo wasn't interested?"

"I didn't tell him about it. It wasn't his kind of thing really. Nudes never have been, not female nudes anyway. And as I said, it was out of my possession or in storage until last week." She became serious. "Look, I told Leo and I'll tell you the same, if you need help – any help – ask me. Neither of you are poor, but I'm loaded. You need extra cash to get yourselves out of a scrape, just ask."

266

"You're a good woman, Ruby."

She nodded. "Yes, I rather think I am. But then again, I'm also a clever judge of character and I know neither of you are evil men. Stupid, probably, all men are stupid, even the clever ones, but not evil." She yawned loudly. "I'm tired and I'm off to bed."

"We'll speak soon."

"Yes, Vincent," she said evenly, "I know we will."

Thirty Nine

People don't sleep when they are in crisis. Or in love, in debt, in pain, in sorrow. Sometimes night becomes the time we dread throughout the day, every hour taking us closer to the dark. When we most need her, sleep turns her back; Hypnos and Nyx join forces, play Cinderella games but keep their sombre slippers on. And midnight and the early hours yawn with the promise of a rest that never comes.

Or one that lasts too long.

In his gallery Tyland Bray was working on the catalogue for his new exhibition, ducking his wife's wearisome attentions. He had received the last anonymous letter and torn it up, throwing it into an outside bin, but the words were burned into his skin like a tattoo and made him vicious.

"Why are you going out at this time, Tyland?" Marina had asked tentatively. "You should be resting, you're not well."

"Oh, for God's Sake! I passed out because I took too many painkillers and the auction hall was stuffy. How many times do I have to tell you that, Marina?" He had railed at her, wanting her to fight back. As she would have done when they were younger. "Look at yourself, can't you get some new clothes, spruce yourself up a bit? I'm going to be Minster of Arts, I need a proper wife, someone who looks the part."

He had been cruel. He could see *how* cruel now he was sitting alone in the gallery, in the upstairs flat, the windows barred for the night, the burglar alarm set. His cruelty had been a reaction to what was unravelling before him, and what he could see slipping away - the future, the height of his ambitions balanced like a tight rope walker without a wire.

He would be Minister of the Arts, he *would,* despite the woman coming after him. *A freak,* she had called him. Well, he would show her what a real freak was. A man driven to becoming a freak, a quirk of malicious nature... His mind turned back to the present, to Stella Nicholson, and thought of what Vincent had told him. How the Nicholson woman had dug up his past activities and laid them in front of the poisonous gnome of a detective like Salome offering John the Baptist's head.

Oh, he knew what she doing. Taking suspicion off the lecherous Jimmy Nicholson, sacrificing four men to absolve the reputation of one bastard. *Bitch*, Tyland thought, as he pushed aside his papers and thought of the message Sox had left on the answer phone to say he was coming to the gallery. *For a chat.* How delightful, Tyland thought bitterly. He could imagine exactly what the chat would be about – the fakes. And Clive Shawcross.

If only he could sleep he could recover his wits. But sleep wouldn't come, so instead Tyland was sitting in the cold flat staring out of the window, down into Dover Street, W1. There were only few people around, a man walking a dog, a couple coming round the corner, huddled under an umbrella. Nothing important or out of place. Nostalgia – unexpected and unwelcome – hijacked him. Took him back, down all the years, to his father, when Leonard Bray was running the gallery. Strict, humourless, gifted.

'Watch and learn and you'll get somewhere.'

He had been right, and Tyland *had* watched and he learned, but he wasn't his father and when he was young he had – yes, admit it – a reckless streak. Time had hammered that out of him, but not before once gambling with his reputation. Tyland winced at the remembrance. He had done it for the risk. Not for the money, but to protest against the straitjacket of his father's way of life.

In pain, Tyland rubbed his shoulder, then his arm. That morning another bruise had developed, probably from when he had slumped, so lumpenly, onto the auction floor. The colleague who had greeted him earlier had helped him to his feet, asking if he needed a doctor, and behind their backs Tyland had heard people talking.

'Poor Tyland, he's lost two of his closest friends.
It's affected him badly... I wonder if he thinks he might be next?
I mean, Jimmy Nicholson was a dealer too.
Ssshhh, he'll hear you...'

Embarrassed, he had murmured about the temperature being too high in the hall and how he needed to get some fresh air. And his colleague had followed him out, like a carer, pretending to be concerned, but really wanting any grim kernel of news he could scuff up and pass on.

Tyland rolled up his shirt sleeve with effort and then scrutinised his upper arm. Bruised, purple as a ripe plum, and as he rubbed it he thought back to the past. To Clive Shawcross ... He remembered the man well. Slick haired, wearing a cheap suit and a fake leather jacket, teeth too big for his face. Wily. But not that wily. Tyland had caught him stealing a drawing from the Bray gallery and had called the police, instructing them to charge him with theft. A charge that Tyland then dropped, saying that there had been a mistake.

There had been no mistake. Tyland had simply recognised an advantage. And from that moment on Shawcross had been in his debt. It had been thrilling. Adrenalin days, an overheated summer spent travelling from France to London and back again. Forged canvases secreted in the boot of his sports car, and Marina, still full breasted and full lipped, eager in bed. God how long ago was that? How long since he could climb on top of her and release his frustration in sex. How long had it been since his body had functioned efficiently, before forcing him into resented celibacy? Transforming into a malfunctioning machine of blood and bone and endless breaks and bruises.

There were dry crickets and the sound of a mill wheel turning close by. You kissed my stomach, ran your hands along my thighs, teased me under a wicked sun that burned the summer leaves.
I had a whole, well body then, before illness claimed every inch of me, except my brain...

That rumbled on, snake charmed its way to the
zenith of my career
And the apogee of my days.

You didn't know about the forgeries, Marina. Or did you? You never said, but sometimes there was a look about your eyes, as though you weren't innocent of what I was doing. And I liked those secret moments between us; liked that we hid parts of ourselves to find later. Saving them for our middle years and long old age.

Tyland rolled down his sleeve again. What good was it being sentimental? That Tyland was gone. That Marina was gone. And as for Clive Shawcross... His thoughts turned back to Stella Nicholson – so she would try and ruin him, would she? There was no proof of what he had done and his friends were hardly likely to speak up about their involvement and risk their good names. No one would speak out - except Shawcross. And where was he? Tyland wondered. Dead, he presumed. Or abroad. He had kept some of the fakes, probably milked them out into the art market over the years to give himself a comfortable living. There *had* been moments when Tyland had wondered if Shawcross would get back in touch, but as time passed he had relaxed. Their paths had crossed, then uncrossed, each going their separate ways. Stella Nicholson was a liar. That was what he would insist. But then again, who cared, if it kept the police on the wrong track? Let them believe her story. Let them wonder about his past. There was no *evidence*, nothing to stop him running for the tape. For the prize, Minister of Arts.

But for all his bravado Tyland was uneasy, a sentence constantly replaying in his head, the words written by the red haired girl he had encountered so many years before.

You ruled over me once, now I rule over you. And I will bring about the fall of all you hollow kings.

Forty

"Let me help, you look dead on your feet." Milas said, watching his uncle from the doorway.

Vincent turned. "I'm taking some time off from the hospital. I've just organised cover. I need to have a break."

He didn't say that he wasn't fit to operate any longer, afraid that he might jeopardise his patients. He didn't say that every face he encountered at the hospital seemed like a threat. St Thomas's had become an anthill of menace, full of dark corridors and old lifts. How easy it would be for someone to hide in any of the numerous wards and passageways; how simple to ascend or descend on the bleak back stairs. In the past Vincent would walked around the hospital at night confidently, now every footfall was a threat and every noise a warning.

Home was safer. Vincent knew his own house, knew how it sounded, which creaks were normal, which were not. He knew the doors and windows, the safe entries and escape routes. A sound in his home he could identify, place, accept. He knew the floorboards that shifted in December and the ivy tapping on the conservatory glass roof. The pantry door might rattle and the boiler hum uncertainly, but the sounds were benign. Familiar. Safe. Yes, thought Vincent, if he stayed in his own house, he had a chance.

"I think it's a good idea to take time off," Milas agreed, "and when Leo's arrives, you can relax."

Vincent studied his nephew; the fine fair hair, the glasses, the slim hands holding papers. He was proud of Milas's brain; quick, clever, adept at picking up details. The perfect researcher and proof reader. But he found it difficult to reconcile Milas's intelligence with his lack of ambition. Perhaps he had missed his vocation, slipped past his goal in life? Perhaps, with the right advice, he could still achieve something worthwhile.

"What is it?"

"I was thinking, Milas. You're smart, the work you've done for me is impressive. I could recommend you to my colleagues, they need quick research brains." A shutter came down. Vincent saw it and backtracked. "I'm not trying to rule your life, it was just that I thought --"

"My mother was ambitious for me too. But with her it was always a criticism."

"I'm sorry." Vincent said, embarrassed, "I didn't mean to bring up bad memories. Weren't you happy at home?"

"We weren't happy or unhappy. We just were."

Usually judicious, for once Vincent's curiosity gained the upper hand. "I never got to really know your father, but he seemed like a reasonable man."

"He was."

"I suppose he wanted you to stay in Denmark?"

"He never said. I suppose so," Milas agreed. "I don't know for certain. That was the problem, no one talked very much. Occasionally we argued and then all the irritations came out, but most of the time we just rubbed along. Until they died. Then I missed them."

"You should have come to me straight after the accident."

Milas shook his head, glancing away. "I couldn't. I didn't know what I wanted and I needed to try and work things out for myself. And then there was the house to sell and their possessions to sort out. It took time. I wanted to come to London, but I wasn't sure if you'd welcome me; if the argument you'd had with my mother had left too much ill feeling." Milas looked over to his uncle. "You don't know how much it means to me being here."

"No more than it means to me. I just worry that you haven't made any friends. You spend a lot of time in the house, or working. You should get out more, you're still young."

"Oh, I've had enough socialising for the time being," Milas replied, laughing, then becoming serious again. "Look, Vincent, there's something I should tell you. I've been meaning to for quite a while, but I lacked the courage… After my parents died I spent time in rehab." Vincent was surprised by the confession but didn't show it, Milas continuing to talk. "I was on drugs. Had been for a while. I'm off them now – for over four years - but I wanted you to know. Apparently I've an 'addictive personality,'" he smiled. "That was the view of my therapist. My view was different – I was in a fucking mess and I didn't know where to turn. My father wasn't the kind of man you emulated. It wasn't his fault, but he didn't set any kind of example. I didn't admire him. My mother knew that; she didn't admire him either. That's why she was so jealous of you, because people thought of you as a hero. My parents didn't talk about you, but I knew all about you and I was proud of you. Bragged about my famous uncle. I kept the newspaper cuttings about your work and watched your speeches online. I was quite the stalker."

Vincent didn't reply. What would Milas think if he knew the truth? If he knew *why* his admired uncle was taking time off from his profession. Why he was being questioned by the police. Why his friends were being murdered… He wanted to be honest, to explain, confess. But he craved the admiration too much, and hesitated.

"Look, Milas, I'm not what you think."

"I know what you are."

"No, you don't." Vincent replied. "Don't make me into a hero."

"Even if you are one?"

"I'm grateful for what you said, it means a lot to me, but you don't really know me --

Milas cut him off. "Why? What have you done that could possibly make me think less of you?"

A moment hung out between them, taut as a washing line, the question unanswered, Milas tapping his uncle affectionately on the shoulder as he left the room.

Later that night, much later, when Vincent couldn't sleep, he thought over what Milas had said, because something was nagging at him. He couldn't grasp it, and brooded, at three am finally remembering what his nephew had said about the time after his parents were killed.

'And then there was the house to sell and their possessions to sort out…'

Vincent turned over in bed, frowning. It was a small thing, hardly of any importance, but it rankled. His sister and brother in law had never bought a house. They had always rented. It was a matter he had discussed with Adela a number of times, but she had been adamant. Rental was the best way to go, she had insisted. *We'd never buy a house. Never.*

Maybe she had changed her mind, Vincent decided, people changed their minds all the time. She must have done, because otherwise Milas wouldn't have talked about selling the family property. He would know, after all. He was their son, it had been his responsibility to settle matters after his parents' death. Vincent rolled over onto his back, closing his eyes and reopening them moments later, a doubt beginning to surface in his mind. Was Milas lying to him? And if so, why?

He had come to Vincent as his nephew and no one had doubted it. But there *were* areas of his life he avoided, patches that Vincent had not pressed him on, afraid of alienating him, of driving away this surrogate son. Had his guilt, his desire to make amends, welcomed a cuckoo into the nest? It was ridiculous to even think it, he told himself, Milas knew personal, intimate details about Denmark and Adela that only a son would know.

Vincent closed his mind against the thought.

He was paranoid because of the murders.

Suspecting everyone.

Milas was his flesh and blood.

There had been no reason to doubt it.

Until now.

-oO0o-

Punchy from jet lag, Leo slept most of the following day, finally coming downstairs at noon to find Vincent in his study, working at his desk, a mug of cold coffee on the window ledge beside him.

Hearing footsteps, he looked up. "How are you feeling?"

"Not bad," Leo replied, "but I don't sleep so well at the moment. Not since the murders started. I dream too much. In fact, I was just dreaming of Barend."

He trailed off, moving towards the window and looking out. The garden was downy with mist, Arthur Brooks directing some men who were felling a sycamore. A moment later a chainsaw started up, a scatter of birds making for the naked winter sky.

"Where's your nephew?"

Vincent was wondering the same. Apparently Milas had left the house earlier and hadn't returned. "He should be back any time."

Leo nodded, still looking out into the garden. "Are you having the trees cut down?"

"Just the ones closest to the house. I told you about someone breaking into the gallery. I didn't see a thing, so they probably used the trees as cover. Sox suggested I cut them down."

"The detective?"

Vincent nodded. "He fluctuates between suspecting me and protecting me... I've sent Charlotte to stay with her mother."

Leo was still staring at the gardeners outside. "Are you sure you don't mind me being here?"

"Of course I don't."

"I spoke to Ruby just now, she told me about the sculpture. The *Danaid*, the piece that started all this off!" He turned to Vincent, his expression incredulous. "Did you know she had it?"

"No," Vincent admitted "and it was a shock when I found out. I knew that Tyland had sold it on, but until the other day I had no idea who bought it."

"He never told me it was Ruby!"

"It wouldn't have occurred to him. He doesn't know Ruby had a connection to you –"

"Why Ruby?"

Vincent frowned, baffled. *"What?"*

"Why would Ruby buy it?" Leo asked. "Why her, of all people?"

"She collects art, always has done –"

"You never saw the *Danaid* in her London home?"

"If I had, don't you think I would have mentioned it?" Vincent replied, taking in a breath before he continued. "Apparently she's loaned out the piece to various galleries and then kept it in storage for a while –"

"But not now?"

"What are you're getting at?"

"Ruby had it locked away and now its back, on show, in her house." He stared at Vincent. *"Think about it!"*

"Think about what?"

"Why did she suddenly put it back on show?" Leo persisted. "Now, just after Jimmy Nicholson and Barend de Vries have been murdered by the girl we hired to recreate the *Danaid*!" His voice wavered. "It's not co-incidence, you must see that. It's all part of her plan. "

"Leo, it can't have been. How could she know what Ruby was going to do?"

"I DON'T KNOW! How could she do any of the things she's doing? She's just does them. She's tormenting us." His shoulders dropped, limp with fear. "Ruby said you asked her to look for something on the sculpture. What did you think you'd find?"

"I don't know. Something, anything that could give me a lead to the girl –"

"You were the one that hired her! Why don't you have a record?"

"It was over twenty years ago! Someone sent her along to sit for us. Who, I don't remember –"

"You don't remember! **You never remember anything!**" Leo snapped, getting to his feet and walking to the window. There he placed his palms flat on the glass, staring out. "What if she's watching us now?"

"Cut it out, Leo, the house is alarmed –"

"So was Jimmy Nicholson's, but that didn't stop her, did it? And she managed to walk into Barend's chambers without being stopped or even seen. How did she do that? She's not real. She's a demon --"

"*She's a woman!* You have to calm down, you're acting like a child." He could see Leo flinch. "I don't know what you want do, but I'm not sitting here waiting to be picked off. That's *not* going to happen. I'm going to find her."

Leo laughed softly. "Before she finds us?"

"She's *already* found us. She knows exactly who we are, and where we are."

"Oh Christ…" Leo leaned against the window frame, his great body slumped. "I keep rereading that last letter. What she said --"

"*Don't keep reading it!* Don't let it play on your mind, that's what she wants. We've got to keep our nerve --"

"I can't!"

"You can." Vincent told him. "You *have* to hold on, Leo --"

"For how long?"

"For as long as it takes to find her. The police are looking for witnesses, anyone who saw anything around the time of Barend's murder. There was a junior clerk working at the Chambers the night he was killed, but he left just before the attack. Which means that someone was watching, waiting for him to leave, waiting for the right moment. Either outside, or inside, the building."

He glanced over to Leo, could see the terrified expression in his eyes. It had been the right decision to get him over to London. If Leo had stayed in New York alone he would have had a breakdown, certainly he would have confessed to someone. Fear was crippling him, a big man shadow boxing his own terror.

"You're safe here."

"*How can you say that!*" Leo reacted, "you've just said she knows everything."

"She won't come after two of us. That would be too risky."

"You don't know that."

Vincent sighed. "No, I don't know for certain, but logic says --"

"*Logic!* Since when was there any logic in any of this?" Leo countered, his voice plummeting. "I spoke to a priest."

"Why?"

"I had to talk to someone!"

"About what? You didn't do anything that night."

"I didn't stop it!" Leo replied brokenly. "That's makes me just as guilty."

"No, it doesn't." Vincent moved to the door and looked out into the hall, making sure no one could overhear their conversation. "She blames me the most. You've seen the letter she wrote –"

"*It was Jimmy,* it was all his fault."

"Was it?" Vincent threw up his hands, exasperated. "I keep trying to remember what happened that night, but I can't, so much was going on. Nancy and I had an argument, I'd been fighting off an infection and taken antibiotics. I knew I shouldn't have been drinking --"

"So that's why you were so drunk?"

"Yes," Vincent agreed "but surely I should remember *something?*"

"It was a celebration, we were all preoccupied with the Rodin acquisition and the magazine article. A journalist had come and then a photographer and we posed for a group shot –"

Vincent stared at Leo hopefully: "Did they photograph the girl?"

"No, just the *Danaid.*" Leo replied, his voice dropping. "You don't remember her because it was a big night and she meant nothing to you. Why would you remember her name? You probably never knew it."

"I remember one thing. She left in a hurry and Jimmy was blustering around, red faced."

"He took her somewhere --"

"*Where?*"

"I don't know. Just that he took her into another room … I *knew* what he was going to do, I guessed, but I didn't stop him..." Leo pressed his palms against his closed eyes. "Barend and Tyland were arguing about politics, they always argued. It was freezing cold, coming up for Christmas --"

Vincent was staring at him. "How long was the girl with Jimmy on her own?"

"I don't know. Five minutes, ten at the most."

"You never told me this before."

Leo looked up, his eyes bloodshot. "I couldn't! What if they had just been talking, or going to get some more drinks? And besides, what did I *really* know? So I kept reassuring myself, telling myself that maybe nothing had happened... But when she came back she looked at me and I knew. *I knew.* And I still said nothing."

Another vague memory came back to Vincent. "Jimmy had wanted that sculpture so much, but then suddenly he said he hated it, said he didn't want it in his collection. Said the whole evening had been ruined."

The doorbell rang suddenly, Ellen Brooks's footsteps scurrying towards the sound. A muffle of voices were exchanged, then a tap on the study door.

"Dr Lund, there's a parcel for you."

Hurriedly he took it from her, waiting until she had returned to the kitchen before closing the study door. The parcel had his name and address clearly marked, hand delivered by a courier. Vincent laid it down on his desk and stared at it. He knew - without knowing how – that there was something in the package he dreaded. Something he would regret seeing and for an instant he was tempted to throw it away unopened. His hands reached out towards it, hesitated, then he ripped off the wrapping.

Inside was a cardboard box which had once held biscuits, Leo coming over to look as Vincent cut open the Sellotape which was wrapped around it. Then he lifted the lid, the daylight coming in and illuminating the object inside.

Forty One

As he lifted the garment out of the box, the long Oriental gown unravelled, its hem sinking slowly to the floor. His hands were shaking, the red dragons fluttering in the silk.

"Oh, God," Leo stared at it "it's the robe she was wearing that night."

There was no damage, no smudge of make up around the neckline. It was pristine. And terrifying. A moment passed, then Vincent moved to the door and called for Ellen.

She came out wiping her hands on a tea towel. "Yes, doctor?"

"Who came with this parcel?"

"A courier on a bike."

"Did you get the name of the company?"

"No."

"The delivery driver?"

"No, and I didn't get their inside leg measurement either," she said exasperated, shaking her head. "It was just handed to me."

"But I heard you talking."

"He just said, *'This is for Dr Lund. Is he home?'* and I said 'Yes, I'll give it to him.' That was it. Is there a problem?"

"Was it a man?"

"Wearing leathers with a helmet on his head?" She replied dryly. "Yes, I think I could safely say it was a man."

"But he didn't take his helmet off?"

"No, doctor."

"And it sounded like a man?"

"Yes, but it was muffled. It sounded like someone talking with their head inside a helmet. Which it was." She looked at him, suddenly anxious. "Are you alright?"

Without answering, Vincent moved back into the study. Leo was still staring at the Oriental robe, transfixed. He had wrapped his arms around his body, his great hands clutching at his torso. He didn't need to say what he was thinking: that the woman knew he had left New York and was staying with Vincent Lund. She had come – or sent someone – to deliver the parcel whilst they were both in the house, letting them know she was watching.

Vincent picked up the robe again, Leo flinching. "Shouldn't you leave it? It might be evidence."

"Of *what*?" He countered. "We're not handing it over to the police, are we?"

"I wish they'd cut down all the trees! There are still so many of them. So many places to hide. " Leo said, glancing out of the window. "You think someone was outside, watching?" He stepped back from the window. "D'you think she's watching now?"

"I don't know," Vincent replied, lifting up the robe to scrutinise it.

He ran his fingers along the seams, then down the front trimmings, and then finally he reached into the pocket. It was empty. Or was it? He felt again, his fingers rubbing against the lining and feeling something move.

He glanced over to Leo. "Go back upstairs and have a rest."

"I can't rest!" He said frantically. "Not when this has just happened. That was the robe we gave her to put on. She's kept it all this time. And now it's back here!"

"Leo, relax, please. I'll give you something to calm you."

"I just wish they'd cut down the trees."

Vincent could see the imminent signs of hysteria. "Listen to me, Leo --"

He was immediately interrupted. "If the trees were gone we could have seen more, Vincent. We could have seen *her* --"

"*Listen to me!* Go upstairs, I'll give you a sedative."

"She might still be out there --"

"Go upstairs!" Vincent snapped. "Let me handle this."

Nodding, Leo stumbled out of the room. Vincent waited until his footsteps had faded overhead, then took a pair of scissors and unpicked the pocket seam. He was a surgeon, dexterous with his hands, slowly drawing out a piece of paper hardly larger than a business card. Then he reached for his reading glasses and read:

18 Barlow Street
Oldham, Merseyside

An address. Simple, very easy to read, Vincent moving over to his laptop and entering it. It came up on Google Maps, an impoverished area, with terraced housing and alleyways, a pub called **The Nightingale** on the corner of Barlow Street. So it was real. He looked at the piece of paper again. It was obviously new, certainly not dating from the night which had changed everything.

So had the woman put it here? Hidden, but not that hidden. It made sense that she would send it to him. After all, it had belonged to Vincent, part of his collection that she had worn it at *his* house... So she had taken it that night, Vincent thought. He had often wondered about that, wondered where it had gone. He could imagine her rolling it up, the silk dragons crushed as she pushed the gown into her bag and left that rainy night. How often had she looked at it over the years? How far had it gone with her? Other towns? Other countries? Had it been hidden on top of a wardrobe, or shifted from bedsit to bedsit. He knew she had never worn it again; it would have been ugly to her. But she *had* kept it - and now she had sent it back to him.

The address was his summons, his call to arms.

The clock is ticking.

It's ticking.

Forty Two

Bray Gallery
London W1

Asking his secretary to make coffee, Tyland showed Detective Sox into his office at the back of the building. All the ephemera of the Bray gallery was either hung on the walls, or propped against them. Invitations from Private Views, catalogue covers and photographs of various dignitaries attending exhibition openings. Sox looked round, some of the published catalogues dated back forty years, the volumes arranged chronologically on dusted mahogany shelves, a photograph of Tyland Bray greeting the Prime Minister conspicuously visible on his desk.

"Terrible weather," Sox began, watching as the secretary poured their coffee and left. "Forecast says the rain is set in for the week."

Tyland's turtle eyes watched him: "Really?"

"Yes, the whole week. Mind you, it's mild for this time of year."

"You said you wanted to talk to me about something, detective. I'm rather busy, could we get on with it?"

Sox nodded pleasantly, but he was thinking that the dealer was an arrogant sod. "I believe you knew a Mr Clive Shawcross?"

"I hardly knew him. The man was a thief --"

"Yet you dropped the charge against him – the theft of a drawing from this very gallery, I believe."

Tyland didn't even blink. "Many years ago I was rather stupid, more trusting than I am these days. Shawcross spun me a sob story about his children and I felt story for the man so I dropped the charges."

"What was it?"

"What was *what?*"

"The story."

Sox studied the dealer, but he had to admit he was impressed. Bray wasn't showing the slightest sign of nerves.

"Apparently he had two children – both boys – and one needed medical treatment."

"He was ill?"

"That's usually when you need medical attention." Tyland replied, his tone chilling. "I can't remember any more about him. It was a long time ago."

"But your paths crossed later, didn't they? When you were called to give evidence at Clive Shawcross's forgery trail." Sox pretended to check his notes. "That's right, isn't it?"

"Yes, that's right. My expertise was called upon."

"Were you paid for your expertise?"

"No."

"Why not?" Sox countered. "Specialist witnesses are usually paid for their opinion."

He could see the turtle eyes blink. One, two, before Bray responded. "I have a feeling that you already know the answer to that, detective. Surely you've researched the trial? And if so, you would have discovered that Mr Shawcross was defended by the legal firm of *Oakley & Wyman* --"

"Which later became *De Vries, Oakley & Wyman*."

Tyland leaned back in his seat, looking down his nose at the little detective. "Exactly. I gave evidence as a favour to a friend, Barend de Vries."

"Ah, that explains a lot," Sox replied, glancing back to his notes. He pretended to read them, knowing Tyland was watching him, and then he frowned and looked up. "So you had nothing to do with the forgery case itself? You weren't dealing in fakes?"

"I beg your pardon!"

"You see, I've been given some information that you were trading in forgeries."

He waited, but whatever Tyland Bray was thinking it wasn't showing on his face. Instead he sipped his coffee, then put down the cup. His hands were steady.

"That's a very serious accusation, detective."

"Oh, I wasn't accusing you, Mr Bray, merely repeating something that I'd been told."

"May I ask who told you this nonsense?"

"It's confidential, sir. Sorry, I can't say."

Tyland smiled sardonically. "You must understand, detective, that there's a lot of competitiveness in the art world; people can be jealous, envious. Mischievous people spread rumours. Rumours that they can't prove."

"But if they *could* prove them, that would be different."

Still not a flicker in Tyland Bray's eyes, Sox noticed. So was he innocent? *Had* Stella Nicholson made up the whole story? Or was the dealer so well-rehearsed he could hide his emotions?

"So this person has proof, do they?"

Sox changed the subject, hoping it would throw Tyland off guard. "I suppose you'd have liked a son to inherit your gallery? I mean, like you inherited it from your father. Every man wants a son --"

"I don't understand what you're talking about."

" -- your children, or *lack* of children." Sox continued. "I don't want to pry, but sometime I have to ask difficult questions. Like now. You don't have children. Was that natural selection, or choice?"

Finally, Tyland Bray was rattled. "What the hell's that to do with you!"

"I was just wondering if that was why you were so concerned about Mr Shawcross's sons," Sox continued blithely. "Letting Shawcross off like that was very generous. There's not many men who'd be that understanding. Did you ever meet the sick boy?"

"No."

"But I imagine Mr Shawcross, after what you did for him, let you know how the lad got on. Whether he recovered, or not."

The dealer hesitated, Sox saw it and pushed on. "Did Mr Shawcross never get back in touch? Not even to say thank you?"

"I never saw him again."

"Oh, my apologies, Mr Bray. I think, like you say, someone's been spreading rumours. Trying to discredit you. Stir up trouble. I mean, you're a very important man, with a pristine reputation and, if I hear correctly, the chance of a post in Government. Hardly someone who'd risk their good name dealing with criminals or getting involved in forgery. Besides, Mr Shawcross never mentioned you at his trial..." The dealer was staring at him, breathing a little faster as Sox continued. "… which he would have done if you *had* been involved."

"I have no doubt that you know exactly what was said at the trial."

Sox nodded. "Yes, I do. But my informant was talking about a motive for the murders of your friends and I just wondered if – sounds silly, I know – but if there was any bad feeling from the past? If Shawcross or maybe his offspring were trying to settle an old score with you. This rumour I was told – forgive me, it's embarrassing to even repeat it – was that you'd involved your *friends* in the crime and that Shawcross's wife committed suicide after her husband was jailed. And that's why he had a grudge against all of you." Sox tilted his head to one side. "Which would make sense, in a way. I mean, here we have five powerful men who are all prominent in their fields, five men with a lot to lose, and suddenly up comes someone from the past who wants to destroy them."

"It's absurd!"

"Then naturally the five of you *would* band together, not wanting to reveal what was going on, even to the police – and in that way you'd keep your secret. And protect yourselves."

"Well, *if* we did such a thing, we failed. Two of us are already dead." Tyland sneered. "You can't be taking a rumour seriously."

"Even if it connects all five of you?"

"Who said that? I've not been threatened, and to my knowledge neither has Dr Lund or Leo Parks." The dealer paused, his confidence returning full force. "The only person who could verify this rumour is Clive Shawcross."

"And we can't find a trace of Mr Shawcross. He seems to have disappeared after he came out of jail."

Tyland breathed in. It was barely perceptible, but Sox caught it, impressed by the speed at which the dealer was recovering.

"There's no truth in any of it, detective. It's a rumour, an unfounded rumour, no more. The whole story is nothing but slander, lies, and you have no evidence to prove otherwise."

Sox stood up, glancing round the office. "Fascinating, the art world. All this beauty and money, all this rivalry and jealousy - and we *do* have these nasty murders, Mr Bray. We do have those. And we *do* have a motive."

"But no proof. And no Clive Shawcross."

"No, Mr Shawcross has disappeared." Sox agreed, walking to the door and then pausing. "Lucky we found one of his sons... I'll be touch."

It was a bluff.

But Tyland Bray didn't know that.

Forty Three

"Where have you been?" Vincent asked as Milas came home just after noon.

He was whistling under his breath and smiled. "I went out walking."

"All night?"

"No, I went out really early this morning and walked around Richmond. So many dog walkers in the park, you should get a dog, Vincent. I'd walk it for you." He was cheerful, putting down the holdall he was carrying and taking out some papers. "I finished that research sat on a bench. It was peaceful, quiet." He passed his uncle the notes he had made. "It was pretty cold though, but nothing compared to Denmark in the winter."

Vincent took the papers from him, uncertain how to approach the question which had plagued him all night. "Did you never think to keep hold of your parents' house?"

"Why?" Milas asked, "I had no need of a family house. Better to sell it. Anyway by the time I'd paid off the mortgage and the bills my father had left behind there wasn't much remaining. Why d'you ask?"

"I was just wondering. You know, family home, sometimes offspring like to keep hold of it."

"Maybe married offspring with kids, but not me." Milas replied, still busy shifting through the papers. He was unusually high spirited, Vincent edgy.

"Was it difficult? Coming off the drugs, I mean?"

Pausing, Milas stared down at the papers. Then he straightened up, his tone cool. "I wasn't lying when I said I'd given them up. Not touched anything for five years. If you're worried about Charlotte, you don't have to be, I'd never hurt her or involve her in anything --"

"I never said you would."

"No, but you're wondering," Milas replied, on the defensive. "I don't blame you, addicts aren't the most responsible people, are they? But it's over, that part of my life is done with. I was stupid, and I wasted a lot of money and even more time - but I learnt my lesson. Never again, you have my word on that. I'm clean, Vincent, and I'm staying that way."

"How did you get hold of the drugs?"

"In the same way you'd get drugs in London, it's not difficult." He stared at his uncle, then shook his head. "I wasn't looking for drugs today! I was walking, that was all…."

"I wasn't suggesting --"

"… and I wouldn't lie to you! I respect you too much for that."

But Vincent was uncertain. A doubt had formed in his mind and was niggling at him. "Did your family always live in the house where you were born?"

"Yes, we never moved."

"I remember that house well. Adela liked it."

"Not that much, my mother wanted to move, talked about it now and again, but we never did."

"Like you say, they had to pay off the mortgage."

"They should never have bought it."

A flicker of hope.

"So they didn't always own it?"

"No, my mother used to argue with my father about that" Milas replied, his voice assuming a woman's higher tone *"'Why did you buy it if you couldn't afford the upkeep and the mortgage? Why didn't we keep renting? We could have managed the rent without struggling...'* It was always a bone of contention between them." Milas paused, "What is it?"

Vincent felt the relief flood through him, along with guilt. What was happening to him that he could seriously doubt his own nephew? Of course Milas hadn't been lying! What would have been the point?

"Are you OK, Vincent?"

"It's nothing, I had a bad night." He replied, "they've been many of those lately."

But as he said the words he could feel a tension between them that had not been there before, his nephew the first to speak.

"I saw Tilly de Vries on my way home, she's always walking their dog. Courting attention." Milas went on. "Strange girl, she seems to be enjoying the interest she's getting because of her step father's murder."

"You don't like her?"

"Not as much as you once liked her mother," Milas said, smiling. "Hey, your affair's got nothing to do with me, it was Tilly who mentioned it. Were you very fond of Alicia de Vries?"

"She was fascinating. But then again, a lot of men find her fascinating." Vincent replied carefully. "It's over, if you're wondering. We're still friends, but not involved."

Milas nodded, his gaze falling on the cardboard box. "What's that?"

"Nothing important."

But Milas had already flipped open the lid and was looking at the Oriental robe inside. "You bought something else at auction apart from '*The Bearded Woman*'?"

The lie was automatic. "I couldn't resist it."

"I didn't know you were still collecting Oriental things. I thought that was more in Leo Parks' line."

"Who told you that?"

"You did, Vincent." He said, frowning. "God, you're jumpy, you *must* have had a bad night. Are you going out today?"

"Actually I'm going up North. I've got to see a colleague about some research and I'll probably stay over."

"You think that's wise?"

"You think I'm going to be murdered in Manchester?"

The joke fell flat, Milas anxious. "You want some company?"

"No, thanks. It's a long trip and I'd rather just get there and come back quickly." Vincent replied, watching as Milas touched the Oriental robe, his fingers lingering over the silk as something came into his mind and he spoke without thinking. "Could you put that in the gallery for me?"

"Sure."

And then Vincent wondered how his nephew could get into the gallery. Had he been there before?

As though he read his mind, Milas put out his hand. "I need the key."

"Yes, yes, of course you do," Vincent stammered, taking the gallery key off the main ring and handing it to him. "Don't forget to lock up when you leave."

Forty Four

Ashamed of his outburst, Leo avoided Vincent and the following day visited the Bray gallery alone. He hurried in from the cold and walked disconsolately around the new exhibition of early Dutch paintings, feeling out of control, unnerved. Vincent wouldn't talk about the package he had been sent, refused to discuss the damned Oriental robe, and had left for the North on a hurried trip. A trip to see a medical colleague, he said, but Leo wasn't convinced. Nervous, suspicious and unwilling to be alone in the Richmond house, Leo had just arrived at Tyland's gallery when, to his surprise, Sox walked out of the dealer's private office.

"Mr Parks, isn't it?" The detective greeted him. "That's the beauty of talking to people on Zoom, you can always put a face to the name. Not like the old days over the phone." He shook Leo's hand vigorously. "Are you here on business?"

Uncertain, Leo nodded. "Yeah, I came about the Ribera painting."

"You were pipped to the post though, weren't you? Dr Lund bought it. Pity, seems like rather a wasted journey for you."

"Not really, I'm staying with Vincent for a while."

"Oh," Sox managed to imply a lot with the one syllable. "For how long?"

"Not sure."

"I thought you only came over once a month," Sox continued, Tyland standing in the doorway behind him and beckoning for Leo to approach. Unconcerned, Sox kept talking: "I'm sorry about your friends, Mr Parks, it must be hard to come to England under such circumstances."

"Yeah" Leo said uncertainly. "it's hard…."

Tyland was still gesturing.

"… losing friends is difficult."

"Especially in these circumstances." Sox said, his tone sympathetic. "Death is always hard, but murder – that's another thing altogether. It's lucky I bumped into you, Mr Parks, I wanted to have a chat."

Tyland rolled his eyes behind the detective, Leo trying to get away. "Shall I call you, detective?"

"Oh, don't worry about that, I'll pop by Dr Lund's house later. Will you be there?"

"Well, I'm not sure --"

"See you around five then." Sox said happily, walking off.

In silence, the two men watched the detective leave, then Tyland gripped Leo's arm and steered him into the office, slamming the door shut behind them.

"What the hell are you doing here?"

"I just thought I'd call by --"

"You certainly picked your moment," Tyland replied, "that bloody detective has been here for the last hour, regaling me with Stella Nicholson's version of events. Did Vincent tell you what she'd done?"

"Yeah… but it's not bad for us, it is?"

"What?"

Leo's tone was plaintive. "I mean, it gives the police a motive and takes their attention off the woman. Anyway, they can't prove anything about the forging."

"Maybe they can. Sox has found Clive Shawcross's son."

"Oh, Jesus…"

His hand reaching for a chair, Leo sat down, breathing through his mouth. His mind was fizzing, thoughts coming and going without order, confusion making a maze out of logic. He felt a desire to run, to leave London. It had been a mistake, if he had stayed at home he would have been safe. He had to get back. Back to New York.

"We can't flap about this," Tyland said, interrupting his thoughts. "Shawcross's son might not know anything. It could have even been a bluff. Sox was just trying to unnerve me."

"But what if it's true? What if he *can* expose you? All of us?"

"*He can't!*" Tyland snapped. "If he'd known anything he would have come forward before now. I don't believe that little runt Sox, I think it *is* a bluff."

"We should have gone to the police at the start," Leo said brokenly. "I said that all along –"

"And tell them the truth? Good thinking, Leo. Let's confess about the girl. Why not? We don't have anything to lose, do we? Only our bloody reputations!" He snapped. "Let Sox believe the forgery story."

"It was true --"

"But he can't prove it!" Tyland countered, thinking back. "There's no evidence that I was involved. No proof that you were, or any of the others. If Shawcross's son says anything I'll deny it. Say it was just malicious revenge for what happened to his mother."

"But what … what if it *is* the son coming after us?"

"The killer is female!" Tyland shouted and leaned towards Leo. "Think clearly, and stop panicking. If the police think it was Shawcross junior, that's good for us and it will take them further away from the real killer. Remember, only we know it's a *woman*." Tyland relaxed and changed the subject. "Where's Vincent?"

"He's gone up North."

"Up North? What for?" He stared into Leo's face. "What's happening?"

"I don't know.""

"You're a bloody awful liar. Something's happened, what is it?"

"The robe… the Oriental robe the girl was wearing that night. It was sent back to Vincent."

"So she *did* take it." Tyland rubbed his arm thoughtfully. "And she kept it. Which means that she must have been planning all this for a long time."

"I want to go back home --"

"*Shut up, Leo!*" Tyland snapped, "You're in this up to your neck and you're not going to lose your nerve now. Before you start pitying that girl, remember this – she killed Jimmy and Barend. She murdered them. Whatever happened that night is *nothing* compared to what she did to them."

Rebuked, Leo left the gallery and walked down Dover Street. His reflection looked back at him from the shop and gallery windows as he passed, a tall black man, his coat stained by rain. He had some notion of going to the Royal Academy but dismissed it, heading across the road towards St James Church. There was a choir practice going on, the rain hardly audible over the melting chords as Leo took a seat on one of the pews at the back. Cold, he hunkered down into his coat, and turned up the collar against the draft coming from under the heavy wooden doors. His mind, restless and unquiet, forced him to his knees, his head pressed against the wooden pew in front. Prayers – known and repeated for years – stuck to the roof of his mouth, his lips forgetting the habit of decades. He thought of the priest he had seen, of the confession he had made, of the promise of forgiveness, and felt no relief.

He wondered how he would die. If it would be slow and drawn out, or bloody. If he would feel the poison burn through his belly or the knife blade entering his throat or his eye. If he would have time to try and defend himself, attempt some kind of resistance. But most of all he wondered if he would have time to look into her face and see her, recognise her from that night. If she would still be the same girl with red hair, and if, just *if*, she would give him time to beg her forgiveness.

He admired Tyland Bray's defiance and was impressed by Vincent's determination to find the woman. He even suspected that his sudden trip was connected. To have a determined focus enabled a man to live and seek purpose in his life. But Leo had no such purpose. He felt like a fraud; as much a fake as one of Tyland Bray's forgeries. He was tired, exhausted by his own mind, his own guilt, and wanted nothing but silence.

Leo stared ahead at the altar, the candles burning, a crucifix suspended above, and wondered at his own hypocrisy, how any of his pleading could create even a dent in his sin. Minutes passed, his hands now gripping the wooden pew, his eyes closed as the choir practice ended, the choristers leaving en masse. The glass stained windows threw only a little light from the darkening day outside, the rain making its own pattern against the muted panes.

Finally he raised his head and glanced across the church. He saw a couple sitting together and felt a shift of longing, for companionship, for someone who could soothe him. For someone who could quieten his incessant guilt, the sickening anguish inside his body. Then yards before him, in another pew, he noticed a figure sitting alone, a woman staring ahead. She did not move, or turn around. She just sat immobile, her body erect, her whole attention focused on the altar before her.

Fear came like a blessing to him; a cessation of despair, an absolution offered. But despite him willing her to turn she did not move, and as the rain continued to fall outside he waited. And he knew her for who she was.

Forty Five

Stella was reading as the housekeeper showed Marina into the breakfast room.

"Hello," she said, without any trace of a welcome, "it's good to see you."

"And it's nice to see you…" Marina replied uneasily, as she hovered about the chair facing Stella, then sat down, perched on the edge as though she didn't belong there and was ready to run. "How are you?"

"As you see, almost back to myself."

"The doctors are pleased with your progress?"

"I would hardly have been allowed home if they weren't." Stella continued imperiously. "Apparently the shock of Jimmy's death had more of an effect that I thought. But luckily it was only a minor stroke, nothing to worry about. I should be completely recovered in another couple of weeks."

Marina nodded, holding the flowers she had bought with her. She glanced around for a vase, but, seeing none, didn't dare to ask. Instead she unbuttoned her coat and smiled nervously. "We are all very worried about you."

"All?"

"Me, Tyland and Alicia --"

307

"Hah!"

" – she *was* worried."

"Guilty conscience," Stella said shortly. "Probably thought she'd have my death on her conscience if I didn't recover."

"Oh, Stella, don't say that!"

"You don't like Alicia de Vries any more than I do, why are you defending her?"

"You've both suffered, lost your husbands. Alicia's changed a lot."

"That can only be an improvement," Stella replied, laying down her crossword and taking off her glasses. "I suppose she's sniffing around Vincent Lund, trying to get back with him? Lost cause, he's not that big a fool. At least no one else has been murdered since I've been in hospital."

"Oh, Stella..." Marina said, shocked. "You say the most terrible things."

"Come on, my dear, it's just my way. Besides, I know you're worried about Tyland. Wondering if he's going to be next."

"Why would anyone come after Tyland? He's not done anything wrong."

Stella leaned towards her. "Not that we know of." She let the implication hang in the air between them. "But let's face it, Marina, how well do we know our husbands? I thought I knew Jimmy, but apparently he had even more secrets than I thought. Tyland must have secrets too. Think about it, you've been married to him for over twenty years – but *before* you met? Don't you wonder what he was doing then? Who he was seeing then?"

Marina *did* wonder about that and was surprised how easily Stella had picked into her thoughts, unravelling them like oakum. "Tyland is a good man --"

"Bad tempered, patronising and domineering, my dear. But if you say he's a good man, I'll take your word for it. Sadly I don't see him like that, he's always belittled you and you've allowed it." She paused, shrugging. "You let everyone bully you. Strange, you weren't like that when I first met you. Quite the rebel then."

"People change."

"Because other people change them."

Marina could tell that Stella was in an argumentative mood and was sorry she came. In fact, she was wondering how soon she could leave, when Stella sighed and smiled at her.

"Forgive me, I'm being horrible. Circumstances change all of us. And in my case not for the better. I can't quite work out if its bitterness or shock at the jolt my life has undergone. Everything is so untidy now." She put her glasses back on. "I never thought I'd miss Jimmy, but I do. I didn't care for him overmuch, but I was used to him around. I suppose if I had family it would help."

"What about your son?" Marina asked, immediately regretting the question as she saw Stella stiffen.

"Dominic? Oh, I don't want to see him. Too much unpleasantness in the past. It's no good picking at old wounds. Besides, he didn't even come to his father's funeral – what kind of son is that?" Her tone was brusque but Marina could feel the wound underneath. "I'm afraid Jimmy was right about Dominic, he didn't turn out the way I expected. I can only hope he treats his own family better."

"I didn't know he had children."

"A son." Stella said crisply.

"So you're a grandmother?"

"In name only." Stella replied, changing tack. "I know how much you wanted children, Marina, but, believe me, you didn't miss much."

"Tyland said --"

"Ah, Tyland. He makes all the decisions, doesn't he?" She interrupted, almost sympathetically. "I pity you, Marina. I mean, aside from Tyland, you have no family."

"Apart from my sister."

She could sense the shock as it registered in Stella. "*A sister?* You never mentioned her before."

No, she hadn't, because Rachel had been a secret. Cordoned off, Tyland forbidding all reference to her, only once confiding in Vincent. But lately Marina had begun to wonder about her sister. She had even considered – although she could hardly bear the thought – that if anything happened to Tyland she would get back in touch.

They had been close once, decades earlier: Rachel pretty, mercurial, unstable. Needing psychiatric treatment for schizophrenia – with all the shame that dreaded diagnosis had instilled in their late parents. For several years Rachel had been in and out of institutions, her condition stabilised with medication, her see-saw temperament temporarily steadied. But only for so long; then she would neglect herself, stop her medication and disappear back into the stew of London. Only to re-emerge, disorientated, begging for help.

Time grabbed Rachel by the scruff of her neck and shook off her beauty. Her charm petered out and the medication dampened her clever mind. At times she railed against it, at other times she was subdued, defeated. Then she met someone and the last Marina heard of her sister was that she was moving to Holland to marry. There had been only a listless connection after that, a few Christmas cards and a garbled telephone message a year earlier asking for money. Marina had assured her sister she would send funds, but Rachel never sent her an address or bank details. After that, nothing.

Stella's voice persisted, curious. "*Why* did you never say anything about having a sister?"

"Tyland thought it was for the best....He didn't like Rachel and we grew apart. I haven't seen her for years. She lives abroad." Marina blustered on. "Well, she moved to the Netherlands and married, but I don't know if she's still there." Uneasy, Marina picked at the stems of the flowers, Stella watching her. "I should get some water for these, and a vase."

"It's ridiculous how many families break up," Stella said shortly. "Why do we have siblings? Why bother to marry and have children? Look how I've ended up. Alone, like so many women. A widow."

"But *I'm* not a widow."

"Not yet," Stella replied, callously. "I don't suppose Tyland has confided in you?"

"No, he doesn't want to worry me, says my nerves wouldn't be up to it." Her voice dropped. "But I *should* know what's going on --"

"There's a man for you." Stella replied crisply. "Why bother talking when you can sulk?"

"He's not eating properly or sleeping because he's so worried --"

"And you aren't?" Stella countered. She was getting agitated, Marina could see the spots of colour rising on her cheeks.

"Don't get upset. Please, it's not good for you."

"Shouldn't I be saying that to you? I mean, my husband's dead, you're still waiting for Tyland to –"

"Stop it!" Marina said heatedly, "you talk about it as though it's bound to happen."

"Perhaps it is. And perhaps you should press Tyland into giving you reassurance. It's the least he can do. I would insist that he talks to you. Your husband must have some thoughts about his friends' deaths." Her voice had a guilty tone to it, a slyness that Marina hadn't expected.

"I've told you, Tyland won't confide. And I keep thinking... I keep thinking that he *could* be next. I mean, the five of them were all friends." She began, very softly, to cry. "You don't know anything, do you?"

Stella looked shocked. *"Me?* No."

"I overheard part of a phone call. I wasn't eavesdropping - it was just that I had to listen - I *have* to find out what I can."

"What did you hear?"

"Tyland was talking to Detective Sox and he mentioned something about an old court case where he was giving evidence... It meant nothing to me then, but now I'm wondering ... I'm just wondering if Jimmy had ever mentioned it to you? That's why I asked you if you knew anything."

"No," Stella replied, her expression guileless. "I'm as much in the dark as you are."

"I'm so scared." Marina said, her voice barely audible. "If anything happened to Tyland, I don't know how I'd cope. I *couldn't* cope." Her eyelids were beginning to swell, tears diluting the blue pupils. "You *would* tell me if you knew anything, wouldn't you? You'd help me, wouldn't you?"

"I know nothing or I'd warn you, my dear." Stella tapped the back of the other woman's hand. "After all, that's what friends are for."

-oOo-

When Marina returned home she was surprised to find Tyland's car outside and for a moment was tempted to walk on. But just as she thought it a journalist approached her on the road, asking for a statement about the murders. Startled, Marina managed to stammer 'no comment' and hurried into the house. As she entered she tripped over the mat, one shoe coming off as she scrambled to pick it up.

Tyland was waiting at the study door, watching her. "Where have you been?"

"I went to see Stella," Marina replied, embarrassed as she pulled her shoe back on. "She's much better."

"Pity." Tyland said and moved away.

Marina ran after him. "I went to talk to her about what's going on... *Tyland*," she said plaintively, "please, we have to talk."

He spun round: "Since when does Stella Nicholson tell you what to do? Since when do you take advice from her?"

"She didn't... I don't... she just --"

"Just *what?* Just what did she suggest, Marina?" He towered over her, a tailoured scarecrow in a three piece suit. "Do you realise what's at stake here? My post as Minister of Arts. Do you really want to jeopardise everything I've worked for all these years? I always thought you were a loyal wife --"

"Tyland" she said desperately, "I *am* loyal, I didn't tell Stella anything. I couldn't tell her anything. How could I? I don't *know* anything." She put her hands over her face, sobbing quietly. "I just don't want anything to happen to you."

"Why is everything about you? You think *I* want something to happen?"

"No, of course not," she replied, her voice muffled "but if you've got any idea about --"

"Oh, I see," he countered, cutting her off. "You're implying that these murders are somehow *my* fault."

Marina's hands dropped from her face, her voice desperate. "No! I didn't say that!"

"You implied it."

"But I didn't *mean* anything like that! It's just that I don't understand. People are talking about the murders, that the victims were your friends, and the neighbours keep asking me --"

"Neighbours, hah!"

" – if you've been threatened. And now there are journalists --"

"*Journalists!*" He grabbed her arm. "You haven't been talking to journalists, have you?"

"No!"

"You mustn't say a word, Marina. You don't know how to deal with those types. You know how you struggle to communicate with people." His grip loosened, his tone softening. "Let me handle this, my dear."

"I *want* you to handle it, Tyland, I really do...." She said helplessly. "But if I just knew more about what was going on. Just a little bit, it would be easier for me. I worry so much about you. Are you in danger?"

"You need to calm down, Marina, you really do. I can't cope with a hysterical wife at the moment, not with everything else going on." His voice hardened again. "I think you should consider your loyalties and decide where they lie. No loving wife would be running off discussing personal matters with the likes of Stella Nicholson --"

"*How could you say that, Tyland!*" Maria wailed. "I've never done anything to betray your trust, or shame you --"

"*And I have?* I've been a loyal, faithful husband, Marina, perhaps you should remember that when you're so busy criticising me. I worry about you, I honesty do. You're losing your senses, I don't know what to say to you anymore --"

"Tyland, *don't.*"

" -- perhaps you should talk to someone professional, these outbursts of yours are getting worse. When I see you like this, I remember your sister."

Stunned, Marina stopped crying and stared at her husband. *"What?"*

"Rachel was unbalanced, perhaps it runs in your family." He paused, taking aim. "I've never said this before because I didn't want to hurt you, Marina, but why do you think I didn't want us to have children?"

Stunned, she watched him turn away and then leave the house, her head humming with the words

… Why do you think I didn't want us to have children?…

But **I** wanted children, she thought, I longed for them. And you said you didn't want children; that we would be enough together. That we didn't need children to be happy. But **I** did. And all the time you were lying. You cheated me, and I let you. You stole a future from me, and I let you. You bullied and bellowed your rules at me, until every one of my wishes was subjugated. *And I let you.*

Slowly, in shock, she climbed the stairs. His words repeated endlessly in her head as she walked into the bathroom.

... Why do you think I didn't want us to have children?...

Turning on the bath taps, Marina walked to the cabinet and took out her sleeping pills, swallowing a handful with some water. Then, still fully dressed, she climbed into the tub and waited until the bath filled. It took a few minutes, the drug slowly taking effect. Nauseous and drowsy, Marina's eyes closed, her head lolling to one side. Finally, when the bath was deep enough, she slid under the water, her eyes half open, bubbles coming from between her lips.

Forty Six

One of the vergers had lighted the incense in the burner, then hoisted the chain so that it rose ten feet above the church pews. The hazy scent trickled downwards to where Leo was sitting, his gaze fixed on the seated woman ahead of him. He had stopped praying, no incantations left, no novenas nor supplications, only the sickly odour of the incense and the thumping of the mindless rain.

She was only a shape to him, her head covered, her shoulders rigid in a dark coat. He braced himself for her movement, for the rush towards him, but it didn't come. Instead the incense continued to burn and the rain continued to fall. He waited, she waited. After another few minutes the other congregants left, the door creaking on its hinges as it closed behind them. Slowly, Leo looked around, but the verger had gone and there was still no movement from the solitary worshipper.

But she wasn't worshipping, was she? Leo knew that, knew in the pit of his gut that she had not even a nodding acquaintance with God. She did not need His approval. She had no god and her congregation consisted of only five. Two of whom were already in some other existence, facing their own deity. He thought for a moment to call out, but hesitated, closing his eyes against the figure in front of him.

The minutes dug their fingers into the time, dragged the clock hands round until an hour had passed and Leo was still waiting. Finally he saw her move, rise to her feet and genuflect as she left the pew. The light was so dim he couldn't make out her face and it was only as she drew level with him that Leo could see her clearly.

Confused, he stared at the woman, then realised she was old, well into her eighties. Too old. He had been waiting for the wrong woman. She stared back at him, bemused, tipped her head slightly, then passed. He heard the creaking door open, a moment of traffic noise, then it closed, and the church was empty and silent again... Unmoving, Leo stared ahead, the incense drifting down, the rain a tom tom on the church roof, and the crucifix with its watching Christ standing guard over him. It was then that Leo realised he longed to die; the sheer effort of living too much when all hope had gone.

He wanted the end.

And it came to him, the blow landing at the back of his head, splitting the great skull and sending him forwards, his knees buckling into his last and final prayer.

Forty Seven

With his head bowed down against the sharp wind, Detective Sox moved up the steps towards Vincent's front door and turned. Curious, Arthur Brooks watched him, standing in amongst the trimmed bushes and cut trees, a chain saw on the grass at his feet.

Hearing the bell ring, Ellen answered the door and let the detective in. "Dr Lund's away."

"And I can't seem to get him on his mobile."

Ellen's eyebrows rose. "Really? That's odd, I called him about an hour ago. Anything I can do for you?"

"Do you know where he's gone?"

"Up North."

"Where up North?"

"The doctor doesn't tell me his plans."

"Is he on business?"

"Like I say, I don't keep the doctor's diary. When he gets back I'll let him know you called. Mr Parks isn't here either. He left earlier." She paused, caught the look on the detective's face. "What's the matter?"

"I'm very sorry to tell you that Mr Parks has died --"

"What!" Ellen stared at him. *"*He was here only a few hours ago. He can't be dead."

"I'm afraid he is --"

Her voice faltered. "Was he murdered?"

"Yes," Sox nodded. "Yes, sadly he was."

"Then why aren't you doing something about it!" She snapped. "I know these men. I knew all of Dr Lund's friends, and how many have been killed now? *Three*!" Her voice rose. "Dear God, you don't need a bloody map to show what direction this is going in." She called for her husband across the garden, Arthur hurrying over.

"What's up?"

"Mr Parks has been killed, and no one can get Dr Lund on his mobile,"

"The connection was fine when I was talking to him. I spoke to him a couple of hours ago about the trees --"

"I spoke to him too" She replied then turned back to the detective, "but apparently the police can't reach him."

"Maybe he's just out of range --"

"**Maybe he's dead!**" She snapped back, Sox flinching. "For all the good you lot have been, he might well be."

Embarrassed, Sox persisted. "You've no idea where Dr Lund went up North?"

"No, and stop asking me that! He didn't tell me. And for the record I've told you – and my husband's told you - *everything* we know about Dr Lund and his friends. You've asked us repeatedly and we've answered repeatedly, but it's done no good, has it? And now you're telling me that you lost touch with the doctor." She was flushed, shaken. "You should have given him police protection --"

"Dr Lund told me he had received no direct threats."

"*Three of his friends have been killed!* How direct do you need it?" She snapped. "Where was Mr Parks killed?"

"St James Church in Piccadilly."

"In a church..." She mused. "How was he killed?"

"I can't disclose that --"

"Look, detective, I've got an unmade bed upstairs that the American was lying in only hours ago. I've got his clothes to sort out and his books to send on, and I've got to deal with Dr Lund coming back to hear that *another* of his friends has been killed. So don't give me half a bloody story --"

"Leo Parks was bludgeoned to death."

She flinched, took in a breath. "Someone *must* have seen the killer leaving the church. You can't murder a person that way without being messed up. They'd be covered in blood."

She was right; no one *could* have killed Leo Parks without being splattered with blood and brain matter. The scene at the church had been a slaughter house, the smell of blood overwhelming, traces spraying the pews and the aisle. And yet the killer had taken care not to step in the blood, anxious to leave no trace of themselves, Sox suspecting that when they tested for fingerprints there would be none. The murderer was certain to have been wearing gloves. And as with the other killings, when they checked for DNA and hair samples – should they find any - they would fit no one on police files.

They only matched the person who had come off the busy thoroughfare of Piccadilly, bludgeoned a man to death, smashed his skull into a pulp and then walked back into the crowds.

Unseen, unnoticed. Unknown.

-oOo-

The Bray House

Relieved to see Tyland's car pass by her on the road, Alicia walked towards the front steps, surprised to find the front door open. Marina was always cautious, especially now.

Anxious, she called out: "Marina?"

No reply.

"Marina? Are you here?"

She moved further into the hallway. The cleaner would have left at lunch time, but Marina was always around in the afternoons. Besides, if she had gone out she would have locked the front door and taken her handbag. The handbag that was lying on the hall table. Anxious, Alicia moved to the bottom of the stairs, her left hand on the banister rail as she called up.

"Marina, it's Alicia, are you up there?"

The continued silence prompted her to move fast, taking the stairs two at a time and then running towards the master bedroom. It was empty. Unnerved, she then hurried towards the dressing room, again empty. Some instinct directed her, forcing her to retrace her steps back into the bedroom and into the bathroom beyond.

"Oh, shit!" She screamed, bending over the bathtub, trying to lift Marina out of the water. But she was heavy, Alicia straining and then finally losing her foot-

ing on the floor and falling backwards, dragging Marina out of the bath to land alongside her on the floor.

"Marina!" she shouted, slapping her face. "Breathe, for God's Sake, *breathe!*"

Frantically she began CPR, repeatedly pausing to see if Marina would revive.

"Come on! Don't give up! **Jesus, Marina, come on!**"

For over three minutes Alicia de Vries tried to resuscitate Marina Bray, waiting for the gasp of breath, for the lifting of the chest. But it didn't happen. Instead Marina lay on the bathroom floor, on the unforgiving marble, her eyes closed, her lips parted.

Crying, Alicia railed at her.

"**You stupid bitch!**" She shouted, "You stupid, stupid, bitch! Why did you do it? *Why?*" Distraught, Alicia pushed the body with her foot, punched the chest, then gently wiped the wet hair away from Marina's forehead.

And in that instance, she coughed.

Alicia jumped.

Marina coughed a second time, gagging and rolling over onto her side, water coming from her mouth, her lungs finally taking in air.

Forty Eight

18, Barlow Street,
Oldham, Merseyside.

Vincent drew up at the corner and parked. It was a terraced street, each house butting against its neighbour, many of them boarded up, the brick walls covered in graffiti on the ground floors. Surprised to find that he still couldn't get a signal, Vincent put his mobile back in his pocket and walked towards No 18. He was aware that two men were watching him and nodded as though to imply he was no threat, but they didn't respond. The rain that had marked his journey had faded when darkness fell, but the winter cold was building, vapour coming from Vincent's lips as he walked.

No 18 was not boarded up and he knocked. Then knocked again. Finally an old man answered. He was wearing a cardigan with cigarette burns down the front, his voice querulous.

"Who's there?"

"Can I come in?"

"Bugger off!"

Vincent moved closer so that the old man could see his face illuminated from the street lamp inside. "It's very important that I speak to you. I've come a long way. My name's --" The door began to close, Vincent putting his hand around it and holding it open. "Please, hear me out. My name's Dr Lund --"

"I don't need a doctor! I told that bloody nurse that I didn't need a doctor."

"A nurse didn't send me, I just want to talk to you."

"Ah, that what they all say, then they get in and start going on about putting me in a home. Well, you can bugger off! *This* is my home."

Determined, Vincent pushed the door open and walked in. "I'm sorry, but I *have* to talk to you."

The old man stepped back and wiped his nose with the back of his hand. "It'll cost you."

"Fine. How much?"

"How much you got?"

"I don't know if you've got the information I want yet."

He coughed again and walked into the kitchen, Vincent following. There was a wooden rack in front of a coal fire, the clothes steaming, condensation running down the windows. Jerking his head to indicate that Vincent should sit down, the old man took out his cigarettes.

"Want one?"

"No, thanks."

He shrugged, lighting it slowly, then shaking the match to put out the flame. On his feet he was wearing tartan slippers that zipped up at the front over a pair of socks printed with the Union Jack.

"So what d'you want to know?"

"It's about a girl."

"I thought it might be. You coming all this way in your big car and your expensive clothes, I thought it'd be about a girl."

"It's not like that." Vincent replied, "it's about something that happened a long time ago. Over twenty years. How long have you lived here?"

"Forty one years."

"Alone?"

"Nah, I were married for forty of those. My wife died last year." He inhaled deeply, nicotined fingers wrapped tight around the cigarette stub.

"Did you... *do* you have a daughter?"

"Why would you want to know that?"

Vincent was patient. "It's important that you answer. Please tell me – do you have a daughter?"

"No, two sons. And both of them in Liverpool now." The old man spat into the fire, the spittle making a hissing sound when it landed on the hot coals. "Never had a girl. My wife wanted a girl, but we got boys... Is that what you wanted to know?"

Vincent shook his head. He had come a long way, driven for hours in bad weather, it couldn't be for nothing, could it? Another thought occurred to him then – had he been drawn away from London for a reason? Called away from his home on a wild goose chase?

"Hey! doctor!" the old man shouted, breaking into Vincent's thoughts. "I said – *is that what you wanted to know?*"

"No, I need to know more. Did you ever have a young woman living here with you? I mean renting a room?"

The old man threw his smoked stub into the fire, then lit another cigarette. The room was damp, a thick fug hanging over both men.

"We had a few girls stay here in the past."

"Any with red hair?"

The old man clucked his tongue. "One red haired girl stayed here, long while back. A model she said, I know she danced in Manchester at one of the clubs. She wasn't on the game - not a like that. My late wife said she were a decent girl - kept herself to herself."

Vincent could feel his heart speeding up. Had he found her? He had been sent this address, so she *wanted* him to find her.

"What was her name?"

"Oh, I don't remember that!"

"What did she look like?"

The old man laughed. "Oh, I remember that! She had red hair, like you were asking about, and very dark eyes – almost black. Tall girl, but very thin, and so quiet. Bloody hell, I used to say to my late wife, it's like having a flaming ghost around."

"How long did she live here?"

"About eighteen months." The old man replied, relaxing, glad of a reason to talk and remember. "My missus worked at the **Nightingale Pub,** that's the one just on the corner, and the girl helped out now and again."

"What about family? Did she have any?"

"The girl?"

"Yes, the red haired girl."

"No. Said she were on her own. I never saw her with anyone and no one came to see her either. Never had a boyfriend, although there were plenty who wanted to get with her. And she were always hard up, always just scraping by. No qualifications, I suppose, only had her looks."

"But you said that she worked as a dancer?"

"And pub bottle washer, babysitter, cleaner," the old man paused, remembering. "and she modelled a bit. Nothing iffy, just some catalogue stuff. You know the kind of thing, models showing off fridges and bloody radiators. Nothing sordid. No glamour modelling, not for her Page 3 of The Sun. No, she were shy. Like I say, she weren't the type to draw attention to herself."

"So why did she leave?"

He shrugged. "She went to London. Had the offer of a job. That's what she told us, and then one day my wife took a phone message for her. It were from a doctor in Harley Street. Well, his secretary anyway, saying that had an appointment for her!" He laughed, wheezing, "bloody Harley Street! And we thought she were hard up. Must have been saving every penny to pay for that."

Puzzled, Vincent leaned towards the old man. "Why did she need to see a doctor?"

"*How the bloody hell would I know!* God, this is so long ago, I only remember her because she were beautiful. Striking face, you know? Nothing like other girls, nothing flashy. We had a few lodgers over the years, but she stood out."

"Did she keep in touch after she moved to London?"

"Yeah, she did for a while. Said she were doing some more modelling work, but it was different, she were posing as an *artist's model.*" He blew out his cheeks. "You don't need a drawing to work out what that means."

Vincent watched the old man stub out his cigarette and immediately light another. The smoke circled up towards the yellowed ceiling.

"Did she say *where* she was posing?"

"Nah. She just wrote to my wife and said she were meeting some very 'powerful people' and that it might be the start of an upturn in her life." He paused. "God only knows if it were, we never heard from her again."

*I <u>was</u> drunk that night. I remember arguing with
my wife, and her leaving... I could hear voices
in the drawing room and turned when the lights
on the Christmas tree flickered....I <u>was</u> drunk...
The girl was oddly defiant, blaze of red hair,
quiet, but fierce around the eyes.
When she looked at me I was the one that
felt naked....*

"Hey!"

Vincent snapped back to the present. "Sorry, I was thinking."

"To right you were," the old man replied. He had stood up and was hovering by a ragged desk, twirling a piece of paper in his hand. "Her name was......"

"Tell me, please."

"Pay me."

Vincent reached into his wallet and handed the old man a fifty pound note.

He took it, then shook his head. "Nah, I think a name's worth more than that."

And Vincent knew that this old man with his heavy smoking and hard, nicotined fingers, had wanted the girl. He could see him – in his mind's eye – watching her, watching those black eyes and red hair, wondering. Waiting perhaps for when his wife went out. Waiting for his moment. But it never came, did it? She left and now you want money, compensation for her refusing you.

"A hundred pounds. That's all you're getting." Vincent said, handing the money over. "Now what was her name?"

Forty Nine

Sox didn't like what was going on, not at all. He told his superiors the same and they told him that he had *… better start getting some results…* As if he didn't know that already. Three murdered men, all friends, and every detail, known or fabricated, drizzled over the papers and online daily. The glamour of the people involved had made it all the more newsworthy; Barend de Vries, the KC to be, Jimmy Nicholson, art dealer and raconteur, Dr Vincent Lund the heroic Dane, Tyland Bray with his articulate English contempt, and Leo Parks with his African American gravitas.

Only Leo Parks was now dead, his murder timed to hit the six o'clock news, together with a photograph of his corpse in a body bag being carried out of St James's church in Piccadilly. Conspiracy theories were increasing hourly, jobbing nutters suggesting that the five men were part of a cult involved in the smuggling of children from the Congo. Another theory was that the five men were all related and had some disease that the murders prevented from spreading. Homicidal birth control. Unpoliced, the internet hissed and writhed with anecdotes; the dead men were picked over like the lantern of a chicken, whilst the two remaining survivors began their own road to a public Calvary.

And Vincent wasn't aware of any of it.

His mobile – which had always been reliable before - had failed him and he was desperate to find a phone. Pulling into the carpark of a grim commercial hotel, Vincent walked into the Reception and then stopped dead when he spotted the evening paper – and a photograph of Leo Parks on the front page. And next to his image a photograph of Barend, Jimmy Nicholson, and *him*... Vincent snatched up the paper and sat down before his legs gave way. Blindly, he stared at the photograph of Leo, the man who had been staying at his house, the man he had been talking to earlier, the same man he had promised to keep safe. His gaze settled on the image of the stretcher, Leo's body carried to an ambulance in a London street. *Leo Parks was dead.* The realisation did not register. No, he was staying at his house, he was resting, maybe reading one of Vincent's auction catalogues. Or maybe he was on the phone, talking to someone at his magazine's head office in New York. Maybe he was taking a nap. But dead? No, not dead.

But he *was* dead. So were Jimmy Nicholson and Barend de Vries. And Leo had become the third victim... Vincent loosened his tie and unfastened the top button of his shirt, his hands shaking. How could he have been so stupid? He had fallen into a trap that he been set for him. He had left Leo, left London, believing that he would meet up with the woman – whilst she stayed behind, ready to make her move.

Vincent put his head in his hands, despairing. The mobile hadn't worked all day and it always worked. Had she somehow managed to disable it? But how was that possible? His mind scrambled to collect his thoughts. She had been in his house before, in the gallery, why not again? And whilst he was uncontactable, out of reach, Leo had been murdered. She had planned it all, and he had done exactly what she wanted... Grief mingled with despair. When Vincent had received the Oriental gown he had seen it as an omen, that he was to be the next victim, but now he realised that her revenge was to be more intricate, more prolonged.

"Can I get you a drink?"

Vincent looked up at the waitress; a woman in her fifties, running to fat, hair dyed too dark. He shook his head. "No... I just need to use your phone."

"I can't let you do that, sir, it's management's phone, it's more than my job's worth if I let you use it."

"It's an emergency, I'll pay for the call."

She shrugged, plump arms in a nylon blouse. "If it was down to me, I'd let you, but --"

"Who will know?" Vincent asked, his tone pleading. "Just let me use the phone, I'll be quick. It's serious, it's really serious." He heaved himself to his feet, the woman looking round, then beckoning him over to the bar.

"Hurry up, but don't let the Manager catch you." She said, "I'll watch by the door."

Vincent punched in the number, then repeated it, the digits scrambling in his head. After a couple of seconds, Ellen answered. "Thank God!" she said, "Where are you? Mr Parks has been killed --"

"I know, I've just seen the paper. When?"

"This afternoon," Ellen replied, "that fool detective was here looking for you. When are you coming back?"

"I was going to stay over, but I'll be home tonight. Don't wait up, it'll be late when I get in. Where's Milas?"

"He's fine, he's here."

Relieved, Vincent pressed on: "Why did Leo go out? He said he was staying in all day. Did anyone come to see him?"

"No."

"Did he seem upset?"

"He seemed nervy, like you."

"But he got no phone calls? No visits?"

"I've told you, no!" She replied, unnerved. "And frankly I'm getting a bit worried, Dr Lund. Me and Arthur are fond of you and your family, but these murders are too close to home. You *knew* all these men, they were your friends. I've cooked for them over the years, poured their drinks, tidied up after they've gone. And now *three* of them are dead - what the hell am I supposed to think?"

"You and your husband aren't in any danger." Vincent reassured her. "This concerns me, no one else."

"You can't be sure –"

"I can," Vincent insisted.

"And what do I say if that ginger copper comes back?"

"Tell him I'm on my way home."

"Well, just make sure you get back in one piece." Her tone was anxious. "Drive carefully. Concentrate on the road, not what's happening. Just get home safe."

"I will." He said, turning to find the waitress watching him, her mouth open. Her eyes moved from Vincent to the evening paper, then back again, her voice a whisper. "You know him? That man that was killed?..."

Vincent handed her the money for the phone call and moved to the door.

"… I thought I recognised you. Yes, I *do* know you. You've been in the papers, haven't you? You're connected to those murders, aren't you? It's *your* friends getting killed. Oh, that's awful…." she followed him out, Vincent pausing on the hotel steps.

"My name is Vincent Lund, I'm a doctor and" he checked his watch. "you were talking to me today at six fifteen pm. Have you got that?..."

She nodded, dumb struck.

"… Can you repeat it?"

"'I was talking to you today at six fifteen, and your name's Vincent Lund.'"

"Perfect. If the police ask you any questions, you tell them exactly that." Vincent paused. "Can you do that for me?"

"Yeah."

"Good. What's *your* name?"

"Sandra."

He took her hand and shook it. "Thank you, Sandra. Thank you for being my alibi."

Fifty

Marina had stopped coughing and was vomiting instead as she hung over the lavatory bowl, Alicia holding her hair back from her face. She heaved and brought up some of the sleeping pills, then heaved again, and again, until her stomach was finally empty. Grimacing, Alicia put down the toilet seat as Marina slumped onto the bathroom floor, her head on her knees, crying.

"You wrecked my leather trousers," Alicia said, putting a towel around Marina's shoulders and sitting down next to her. "What the hell *were* you thinking, taking all those pills? I'm going to call a doctor, have you checked out --"

Marina's hand gripped Alicia's tightly. "No doctor!"

"You should –"

"*No doctor!*"

"Ok, ok," Alicia looked at the toilet. "you've puked up the pills anyway. How many did you take?"

"I don't know....I'm Ok.... I'll be ok... I don't want Tyland to hear about this... he wouldn't understand."

"He wouldn't be the only one," Alicia replied, "what happened?"

"It's my fault."

"I doubt that, what did he say to you?"

"I'd been to see Stella. She's out of hospital and somehow we got talking about my sister.... I know I've never told you about her --"

"You must have had your reasons."

"*I did! I **did** have my reasons....*" Marina retorted helplessly. "Rachel has problems, mental problems, and Tyland never wanted me to be in contact with her.... so I let our relationship go... but this morning I was thinking that if anything happened to Tyland....." her head bowed, water dripping off her hair onto her jumper. "... I'd have someone. You know, if I got back in touch with my sister... It was a terrible thing to think. Then I realised that I probably couldn't find her and..."

"And?"

"I'd be alone, a widow. And I knew I couldn't cope with that.... I'm not like you, or Stella," she said brokenly, "I'm not tough.... I couldn't live alone."

"And suicide was a better option?"

"You can't tell Tyland!"

"If you'd succeeded, he'd have found out anyway." Alicia replied, putting her arm around Marina. "What's the rest? I know there's something else."

She could feel Marina flinch. "Tyland said...Tyland said.... that I was getting like my sister and that Rachel was why he would never agree to us having children."

"He really is a bastard –"

"He'd never said it before! All the years we'd been married and I didn't know *why* he wouldn't let me have a child until today.... He used to say it was because of my nerves....but that was a lie too.... And suddenly when he said that about Rachel, and when

I thought about being alone... and him dying. Suddenly it was all too much. I wanted it to stop. Just stop. I wanted my life to stop......"

She shivered again, weeping without making a noise, as Alicia stared at the enamel side of the bath, rocking her. I never really liked you, she thought, and you never liked me. And yet here we are, me in my ruined trousers, you in your ruined life, sitting on a bathroom floor together. And she understood exactly what Marina wanted, her life to be over. The only difference was that Alicia wanted a temporary pause and Marina wanted closure.

"You won't try it again, will you?"

Marina shook her head. "No, no.... It just seemed like the right thing to do... I know I'm a coward, but I don't see anything ahead and the emptiness that scares me."

"It scares all of us. Life's fucking hard.... You know something? When I bought these trousers Barend said that only whores wore leather. Cretin." She paused, thinking. "But I miss him and it wasn't fair how he died. I think about it all the time, wondering what he felt, *how* he felt, and if he thought about me. I suppose the crack about whores wearing leather was for my benefit, but we did care for each other. We weren't soul mates, but then I've never believed in that crap."

Marina wrapped the towel around herself and huddled into it. "What about Vincent?"

"*What* about Vincent?"

"You care about him, you know you do."

"I daren't care about Vincent anymore – what if something happened to him?"

She didn't look at Marina, didn't tell her that Leo Parks had just been found murdered. Didn't mention the obvious – that three out of the five friends were now dead. It would have been cruel, and serve no purpose to remind a desperate woman that there were only two men left, and that one of them was her husband.

So Alicia sat with Marina on the bathroom floor a little while longer, then she took her into the bedroom and made her change into dry clothes. She brushed her hair, put concealer around her puffy eyes, and then went back into the en suite. The bath was still full. Jerking at the brass chain, she pulled out the plug, the water gurgling like a drowning man as she flushed the toilet and left.

-o0o-

The Lund House

It was past midnight when Vincent finally returned, parking outside and avoiding the garages. Hurriedly he entered the front door and then bolted it behind him, jumping when he saw his nephew in the doorway.

"Jesus! You scared me --"

"Leo Parks is dead."

"I know." Vincent said quietly, moving passed Milas and walking into his study, his nephew following.

"For God's sake, you need police protection. I've been trying to call you all day --"

"My mobile doesn't work!" Vincent snapped, throwing it onto a chair under the window. *"No one could get me. I had to use a fucking phone in a hotel and there it was – all over the newspaper – Leo murdered. What's wrong with the bloody phone?"* He shouted, pouring himself a drink and then leaving it untouched. "I'm sorry, Milas, I can't think straight –"

"D'you want something to eat?"

"No." Vincent shook his head. "I should never have left him, Milas. I should have stayed with Leo, stayed here. If I had, he would still be alive."

"Where did you go?"

Vincent hesitated, "It was business –"

"Urgent?"

"It was urgent! Does it matter!" Vincent snatched up the glass and drank half the whisky, avoiding his nephew's questions. "Don't worry, I this will last much longer, I'll be dead any time now." He dropped into a chair, his legs stretched out in front of him.

"Don't say that, Vincent –"

"All I could think about on the way home was Leo, then Barend. Not Jimmy, I don't know why, but not him." He looked over to Milas. "I stopped at a service station to get some coffee to keep me awake and I read *The Standard* and how Leo had been bludgeoned to death. Bludgeoned is such an old fashioned word, so mediaeval..." He reached for the drink, then left it. "He was hit so many times, but they say he died with the first blow. That's what the pathologist told me anyway... It's wasn't like Barend. I mean, Barend died slow, that was messy. Cruel, like Jimmy's death. It makes me think that the killer felt more kindly towards Leo than the others..."

Milas didn't say anything, just let his uncle talk.

"... and they killed him in a church. That was making a point, wasn't it? Like they were playing God, on His territory. They do say that killers are egotistical."

"You've got to get police protection now. No more excuses."

Vincent reached for his drink, sipped it, holding the glass with both hands, then put it down again. Keep your wits about you, he told himself, don't slip up. You're tired, confused, don't start confiding. This is Milas, your nephew, don't lose face with the person who admires you most... He remembered Adela's hostility, her envy of what she saw as her brother's escape. All those years of bitterness which he had done nothing to resolve, but then Milas came to him and he had *finally* corrected the past. He wasn't going to fail now.

He wasn't going die either.

Instead he was going to find the woman, the red haired girl called Angela Patterson. The name on the piece of paper the old man had given to him... Vincent rolled her name around his tongue, thought about it, counted down the letters. Such an innocuous name, Angela, Angel. No angel she. Unless it was some fallen angel, some sister of Lucifer, coming up from the dark. But it wasn't *her* darkness, was it? It was the darkness in which they had thrown her.

"You think the murderer *cared* about Leo?"

"*What*?" Vincent glanced over to his nephew. "I don't know. Maybe... they... they did." Be careful, he told himself, you nearly said *she*. And then what? Milas would know that you had been lying, that you knew who the killer was. And he would probe and dig and if you didn't tell him he would mistrust you. And then you would fall off that pedestal like a shot bird.

"I'm going to bed, I have to get some rest --"

"You should ask Sox for police protection. *Demand* it." Milas persisted. "Phone him in the morning."

"Oh, I don't think I'll have to phone him, I think he'll be here first thing. He'll be wondering what's going on. And perhaps he won't believe that m*y* phone wasn't working. That there was some other, more sinister reason, why I wasn't contactable all day. Ellen told him I'd gone up North, but he'll be wondering if I *did* go. If, in fact, I was in London. With Leo."

Milas frowned, wrong footed. "But you weren't with Leo."

"No, and I have a witness. Someone who can say I was up North."

"Good. So what are you worried about?"

"Sox might think I had time to kill Leo *before* I left --"

"This is fucking ridiculous! *Why* would you kill him?"

"I wouldn't. *I didn't.* But someone might want it to *look* as though I did. They might want me to be blamed for his death."

"I don't understand," Milas said, exasperated. "Why would anyone frame you?"

"To take the blame off themselves."

"Why use *you* as a scapegoat?" Milas countered. "Why would anyone think you killed your friends! They *were* your friends, weren't they?"

"Meaning?"

"You don't trust me!" Milas replied, bitterly. "I can't help you if I don't know what's going on –"

"I didn't ask for your help. I just need to sort this out for myself."

"Surely you can prove where you were when Jimmy Nicholson and Barend de Vries were killed?"

"Up to a point. But I could have got into Jimmy's house at any time, we were friends. And I'm a doctor, how easy would it be for me to change his insulin? Jimmy always had a stack of it in a small fridge in his dressing room, I could have changed one of the vials. He could have died the night he did, or a week later."

"But you *didn't* do it."

"**I know that!**" Vincent snapped, "But Sox could make a case for my being the murderer."

"What about Barend? You said they were all here the night he died, apart from Jimmy Nicholson, who was already dead. You told me that Barend left on his own and was killed in his Chambers. How could you have been in two places at the same time?"

"There *were* four of us here that night. And yes, you're right, Barend left early…"

"*And?*"

"Tyland and Leo were looking at an auction catalogue, arguing over a painting. Barend had caused a scene and stormed off and I went for some more wine in the cellar." Vincent paused, avoiding Milas's gaze. "I could hear them arguing, and I didn't want to go back in there. Not for a while anyway…"

"So where *did* you go?"

Vincent shrugged. "I went to see Alicia de Vries."

"Oh."

"It wasn't like that, Milas! We just talked. I was with her for an hour and a half, two hours at the most. When I got back Tyland and Leo were going on about Jimmy Nicholson's collection. Tyland wanted to offer Alicia a deal for the whole lot. They must have known I'd gone out, but they were too busy to notice how long I'd been gone."

"They didn't miss you for two hours?"

"They were used to me being called to the hospital. They probably thought I'd gone in to check on a patient. It was something that happened all the time. I got called out of parties, weddings, meetings. It wasn't anything out of the ordinary --"

"So why are you worried about it?"

"Because I *could* have followed Barend and I *could have* killed him."

"Was there enough time to have driven to Lincoln's Inn and back again?"

"It was late at night, the roads are quiet. It's possible – but I didn't do it! I'm just saying that I *could.*" Vincent dropped his voice. "You see how it would look to the police?"

Milas shook his head. "No, I don't. It doesn't make sense. Why would you kill Barend de Vries?"

"Alicia and I had had an affair. That's a motive, if ever there was one."

"Alright, say that *is* a motive. But it doesn't explain why you would have killed Jimmy Nicholson, does it?"

Vincent shook his head. He was exhausted by the drive, by the trauma of Leo's death, and desperate not to give himself away. "I didn't kill either of them. But the police might *think* I did."

"When they find the killer you'll be cleared --"

"Unless they think I'm the killer and stop looking."

"Then we do this" Milas said defiantly. "I'll say I went up North with you today and I was with you all the time."

"And perjure yourself? I won't let you do that."

"So what *are* you going to do, Vincent? If you think someone's trying to make it look as though you're the murderer you can't let them get away with it. You can't lose everything you've worked for - you

can't let that happen! If someone wants to ruin you, there must be a reason. Someone set out to kill five prominent, wealthy men – who happen to be friends – *there must be a reason for it*." He stared at his uncle. "It's obvious, isn't it?"

Vincent stared at him, dry mouthed. "What is?"

"You'll have to find out what the reason is. Then you'll find the killer."

Book Four

This is my fourth and last letter.

Out of the five Kings there are only two of you left. Vincent Lund and Tyland Bray. I imagine you have worked out my plan – either singly, or together – and you're tempted to go to the police. But you can't, or you would have already confided in the little detective Sox. You can't confess now, because the truth would come out and it would be worse for both of you – now that you've sacrificed three friends by keeping your silence. Yes, Vincent, I did say sacrificed, although you'll see it differently. You could have saved them, you know. You could have saved yourselves if you had just been honest, owned up to what happened that November night.

Jimmy Nicholson raped me in the room next to your drawing room, he was waiting for me when I had finished posing and grabbed me as I headed for the cloakroom to change. He was a big man, easily over-powering me as he pulled away the Oriental robe. There were bruises on my thighs and breasts for weeks afterwards. They would have proved to the police that I had resisted, but I didn't report the rape. I was ashamed.

When Jimmy Nicholson had finished, he laughed. He isn't laughing now. Barend de Vries thought it was amusing too. I saw him through the window when I ran out. Standing next to Jimmy Nicholson and grinning, his Humpty Dumpy head tilted towards the dealer, listening. Leo Parks didn't laugh, but he didn't help me either. And he could – should – have done.

As for Tyland Bray, he bullied me, criticised me; impatient because I didn't hold the pose exactly as he wanted. As if it mattered. He was talking about Rodin, that great pot-bellied bully who drove his lover into an asylum. How much you all admired the Frenchman, despite there being doubts that Rodin sculpted the Danaid. But it would hurt your male egos to have it attributed to poor Camille Claudel.

Tyland Bray, the name suits him as he brays like a donkey.

His time is very nearly up.

*Incidentally, Tyland, I don't like the exhibition you have at your gallery at the moment, and that accountant of yours isn't honest. But I don't suppose that matters to you, does it? Marina's struggling too, wondering when **she** will be a widow. I'm sorry for her, but I can't save her. You could have done, Tyland, but you can't ask that of me.*

And you, Vincent, you have such an ally in your nephew. He stands by you, he worries about you. I see him at the window sometimes, and watch him walk with you in the garden. The trees are such a mess now. Did you cut them down for me? Did you hope it would make it easier to keep me out?.... I can see what you're thinking. If you go to the police you might still save yourselves, but you won't. You've got my name now, Angela Patterson, but nothing else. You have to keep digging Vincent. Hurry up! You might find me before I get to Tyland Bray.

It's not you, it's Tyland next. And you know why? Because I'm dancing again, like Salome in front of King Herod, and my reward? Your head on a platter, Vincent Lund. You're the killer of them all.

Oh, you and I know that's not true, but no one else will. Who but a doctor would know about poisons? Who but you had access to all four men? And motives to kill them... Jimmy Nicholson, because he was a rival for Alicia's affections. Barend de Fries, because he was her husband, another rival, Leo Parks, because he had discovered you were the killer and was about to expose you. After all, didn't you insist that he left his home in New York and come to stay with you? Lastly, your motive for killing Tyland Bray – that's simple. He involved you in a forgery scam a long time ago, illegal dealings which are going to be exposed and will ruin you.

You see how it all falls into place?

That wasn't by accident, I planned it. I used the facts of your lives and wove them into a cat's cradle of interlinking lies and secrets. And so the five of you, now Kings, took possession of your thrones and I watched you rise higher and higher. I infiltrated all your lives – that's how I could get to you. You don't see someone who doesn't look out of place. And I always knew my place. Sometimes I was behind you, sometimes beside you, sometimes ahead of you. As I am now.

I won't tell you anything to make finding me easier, but I will tell you this – I am not the girl who was raped that night. You wouldn't recognise me now. Even if I were to stand in front of you, you wouldn't recognise me now.

I'm relying on that.

Fifty One

People can be very deceptive. We see a beautiful face and we think the character must match. We see ugliness and suspect a person merely on their features. Bill Falmer was neither handsome or ugly; he was indistinguishable from a thousand other men. Average in height, weight, colouring, he was animated wallpaper, blending perfectly into the background of wherever he chose to be.

And at this moment he was sitting in Vincent's study, in the chair opposite Vincent's desk.

"You want me to find a woman called Angela Patterson." He said. His voice was even, no highs, no lows. Average.

Vincent nodded. "The last address I have for her was 18, Barlow Street, Oldham, Merseyside. That was more than twenty years ago."

Falmer didn't even blink. "Nothing since?"

"She moved down to London and worked as an artist's model."

"Art school?"

"I don't know."

"Age?"

"Seventeen or eighteen. No more. Not now, obviously, I mean then."

"Any family?"

"No."

"Was she married?"

"Not that I know of. Apparently she was very shy." Vincent thought back to what he had been told. "Sometimes she helped out at a pub on Barlow Street, called The Nightingale."

Falmer wrote the name down. For a moment his cuff rose up and Vincent caught sight of a small tattoo. Discreetly, Falmer pulled down his cuff and continued.

"Description?"

"Red hair, dark eyes. Tall --"

"How tall?"

She was tall, standing beside the sculpture, five feet nine, tall for a girl but not clumsy. Her limbs were long, straight, her hands white, without colour at the tips because she was cold....

"About five feet nine or ten."

"Build?"

"Thin."

"Thin?"

Vincent nodded as another memory came back.

'Just hold the position! Good God, that's all you have to do'... Tyland exasperated, wearing a plaster cast on his broken wrist, Barend drinking a gin and tonic, the ice chinking against the side of the glass... 'She's no bloody good, we should have got a professional'... and then her head bowing as the long red hair fell over the shadowed eyes...

354

"Scars?"

"What?"

"Scars?"

Vincent shook his head. "No, not that I know of."

"Any distinguishing features?"

"No."

"Any deformities? Illnesses?"

Vincent could hear the old man's voice '.... *then one day my wife took a phone message for her. It was from a doctor in Harley Street...*

Falmer repeated the question. "Any deformities? Illness?"

"Not that I know of."

"So she would be approaching forty now?"

"Yes."

"Accent?" Falmer expanded the question. "Did she have an accent?"

"Northern."

"Northern? Manchester? Yorkshire? Newcastle?"

"Manchester, I suppose," Vincent offered. "I mean she lived there, so I imagine she came from there."

He didn't say that he had heard her voice. Once, a long time ago.

"Clothes?"

Shabby, no colour, poor material, dye faded.
Shoes that had let in the rain, bought off
the market.
But – for a little while – she wore silk, the Ori-
ental gown, with its field of dragons.

"I don't know about her clothes." Vincent said at last.

"She was naked?"

"She was recreating one of Rodin's sculptures of a nude –"

"But she wore clothes when she arrived?"

"Of course she did!"

Falmer didn't react. "Remember anything about those clothes?"

"They were normal day time wear. A dress and coat."

"Do you know anyone who knows her?" Falmer continued "Anyone I could talk to?"

"Stanley Arnold. He lives at 18, Barlow Street, Oldham." Vincent thought of the smoggy kitchen, the wet clothes on the wooden rack. "Apparently the girl lodged there a long time ago, with Mr Arnold and his wife. Mrs Arnold is no longer alive, but he'll be able to tell you about Angela Patterson. I spoke to him myself the other day. If you talk to him, you'll have to pay."

"Expenses should cover that."

"I'll cover your expenses," Vincent said quickly. "Any expenses you incur. As we agreed."

Falmer put his notepad back in his coat pocket and stood up, Vincent surprised. "Is that it?"

"For now."

"And everything's we talked about is in the strictest confidence?"

"Naturally." Falmer glanced at the newspaper lying on top of Vincent's desk, with the photographs of Jimmy Nicholson, Barend de Vries and Leo Parks under the headline THREE PROMINENT MURDER VICTIMS. His gaze moved back to Vincent. "How long?"

"*What?*"

"How long have I got to find the girl?"

"It's urgent."

"Yes, Dr Lund, I thought it might be."

Fifty Two

New York

"I thought you were going to look after him! Ruby snapped down the phone line. "I knew Leo shouldn't have gone back to London, I told him not to go. But *you* persuaded him, Vincent, it's your fault. You should left him alone –"

"I thought he'd be safer here --"

"But he wasn't, was he? What happened?" She asked, her voice breaking. "It said in the news that he had head injuries and he was killed in a church! Jesus, a *church!* Why weren't you there?"

"Ruby, I can't explain --"

"That's the point, isn't it? No one has explained *any* of this. Not you, not Leo. And now I'm sitting here having lost the one person on this fucking planet that I cared about and *I don't even know why!"* Her voice rose. "He could have told me anything and I would have helped him. I offered help to you as well, but no, you didn't want it and now Leo's dead. He's dead and the news is full of him and two of your other friends and all kinds of theories about why they were killed. And **you,** Vincent, have the fucking nerve to come on this phone and tell me you won't explain!"

"Ruby, it's --"

"What? What it is, Vincent? Some dark deep secret? Something you all did in the past? Something criminal? Maybe you all murdered someone and kept it quiet, covered up for each other. That would make sense, you all have a lot to lose and people get antsy when the see their reputations and livelihoods threatened. But then again, murder isn't your style, or is it? But it wasn't Leo's. He'd never have killed someone, but he might have got involved in some scheme. He was always so impressed by you, desperate to be accepted by the elite. You and your frigging friends, what did you do to him?"

"Ruby, please –"

She couldn't, wouldn't, stop.

"I asked him if he was being blackmailed. If someone was going expose him – but I couldn't see that happening, Leo was open about his sexuality. Or then again, maybe you're *all* gay." She laughed coldly. "With your art collections and your nudes. Yes, I know about them, Leo told me. It wasn't much of a secret, who cares?"

Vincent flinched, desperate to calm her down. Ruby Schulman had loved Leo for many years, but she had a wicked tongue and a knew a lot of people. Better to keep her on side, rather than risk alienating her.

"Ruby, please listen to me –"

She cut him off at once. "Have you read the theories online, Vincent? Some people think the killer is someone with a grudge against rich, powerful men. Perhaps someone who was prosecuted by Barend de Vries? Or cheated in an art deal by Jimmy Nicholson? Or maybe someone Leo fell foul off, libelled in his magazine? Could be. But you know what's *really* odd?

These aren't five random men; they are all friends of yours. **You** are the common denominator, Vincent."

"I'm being framed."

She stopped dead. Took in a breath. *"What?"*

"Someone's trying to make it look like I'm the murderer. As you say, I'm the common denominator."

There was an extended pause before Ruby spoke again. "If someone's coming after you you'll be the last victim."

"How d'you work that out?"

"Because it has to look as though you killed the others. You can't die next, or the plan's ruined. You're supposed to be the killer, Vincent, how can the killer die out of order?"

"Jesus...."

"Has nothing to do with it." Ruby replied. "If this is the plan, you *have* to survive, or you won't get out of this mess."

"I don't understand."

"Concentrate, Vincent. Whoever's framing you will kill you last. They have to make sure you live long enough for the police to determine that you're the killer --"

"But it's not me!"

"That's not the way it will seem to the police." Ruby paused, brutal, practical. "It's ingenious, in a way. The only thing that worries me is how they will kill you. If you're in police custody, how can they get to you? They will have make your death look like a suicide. Make it seem that you killed yourself after you'd murdered your four friends –"

"This is madness!"

" -- and they will want to know why."

"Why *what?*"

"What *I* keep asking you, Vincent. Why are your friends being butchered? Why did you murder them?"

"I didn't!"

"The police will ask for the motive, and they won't stop asking you why. Why your friends are dead, why, why. *Why.*"

Vincent moved away from the window in his study, away from the pruned trees and the cropped bushes. The garden yawned out before him, the drive an invitation, not a barrier. In his pocket was his mobile, working again, and the gallery doors were locked. Upstairs, hidden at the back of his wardrobe, was the Oriental robe, almost as though it was waiting. Inviting her to wear it again.

He had to admit that the plan was clever, she must have spent many hours perfecting it. Maybe she had kept newspaper cuttings of their lives, five men charted out like an explorer navigating unknown territory. She would have read about Vincent, feted for his surgery; Barend up for KC; the success of Leo's magazine; Tyland hovering around the post of Government Minister for the Arts; and Jimmy Nicholson triumphant in the art world. All her sordid Princes becoming Kings. And in what cramped bedsit did she sit and envy the jewels of other people's lives?

Still staring out of the window at the clipped hedges and felled trees, Vincent finally spoke. "I need to tell you something, Ruby."

"Ok, so tell me."

"I'm going to need your help."

"About bloody time," she said crisply "what d'you want?"

Fifty Three

Detective Sox waddled into the gallery at around two, Tyland seeing him and standing with a painting in his hands as he waited for him to approach.

Sox looked at the picture and frowned. "I never cared for the Dutch painters."

"That's a shame, they speak well of you."

The barb went over Sox's head. "Could I have a word?"

"I don't see why, all the *words* we have don't seem to be getting us anywhere, do they?"

Tyland was unnerved, but he wasn't going to show fear. Not to some creepy little policeman or to the woman who was coming after him. Her last letter had spelt out the threat, his imminent death mapped out - and Tyland's bravado had finally melted. But he wasn't going to give *anyone* the satisfaction of seeing him weak. That was the last vestige of his pride and he was going to hand onto it. His past actions mocked him. Hadn't he sneered at the thought of a female killer? Smirked with Barend der Vries? Who was now dead. Like Jimmy Nicholson and Leo Parks. How ridiculous it had seemed only weeks before, but now, three deaths later, Tyland wasn't sneering anymore.

As the dealer showed detective Sox into his office, the receptionist watched both men from her desk at the front of the gallery. She would ring Tilly de Vries later, pass on to her friend that the odd little detective had come calling again. Tilly would like that, loved to be kept in the loop.

Sighing, Tyland closed the office door and sat down. He had received the last letter that morning and put it, with the others, in his safe. To which he had the only key. Another sleepless night had left him limp as a glove. In the early hours he had woken and – for a fleeting moment – considered going into Marina's bedroom, but resisted. His wife was no good to him. She would panic and besides, she was acting oddly. Even more than usual, prone to crying, to the tearful outbreaks he had always found distasteful.

"This is all rather difficult…" Sox began.

Silent, Tyland stared at the detective, forcing him to continue.

"…The murder of Mr Parks has changed matters, made me consider some other options."

"Well, the options you've been considering so far don't seem to have got us anywhere, do they?" Tyland marvelled at his own composure, his sarcasm intact.

"I want to talk about Dr Lund."

"What about him?"

"You've known him for many years, haven't you?"

Tyland nodded. "Over twenty five."

"Have you ever known him to be violent?"

"Violent? Vincent?" Tyland paused, his mind was shuffling through a variety of responses as he picked

the one least likely to incriminate him. "Whatever makes you ask that?"

"This is in the strictest confidence, but I wondered about the doctor's divorce. Do you know the reason for it?"

"His wife was unfaithful."

"Ah." A pause. "But Dr Lund was also unfaithful, I believe?"

"Vincent's affair with Alicia de Vries happened after he and his wife separated."

"And there was no ill feeling?"

"Between whom?"

"Dr Lund and his wife."

"No, Nancy left him." Tyland replied, "and before you ask, Alicia and Vincent had an affair when the de Vries were 'taking a break'. I think that's the term."

"But Mr de Vries – forgive me stating the obvious - can't have been happy about it."

"Barend was used to his wife's ways."

"Because she'd already had an affair with Mr Nicholson?"

"Alicia is not typical wife material. But Barend accepted her for what she was. He didn't hold it against Vincent."

"Never expressed anger?"

"Barend? Or Vincent?"

"Either."

"No. They were friends, they stayed friends."

"Even when Mr de Vries knew that his wife was in love with Vincent?"

"Who knows if she was --"

"Is."

"Is?"

Sox nodded. "I believe, from what I've been told, that Alicia de Vries is still very much in love with Dr Lund."

"Who told you that?"

"A few different people."

"I wouldn't know, I'm not interested in love affairs." Tyland replied, feeling his way along and wondering what the detective's point was. "Anyway, why bring it up now?"

Sox ignored the comment and continued. "I've spoken to Dr Lund's previous nurse, she said that he once threw a surgical instrument across theatre when he was operating."

"Vincent's surgery is high risk and he works long hours. Not surprisingly he might get frustrated now and then. I don't imagine he threw the instrument meaning to kill someone."

Sox smiled. "No, of course not. My wife always says that being a doctor must put a man under great pressure. You know, someone's life in your hands and knowing that if you messed up it could be dangerous. Lethal, in fact."

"Vincent hasn't killed any patients that I'm aware of," Tyland replied dryly. "And I've never seen him hit anyone, or even lose his temper violently. He's not that type of man. And I'd know, we've been friends a long time."

"Would you say he was strategic?"

"In his operations, yes, he has to be. In his private life, no, I wouldn't say so. Vincent was devastated when his wife cheated on him, but he loves his daughter and welcomed Milas –"

"His nephew?"

"Yes. Milas was accepted as part of the family when he came to London. I'd say that Vincent longs for a normal domestic life, but has never quite achieved it."

"Yes, I see…" Sox nodded. "I spoke to his old colleagues in Copenhagen, at the hospital where he used to work."

"My, my, you *have* been busy."

"They said Dr Lund was an excellent surgeon, very ambitious."

"We're are all ambitious, it's hardly a crime."

"No, you can't penalise a man for wanting to get on, can you? As for myself, I've never been that driven. I like my work, like to solve puzzles, but the politics, no, they wouldn't suit me. Wouldn't suit me at all." He smiled, Tyland was stony faced. "You see, this is my problem, Mr Bray, three men have been killed and I can't find a motive --"

"I thought you *had* a motive. The one Stella Nicholson supplied you with."

"No evidence."

"No homicidal Shawcross offspring?"

Sox smiled again. "Shawcross junior turned out to a carpenter in Scotland. I spoke to him at length and apparently, although he knew about his father's criminal activities and imprisonment, he hasn't seen him for over fifteen years."

"But you told me his mother committed suicide, wasn't that allegedly the motive for Shawcross's revenge?"

"You have a good memory."

"I enjoy a good story." Tyland countered. "So the revenge theory was nonsense?"

"The son told me that his mother had been unstable for years and that she hadn't wanted the baby she was carrying. When Clive Shawcross was jailed it was the last straw. She left a note to say she was killing herself and the child. The two sons went to live with their widowed grandmother. She brought them up. Sadly the elder son died from leukaemia."

"And the other son hasn't seen his father for…. how many years?"

"Your long term memory seems to be better than your short term one." Sox replied deftly. "The son hadn't seen his father for *fifteen* years. He believes he's dead."

"Why would he believe that?"

"Clive Shawcross wasn't in good health. He had developed heart problems."

Tyland's expression betrayed nothing. He was relieved, but also slightly disappointed that Sox was now looking for another motive. If Sox continued to overturn the dirt, he might uncover something that would lead him to the red haired girl. Tyland's government post was hovering just out of reach and he had a sudden memory of his trip to Australia where he had been told about 'lamping'. At night the men would go out in the darkness to hunt, when they saw a kangaroo they would turn on a spotlight, blinding their prey to catch it off guard before they killed it.

Tyland Bray had the unpleasant sensation that Sox was just about to flick the switch.

"Where are you going with this, detective?"

"Do you think Dr Lund could be the killer?"

The light was on, but it wasn't pointing in *Tyland's* direction.

"What makes you ask that?"

"I've been looking into the timings of the murders. Dr Lund could have killed Jimmy Nicholson and Leo Parks. As for Barend de Vries, that was what I wanted to ask you about – you told me before that the three of you were visiting Dr Lund that night, but that Barend de Vries left early."

"That's right."

"Did Vincent go with him?"

"No."

"So he was with you, and Mr Parks, for the remainder of the evening?"

No, he wasn't, Tyland thought. He went to get some wine from the cellar, but he didn't come back for a while. I was arguing with Leo Parks about some bloody painting. We didn't notice he was gone at first, then we decided that he'd been called to the hospital and thought no more of it. When Vincent came back we still arguing…Tyland Bray was a consummate politician and he had always played the long game. His interests came before anyone else's. It was his instinct to protect himself and sacrifice others. So for a fleeting moment he wondered if telling the truth would serve him better than a lie. If throwing suspicion on Vincent would move it further away from the girl.

It took him only and instant to decide. "Vincent was with us all evening. We stayed late actually, drinking a little too much."

"Did you drive home?"

Tyland was ready for him. A taxi fare could be checked out. "No, we only live five minutes away from each other. I walked home."

"Alone?"

"Oh yes, Leo was staying in a hotel but he slept over at Vincent's house. As I say, we had been drinking."

"Dr Lund likes to drink, doesn't he?"

"We all do."

"But you have a condition that prevents you drinking heavily."

Tyland leaned across his desk towards the detective. "You're on the wrong track."

"How so?"

"Vincent Lund is not a violent man. He is not a nasty drunk, and he has never – even provoked – thrown a surgical instrument, or any other object, at me." Tyland surprised himself with the next words. "He's a good man. In fact, he's a better man than I will ever be."

"Well," Sox said as he got to his feet. "I'm very pleased we've had this chat and you've managed to provide Dr Lund with an alibi –"

"I didn't provide it, I *related* it."

Sox nodded. "Of course. I'll have to follow up on my own theory about Dr Lund, but your insight has been a great help. I must say he seems an unlikely suspect, but you can never tell. People lie all the time. Of course we *will* find out, one way or the other."

Tyland's lizard eyes stared at the detective. "How so?"

"Well, if anything happens to you, Mr Bray, there's only Dr Lund left."

-oOo-

18, Barlow Street,
Manchester

It was hard graft lifting the loft hatch, Stanley Arnold grunting as he pushed it back onto the attic floor. It was a stupid bloody idea putting his winter shoes away, but you didn't think that when it was summer and your feet were sweating. He reached up, grabbed the bag he wanted and was about to descend again when he felt a small case. His wife's. He'd forgotten it, never looked for it since she died. Well, why would you? No point digging up old photos and memories that only upset you. But this time Stanley felt a nudge of curiosity and after he took down the shoe bag, went back for his late wife's case.

It was what she called her 'vanity case' which didn't sense to him because his wife had had no vanity and no interest in makeup. So after he had sorted out his boots from the mess of shoes, he turned to the case and flipped open the lid. There was an old Cadbury's chocolate box full of cottons and darning wool and a couple of baby shoes – their sons' – and underneath those a set of house keys. Spares, good, he thought, saved him having others cut. He tucked them in his pocket and turned back to the case, a lipstick, never used, tucked into a ruched side pocket. And with the lipstick were a couple of postcards, one from his late wife's mother and another in a stilted uncertain handwriting he didn't recognise.

Dear Mrs and Mrs Arnold
I am living in Vincentia now, just one room, but comfortable enough. I've got work and I'm doing some dancing like I did up home. My phone no is 01745 505 877 – if you could pass it on to Dr Rickards

if he calls. I don't have his number down here or his address since he moved from Harley Street.

Thank you for being so kind,
Angela

Stanley read the postcard again, Dr Rickards, oh yes, he remembered now, that was the name of the doctor on Harley Street that the girl was going to see, but according to the postcard he had moved on long ago. The postmark was dated nineteen years earlier.... Stanley sucked in a breath. What a find! This would be worth money, he thought. Oh yes, he could get some cash out of Dr Lund for this bit of news.

-o0o-

Tilly was sauntering along the road walking her dog when she saw Milas and waved. He returned the wave and crossed over to greet her.

"Hello there, how are you?"

She smiled at him, flirting. "I was fed up, but I feel much better seeing you. How's Vincent? I mean, he must be terribly upset about Leo Parks being killed." She tugged at the dog lead. "My mother's so worried about him."

Milas pulled his collar up around his neck as a wind started to build. "You want a coffee? It's freezing out here."

Smug, Tilly nodded, seeing a friend across the road and waving. Good timing, she thought, the friend would be bound to pass on the gossip about Tilly de Vries walking with a good looking blonde man. Confident, she walked in the café with Milas and slid into a seat by the window - just to make sure they wouldn't be missed - then she leaned towards him.

"Is he OK?"

"Vincent? No, he's not good at all, but he tries to cover it up."

"It's just incredible what's happening. I mean, *Leo Parks* – he was staying with you at the house." She paused as Milas ordered their coffee then started talking again. "Thank God he wasn't killed there. Can you imagine? Finding someone's corpse." She shuddered. "He must be looking over his shoulder all the time. Vincent, I mean." Her hand went out and covered Milas's. "If there's anything I can do to help, just ask."

Smiling, he slid his hand away. "I'm Ok, I'm just glad I'm with my uncle and he's not on his own --"

"But if someone broke into the house, you might be in danger too! Think about it, they got to Jimmy Nicholson in his *bathroom*…. Does Vincent talk about the murders?" She paused, wanting the details to pass onto Alicia and her friends.

But she was disappointed, Milas shaking his head. "No, my uncle keeps it all inside."

"You know, you could always stay with us. You and Vincent, I mean. The house is plenty big enough –"

Milas laughed. "That's a nice idea, but we're Ok where we are."

"Well, the offer's there if you want it …." she trailed off, looking at Milas thoughtfully. "Do you need those glasses?"

"What?"

"I mean, take them off, I want to see your eyes."

He leaned back in his seat, suddenly uncomfortable. "I need them."

"Not for drinking coffee." She reached out, taking them off. "You've got beautiful eyes."

Annoyed, he snatched the glasses from her and put them back on, but not before Tilly had looked through them herself.

"I don't know why you wear them! They look like clear glass, there's no prescription in the lens."

"I've got a stigmatism." Milas said curtly.

"You could wear contact lens."

"Why? I'm don't mind wearing glasses."

"It was just a thought. Sorry." Tilly replied, annoyed that she had upset him. "It's nice having coffee with you. You know, we could go and see a film if you wanted." No response. "There's a thriller on --"

Without saying a word, Milas stood up, put some money on the table, and left.

Fifty Four

Stella was reading when Tyland was shown in, his lanky frame towering over the seated woman.

"What the hell is the matter with you?"

"You can drop the aggressive tone, Tyland. I've been ill, I don't need an argument --"

"You need strangling."

"Really?" she replied coolly. "That's an interesting comment. What d'you want?"

"I want the answer to three things. Firstly - what the hell did you say to Marina? She's been odd since she talked to you. Secondly - why did you tell bloody Sox about my so called 'forgery dealings'. Thirdly - stop spreading rumours about Alicia de Vries being in love with Vincent."

She laughed; the sound was almost a bark. "What a ridiculous man you are. Coming in here puffing and blowing like an actor in a Victorian melodrama --"

"Don't laugh at me!"

"Don't laugh at you?" Stella repeated, getting to her feet. "Yes, it's very hurtful to have people laugh at you. Mock you, make fun of you. It can really go deep, that kind of unkindness. It's the kind of casual cruelty from which some people never recover." She moved

over to the desk by the window, took something out of a drawer, and walked back to Tyland. "You see this? Look familiar?"

He saw the letter and recognised it at once.

"Ah, I see it strikes a chord."

Tyland knew pleading ignorance was useless. "How long have you had that?"

"I found it just after Jimmy died. After Jimmy was *murdered,* I should say. Quite a revelation. Not about my husband, Jimmy was always a pig, but the fact that there was a *woman* coming after all of you." She smiled bitterly. "You really should be grateful to me, Tyland, my chat with detective Sox steered him right away from the truth."

"You sacrificed me to save your husband's name!"

"Yes, I did. But I knew you were clever, I knew there would be no evidence, so the police would never be able to prove it."

"Prove it or not, if it came out, I'd be ruined!"

"Well, you certainly wouldn't make Minster of Arts and that's a fact." Stella replied calmly. "But then again, if it had come out that five friends had been privy to the rape of a young girl --"

"Rape!" Tyland glowered at her. **"**Where d'you get that ridiculous idea?"

"It's in the letter, and your reaction has just proved it. Besides, it's motive enough for a woman to kill. If exposed it would have blown all your careers to smithereens. Forgery is one thing, rape is another."

"You keep talking about a rape that never happened –"

"Enough!" She snapped. "Stop lying, Tyland, you might not have been directly involved – you're not the type – but she's picking you off, one by one. No one commits murder unless something terrible happened to them. I'm not surprised about Jimmy. But the rest of you?"

"No one touched her *apart* from Jimmy!"

"No one saved either, did they?" Stella replied bitterly, reading from the letter.

> *"...you came so close I could feel your breath on the skin of my legs, stomach and breasts and I knew I would never leave that house whole..."*

She shook the letter in front of Tyland's face. "Just try, with your limited compassion, to imagine what that girl was feeling. She was in a strange house, naked and surrounded by men, all of you drinking and baying like a pack of wolves. She was afraid of what was going to happen to her."

"We are – *were* – not animals!"

"How did she know that?" Stella retorted. "She was only a girl, and it's obvious from the letter than she was naive."

"She willingly took the job --"

"Because she needed the money! God knows how frightened she was when she realised what she'd got herself into. Why didn't you hire a model from the art school? You hired a professional before when you were exhibiting the Byan Shaw nudes. Why not this time?"

"There was no one available."

"So where did she come from?"

"I don't know," Tyland replied, his tone haughty. "I think Vincent hired here, or maybe it was your husband. All she had to do was to recreate the Rodin sculpture. I'd just bought it for my gallery, but we couldn't celebrate there because the builders were repairing the ceiling," he sighed expansively. "It was all so long ago! An hour's work. That's all it was. All she had to do was to hold a pose. And she couldn't even do that properly." Stella regarded him coldly as he continued. "She didn't say anything that night. If something had happened, why didn't she complain?"

"Shame, fear." Stella shuddered. "My husband… what a bastard he was."

"Yet you still want to protect him."

"Not him, Tyland, *myself.*" Stella replied, setting down the letter and sighing. "You were unlucky with that girl, but you're lucky with me. Not that I care what happens to you, or the others. I could have ruined you all, but then I'd have ruined myself, and I was never going to do that."

"You knew about this for a long time?"

"No," she shook her head. "I knew about the forgeries, but not the rape –"

"You keep saying rape!"

"Tyland, be quiet and listen. I like being a rich, *respectable*, widow. That's why I didn't expose you, that's why I never will. Besides, if this girl keeps her word, none of you will be left to tell the tale anyway."

He stared at her: "You bitch."

"And you, Tyland? Bullying, arrogant, lying, patronising, belittling tyrant. You ask me what I did to your wife? *I'm* not the one who's been married to her for over twenty years. You ruined her, just like you ruined the girl in the letter –"

"*I* didn't rape her!"

"I imagine you played your part. Did you humiliate her? You didn't protect her, and I'm pretty certain that you mocked her. You've just admitted as much: '.. *she couldn't even do that properly…* '" Stella paused, considering Tyland's previous words. "And why shouldn't I talk about Vincent Lund and Alicia de Vries?"

"Because the police are beginning to wonder if Vincent is the killer. And Alicia would be his motive for murdering your husband and Barend."

"Dear Alicia," Stella said, her voice icy. "she might turn out to be a real femme fatale, after all."

"I don't understand." Tyland was baffled, confused by her stance. "What have to got against Vincent? Or me? What have we ever done to you?"

"You expect me to feel pity for you? You're all guilty, to varying degrees, and now you're paying for it."

Tyland put up his hands as though he was warding her off. "Oh no, not me. She's not going to kill me --"

"She killed Jimmy and Barend and she murdered Leo Parks two days ago. Jimmy wasn't expecting it, neither was Barend – not really. But Leo? He knew the danger he was in and she *still* got to him. Do you think all your shiny new alarms will keep her out, Tyland?"

"I am *not* going to die!"

"Really? How are you going to avoid it? Go to the police and have the truth exposed?"

"It was your husband that did the most damage --"

"Ah, but Jimmy is dead and it would look like you were using him as a scapegoat. After all, how could a dead man defend himself?"

"I didn't rape that girl!"

"I believe you. But you didn't stop it, none of you did. Remember, I read the letter, Tyland. You all laughed at her, you belittled her, you *misused* her, and that's how it will look to the public if it comes out. How could you face the disgrace if you're charged with abuse? *Why didn't you come forward before?* People will ask. Because you were scared and your reputation was worth more to you than the lives of your friends --"

"This is not all down to me! No one else stepped forward either, you can't lay all this at my door." Tyland snapped, wincing as he rubbed his shoulder fretfully. "I never thought she'd go through with it! I thought it was just a threat."

"Well, she's certainly proved otherwise."

"The bloody woman must be mad."

"Mad? Maybe. Dangerous, certainly. She's obviously planned it to perfection, taken years to plot and refine her revenge. I suppose seeing all her 'Kings' prosper incensed her even more. Who knows how hard her life has been whilst you five were living off the fat of the land." Stella regarded him thoughtfully. "If this comes out there'll be no more Garrick Club for you, no more gallery openings. You'd be a pariah, shunned and despised --"

"I supposed you'd relish that."

"Not at all. I don't want the truth exposed, because it would ruin my life. Besides, you have to think about your career, Tyland. After all, that's what matters most to you. In the end that's the choice - *your career or your life.*" She moved over to him. "Either way, you're not going to make Minister of Arts."

He was wavering under the onslaught of her bitterness. "That woman is *not* going to kill me!"

"Really? Well there's only way you'll survive this, Tyland --"

"How?"

"Find her."

"We've tried that!" He snorted. "Vincent's doing everything he can, but we haven't enough to go on. She could be anyone!"

"Indeed she could." Stella shrugged. "But if you don't find her, she'll certainly find you."

Fifty Five

The Lund house

It was a reserved Bill Falmer who walked into the study at Richmond and sat down, his case on his lap. He then passed a folder over to the desk and waited expectantly.

"I'll read it later," Vincent said, "just tell me what you've found out."

"Angela Patterson worked for a club in Beak Street, Soho. Fifteen years ago. There are some photographs of her in that file."

"Then where did she work?"

"No record of Angela Patterson after that."

It was not what Vincent was expecting. *"What? She can't have disappeared."*

"People do." Falmer replied, "I'm hired to find people all the time."

"So you *can* find her?"

"Maybe. It'll take time."

"Oh, come on!" Vincent retorted, "you know what's going on, time is the one thing I don't have. You *must* have some ideas, some thoughts where we can look."

Falmer put his head to one side. "How did you find out about Barlow Street?"

"Angela Patterson sent me a note with the address. She wanted me to go there. But before you ask, she's not sent me anything else."

Falmer bent down and reached into his briefcase, drawing out the postcard.

"Mr Arnold - at 18 Barlow Street - found this. I went up to Manchester to collect it. Always better to have the evidence rather than a photograph."

He pushed it across the desk, Vincent reading it. "...*Dr Rickards*..." he looked up at the investigator. "We need to find out if there was a doctor with that name working on Harley Street twenty years ago."

"There was."

"Have you spoken to him?"

"He died five years ago...."

Vincent felt his stomach lurch.

".... but his son's a doctor too and he took over his father's consulting rooms. His name is" Falmer checked his notes. "Ian Bellingham. His mother divorced and remarried again and he took his stepfather's name."

"*Bellingham?* Ian Bellingham?" Vincent frowned. "I know him. Not personally, but I know him by reputation. He's a surgeon, gastro-intestinal." Vincent stared at Falmer. "What was his father's specialty?"

"Plastic surgery reconstruction, accident victims. That's more your line, isn't it?"

But Vincent wasn't listening, instead his mind was running on. "Have you contacted Ian Bellingham?"

"Not yet."

"Good. Don't. I want to talk to him myself."

-o0o-

New York

The first full snows had started, Ruby entering Leo's old apartment block and nodding to the porter. He seemed about to say something, but thought better of it, smiling sympathetically at her instead. Alone, Ruby entered the lift and watched as the lights marked out the rising floors, finally exiting and making her way to Leo's apartment. At the door she paused, key in hand, then unlocked it and walked in.

The cold was punishing, Ruby flicking on the lights and then the heating as she moved from the sitting room into Leo's bedroom. His bed was immaculate, the hangings ornate, the pillows arranged to perfection, like one of his magazine shoots. By the window a cheval mirror reflected the room, Ruby sitting down heavily on the side of the bed. She had had some hope of the apartment being a comfort to her, but there was nothing of her lost boy remaining. It was perfectly imperfect, his soul long gone.

Ruby had requested that the body – when it was finally released – be shipped back to New York where it would be buried. Leo's will had left no requests, no instructions, but he had kept his word and bequeathed her his collection. Despite the temperature rising in the apartment Ruby shivered; a long shudder of something other than cold. She felt, in amongst his belongings, the terrible impermanence of life and wanted to be gone, to follow him.

"You weren't supposed to fucking die. I'm old, it was supposed to be me going first," she said out loud. "Jesus, Leo, I miss you."

Her hand slid along the cover, her gaze falling on Leo's slippers, laid side by side by the bed. The sight was like a thorn through her heart as Ruby took out the roll of black bin liners she had brought with her and opened the wardrobe. Of all the duties, the clearing up of a life is the most poignant. The clothes that will never be worn again by that person, who had been once been breathing. Once warm, now removed, out of earshot, the familiar face beginning its slow blur into memory. And the personal sadness of the bathroom cabinet, the toothbrush, the water glass with the remaining inch of liquid drawn without realising it would be the last.

Turning round, Ruby glanced over to Leo's shower, to the giant platter of a shower head that she had teased him about. *Dear God, you could irrigate Africa with that thing…* and he had laughed, just like she had known he would. Distressed, Ruby hurriedly emptied the contents of the cabinet into a bin liner and walked out into the sitting room. Leo's antiques would be sold and the money donated to his charities, those unknown people he had helped down the years. All the auctions Leo had arranged, making money, multiplying money, donations growing like ripe apricots in a hot sun.

His diligence had fascinated Ruby, his dedication inspiring. Leo had never explained why, just that he wanted to give, endlessly give, in the way people who don't receive enough always give… She paused, tried of the old questions. *What did you do? Why did you die?* They were pointless, useless, dry seeds that could never live again. Dead twigs broken off from a tree that she wouldn't have recognised, in a wood she had never known existed. Getting to her feet, Ruby walked over to Leo's desk, her fingers running over the polished top. Curiosity made her look in the drawers, but aside from bills and business paperwork there was nothing else. Disappointed, she moved over to the armchair Leo had always used, sinking into the seat and resting her head back against the leather.

Surprised, she jerked forwards; the chair was uncomfortable, the leather on the high back, hard and unyielding. How unusual for Leo, she thought, her hand running over the top of the chair. How unlike him. Her fingers moved over the leather, then stopped, Ruby staring at the row of metal studs. They were slightly uneven. Grabbing the letter knife off the desk, she eased out the studs one by one and slid her hand inside.

The three letters were folded tightly together, Ruby reading each of them, then thinking of Leo. Why didn't you come to me? Why? I would have helped you, I would always have helped you. Whatever you had done... She read the letters again, the words damning, ominous. And she thought of Vincent asking for her help.... Vincent, as secretive as Leo. Only Vincent was still alive.

For now, anyway.

-o0o-

Upper Harley Street
London W1

The rain had stopped, but only temporarily, Vincent dodging another shower as he left the street and was shown into Ian Bellingham's consulting room. Five minutes later he was surprised to be greeted by a young man with dark curly hair and an impressive beard.

Vincent put out his hand. "Thank you for seeing me on such short notice."

Bellingham exchanged the handshake. "I've heard a great deal about your work. It's good to meet you. Sit down, please." He gestured to a seat. "Is there something I can help you with?"

"It's actually about your father. One of his old patients," Vincent began. "I'm afraid it's rather a long shot, but I wondered if you still have your father's patient notes."

Bellingham blew out his cheeks. "There are a lot of files stashed away upstairs. I don't know how far they go back. But my father was a stickler for keeping records so you could get lucky. What was the name of the patient?"

"Angela Patterson. She saw your father twenty years ago, and then again fifteen years ago, but I don't know for how long he treated her, or what he treated her for."

"That's some time ago. And patients files are confident --"

Vincent nodded. "I know. But it's urgent, you have no idea how important. Could someone see if her file still exists?"

Bellingham rang for his secretary, a middle aged woman entering.

"The old files are stored upstairs. The ones we kept, that is." Her expression was curious. "Some of them go back years, it might take me a while to go through them. But if you're willing to wait..."

"I am, thank you." Vincent replied, taking a seat in the waiting room.

Patients came and went, the doorbell rang regularly, then fell silence at lunch time. Soon afterwards a child ran in, his mother following and pulling the little boy onto her knee. But the secretary didn't reemerge.

Agitated, Vincent paced the room, repeatedly checking his mobile for messages. Any messages, from anyone. There was nothing. He kept waiting. Finally, Ian Bellingham put his head around the door and signalled for him.

"I have to go to operate now, but you're welcome to stay. My secretary's still looking for that file."

"I'm sorry, I know this is a lot to ask –"

"It's fine," Bellingham replied, ushering Vincent into the hallway, his voice lowered. "Look, please don't take this the wrong way, but it's been all over the papers about your friends being murdered and your name's been mentioned a few times… if I can help in any way, ask."

Vincent was moved by the offer. "Thanks, but I just need the file."

Bellingham nodded. "Well, let's hope my secretary finds it, hey?"

The hall clock was chiming two thirty when she walked into the waiting room, Vincent immediately on his feet and following her out into the hall. Her hands were dusty, the palms grubby from rifling through old files, her expression resigned.

"Angela Patterson." She said wearily. "Her main medical file is in another storage collection, which isn't here so I can't get to it today. Sorry. If you leave me your details I'll get back to you as soon as I can." She passed Vincent a battered Rolex card. "But I found this note in the doctor's old listings. The patient you're looking for, Angela Patterson? I can only tell you one thing for certain - she's deceased."

Fifty Six

"Missing?" Sox stared at the junior officer. "*What d'you mean, missing?*"

"Mr Bray was reported missing an hour ago by his wife." The young officer said timidly. "Apparently she hadn't seen him since last night --"

"And she didn't report it until this morning!" Sox snapped. "He can't be missing! Get her on the phone now. No, don't! I'll go over to see her."

Marina Bray was sitting perched on the edge of the sofa, Alicia de Vries beside her, when the detective walked in. He wasn't expecting Alicia and was irritated.

"May I speak with Mrs Bray alone?"

"No," Alicia replied, crossing her legs. "I'm staying put."

"I *want* Alicia to stay," Maria said plaintively, "she's been here since seven o'clock... I need her to be here..."

Sox stook in an impatient breath. "You reported your husband missing –"

"What are you so needled about?" Alicia asked, looking the detective up and down. "Mrs Bray is upset. And frankly, it's not your place to be put out. *You're* supposed to have found the fucking maniac who's kill-ing everyone."

"Tyland isn't dead!" Marina gasped, looking over to Sox. "*Is Tyland dead?*"

"No," he replied, regarding the two women and struggling to keep his composure. "I just need some details, Mrs Bray. When did you last see your husband?"

"Last night, around eleven."

"You didn't see him after that?"

"We sleep in separate rooms," Marina explained, embarrassed, adding. "Tyland is very restless at night and he needs his sleep. I would only irritate him if we were in the same bed, so when he retires he doesn't like to be disturbed until morning....."

"So you last saw him at eleven pm? When did you notice he was missing?"

"At six o'clock this morning. I make his break-fast everyday.... Tyland goes to the gallery very early, avoids the traffic and does his paperwork before they open to the public... he wasn't in his room. And his bed hadn't been slept in...." she stared at Sox, then glanced over to Alicia. "He could have been gone all night!"

"Or he could have made his bed before he left this morning."

"Tyland never makes his bed...."

Sox could believe that. "What about his car?"

"It's still here."

"So he didn't drive to work?"

"Oh, genius," Alicia said derisively, "fucking genius."

Sox ignored her. "Did your husband ever take the bus to work?"

"Tyland?"

"Did he use any form of public transport?"

Marina shook her head. "Tyland drives to work every day..."

"I hate to state the obvious, Mrs Bray, but this is a big house and you do have outbuildings. Have you looked around?"

"Unbelievable."

"Mrs de Vries! I need to ask questions and you're being obstructive! I'm doing my best here --"

"If this is your best, no wonder the murderer's not been caught." She put a protective arm around Marina. "Yes, of course we checked everywhere before we called the police. I thought that Tyland might have collapsed, been taken ill, so we looked around the property. And we didn't find him."

"What about the gallery?"

"No, he's not been there."

"Have you looked?"

"Tyland has the only key to get in. The key is still on his nightstand."

"What about the cleaners?"

"Like Marina said, Tyland gets into central London early, he lets the cleaners in at the gallery." Alicia replied, "No one else has a key. He's very careful."

The detective rose to his feet. "Can I have a look round?" He asked, then motioned for them to remain seated. "On my own."

"Tyland's bedroom is the third door on the right." Marina said, her tone lost. "You won't disturb anything, will you? Please, don't....Tyland likes to keep things in order."

Leaving the women downstairs, Sox made his way up the stairs, passed a large bronze statue on the landing and down a corridor hung with sporting prints. He walked into Tyland Bray's bedroom and paused. The room was panelled, masculine, with a faint aroma of cedar wood, the bay window looking out over the garden, the en suite as large as his sitting room at home. Who needed so much space? Sox wondered, staring at a Victorian lavatory with a mahogany seat and overhead cistern. He grimaced, then turned. There were two bathroom cabinets, side by side, Tyland Bray's toiletries in one, the other holding his medicines, ointments and bandages. Sox stared at the labels on the bottles of medication, made notes, then moved back into the bedroom.

There was no sign of disturbance, either in the room or in the corridor outside. In fact, it was pristine. Curious, Sox moved to the window, unlocking the French doors and walking out onto the small balcony. There was nothing out of order. Then he bent over the wrought iron railings and noticed a couple of deep indentations in the soil of the flower bed below.

"Did you find anything?" Alicia asked as Sox came downstairs.

He ignored her and walked out into the garden. The indentations were very deep in the soil and placed about fourteen inches apart.

"So?" Alicia asked, walking up behind him. "What is it?"

"Please, just let me do my job." Sox replied, walking towards the garages. Alicia frowned, then followed, watching from the doorway as Sox pulled out a ladder. In silence, he moved back to the house and placed the feet of the ladder in the two indentations. They fitted perfectly.

"Mrs Bray," Sox said as he walked back into the sitting room. "When did you last have your windows cleaned?"

"What?....oh... over a week ago. Why?"

"Have you had any repair work done on the outside of the house? On your husband's bedroom wall? Any pointing? Any re-wiring? Any maintenance on the balcony?"

She shook her head. "No, nothing... why?"

"Your husband has a medical condition, hasn't he?"

"Tyland has Ehlers-Danlos syndrome. He's often in pain...but he copes... "

"Does it affect his mobility?"

She nodded. "Sometimes. But Tyland manages very well...."

"Could he climb down a ladder?"

Alicia's eyebrows rose. *"What?"*

"Is he physically capable of climbing down a ladder?" Sox repeated, "Could he have climbed down from his bedroom to the garden?"

"I don't know... I'm not sure..." Marina said, baffled. "Why would Tyland *want* to do that?"

"Why?" Sox asked. "To escape. Why else?"

Fifty Seven

Angela Patterson was dead. No, Vincent thought, no. He didn't care what it said on the doctor's card, she wasn't dead. She might pretend to be, but she was alive, living, breathing, planning her demise as skilfully as she was planning theirs. After all, what better way to disappear than to be dead? The police wouldn't be able to find her, wouldn't look for someone recorded as deceased, and Vincent would be the scapegoat. He felt a bitterness, an impotent fury. How clever it all was, how well planned. He thought of ringing Bill Falmer, but dismissed the idea. The detective couldn't find out any more than he could. And anyway, there was no time left.

Vincent could hear Ellen Brooks in the kitchen and see her husband in the garden, burning leaves. The debris from the tree cutting had been removed, offering a clear view to the garages and the gallery beyond, Vincent's gaze moving back to the drive. His eyes were itchy from tiredness, Marina's hysterical phone call dragging him out of a sweaty half sleep. *Tyland was missing.* Tyland was missing - and he knew immediately what that meant. He was now alone, exposed, set out like a penitent about to be garrotted for his sins.

A leaf blew down the drive towards the house, it scuffed its way along, spinning, then thrown against a hedge. Stuck against the living greenery. Dead against the flush of life. There was nothing more Vincent could do. He would never find Angela Patterson, because she was, to all intents and purposes, dead. So was her ghost coming after them? Had her spirit poisoned, stabbed and bludgeoned her victims to death?

Uneasy, Vincent sighed when the intercom rang in the hallway. "Hello?"

"It's Detective Sox, can you let me in, please?"

"Why?"

"We need to talk." A pause. "Dr Lund, please let me in."

He entered shaking his head and clucking his tongue. "Terrible weather. Still, it's winter, after all."

"Have you found Tyland?"

"Oh, so you know he's missing?"

"His wife called first thing this morning." Vincent replied.

"I have to ask you --"

"Where I was last night? I was giving a talk at the hospital. I was never alone and I have at least twenty witnesses." He turned away from the detective, moved to the window. "I can give you names and they will vouch for me."

"I thought you weren't working at the moment."

"I'm not operating, but the talk was arranged months earlier, I had honour my commitment." He turned back to Sox. "I don't know where Tyland Bray is. I wish I did. I wish I could call his wife and tell her that he's fit and well. I wish I could, but I can't. It's your duty to find him."

"It doesn't look very good for you, doctor."

"You think I killed him and disposed of the body? How could I have done that?"

"Mr Bray went missing some time between 11pm and 6am this morning –"

"Which is when **I** was here." Both men turned, Alicia walking into the sitting room and moving over to Sox. "Sorry to disappoint you, detective, but Dr Lund was with me all night."

Sox took in a long breath, looking from Alicia to Vincent and smiling. "Really?"

She was calm, avoiding Vincent's gaze. "Oh, don't look so shocked, detective, we go back a long way. We spent the night together, all the night, in the same bed. It's not against the law. Yet. *"*

Irritated, Sox studied her. "So why are you wearing an outdoor coat?"

"I've been walking round the garden," Alicia replied, "that's not against the law either." She glanced over to Vincent. "I took those cuttings you offered me. Thanks."

He nodded, too surprised to risk his voice, Alicia perfectly composed. There had been no night of passion, no walk in the garden, no cuttings, she had just arrived at the consummate moment to provide him with an alibi. For an instant he was tempted to say that she was lying, but resisted, Sox still staring at Alicia.

"But you were at Mrs Bray's house a little while ago."

"Yes, I was, you saw me. But when I was *there* Mrs Brooks, Vincent's housekeeper, was *here* – and she can vouch for him all the time I was absent."

"Was she in the doctor's bed too?"

Alicia laughed. "Was that sarcasm, detective?"

"Why didn't you tell me you were with Dr Lund when I spoke to you earlier?"

"I didn't want Marina to know. She would have thought it was in bad taste." Alicia was calm, still as a mill pond. "When she rang Vincent to say that Tyland was missing I was with him. Then I went over to see her whilst Vincent stayed here."

"I see" he turned to Vincent "and I suppose Mrs Brooks made you breakfast?"

He nodded. "Poached eggs."

Looking from Vincent to Alicia, the detective's expression hardened. "How convenient to have such a ready alibi."

"Not convenient, true." Alicia replied, "did you tell Vincent about the ladder?"

"No, but I will now... Mr Bray went to bed last night," Sox explained "then sometime during the night he left the house, descending a ladder from his bedroom window to the garden."

Vincent frowned. "Why didn't he use the front door?"

"Ah, Dr Lund, that's what *I'd* like to know. Was Mr Bray trying to make sure that his wife didn't realise he had left the house? Or did someone *help* him leave?"

"Tyland isn't fit and he's also a very tall man, I doubt anyone could have taken him anywhere, least of all down a ladder, against his will."

"I agree. Which means that he left voluntarily. Secretly. Which means only one thing – he didn't want anyone to know exactly *when* he left."

"For the last couple of days Tyland has been very agitated," Vincent explained. "he was nervous, really shaken after Leo's death. Maybe he took fright and thought he'd be safer away from the house."

"And go where? He isn't at his gallery. We checked." Sox replied, "I don't like to accuse you of lying, Mrs de Vries, but I don't take anything anyone says on trust. Bad habit, but there you are, people lie and we have to make allowances for that." He turned back to Vincent. "If *you* were in fear of your life would you leave your home?"

"If I thought I might be safer elsewhere, yes."

"But Mr Bray didn't come here?"

"No, detective, he didn't come here. You're welcome to search the house. But you won't find him, I can promise you that."

A disgruntled Sox left soon after, driving off as Vincent watched from the window. When he was certain the detective wasn't coming back, he turned to Alicia.

"Why?"

She shrugged. "You needed an alibi. And I know you've never killed anyone. I suspected that little tit of a detective would come over and I was right... You have to admit my timing's impeccable."

The shrill sound of a mobile ringing made her jump, both of them looking at the phone lying on the coffee table. An instant later a text appeared onscreen, simple, and to the point.

I KNOW WHAT YOU'VE DONE.
WE NEED TO MEET UP.
WAIT UNTIL I CONTACT YOU.

Before he could stop her, Alicia had read it. "What does it mean?" she said, her eyes widening. "Vincent, *what does it mean?"*

"It's probably just a patient --"

397

"Bullshit! What patient would write that!" She was suddenly afraid. "Is it the killer?"

"It's just a text."

"Oh come on, I'm not stupid!" She snapped. "What does it mean?"

"I don't know."

"It's a bloody trap!"

"I still have to go!"

She grabbed his arm. "**No, you don't!** Get Sox to go. You know who fucking sent that message, don't you? The person who's killed three of your friends and has probably got hold of Tyland."

He shook her off. "Alicia, I'm grateful for what you've done for me, but I have to see this through --"

"Why?"

"Because I have to! Because all of this is my fault!" He shouted. *"Because three men are dead because of me!"*

"Oh, Christ," she said, stepping back, her face ashen. "What have you done?"

And then he told her.

Everything.

Fifty Eight

"You won't believe it," Tilly said, leaning towards Mila. "Tyland Bray is missing."

"I know, Vincent told me, and that detective's already been round to the house this morning."

"Well, you could have told me." Tilly replied sullenly. "But at least you're not angry with me anymore."

"Look, I'm sorry about that, I'm just pre-occupied, I'm worried about Vincent. Come on, Tilly, surely you can understand that?"

She blew on her coffee to cool it, her hair falling around her face. "Yeah, I understand, but life should go on. I mean - not that anything's going to happen to your uncle - why would it, he's not done anything bad – but at the moment everything's just in limbo. Everyone's waiting for what's going to happen next. It's weird." She could sense that Mila's attention was drifting and hurried on. "I heard that you went with Vincent when he gave his talk at the hospital. That you took the minutes."

He nodded. "Yeah, I did. He's a great speaker. Didn't seem to show any nerves. But he was pissed off with people coming up to him and talking about the murders."

"People are so curious, ghoulish. Like me, I suppose..." Tilly replied, wanting to snatch Milas's glasses off and look into his eyes. His detachment was like a flame to a moth, her self-esteem resting on his attention. "Your uncle must be glad to have you around."

"I think so."

"Do you know..." she began, her voice lowered. "... that my mother and Vincent are back on?"

He seemed amused. *"What?* You know more than I do."

She smiled, but she was annoyed. Her plan to triumph over her mother had failed, but Tilly wasn't going to give up. If Alicia could reconcile with Vincent, she could win over Milas. It would just require a little guile.

"My mother's always been crazy about your uncle," Tilly continued, "I suppose I shouldn't be surprised, good looks run in your family...."

Milas smiled again, seemed slightly embarrassed and glanced out of the café window.

"... maybe they'll get together properly."

"Does she care for him? I mean *really* care for him?"

Tilly laughed. "God, you're not his mother!"

"Vincent's all the family I have now. Of course I worry about him."

"Yeah, I get that" Tilly said hurriedly. "and my mother really cares for your uncle. Always has. She's freaking out about the murders, worrying about Vincent all the time, about the victims being his friends. She says what we're all thinking – *could someone come after your uncle?* And now that Tyland's gone missing. You don't think … ?"

"He's dead?"

She nodded.

"Why think the worst, Tilly? He might just have gone off somewhere. Or maybe he's left the country?"

"And not told his wife?"

"He might want to protect her."

"Maybe." Tilly shrugged. "Or maybe not. Who knows what's going on."

"What does your mother think about Tyland Bray going missing?"

"I don't know," Tilly admitted. "She went over to see Marina and stayed with her this morning. Mum said she should come and stay with us, but she won't, so my mother's going to stay the night at the Bray house."

"Is that wise?"

"All the victims are men! God Almighty," Tilly said, suddenly anxious. "You don't think he'll come after the families, do you?"

"No, of course not!" Milas replied, calming her. "I just wish I knew why the murders began. Something must have started them off. I've asked Vincent if he knows, but he doesn't. Or he's not admitting that he does."

"I don't know about any motive" Tilly said, stirring the dregs of her coffee "but no one has a right to kill people, whatever they've done."

"Whatever? What if they hurt someone you loved?"

"I wouldn't kill them!" She pushed her coffee away. "It's bloody gruesome. These are people I've known since I was a kid, Milas, and they're being

401

butchered. It's not a fucking war, what's happening? And the press won't stop --"

"You've got them too?"

"Yeah, on and off. It's not as bad as it was when Barend was killed, but it's starting up again this morning with the news of Tyland going missing." She toyed with her teaspoon, twisting it over and over. "I didn't take the murders seriously enough, did I? I should have done, but I didn't."

"You are now."

She nodded. "Yeah… it was shitty what happened to Leo Parks. He was a sweet man, really sweet, I don't know why anyone would hurt him."

"Maybe he wasn't what you thought he was."

"I know what he was!" Tilly replied heatedly, "He was kind and did all that charity work and raised all that money. He never came to London without bringing a present for me when I was growing up. Even took me to some shows in the West End and introduced me to the actors afterwards. God, I used to brag about that in school. Leo knew everyone and everyone loved him. You know why?"

"Tell me."

"Because he was never cruel, always giving, giving…Why someone would kill him is *ridiculous* and it's bloody unfair. It sounds terrible, but Barend being killed I can understand more. I mean, he was tough, I can imagine someone bearing him a grudge. And Jimmy Nicholson, well, he was a creep. But Leo? No, that makes no sense… There's are so many shitty people in this world, why pick him? The killer must be crazy."

"We never know people. We think we do, but we only know what they let us see." Milas paused, then changed the subject, looking round the cafe. "Aren't you bored of this place?"

She was, but she hadn't wanted to be the first to say it. "Yeah. why d'you ask?"

"We could go for a meal somewhere else. One night later on this week perhaps."

Overjoyed, Tilly returned his smile. "That's would be great."

"Ok," Milas said, his attention moving back to his coffee. "Let's do it."

-o0o-

Ian Bellingham's secretary brushed the dust off her hands and opened the notes marked, *Angela Patterson*. Normally she wouldn't have been curious, but having spent several hours rummaging through a dusty attic in Upper Harley Street, and getting bitterly cold in the process, she wanted to know just what was important about the deceased woman.

The file photograph dated back twenty years and showed a very striking young woman with long auburn hair and dark eyes. The patient's address had been somewhere up North, but was scored out and replaced with another in Vincentia. Occupation – artist's model. She flicked over the first two pages, reading the notes about height, weight, previous illnesses and hospital admissions. Of which there had been none. Her interest began to fade and she took one last look at the photograph and yawned. What was the point of reading about some deceased patient? She had more than enough to do. Sliding the file into a large brown envelope she remembered what Ian Bellingham had told her.

"As soon as you find the file, contact Dr Lund. He wants it urgently."

"Shall I send it to him?"

"No, take it yourself, or get it delivered by courier. Just do it as fast as you can."

Yawning again, Jo Reed tucked the file into her bag and moved out onto the dark street. As she walked along she dialled Vincent's mobile and when he didn't pick up, she left a message on his answering machine.

Dr Lund, this is Mr Bellingham's secretary. I've found the patient's notes you wanted. Please tell me where to send them and I'll can get them delivered immediately.

Fifty Nine

The disappearance of Tyland Bray was news across the media, his photograph published above that of the three murder victims, with the heading:

ART DEALER MISSING, ANOTHER MURDER VICTIM?

Staying inside his house, Vincent refused all calls from the press and kept the electronic gates locked on the drive. Through the iron railings he could see the journalists waiting as a couple of television vans pulled up outside and incessantly – and ever more insanely – came the internet theories.

His life was being picked over in public, his work scrutinised. The Principal of St Thomas's was sympathetic, but wary, and Vincent knew his status was eroding. The hospital's glamorous mascot was looking fallible and the medical politicians had started to circle. He could be sacrificed at any moment; his career besmirched in an apparent attempt to protect the hospital's reputable name. And as the journalists and theorists dug deeper, Vincent Lund's past was exhumed.

It was an article in The Guardian which revealed his private collection, photographs of his skulls and anatomical models reproduced in full colour, along with an image of the poison cabinet. An object which excited much interest. Hadn't Jimmy Nicholson been poisoned? People asked, suspicions rising, the need to find the murderer urgent, with amateur sleuths making merry online. Where did Vincent Lund come from originally? He was Danish, a foreigner, born in Copenhagen. Why did he come to London to practice? Why not stay in his own country? Was he hiding something? Something he might kill to protect? Wasn't it relevant that the dead men were known to Vincent Lund and that he had easy access to them all.

And now Tyland Bray was missing.

Was he dead too?

Sox was wondering the same and had arranged for Vincent to be watched, to make sure he did not leave his house. There wasn't sufficient evidence to warrant an arrest, but, as a suspect, he could be put under surveillance. And as Vincent watched the police car outside the gates and the aggressive milling of the impatient press, he walked from the house to the gallery and locked the door behind him. His heart hammering, he turned on the lights and then stopped dead.

The painting of *The Bearded Woman* had been slashed from the top left hand corner to the bottom right, Magdalena Ventura cut across the face and breast. Disbelieving, he moved over to it then hurried to his office at the back of the gallery. Urgently he searched, flung back the blinds, the doors and looked around the cabinets, then stopped, breathing hard.

"Where are you?"

Silence, only a little shuffle of moonlight coming through the top of the closed shutters.

"Come on, you bitch! You want blood? I'm here, let's stop playing around, shall we? I'm ready."

There was no response. Alert to any sound or movement, Vincent walked over to a store cupboard, pulled open the doors, flung out the papers and rolled up canvases, then paused again.

"Nothing to say? Well, I have. You want to frame me, do you? You can't." He looked around, listening, waiting for someone to come up behind him. "And do you know why? *Because Tyland Bray is alive and staying that way.* You can't find him, you can't reach him. Your plan's ruined because it won't work unless you kill him and make me the last survivor." Cautiously, he moved back into the gallery, the overhead lights illuminating the cabinets and the ripped painting. "Well, come on, *come out!* I want to see you. I want to see your face. You owe me that much. You've been spying on me long enough, time you showed yourself."

The silence continued, but he had the feeling he was being watched, that there were a pair of eyes following him. He moved across the gallery, pulling down medical charts, throwing others aside to check that no one was hiding behind the prints propped up against the wall.

"Come on! Come out! **Face me**!"

Still no response.

"You're not a ghost. You might seem like one, coming and going through locked doors," he was sneering, provoking her. "But you're no ghost. You're flesh and blood, like the men you killed. **Talk to me!"**

No one was talking. No one was listening. They had been there, but no longer. He could sense it, feel the shift in atmosphere. The place was empty. There was no one watching. There *had* been someone in the gallery, they had slashed the painting, but now they had gone. Outsmarted him. Again.

Crossing the drive, Vincent returned to the house and secured the doors and windows, and turned on all the outside lights, throwing illumination across the lawns and the winter trees. Upstairs he could hear Milas playing music and wandered into the kitchen, checking the back door was bolted. His hands were shaking as he reached into his pocket for the studio key. *How* had the woman got in? For the last two weeks he had made a point of keeping the key with him, putting it by his bedside at night. No one could get in, but him.

Distracted, Vincent ran his hands through his hair, trying to calm himself. *She* had got into the gallery. How? Maybe she had made a copy of the key when she first broke in. Yes, Vincent thought, that was it. He would have to get the locks changed in the morning. For an instant he almost laughed, making plans for a morning he wasn't sure he would even see… The music from above filtered downstairs, oddly comforting. He wasn't alone.

Then a shadow passed the window outside, throwing a shape against the kitchen blind as Vincent snatched open the back door.

"Who's there?"

No one.

"I'm not fucking about any longer! Who's there?"

Calm down, he told himself, calm down. Keep your head. It was probably a bloody journalist, snooping round the house. He moved back, relocked the door, sweating, aware of just how frightened he was. How *could* it be a journalist? They couldn't get to the house because the electric gates were locked. No one could get in. But someone had… Blundering into the hall, Vincent checked the alarm system, the green light flashing. It was working, so the gate *had* to be working.

Calm down, think, think.

Outside he could hear shouting. Was someone trying to get his attention, trying to draw him out? Then he wondered if Sox was in the police car, scratching his ginger head and making more useless, scribbled notes. Or maybe he had left another of his rambling messages on voice mail…Vincent checked his calls. There *was* a message, but not from Sox, from someone he never expected. A funeral director in Copenhagen.

They had left two numbers, one for a business and one for a personal mobile. Drawing the curtains and moving away from the window, Vincent punched out the mobile number and waited for it to be answered.

"Hej?"

"Dr Vincent Lund returner edit opkald."

"Doctor, thank you for getting back to me," a man replied, obviously elderly and nervous, struggling with his English. "I'm sorry to ring you so late, but --"

"What can I do for you?" Vincent asked abruptly, lifting up the side of the curtain and looking out. He could see people at the gates, clamouring for a glimpse of him and wondered what the undertaker wanted. News of the murders – and his supposed involvement - had obviously reached Denmark.

"I've been trying to contact you for a while. Years, in fact, but I had no address for you. I just knew you had moved to London a long time ago. Then lately you've been in the papers – I'm so sorry about what happened to your friends – and they said you were working at St Thomas's Hospital. Your secretary there gave me your mobile number, but only after I had explained what I wanted to talk to you about --"

Vincent was losing patience. "Can't this wait until morning?"

"I need to get it sorted now. Please, Dr Lund."

"Alright, go on."

"It's about your sister's ashes…"

It was the last thing Vincent was expecting

"… this is very difficult, doctor, but I wondered, you being family, if you wanted to take possession of them? Most families do, and normally it would have been sorted out a long time ago, but with you leaving Denmark and there being no one here to claim them --"

"My sister's ashes? *Adela?"*

"Yes, her ashes. And the others too. It was such a tragedy to lose everyone in that car accident."

Vincent didn't understand what he was talking about. *"Everyone?* But it was just Adela and Noah, her husband, that were killed."

A pause on the line.

"Dr Lund, I know you and your family were estranged, but surely you must know the circumstances."

"I *do* know the circumstances." He replied testily. "My sister and brother in law were killed and you want *me* to claim their ashes. But I don't understand," Vincent continued, thinking of Milas and what he had told him about the accident and its aftermath. "surely their remains have already been claimed?"

There was an uncomfortable pause on the line before the undertaker spoke again. "No, no one has claimed the family's ashes."

"You keep saying *family!* But it was just my sister and her husband who were killed."

"No, Dr Lund," came back the reply, "I'm so sorry to have to tell you this, but it was all three of them. Your nephew died too."

Sixty

Hearing footsteps, Vincent clicked off his mobile and walked into the hall just in time to see Milas coming down the stairs. He was smiling his easy smile, a sheaf of papers under his arm, Vincent trying to return the smile, but all the while thinking - *This isn't my nephew. This isn't Milas.* It was an imposter instead, someone who had inveigled their way into his home. Someone who had lived under his roof, been involved with his work and family, for three years.

Thank God, Vincent thought, he had sent Charlotte away.

"Press still outside?"

Vincent could feel a buzzing in his head, but answered calmly. "Yes, but now it's dark there aren't so many."

If this wasn't his nephew, who the hell was he?

"You want something to eat, Vincent? I'm just going to make a sandwich."

Who are you?

"No, I'm not hungry."

"You have to eat, keep your strength up." Milas replied, walking down the corridor towards the kitchen.

Are you deceiving me for money? What? Or are you involved in the murders?

"Charlotte rang." Milas called out from the kitchen door. "She said your mobile was busy and sent her love."

"There's nothing on the answering machine." Vincent said, glancing over to it. No red light blinking. No messages from his daughter.

He told me he had been a drug addict.

What else? Who are you?

Not Milas. Not the real Milas. Milas is dead…

"Vincent?"

"Yes?"

"I want to talk to you about something."

Was it you that let her into the gallery?

Jesus, do you know her? Did you plan all this together?

"What is it?"

Milas had come out of the kitchen and walked over to him. "Are you sure you're OK? You look exhausted. Why don't I pour you a drink?"

'Still using the excuse of drunkenness, Vincent?'

"I don't want a drink," he replied, a little more sharply than he meant. "I'm going for a shower. Won't be long." He could see Milas look at him suspiciously and tapped him on the shoulder. "A sandwich is a good idea, thanks. I'll have when I come down."

In his bedroom, Vincent locked the door and sent two texts. Both were hurried, urgent. Then he moved into his bathroom and turned on the shower, the water drumming into the tub as he checked his messages. There was one from Ian Bellingham's secretary, asking if he had got the message left on his answer phone. Puzzled, he made a note to call her later, then waited.

Ten minutes passed, then another five, Vincent longing for a response - which didn't come. Finally he checked his mobile once more and then moved out of the bedroom and down the stairs, heading for the front door.

They had all had presumed the killer was a woman, but was it? What evidence did they have? Just a name, the name of a *dead* woman. And a testimony that a *man* could have written… It seemed suddenly to make sense. The murders had been violent, the callous poisoning of Jimmy Nicholson, the stabbing of Barend and the bloody death of Leo. All his friends. *And all people that Milas knew and had access to…*

Vincent could hear him moving in the kitchen beyond as he held his nerve and waited for the police to arrive. The time seemed eternal. The seconds juddering past, sticking on the minutes. One after the other, they ground on, whilst Milas clattered the dishes in the kitchen and turned on the dishwasher.

Then finally Vincent heard the sound of screeching tyres and wrenched open the front door just as a car crashed into the electric gates. In the chaos that followed he made a run for it, clambering over the shattered wall and running down the road where he hailed the first taxi that came into view. Only then did he look back to catch a glimpse of the press and the police gathering around a tall woman. Ruby Schulman, leaning on the bonnet of her wrecked car.

Sixty One

As the taxi moved into the traffic the cabbie turned on his radio, Vincent taking out his mobile and calling the number Ian Bellingham's secretary had left for him. She answered almost immediately.

"Dr Lund?"

"Have you found the file on Angela Patterson?"

"Yes, I've got it here."

"Where are you?"

"At my flat. It's off Edgware Road," she replied, "Number 782. Name is Reed. Bell No 6. Are you coming over now?"

"Is that alright? I have to get hold of that file."

"It's fine" she agreed, eager to have the matter over and done with. "I'll be waiting for you."

"Before you go --"

"Yes, doctor?"

"You told me Angela Patterson was dead. When did she die?"

There was a pause on the line as she checked the notes. "Fifteen years ago. She was last seen by Dr Rickards the same year."

"How did she die?"

"I can't tell you that, doctor. There's no cause of death in her notes, they are just marked DECEASED."

Sixty One

Went he arrived at Number 782, Edgware Road, Vincent hurried out of the taxi and searched for No 6, walking to the entrance and seeing a list of names. Finding seeing the name J Reed, he pressed the bell.

She replied instantly. "Hello?"

"It's Dr Lund."

The buzzer sounded, Vincent walking in. A young, fair haired woman was looking at him over the banisters. "I'm Jo, Mr Bellingham's secretary. Second floor."

Moving up the narrow stairs, he passed the first landing and arrived outside her front door where she was waiting, smiling a greeting.

"I'm sorry it took so long to find the file. I had to go through the old storage and dig it out." She handed him the patient notes. "You look exhausted, do you want a coffee?"

He was about to refuse, then nodded. "Have you read the notes?"

"Only the first page. It was getting late and Dr Bellingham wanted me to get the file to you as soon as I could."

Her flat was over decorated, overheated, a cat sleeping in a wicker basket under the window, a large flat screen television in the corner with the volume turned down. As she made coffee in the kitchen beyond, Vincent opened the file and stared at the photograph of the young Angela Patterson. He started to read, taking in the details of her age, address and phone number, then moved onto the medical notes. They were written in a sloping hand, many words indecipherable, others added down the side of the page. Obviously there were gaps, a few portions missing, the notes extensive, Vincent struggling to get them in order.

Apparently when she lived up North she had seen Dr Rickards intermittently, but after she had moved to London her appointments had increased. Vincent continued to read, Jo laying a cup of coffee down on the side table next to him. The cat was purring, the television humming, traffic noises leaking up from the road outside.

He read the notes then re-read them, trying to understand exactly what Angela Patterson's medical condition had been. And what treatment she had received. When he finally understood his hands began to tremble, his mouth drying, his whole focus transfixed on the file notes. It *can't* have been, Vincent thought. No, it can't have been… he flipped through the pages again. Stared at the photograph, re-read the doctor's notes. No, it can't have been…

"Your coffee getting cold."

Vincent looked up. "What?"

"Your coffee," she began, then stopped as she saw the look on Vincent's face. "Are you alright?"

He shook his head, then got up, his legs shaking as he left without saying another word.

Sixty Two

Squeezing through the buckled metal of the crashed gates, Sox hurried towards Vincent's house, Ruby following. As he waited on the front door steps after ringing the bell, had an uncomfortable feeling that he had been tricked and was anxious to see Vincent Lund. In the flesh. Living and breathing.

Irritated, he rang the bell again, then glanced over to Ruby. "Why did you crash into the gates?"

"Driving in heels," she shrugged. "My foot slipped from the brake onto the gas. Stupid of me."

He looked at her suspiciously. "I didn't know you'd come over to the UK."

"Leo Parks was murdered --"

"Whilst he was in London."

She nodded. "Yes, whilst he was here. I had to come to make arrangements for the funeral. You see, I'm all the family Leo had. He had no one else."

"And of course you know Dr Lund. I remember you telling me that when we spoke on Zoom." Sox replied, his smile becoming more benign. "Such a good invention. Allows a person to come face to face with someone even when they're a world apart. I rec-

ognised you the moment you drove up to the gates –
even before you redesigned them."

"My car's not looking too good either." Ruby
said dryly.

"Is Dr Lund expecting you?"

"Not crashing through his gates, he's not."

Sox rang the doorbell again. "Mrs Schulman
I have to warn you, if I find out you put on this act
deliberately --"

"It's Vincent who should be annoyed, they're his
gates." Ruby replied, grinding out the butt of her cigarette under the sole of her shoe. "Ring the bell again."

"I have done! No one's answering."

"Give it time."

Time was the one thing he couldn't give. Scuttling
round to the back of the house, Sox tried the kitchen
door, but it was locked, then he banged on the window.
There were lights on inside, but no one answered.

"I don't suppose you've got a key?"

Ruby shook her head. "No." Then she watched
the little detective, towering over him. "Maybe Vincent's in the shower?"

"Where's the housekeeper?" Sox retorted.

"Night off?" She suggested, adding. "You can't
break in, you have no reason to."

"Unless Vincent Lund turns out to be a murderer."

"Don't be ridiculous! Vincent isn't the type."

Sox smiled, his eyes wary. "You'd bet your life on
that, would you?"

"Yes, I would."

"Even though three of his friends have been
murdered?"

"You have no evidence that Vincent was involved.
He isn't a killer."

"Perhaps you know who the killer is?"

She thought of the letters she had found in Leo's flat, the words written by a red haired woman determined on revenge.

"I'm sorry I can't help you, detective. I have no idea who murdered these men."

"And Tyland Bray?"

Ruby raised her eyebrows. *"Is he dead?"*

"Missing. Which points all the more to Dr Lund, doesn't it? I mean, the killer would be the only person who survived. Perhaps that's why he would welcome your diversion, give him time to dodge the police and run away."

She smiled enigmatically, then pointed to the door. "I'd ring the bell again, if I were you. Vincent might be out of the shower now."

-oOo-

The room was musty with the breath of poor sleep, Tyland getting to his feet. Unable to rest, he had dozed like an animal, on and off, then jerking awake at any unexpected sounds. The hideaway, one of the many properties Ruby owned, had become his temporary prison. He had accepted that, but still peeked through a gap in the curtains, longing for the outside. Usually immaculate, he was unshaven, with a stubble of grey beard, the bandage around his bruised elbow murky with sweat.

At home his wife would have never let that happen. She would have massaged his arm, redressed it with clean white bandages, fussed him whilst he brushed her away like a bothersome insect... He felt a sudden and terrible homesickness for all the things he had lost and staring through the gap in the curtains thought of Jimmy Nicholson, Barend de Vries and Leo Parks, his friends. But never really, he had only called them friends and had felt little for them. His prime emotion had been reserved for himself, for his ambition. Then he thought of his father and what he would have said if he was with him.

> *Hiding away like a thief, what good is that?*
> *Get out there, face what's coming like a man...*
> *'I was never your kind of man, father, liked to*
> *sneak my way, politic myself upwards. I was*
> *never your kind.*
> *Never your kind of son.'*

Tyland sunk onto a sofa and stretched out his legs. Fear had unpicked him; two days in a state of suspended terror had left him ragged physically, a battered puppet of a man. But still mentally defiant, talking to himself. "I fooled them all."

> *Fakes in studios, cellars, boots of cars.*
> *Clive Shawcross, you bastard, dead now.*
> *And nearly – oh, so nearly - Minister of Arts*
> *Until some redhead stopped me.*
> *Well, come on, girl, I'm waiting.*

His disappearance had been an attempt to avoid his killer. With Vincent's help and Ruby's timely intervention he had been hidden in a property Ruby owned. A place under restoration, the sign - DANGER, KEEP OUT – staving off squatters. Another sign, declaring that the premises were protected by dogs, proving to be a further deterrent. Tyland had taken with him a bag containing clothes, food and water, enough to last for a few days, but now he was beginning to wonder how long he could *stay* locked away. How long was long enough? Or was he simply postponing the inevitable? His anger ran parallel to his fear; at times he wanted to confront the woman, at other times avoid her. He would wake, in that unfamiliar place, and look at unfamiliar walls, and wonder how a life could be lived in extended limbo. Then he would remember the dead men and calm himself. Stay still, stay safe.

His disappearance was news, Tyland almost amused at the thought of his rival dealers hoping he was dead, an irritable Titan of the art world felled. Maybe they would name a wing of The Tate after him. Was that worth dying for? Because that was the question Tyland asked himself repeatedly, in the dark. Was this half existence so much better than death? A couple of times he had dressed and walked to the door, opened it, heard the quick shout of traffic, wondered how different free air would feel and smell. But then he would reverse, close off his exit route, settle back into a stew of timeless and perpetual limbo. His medication and pain relief kept his illness dampened, but his body was buckling under the stress and his future was no longer his.

He had only one ambition left, to survive. His pride would not allow him to even consider death at a woman's hands. A man was physically stronger than a woman, he would win in a straight fight. The thought consoled him. From where he was hiding he would hear her coming. He would see her. Even though he had no idea who she was, or what she looked like, he would have a chance to live.

And so he waited.

Sixty Three

Holland Park

Vincent pushed open the door just as Tyland jumped to his feet. He was brandishing a fire iron above his head, Vincent putting up his hands.

"It's me! It's me!"

"God Almighty," Tyland said, dropping the weapon and sitting down. "Why didn't tell me you were coming?"

He gestured to Tyland's mobile. "You're not answering your texts." Vincent replied, hurriedly. "I know who the killer is and we have to get out of here, *now*. Get your things, Tyland."

As he said the words they could hear footsteps on the landing outside, Vincent motioning for Tyland to be quiet. In silence they waited. They could see the shadow of feet under the door, pacing backwards and forwards. Then they stopped, Vincent picking up the fire iron Tyland had dropped and moving over to the wall. He gestured for Tyland to stay where he was, then both of them watched as the door slowly opened.

"What's going on?" Milas asked, looking from one to the other. "Why did you run off like that, Vincent?"

He was still holding the fire iron as Milas glancing over to Tyland. "You're alive, thank God." Smiling, he looked over to Vincent. "You hid him here?"

"Did you follow me?"

"I heard you leave home and then there was a commotion with the police outside, and yes, I followed you." Milas frowned. "What's going on?"

"Who are you?"

"*Who am I?*" He repeated, baffled. "I'm your nephew, Milas."

"No," Vincent replied, "you're not Milas. Milas is dead…"

Stunned, Tyland watched them.

"… my nephew died in the crash that killed my sister and brother in law. I would never have found out if it hadn't been for you forgetting one detail – to pick up the ashes. You left them at the funeral home and never collected them. That was careless. I mean, you'd been so clever up until then. So thorough about everything else, but you slipped up there."

"I don't know what you're talking about! I'm your nephew --"

"No. You're not. Who are you really?" Vincent asked again, the fire iron still in his hand. "*Who are you?*"

"Who am I?" He paused, then shook his head, smiling wryly. "Alright, I admit it. I pretended to be your nephew."

"Why?"

"I knew Milas, we were friends in Copenhagen. He told me all about the break up in your family and... Look, it was the wrong thing to do, but I didn't mean any harm. I didn't have any family, Vincent, I didn't think about what I was doing. I just came here to see you. I was going to tell you about Milas's death, but you supposed I was him and I let you go on thinking that. I got fond of you and Charlotte and I just let it go on --"

"What the hell is he talking about!" Tyland snapped, Vincent gesturing for him to be quiet.

"You're lying." He said, confronting the man who had tricked him for so long. "You *planned* it. You wear contact lens --"

"So do many people."

"Yes, but you wore them so you could change the colour of your eyes. Turn them from brown to blue. Like Milas's eyes. His were blue. I looked in your room before I left, I saw the lens." Vincent stared at him. "And then I knew."

"Look, I didn't mean any harm --"

"Milas was never a drug addict, was he?"

"No."

"But you were. I found all this out" Vincent continued "but I *still* didn't realise who you were. Until about an hour ago."

"I *was* a close friend of your nephew's --"

"No! Try again."

"How else would I know about your family?"

"Easily enough," Vincent replied. "I should have been more suspicious, but I just took you on trust because I felt guilty about my sister. I wanted to make up for it, so I took you in. You did your research very well, I'll give you that. And of course I thought you were Milas, I hadn't seen him for many years, I just remembered him as a boy with blond hair and blue eyes."

"I don't understand any of this --" Tyland interrupted.

"Neither did I," Vincent told him. "until just now. Until I was given the medical notes of a woman called Angela Patterson."

Tyland flinched. *"This man knows her?"*

Vincent ignored him and kept his eyes on the stranger. "It was the painting, wasn't it? *La Mujer Barbuda*, 'The Bearded Woman,' the picture all five of us wanted. I think that's what tripped Angela Patterson into action. It reminded her of the past, of what had happened to her all those years ago. The young girl who was raped by Jimmy Nicholson - and humiliated by Barend de Vries, and you, Tyland. Not by Leo, he didn't belittle her, he just didn't protect her and she couldn't forgive him for that."

Confused, Tyland looked from one man to the other. "Where's all this leading?"

"I'll tell where it's leading, it's leading to your death and my disgrace." Vincent replied. "You were supposed to be the last to die, Tyland. That way only I would be left and everyone would think I was the killer. The police were already suspicious of me. The poison, the fact that I'm a medic, that fact that the victims were all friends of mine. I could easily have doctored Jimmy's syringe, could have killed Barend in a jealous rage because his wife was my lover, and poor Leo – was he supposed to have discovered what I was? The murderer planned it perfectly, but that was what took so long, wasn't it?"

"I don't know what – or who – you're talking about." The man replied. "I'm sorry for what I did posing as your nephew, but I don't know anyone called Angela Patterson --"

"Be quiet." Vincent said simply. "I haven't finished yet. I was the most to blame. The meeting was

held at *my* house, it was *my* responsibility. *My* contacts. I brought in the men who abused Angela Patterson and although I never touched her, she held me responsible. And she hated me the most." Vincent reached into his inside jacket pocket where he had put some of the medical notes. "Angela Patterson had ovotesticular disorder of sex development, an intersex condition where a person is born with a vagina and a penis. Sometimes it's caused by two sperm joining together to form a tetragematic chimera."

"*A chimera*?" Tyland repeated, "that girl was a hermaphrodite?"

"Remember how she looked? Tall for a girl, very thin, small breasts." Vincent paused. "Her old landlord told me she was very shy, never dated. Of course she wouldn't. She had no family, no support, only herself to rely on. So she worked hard to raise enough money to see Dr Rickards, who was a specialist in such conditions. He was in Harley Street, it was expensive to get an appointment to see him. The night she agreed to take the modelling work for us was because she needed money for treatment and we paid her so well."

Shocked, Tyland sat down. "So when Jimmy Nicholson tried to rape her would have found out what she was?"

"Oh, he would certainly have discovered her condition. But I don't think it stopped him. I think he sodomised her." Vincent dropped the medical notes onto the coffee table. "She probably thought Jimmy would tell us all about it, laugh at her, talk about her. What she didn't know was that Jimmy never said a thing about it – he was too embarrassed, because in his eyes he'd been duped. Making advances to a *man* would have ruined his reputation as a womaniser... But Angela

Patterson didn't know that, and over the years as she watched us prosper, she brooded and she changed her life. She changed it so much that no one would ever find a trace of her again. *She died.* Not literally, but in a way she did, because she became someone else. But her new identity didn't change her *mentally.* Inside she couldn't forget what had happened to her. She saw herself as a freak and we knew it too."

"But we *didn't.*" Tyland interrupted.

"*She didn't know that!*" Vincent persisted, "She was damaged, withdrawn. Imagine the terror of a young girl who lived daily with the fear of being exposed? Angela Patterson saw herself as an outcast and we re-enforced that in her mind. I don't know what happened, I'm not a psychiatrist, but after a while she fixated on the five of us. *We* were the instruments of her despair."

"For God's Sake!" Tyland said, exasperated. "It was over twenty years ago –"

"Which is *nothing* if you're obsessed. Time would have passed quickly with all that planning and research. She had to map out five lives remember. Five men with lovers, wives, children, careers. No doubt she kept notes and photographs, watching us. Don't you remember what she wrote? '*You ruled over me once, now I will rule over you and set in motion the fall of kings.*'"

Tyland shook his head. "You said she'd made a new life, so why didn't she move on?"

"She couldn't. She was trapped - and she held us responsible." Vincent laid a small photograph of Angela Patterson on top of the medical notes, Tyland glancing at it, irritated.

"So that *excuses* it, does it? She's a bloody lunatic! She killed three men and she wanted to kill us."

"She gave us a choice."

"I don't remember any choice."

"We could have owned up to what we'd done, been disgraced, lost everything. But we didn't own up, we kept it a secret - and so she punished us."

"Oh please," Tyland replied, sarcastically "don't make this out to be some sort of Greek tragedy. She's no wronged heroine. She's a murderer. You say we had a choice? I say, bugger that! She was the one with the choice. Remember, we didn't kill *her.*"

"Oh, but we did." Vincent replied, "we killed Angela Patterson that night as surely as if we'd knifed her."

A silence fell over the three men, Vincent staring at the girl's picture as Tyland rose to his feet, his old arrogance returning. Then he looked back to Vincent and pointed to the man standing, silent and motionless, by the door.

"So where does *he* come into all this? Is he working with Angela Patterson? Or whoever she is now? Does he know her?"

Vincent nodded: "Yes, he knows her... He knows her better than she knows herself."

Sixty Four

Confused, Tyland stared at Vincent. "What's that supposed to mean?"

"Thirteen years after we met Angela Patterson she had surgery in London. She became another person. Another gender." Vincent glanced over to the man watching them. "She became *him.*"

"Don't be bloody stupid!"

"I'm not lying," Vincent replied. "It's true. The man I took in, thinking he was Milas, my nephew, was *her* all along. Don't look so shocked, Tyland, it all makes perfect sense when you think about it. Who else could it have been? Who else had access to my friends? Who else could come and go from my house? My gallery? Who else could organise the poisoning of Jimmy Nicholson? Who else could get access to Barend's Chambers? Who else could move – unseen – amongst us? The person we accepted, unquestioned, even loved."

Tyland turned to the stranger. "Is this true?"

There was a pause, then a slight shrug of the shoulders. "Yes."

"Jesus…" Tyland said, incredulous. "So who are you now? *What* are you?"

"Ivar. Ivar Jacobson." He said calmly. "I got the name --"

"From an old colleague of mine at the hospital in Denmark." Vincent interrupted. "No wonder you're such a good researcher, you really *do* care about the details."

Quickly, Tyland moved across the room and put his back against the door, blocking the exit, his voice warning as he looked over to Vincent.

"So what now?"

"What d'you mean?"

"Oh, come on, Vincent, we can't let him go!"

"Tyland, don't be ridiculous --"

"He's killed three men, our friends, and he was going to kill us. We can't let him walk out of here."

It was the last thing Vincent expected, the tormentor becoming the tormented. Tyland, enraged, ruthless; Ivar Jacobson, silent, watchful.

"Tyland, calm down –"

"Don't tell me to calm down! You might feel pity for this freak, but I don't. We have to finish this, here and now."

"*Finish it?*" Vincent repeated, "this isn't a joke."

"Oh, I know that. No one's been laughing for weeks." He stared at Ivar Jacobson, looking him up and down. The room was muggy, threatening in the curtained light.

"Tyland, be reasonable --"

"*What?* You want me to be reasonable!" He retorted angrily. "How 'reasonable' was he? We *have* to get rid of him. Think about it, Vincent, what alternative do we have?"

"We can call the police --"

"*Call the police!* For God's Sake, that's exactly what we **can't** do. He'll tell them what we did."

"So what's the option?"

"We kill him." Tyland replied flatly. "We say it was an accident. If you can't do it, I will. I'll say that he came after me and I killed him in self-defence --"

"*No!*"

"You say no! Well, think about it, Vincent. Think very carefully," He pointed at Jacobson. "This *bastard* wants to kill us. Remember that. *He wants to kill us.* So we have to stop him. We have to do what any sane person would do – defend ourselves."

"Listen to yourself! For Christ's Sake, listen to what you're saying!"

"*I say kill him!* When he's dead all this is over." Tyland looked at Jacobson again. "I'll do it and then we can go back to our normal lives. We don't tell the police the whole truth. You're right, Vincent, that would be stupid. We tell *some* of the truth – that he's the killer and we stopped him before he killed us." Tyland was polishing his words, like rehearsing an after dinner speech. "The killer discovered where I was because he followed you, didn't he? He then attacked me - and I killed him in self-defence."

Jacobson was still silent, but his breathing had speeded up, a vein pulsing in his neck as Vincent continued to stare at Tyland. "You don't mean it."

Catching Vincent off guard, Tyland snatched the fire iron from his hands and backed away, keeping a distance between himself and the other men. "If you think I'm going to let that bastard get away with this, you're wrong. What's the problem, Vincent? He's a killer."

"And what will you be if you murder him?"

"Free!" Tyland snapped. "Just as you'll be. Free, without having this freak ruining our lives. Think about it, put your feelings aside for a minute, if he lives he *talks*. He can destroy us. Your career, my career, your family – what would Charlotte think of her father if it all came out? What would the hospital do? You'd be a ruined, Vincent, struck off the medical register - that's if you don't get imprisoned for abuse."

"I didn't abuse anyone!"

Tyland's eyes were expressionless. "Remember how drunk you were that night? So how do you know *what* you did? How can you be sure?"

"I know I did nothing!" Vincent insisted, suddenly finding himself outnumbered – one man against two. Jacobson was a killer and it was obvious that Tyland was prepared to do anything to protect himself. As agitated as Jacobson was calm, he goaded Vincent.

"You think this freak will clear your name? You think he'll tell the truth? Why should he, when he'll be spending the rest of his life in jail? He'll talk, Vincent, believe me. He'll lie and he'll punish you, and me, with the last breath in his body. So we take the last breath *out* of his body before he can use it against us."

"Tyland, this is not who you are –"

"This is who **he** made me!"

"Does being the Minister for the Arts mean *that* much to you?"

"Don't fucking patronise me!" Tyland shouted. "You want to be a hero, do it somewhere else. But don't wave your bleeding heart conscience at me." He kept his distance, his back to the door, as he slowly turned towards Jacobson, his right hand still clenching the fire iron, his body tensed.

"Tyland, stop!"

He spun round on Vincent. "Why should I? Give me one good reason, Vincent. *Just one."*

"You can't kill him."

"You mean, *you* can't. You're a coward. If I have to do it for both of us, I will."

"You can't --"

But Tyland had already lifted the fire iron above his head, bringing it down in an arc, Jacobson ducking out of the way as Vincent lunged forward and knocked Tyland to the floor. Landing badly, the dealer screamed in pain as he clutched his injured shoulder, Vincent trying to wrench the weapon from his hand. But he held on, both men struggling, Vincent landing a blow to Tyland's throat, the dealer finally dropping the fire iron. Choking, on his knees, he clutched at his neck and gasped for air.

And with his left foot Vincent kicked the weapon out of his reach. "No more, that's enough! There's been enough bloodshed."

"You should have let me do it." Tyland gasped, pointing over Vincent's shoulder to the open door. "…. *he's gone."*

Frantic, Vincent hurried down the stairs and out into Holland Park Road, looking in every direction, desperate to catch a sight of Jacobson. Then he began to run, pushing past pedestrians, dipping down to look into and under parked cars, leaning over gates and railings to see into basements and front gardens. But there was no sign of Ivar Jacobson and after fifteen minutes of useless searching Vincent stopped.

What he had hoped would be the end was just another beginning.

Sixty Five

There were no more murders and after a month Tyland Bray's natural arrogance reasserted itself. He believed that he had scared Jacobson off, but Vincent disagreed. Not that they discussed it; neither man was in contact, and as the weeks moved on Vincent returned to St Thomas's Hospital and detective Sox was left with the paperwork and three dead men.

"Why did you run off that night?"

"I didn't like being watched," Vincent replied, "you've asked me this question a dozen times."

"And you've lied a dozen times. You've had no more threats? No break ins?"

"No." Vincent replied. "And why are you asking me that? Didn't you think I was the killer?"

"Are you?" Sox replied, "I mean, it would make sense if you stopped when you thought we were about to catch you. *If* you were the killer, that is."

"Which I'm not."

"Or it could be that you're too clever to get caught." Sox continued. "Or maybe you didn't *need* to kill Tyland Bray, you could let him live."

"Or maybe I didn't need to kill any of them." Vincent replied.

"So you think it's over?"

"Yes."

Sox scratched his head, making a snuffling sound. "Like a little pig…."

"What?"

"…. My wife says I'm like a little pig, sniffing away, snuffling out truffles. Those priceless little nuggets. They're out of a policeman's salary bracket. I've always wondered what it would be like to be rich."

Vincent watched him as he rambled on, knowing he wouldn't give up, that his superiors would demand a resolution to the murders and that Sox would have to endure living with the unsolved killings. Three sharp stones in his shoes.

In the weeks after Jacobson disappeared, Vincent had expected to hear from him. He had waited, uneasily, for the post, checked his mobile and answerphone messages, and every time he had entered his gallery had anticipated more damage. But there had been none. Jacobson had vanished. As tangible as vapour. All his plotting and counter plotting had worked meticulously. Which left the vital question – why had he stopped before the plan was completed?

I am dealing with spectres, Vincent thought. Angela Patterson didn't exist, Milas didn't exist, and the elusive Ivar Jacobson had come and gone, without leaving an imprint.

"Of course," Sox went on, looking round Vincent's sitting room. "the murderer could just be lulling us into a false sense of security." Then he paused, changed tack. "I've not seen your nephew around lately. Is he still living with you?"

Milas, living. Milas, dead.

'I know who you are.' You said that, didn't you?

440

Of course you knew, you had tunnelled your way into my life inch by inch, up through the foundations…

Were you laughing at me, Milas?

You should have left my nephew in his grave.

"He's taken a job in Spain," Vincent said, and could see at once that the detective didn't believe him.

"Spain? That's where that painting came from, isn't it? *La Mujer Barbuda*, 'The Bearded Woman.' I've never seen in real life. I mean, I saw it in the auction catalogue, but not in reality. Could I?"

Calmly, Vincent rose to his feet and together they walked across the drive towards the gallery. After unlocking the entrance doors, he walked in, beckoning for Sox to follow. The painting, fully restored, hung on the main wall, its size impressive. Blowing out his cheeks, Sox walked over to it, scrutinised the canvas and clucked his tongue as he stared into the extraordinary face of Magdalena Ventura.

"Bizarre," he said at last. "Can't say I could live with it."

Vincent folded his arms. "I admire it. The sitter *and* the painter."

Sox shrugged. "Half man, half woman, doesn't make sense does it?" He continued, turning back to Vincent. "Urban myth sort of thing. You know, one of those things you hear about but can't believe."

Vincent said nothing. But he wondered - as he would continue to wonder - just how clever the little detective was. It was a question he would ask himself many times. A question that would scuttle through his days and play hop scotch through his nights. How much did Sox really know? How much had he guessed?

"Well, Dr Lund, I have to go now. Thank you for showing me the painting. She'll be pleased I've seen it."

Vincent tensed. "Who's *she?*"

"My wife," Sox replied, walking to the door and then turning back. "You know, it's only when you get right up to the canvas that you can just make out that it's been repaired...." He nodded. "I'll be in touch."

-o0o-

At seven fifteen am the following morning Tyland Bray suffered a massive aortic aneurysm, dropping to the ground just yards from the entrance to his gallery on Dover Street. Seeing him fall, passersby ran to help him, but he was already dead, his eyes staring up at the London sky, his right hand still holding an auction catalogue.

When news of his death was reported there was another flurry of theories. Despite the pathologist's assertions, and the evidence of the post mortem, Tyland's demise was seen as suspicious, the public wanting the death count to rise; longing for the story of the doomed men to continue. In the end, the punters and conspiracy theorists had been more prepared than Tyland Bray had been, confidently predicting his death whilst he had relished his newly restored, but brief, freedom.

The Times obituary was expansive and complimentary. They mentioned his learning, his extensive writings, and stated that – had he lived – Tyland would have become the next Minister for the Arts. Only weeks after his death Marina left their house and put her husband's collection into auction. And on the advice of Alicia de Vries, she hired Bill Falmer, Vincent's private investigator, to find her missing sister.

It was the end of a bitter winter, spring starting her unfurling of blossom, the London parks silly with buds. Gradually interest in the murders faded, Charlotte returned home to live with her father, and the little detective marked the case file 'PENDING'. It was left on his desk, always in his line of sight. Using the same story he had related to Sox, Vincent told his daughter that Milas had moved abroad. She seemed strangely unmoved.

But he wasn't. Embittered by the betrayal, Vincent longed to hate Ivar Jacobson, but missed him. He often wondered how he *could* miss someone who had planned to destroy him, someone so callous he could usurp a dead boy's grave. But Milas – the imposter Milas – had given Vincent absolution for his past. In giving Milas a home Vincent had homed his own grief and regrets. And oddly he did not see Jacobson as a single entity, but twinned with Angela Patterson. Two melted into one, the abused girl and the man she became.

He wondered how it would end. Because he knew there *was* an end coming. Tyland Bray had been too confident, Sox too slow. And so spring wore on, the trees bubbled with blossom, the days lengthened and in the gallery *La Mujer Barbuda* lorded over the skulls, the poison cabinet and the grisly anatomical figures.

And again, Vincent waited.

This is my last letter, Vincent. All the Kings have fallen, but you. I suppose you're wondering about Tyland Bray. The pathologist reported that he died of natural causes. Of course he did. Or then again, maybe not. What do you think? Could I have arranged his death? You tell me, you're the doctor.

I've finished, Vincent, and I suppose you want to know why. Because you changed your own destiny and because of that you'll remain the one King standing. Why, you're wondering. Let me tell you – it was because you protected me. You defended me against Tyland Bray, because he would have killed me. You might have failed me once, more than twenty years ago, but you've made amends now. I wish I could do the same.

*I was cruel, mad, obsessed. The plan was immaculate – it should have been, I'd worked on it for many years. I began to plot when I was recovering from my operation, my switch in gender. Which was easier than I could have imagined. I was never a girl, you see, at heart I was always masculine. My brain was a man's, I suppose that's why I could kill. And you were right, it **was** the painting that tripped me into action. Mag-*

dalena Ventura, that poor freak, who speaks for all the freaks that suffer in this world.

*When I came to you, when you took me in, it was laughably easy. You were so guilty for the past, so keen to make it right again. And I slid into that home of yours like a eel into warm water. I was there when you put up the Christmas trees and always remembered the tree you had twenty years earlier. So blowsy, so impressively, mightily grand. You **were** drunk that night, Vincent, and you argued with your wife. And as you were arguing, Jimmy Nicholson attacked me.*

You know the rest.

We are old friends now, you and I. We don't have to spend time in the past. It's done. There I've said it, you're free. Forgive me, if you can... You saved yourself, Vincent. Not just that night when you defended me, but with all the little kindnesses - the thoughts, the tiny gestures you would never even remember - that turned my heart. I came to you one person, and you made me into another. You became my conscience. You reminded me there was goodness in a world I had hated so long.

Enough, that's all. Just one more thing. Yes, I have the nerve to ask a favour, after all that I've done. But then again, I have left you with your life... In time a parcel will be delivered to you. Please follow the instructions. They will be simple, very clear. I could always plan well.

Postscript

Five years later, on the 14th March, a package *did* arrive, marked:

FOR THE ATTENTION OF
Dr Vincent Lund

It was delivered by a London funeral director and contained crematorium ashes, labelled, 'Angela Patterson and Ivar Jacobson.' And a note, that said simply:

'Goodbye, Vincent.'

By then Vincent had semi-retired, working part time as a consultant at St Thomas's Hospital. When he received the package he took the handwritten note and had it examined, the prints on the paper and saliva on the envelope tested for DNA and compared with the hair sample he had taken from the time Ivar Jacobson had lived with him.

When they came back the results were conclusive. They were *not* a match.

Printed in Great Britain
by Amazon